For I Have Sinned

A Novel

Michael Deeze

outskirts press

For I Have Sinned
Annonment

v4.0

This is a work of fiction. Names, characters, businesses, places, events, locales, and incidents are either the products of the author's imagination or used in a fictitious manner. Any resemblance to actual persons, living or dead, or actual events is purely coincidental.

The opinions expressed in this manuscript are solely the opinions of the author and do not represent the opinions or thoughts of the publisher. The author has represented and warranted full ownership and/or legal right to publish all the materials in this book.

Outskirts Press, Inc.
http://www.outskirtspress.com

ISBN: 978-1-9772-0856-9

Library of Congress Control Number: 2019900667

PRINTED IN THE UNITED STATES OF AMERICA

About the Cover

Cover artist Lori Pecchia. - https://twitter.com/37zombies

Lori Pecchia, cover artist

Born in the suburbs of Chicago in 1978, Lori Pecchia grew up with a love for drawing and sculpting. She won numerous awards from junior high school through college for her abilities in pencil, charcoal, printmaking, and sculpture in multiple mediums. Lori began tattooing while in college, and a decades-long career followed. She has won multiple tattooing awards, but the real reflection of her art is the amazing clients she has amassed over the years. For Lori, tattooing creates a bond that lasts a lifetime.

In 2017, she followed her dream to move to the mountains with her husband Peter and daughter Cora. She currently tattoos in a beautiful shop in historic downtown Golden, Colorado. Even though a thousand miles separate her from her Illinois clients, she returns regularly to work with them, while also expanding her new clientele in Colorado.

When she isn't tattooing, Lori enjoys both outdoor and indoor hobbies. She has completed the Chicago Marathon three times, and run every other type of race leading up to the marathon. Now she has taken on hiking and paddle boarding in her mountain surroundings. Living on Bear Mountain gives her family a chance to see nature's beauty every day.

She has a passion for board and role-playing games. Lori is involved in gaming convention culture. She loves the social aspects and shared experience of playing games. Most important to Lori, gaming is yet another place for making lifelong friends.

Preface

From the time that the United States entered the war in 1944 until the final armistice, over 100,000 airmen lost their lives in the air war over Europe. That is more than the entire loss of life of the U.S. Marine Corps in the war of the Pacific.

Introduction

My name is Emmett Michael Casey. Depending upon the station of the family member I'm with, I'm Michael, or Mick. People who work with me call me Mick or Casey. I stand five feet, seven inches tall and weigh on both sides of 130 pounds, depending upon the time of day. My friends and close relatives call me Little Mick. I don't mind. People who don't know me very well think I'm an asshole. I don't give a shit what people think anymore. I mind my own business.

Diary of Mick Casey, Army Air Corps Tail Gunner, The Flying Ass

January 15, 1945
Trento, Italy

We hung on for dear life while the captain throttled up the four big engines. We were seriously overloaded with fuel, with ammunition, with eight tons of one-hundred-pound bombs—and us. We would need every inch of the runway we could get. The old girl shook like she was going to explode. I could feel myself leaning against my harness, just like we all were, just like she was, pushing hard against the brakes. She wanted to go. Just when I thought it wouldn't take any more, the brakes released and we were off, hanging on tight, deaf from the roar of the four engines going full tilt into hell, down the metal track that was the runway; thirty seconds behind the last bomber and thirty seconds ahead of the next one.

We faced each other belted to the bulkhead, in our crash positions three on one side, three on the other side of the bomb bay between us, the racks of hundred-pounders within an arm's reach as we were thrown into our harnesses with the force of the release and thc rumble of the runway. We felt every bump and rough spot as we pounded along, too fast to abort, daredevils to the end. I didn't think she could lift her ass. I was praying, thinking, *Come on, baby, get up, get up, come on, baby*. I couldn't hold on any tighter. I didn't think we could possibly have enough runway, and still we kept pounding along. Then we were up, and then we bounced back down and raced on. Then we were up. The landing gear ground its way up into the belly, and the engine noise changed pitch. The captain pulled it into a hard bank, and we began the long spiral up to the other planes. We were off, all of us, we brothers—not knowing what was ahead—all of us ready, all of us sudden converts to Jesus, if we weren't already.

I had to leave my parachute behind me in the bomb bay and crawl down the tight passageway into the turret at the back of the plane where I cranked up the tail wheel. Once I got my flight suit plugged in and my oxygen hooked up, I started to warm up a little. An hour out we got the okay from the captain. and I cleared my two fifty-caliber Brownings, firing a long burst from each one, and settled down to watch my piece of the sky. This was our second mission and I prayed to God that it would be like the first one. I wasn't a kid anymore, I was nineteen, and I wanted to live long enough to see twenty. The first mission was a piece of cake the captain had said. We dropped down, unloaded, and got out of there. The flak was light and all the birds flew home. Today we were heading into Austria, the city of Vienna. At the briefing at 3:00 a.m. they said we'd see stronger defenses and concentrated flak. It was a beautiful sunny day, and I watched the Alps as we crossed them and out of Italy. Looking down I thought about how my brother-in-law Charlie was down there somewhere. He's walking behind Patten, I'm flying. Which is worse? I wondered.

As soon as the mountains got a little behind us, the intercom blasted in my ears. Janssen yelled, "Bogies, eleven o'clock high, they're comin' around!"

Janssen manned the upper turret, so I couldn't see the eleven. In the tail gun turret, I rode backward, facing where we just came from. I pulled my helmet back off my eyebrows a little and got a good dose of sun in my eyes. I didn't see the bogies. They used the sun as cover to get behind us. Then I did; three little dots right dead in our six o'clock and getting bigger real fast.

Then Janssen yelled, "Three more coming in on the starboard, four o'clock low! MEs" (Messerschmidt 109s).

The dots got bigger; we were in the starboard group today, flying tight, getting close to our IP (initial point). At the IP, the formation would turn to the target, drop altitude, arm the bombs in the bay, and line up for our run. The group was vulnerable at both ends of the run; the tighter the group, the more firepower we could bring. During the run, we'd string out. They didn't call these babies Flying Fortresses for nothing though.

The wings and tails of the oncoming fighters defined themselves in my vision. They weren't just dots anymore, they were trouble and they were bringing it with them. I swung the guns up. Six hundred yards is the effective range for the Browning .50 caliber and they would be there soon. I knew what six hundred yards looked like and I wasn't going to wait until they got there. I was ready. I pulled the triggers and the twins roared into life, a spray of tracer rounds racing off toward them, five hundred rounds a minute.

The trio behind didn't reach the gun range barrier. Instead

they peeled off away, two to my right and one to my left. I couldn't swing my turret toward the other three MEs as I only had ninety degrees of rotation in the turret. I had to watch as they made their run. I could see the muzzle flashes of their guns as they swung into attack mode, concentrating on the waist and tail of the right-most B-17, *Moaning Lisa*. They attacked from a lower angle to avoid as many of our gun positions as they could, and almost immediately fragments of her started to peel off the fuselage along with sparkling plexiglass from the gun mounts. They were tearing her apart. The first fighter split away, up to where I could lay strafing fire out for him to fly into, and I opened up on him. Then the second ME made its run, targeting the same position. This time her number four engine belched black oily smoke and the right wing dropped. The bomber heeled over to her right and away from the squadron. *Moaning Lisa* turned nose down and spun down into the cloud cover, out of my sight. They had cut one of us out of the herd.

"Stay tight, close up the formation, steady ahead. Any parachutes on that bird?"

"Negative," shouted Taylor from the Sperry ball turret. "No chutes. Three o'clock, three o'clock level, he's gonna take us end to end."

I couldn't watch for chutes. I picked up the ME as he passed.

"Two more, ten o'clock high, one at six o'clock level, you pick him up, Casey?"

"Yep, I see 'em."

Then, just like that they were gone. None of them in the sky. Captain Brinker came over the intercom. "Damage check?" He was a lot older than the rest of us, almost twenty-five, but he was still a pretty neat guy. I couldn't run a damage check because I was on my knees strapped into the turret and the plane was behind me. But there didn't seem to be any when the rest of the crew checked in. He told us we were approaching our IP, which meant I had to get out of the turret and crawl back into the bomb bay. The fighters didn't chase us into the IP. There was flak to do their job for them. They'd wait for us when we came back out after the bomb run. If we came out from it.

Once in the bay, the Sperry ball (belly turret) gunner, Taylor, and I pulled all the pins on the bombs so that they were armed and would explode on contact. We had to put on our chutes and hook up portable oxygen tanks first. We hurried our way through the process. You don't want to bc in the bomb bay when the doors open, and our oxygen bottles didn't have very much air in them anyway. Although we'd practiced it a hundred times, it was hard to do in our parachute gear and oxygen tanks. The catwalk between the bombs was narrow, ten inches wide, and the footing was icy this high up in the air. The wind blows through, matching our airspeed.

Once I got back in the tail-gun turret, we turned hard to port and started our bomb run in earnest. The fighters would wait until we came back out on the other side. Now it would be anti-aircraft defenses, and flak—it started immediately, and it started heavy. The poor ship rocked up and down and back and forth. There was no defense; we were big dark silhouettes in the sky just asking for them to shoot us in the ass. We had to take the pounding. There are no atheists during the bomb run.

Even with my harness cinched tight, my head was snapping around on my neck like a punch-drunk prizefighter. Behind us, I watched as the sky turned black with the smoke of the explosions and the flash of the flame when they detonated. We were in the lead group, and I couldn't imagine what the last group through was going to get as the blackness got thicker and thicker. I imagined this must be what hell looks and feels like.

Suddenly a piece of my turret shattered and hit me on the side of my head, knocking me silly for a minute. I was okay, but my head hurt a lot. There was so much noise in the plane I could barely hear "Bombs away" coming through the headset. But the light on the floor between my knees flashed so that I would know, just in case.

We were ready for the MEs as soon as we cleared the flak. But there weren't any. They had vanished. We made it home safe. At the debriefing we were told we lost three planes. They lost five. Just for laughs the chief from the grounds crew told us we won the award for most holes punched in the fuselage today. He asked if we wanted to know how many. We all told him, "NO." We were in the air seven hours and fifty-five minutes. It felt a lot longer than that. It took twelve stitches to close the gash in my head. That night I crawled into the tent and got in my sleeping bag. It gets cold in January in Italy. I couldn't sleep. I looked up at the canvas and thought, *We go again—tomorrow.*

Emmett

1956
Chicago, Illinois

I wake up with a start. They're in my room again. Those others, I can feel them crowding in. The room is dark and I can hear my sister's open-mouth breathing in the bunk bed above me. Near the window my brother sleeps with his feet sticking out of the bars on his crib. He's too tall for the bed now. I really have to pee. When I roll over and open my eyes, the room is empty, filled with shadows.

I know there will be something under the bed waiting for me to step out, some nameless terror that will snatch at me if I put a foot on the floor. I'm conflicted between chancing the run for the toilet in the bathroom or just peeing the bed and taking my punishment and humiliation in the morning. It might be worth it, but if I don't make up my mind pretty soon, the decision will be made for me. I decide to make the run for it—but quietly. As soundlessly as I can, I peel off my blankets and head out of the bedroom on my tiptoes; the bathroom is at the other end of the apartment. I've memorized where the floor squeaks are.

As soon as I enter the dining room, the aroma of cigarette smoke hits me, strong and familiar—he is awake. I bypass the bathroom door and peek around the doorway into the living room. His silhouette is defined sharply by the streetlight that glares in through the front window. Silently he sits in his chair facing toward me; then his cigarette tip glows bright and even in the low light I see the cloud of smoke he exhales.

"Bad dream?" comes the voice, so quiet yet unexpectedly loud in the silence of midnight.

"The people are in my room again, Da," I said. "I gotta pee."

"They won't hurt you, Emmett; they're not here for you. Go on, go pee, it's behind you."

I shuffle into the bathroom and pee with the door open, aiming at the side of the bowl so it doesn't make too much noise. I wouldn't think of flushing the toilet in the middle of the night for fear of disturbing any other nearby demons, so once I finish, I turn back toward the living room and peek once more. My night vision is good enough to see the bottle and ashtray perched on the stand next to him.

"Bedroom's the other way."

I hesitate.

"Go on now, morning will be here soon. Gotta go again—tomorrow."

Willy's Tavern

April 1973
Madison, Wisconsin

The old man sat on his bar stool looking at me in the mirror behind the bar. Two empty shot glasses sat between the two half-filled beer glasses on the bar. Even when I was very young, he was an old man. This man I'd known my whole life. To me he hadn't aged a day, a constant in the swirling winds of my life. His speech had always been slow and considered, his movements—the same. Today he had something on his mind and I knew that when he was ready, he'd get around to it. When Thomas Quinn had something to say, the people in my family listened.

Willy's Tavern had been another constant in my life. Just around the corner from both the Quinn and Casey homeplaces, it was close enough to walk to and stagger home from. I'd been coming to Willy's as long as I could remember, the sights and smells of it as familiar as my grandmother's house. As a small boy, the Casey and Quinn men repaired to Willy's every Saturday afternoon, leaving the house to the women. At Willy's they spent long hours nursing their beer glasses, eating pickled eggs and pig's feet, and staring at themselves in this same mirror behind the bar, all of them friends, but only to each other. The young men and boys came with, playing the jukebox and drinking six-ounce Coca-Colas with the nickels sparingly supplied by their uncles.

I grew up watching Willy, a cigarette dangling from the corner of his mouth, pour shots and tap beers while in constant conversation. Willy was always friendly with a wide smile but he also enforced the peace when it was necessary, with a bung starter or the sawed-off he kept handy under the bar. No matter how late the men came home on Saturday night, Willy Donovan would still be in his regular church pew on Sunday up at St. Pat's dressed in the same green tie and jacket. Willy's Tavern was Thomas' go-to place when it was time to hand out advice and wisdom.

When we arrived, Willy smiled big and after wiping his hands on his apron, leaned across the counter and shook my hand congratulating me on my return home. He proudly showed me where my name and picture were posted on the wall above the liquor bottles; my brother Andy, a Marine, next to me. Ours weren't the only pictures; there were several, each with a small red and white pendant and a blue star in the center. Two of the stars were gold, a testament to the price of heroism. Without being asked Willy had set up the glasses and reached high up for the good whiskey, the first one on the house.

We were into our second shot now, and the first beer was moving toward the finish line. Thomas was warming up. We'd already covered the "What are your plans" topic, and the "How do you like your job," as well as "How is your mother and what is Kate up to these days?" It struck me that this man may be the most respected person I knew. I recognized how privileged I was to occupy a seat next to him; or to even know him. With a wave, Thomas signaled Willy to pour three more, and when they arrived he handed one to Willy and then turned, handing me the second.

"Here's to the miles under your boots, and to the blessing of your return to us. It is too long since the last time you sat on that stool. Welcome home, Emmett, we're proud to welcome you home safe. Slainte!"

"Slainte, and by the Saints," solemnly spoken by Willy.

"Slainte Seanathair."

Willy threw back his shot and slammed the glass upside down on the bar, gave me a wink and moved off to the other end, where he turned up the volume on the old television, and began rearranging the bottles under it. Even Willy knew that now it was time, and with a deep breath Thomas began. "They came home different as well, you know."

"They?"

"Your uncles...and Mick."

"You mean when they came home after the war?"

"Yeah, they were changed by it, all of them. And you are too. It shows; you've become more careful."

"It's not the same, Grandpa."

"It is exactly the same. Don't you see?"

"You mean, like they say, the Army makes a man out of you."

"The Army can't make a man out of anyone. That's just bullshit. The man finds out what kind of man he is maybe, but the man himself makes the man. The Army just gives him the environment to find out if he's got the stomach and the spine to do it."

I fished out a cigarette from my shirt pocket. The match

shook a little while I lit it. Thomas Quinn was one of the few men I'd never been able to bullshit; he could skewer me right here on this bar stool and I'd have to tell the truth.

"All the same, it's different. World War II was to save the world, and they came home heroes, all of them. This was a completely different thing altogether."

"You should ask them about it, you know."

"Ask who? Little Mick? No offense, Grandpa, but he's not the easiest guy to talk to when he likes you. He doesn't have the time of day for me."

"Your Da holds up his end of the conversation, when there's conversation worth having."

A pause and another sip of beer. I took the moment to go back through the years, to when I was a kid and all of the boys talked about their dads, and uncles, and the war. When we played war games and killed Nazis and Japs.

"I've asked him, you know, about the war but he won't talk about it. I asked Uncle Charlie, and Uncle Arthur, and Seamus and Danny. They all tell the same things. They talk about the chow, the weather, and how their feet hurt, but they don't talk about it. I don't get it."

"Yes, you do, you get it plenty. He was there all right, your father. Charlie too, all of them in one way or another, but he was in the middle of it, much more so than Danny or Arthur and Seamus. He came home far more changed than the rest did. For him it was the hardest. And I can see it is for you."

My glass was almost empty, and there were no other distractions. Thomas had me right where he wanted me.

"Ahh. I'll get over it, I'm just trying to get used to, you know, workin' and like, you know, payin' bills. Stuff like that."

Thomas turned toward the mirror again and took a sip of his beer. This time he spoke to the mirror.

"You've walked into the darkness. I can see it in your eyes, son. That's the other side—and the darkness leaves its mark. The ones that have walked there—and lived—they can never see this side the same way again. They never completely get used to it, as you say."

"I want to forget about that part, Seanathair, I need to forget about it."

Thomas took a moment to re-light his pipe that had gone dead in his hand. He puffed out a good cloud of smoke and pointed the stem at my image in the mirror.

"You can't and you won't. It's a hard thing—the darkness. What you saw there—that thing isn't something terrible out in front of you somewhere, but inside of you, a frightful, loathsome thing squatting deep inside of you—waiting. Seeing it and what it is capable of, it makes you afraid—and ashamed."

Shocked, I stared at the old man in the mirror, his eyes meeting mine. How could he know this—about the beast?

"Some things are beyond redemption, Grandpa; there are things that you can't take back."

"No, you cannot take it back, Mo Mhac, but the darkness is a living thing. It feeds on sorrow and regret it does. It has a hunger that will eat you from the inside, and if you allow it, you will become it. A little at a time you will become—that thing." He paused and threw down his whiskey. "You will become—darkness itself."

I snatched my beer glass and threw back the last swallow, putting down the glass down. It hit the bar harder than I had meant to, and Willy was there in a flash to refill it. This time he stayed.

"He and I don't talk. I'm pretty sure we're past that. I don't think I could, and I'm pretty sure he won't."

"Your Da holds his own counsel, but there are two sides of every coin. I see the other side from the one that you see, and you'll see it now too." He set his pipe down in the ashtray and took a sip of beer. "A quiet man holds many secrets."

"Grandpa, you don't know how hard it is to get up close to him."

"Do you know what Mick, your father, did in the war boy? Do you know what his job was? Don't you think he prays for redemption? You need to talk to them, but this time you'll be speaking from where they have stood all these many years."

Willy nodded, and stayed put. Then he reached back up to the top shelf and brought down the Jameson and poured three more. Setting the bottle on the bar, he looked down at the three glasses and spoke. "I did a full tour in Korea, you know, 1952, 1st Marine Division," and then almost reluctantly he raised his fist. "Oorah." He threw down the shot and looked me in the eye.

Suddenly, in that moment, Willy changed right before my eyes. I saw it in his eyes; as he looked into mine, I saw the irretrievable sadness, the regret—the darkness.

Then Thomas finished. "I can imagine it though, what you did, what you saw. How much of what you went through does he know about? Have you opened up with him about it? The shit that they did show us on the television was bad enough; you don't have to stretch your imagination too far to know that it was probably worse. Now you come home with that stuff that they pinned on your chest and I know they don't give you those for peeling potatoes. So how about it, Emmett, how much have you shared? You've always had a talent for collecting scars but there are more now. Your hand, and your face. I'm thinking there are more on the inside too."

He poked his finger into my chest for emphasis.

"Purgatory is for the dead, not the living, Emmett. You need to find your way back home. It's time you had a talk—with him—and with them." He paused to finish his beer. "Before it's too late."

Diary of Mick Casey

January 17, 1945
Occupied Austria

Our fighter escort turned back; we're going too far for their fuel reserves today. After the escort pulled out, the Krauts came in hard and fast. Concentrating their attack on just one ship, attacking out of the sun. I can't draw a bead; they're staying out of my turret sights. I can't tell how many there are. The Krauts know not to attack straight on from the rear—we tail gunners have taught them a lesson or two—but we're in a lower plane in the formation so they're above us. My guns won't track that far. We're fighting back, I can hear the guys in my headset, we're fighting back.

ME-109s, gee, they're fast. First, they're there and then they're gone. They flash past above me. Most of them have machine guns, but some of them have cannons. All of a sudden 902, Rosy Lips explodes in a ball of flame—from the waist back the rest of the plane disappears in fire. She's just above us and a little to port, tight in the formation. Her wings fold back against the fuselage and for a second the nose lifts up, trailing a huge ball of flame—she stalls. I can see the tail gun turret as it falls away. Hitchcock is the gunner's name, I don't remember his first one. I think I can see him get a leg out of the turret, but he has no parachute anyway. Rosy Lips is a dead stick; she heels over and turns at us, falling right past me. I can see the boys in the cockpit, fighting the controls. There is nothing but fire behind them. The captain calls on the intercom, "IP approaching, pull the pins." I unbuckle and crawl back into the bomb bay.

Emmett

September 1973
Galesburg, Illinois

The breeze coming in the window above the bed blew the curtains and I woke with a start. I hadn't meant to fall asleep. Lying flat on my back, I opened my eyes to a dark and silent room. The girl lying next to me had her head cradled on my chest, my left arm underneath her. I couldn't check my watch for the time without pulling my arm loose; I didn't want to wake her. As gently as I could, I eased off the side of the bed down onto my knees and dragged my arm free and checked my big fancy watch with the luminous face; it was after two o'clock in the morning!

This was a crisis. It didn't really matter what time it was. I was screwed. I needed to be a long way from where I was right now. Yep, screwed. It was early Monday morning and I needed to clock in at work in four and a half hours, give or take one minute. The problem was that I was 180 miles away and not exactly dressed for work.

I climbed out of bed onto my feet, noting that I had a lot of very stiff muscles in my back and the fronts of my legs; it had been a rigorous evening. Reaching around behind me, I flicked the bathroom light on and was momentarily blinded by the bright fluorescents. Squinting, I located my pants, shirt, socks, and boots, sat on the bed frantically pulling them on in random fashion. Without tying my boots, I clomped into the bathroom and confronted the accusing specter in the mirror. My eyes were puffy from the early hour and lack of sleep, my hair was everywhere except where it should be, and my beard was a rat's nest spreading out over the front of my T-shirt. I couldn't fix it. Even if it would make a difference, there was no time to shower and do it properly. I gathered a couple of handfuls of hair and pulled it straight back; scooping a rubber band off the back of the sink, I made a quick ponytail and cinched it tight. I finger-combed my beard as I stumped around the tiny bedroom locating my wallet, new knife, and other gear.

In the half light from the bathroom, I took one last look at her. Her already dark skin was almost black against the white of the sheets; an explosion of black kinky hair framed her beautiful face still stunning even in sleep, her dark lips curled in a barely perceptible smile. She was a captivating mixture of beauty and athleticism that fueled an almost unquenchable sexual appetite, and I had enjoyed every ounce of it. Sadly, it was unlikely I would see her again. She was smart but naïve, and that could be a dangerous combination in a dangerous pastime.

Snapping up my car keys, I headed for the door. The last thing I picked up was the plastic-wrapped brick lying behind the front door. Twenty inches long by six inches high and ten inches wide, it looked like it should weigh more than it did. As it was, it was just slightly under two and a half pounds, one thousand grams; pretty light or pretty heavy depending on the vernacular you're speaking in. It represented almost two weeks of effort and in the end I couldn't have done it without her. She had been my way past the gatekeeper, and I had spent most of the previous evening and night showing my appreciation.

Street value is a fickle thing, depending on which side of the street you're on. The side of the street I didn't want to be on represented probable life in prison; the side of the street I planned to stay on represented thousands of *dólares*. I was committed to my side of the street, but yesterday it had been a near thing. Sometimes those things go as smooth as silk, and then there was yesterday.

I was not a dealer. I was a courier. It was the only skill that my Army career trained me for. I was honest; mostly dependable, even when it wasn't convenient, and I was very good at what I did. It provided extra income, and it made my life more interesting. I have learned that there are a lot of wrong things that happen in this world, but your interpretation of wrong largely depends upon which end of the shit-stick you're on. I've also learned that things that people believe are right in this world seem to revolve around their profit and loss ratios. Good and bad are subjective judgments that are made mostly by people who make those judgments from a distance. Personally, I just don't care. What I did was interesting, occasionally dangerous, always exciting, and which side of the "good and bad" line I was on was irrelevant to me. That was my drug; stress, I was a stress junkie. It helped me feel like I wasn't dead inside.

It started with a friend who knew a guy who knew another guy and so on, the way these things always start. It had culminated with a drive to Knox College in Galesburg to be exact and a displaced inner-city Chicago kid who mistakenly was trying to be a college student. He had plenty of product but no market. Why he had no market became instantly clear when we met him. He was a wigged-out speed freak dressed in clothes that were two sizes too large due to his rail-thin body, his eyes bugged out of his head, and his nose ran constantly, which he wiped with his fingers and then on his filthy pants leg. His face featured an entire crop of acne in varying states of maturity. His apartment was full of trash, dirty laundry, and the aroma of a full back-alley dumpster air freshener. No one in their right mind would have done business with him. He twitched and fidgeted, he would sit only to jump back up on his feet, he paced and checked the windows in his amped-up paranoia. He had put all of his feelers out for buyers, but there had been no bites. Now the walls were closing in on him and he needed to get rid of it. As a result, the price dropped considerably, and my friend, who had a friend who knew a friend and so on, came into the market. To be honest the guy scared the crap out of me. I'd seen what speed-fueled paranoia is capable of.

I didn't make the deals, only the transfers; as a courier, the deal was done before I arrived, and I wasn't there to make friends; or negotiate. The bread was counted and the weed was tested. Both were acceptable by most standards. The burn-out liked the look of my friend; he'd been expecting her. He didn't like the look of me. He didn't like my face, and he especially didn't like my name. Hell, he probably didn't even like my boots. Personally, I liked my boots, a lot.

The more he twitched the more paranoid he got. He started talking about undercover pigs and getting held up. Because of the danger he might be in, he decided that it would be a good idea to shake me down, and to raise the already agreed-to price. I simply turned and headed for the door. I get paid whether I deliver or not, and I had a reliable witness that the deal's failure was not my fault. I get paid a lot more if do deliver though, so I was getting a little agitated myself, maybe a bit more than a little.

He cut me off as I headed to the door, vaulting onto the sofa and running to the end closest to the door, where he balanced on the armrest in his electrified state, eyes twitching in their sockets. Then he made a big mistake. He pulled a knife out of his back pocket. It was a very respectable one. My reflexes were faster than my thought processes and they decided that a sedative would do him a lot of good. Maybe help calm him down a little; I gave him one. By the time I had considered it, he was resting comfortably and my knuckles hurt. He was already on the sofa anyway. I left the money, took the bale of weed, and kept the knife. It really was a very nice knife.

It was cool outside when I hit the sidewalk, but I draped my old field jacket over the bundle just the same and made for the parking lot. Unlocking and opening the door of the Buick coupe, I laid the weed on the backseat and threw my coat over the top. I was well aware of my appearance. Since exiting the Army almost nine months earlier, I had not suffered a single haircut or shave. In addition, after one evening in which I was seriously overserved, I had acquired an earring in my left lobe. After two minutes of deep meditation the next morning in front of the bathroom mirror, I decided that I liked it and that it would annoy a lot of people; so I kept it.

People who looked like me were traffic stopped for all manner of reasons and most of them were bullshit. The stupid ones had their dope sitting in their laps, or on the passenger seat. Others hid it in the trunk. Cops examined the front seat, the lap, and floor from their vantage point outside of the driver's side window very carefully with their flashlights. They also went through the trunk with a fine-tooth comb. These days, even a stray pot seed was reason enough for an arrest. The best place to put things was in plain sight, but not in plain sight, hence the backseat. A low-roofed Buick Skylark coupe made the backseat a hard place to get at for an overweight cop with a utility belt.

Climbing into the Buick, I fired up the engine and headed out of town to the I-74. Even if I had a rocket up my ass, I was going to have a hard time getting back in time for work, but I was going to give it the old college try. I came off the ramp onto the interstate at seventy miles per hour. Because of the time of night and the absence of traffic, I quickly pushed it to eighty and shortly after that the V-8 hammered along at ninety without my even noticing. There were no cars and few trucks, at that speed I thought I was going to make it. I pinched my cheeks to keep me alert and lit a reefer to help me stay awake. Halfway to the Interstate 80 interchange I was practically on top of the state trooper cruiser parked in the median before I saw him.

Almost before he appeared in my rearview mirror, the flashing lights on the cruiser fired up and the headlights danced up out of the grassy median. I was dead-to-rights and knew it. There was no point in waiting for him to arrive, so I opened all the windows and gave it another quarter mile, just to air out the cabin a bit, then eased over onto the shoulder and turned on my emergency flashers and closed the windows again. The cruiser didn't even have to get up to speed but instead eased up behind me with his spotlight aimed directly into the mirrors. I spent the time waiting for him to get out of the car wishing the backseat was empty. Any rummaging around I did he would see as a result of the spotlight, so I sat in my sweat and waited. The Ruger and Stevens twelve-gauge were both cased and locked in the trunk, so I had nothing to worry about there. They were perfectly legal where they were. I was fairly certain that they were both unloaded. It was the bundle on the backseat that was going to get all of the attention; loaded weapons would only increase the egregiousness of the arrest.

It was a slow night, and he was going to take his time, filling the otherwise empty time of a nothing-to-do shift. Eventually, in the flashing strobes of the roof lights, I saw the driver's side door of the cruiser swing open and then the passenger door opened too. The passenger remained behind the open door of the cruiser. Shit, double-teamed, doubly thorough search. I didn't bother rehearsing any lame excuses. I spent the time thinking about prison garb. Still in no hurry, he presented a giant silhouette as he approached backlit by the spotlight; he looked pretty trim from this vantage point, so the backseat was going to be a snap. I rolled my window down and dragged out my wallet. The first twenty seconds would tell the tale. If he asked for my license I might be good, a speeding ticket and then on my way. If he asked me to step out of the car, a search was almost a guarantee. If he walked me back to the cruiser and put me in the back, I was bound for Joliet prison for sure, and the trunk would only be a formality.

The flashlight hit me full in the face, then slowly dragged down across my beard, shirt, and lap. It made a circuit of the passenger side floorboards and then up onto the seat and then back to my face, making me squint up at him. I couldn't make an assessment of the cop because I couldn't see him behind the light. I wasn't even trying to see the other guy on the right side of the car.

"Going to a fire?"

"No, Officer, I'm going to be late for work. Guess I got carried away."

"Ninety-three miles per hour is a little more than carried away."

The flashlight did another lap; then with a long sigh he added, "Please step out of the vehicle, sir."

Shit. If he asks me to accompany to the cruiser, I'll already be half arrested. Once I was locked in the backseat behind the cage, I'd get to watch the rest of my life burn down from a front row seat.

"Please accompany me back to the vehicle and may I see your driver's license?"

Shit.

I still hadn't noticed the other cop, but as we walked back to the car, I took a good look. It was a kid, well, not a kid, but if he was my age I would have been surprised. More importantly, he wasn't wearing a uniform; he was in plain clothes. A ride-along?

I was very politely placed in the backseat of the cruiser, the trooper placing his hand on the top of my head to prevent me from hitting it against the roof of the car as I lowered myself into the seat. Pointlessly I noted that there were no door handles on the inside. Then he and his ride-along got into the front with my driver's license. The trooper immediately thumbed his mike and got on the radio requesting a 10-27 (vehicle registration check) and ran my driver's license number. The cruiser was not really warm, but the sweat was already running down my butt crack just the same. I figured I better do something. I was caught speeding, I was pretty stoned, I was a long way from home, and I had a life sentence on the backseat of the Buick. My brain was doing gymnastics like a Russian Gold Medalist. Checking my shit out was going to take a while, phone calls would have to be made, people who didn't want to be busy were going to have to become busy, and the gigantic law enforcement machine was going to take its time fucking my life up. I was going down without my say.

"Listen, officer, I know I was speeding, you know, I was down in Galesburg seeing my girlfriend," (not entirely true), "well, it got late and I fell asleep, but I gotta be at work by seven back in Elmhurst, so I got a little carried away."

No response. The two in the front seat exchanged glances.

"Well, you know how it is, I don't get to see her very often now that she's so far away, it was hard to say good-bye. You know how it is. Right?"

No response. The radio said nothing.

"There's no traffic, not even a little, you know, so even if I was to have an accident it would only be one car, and well, at that speed, you know, you'd probably be cleaning me up with a shovel, so you know…" I thought it might be humorous.

This time he looked at me in the mirror, and it wasn't really a friendly look, so the humorous approach was probably not the best avenue to pursue. I tried another tack.

"I haven't been out of the service very long, and it's been

pretty hard, you know, adjusting and all, and this is my first girlfriend, she's pretty neat, I don't have a picture of her though. I'm like, you know, getting my life going again, after, you know, being over there."

No response. He looked over at the kid and his eyebrows ticked up. Just a marginal twitch. Aha, maybe an opening. I tried to widen it.

"Yeah, I was in the Central Highlands, 173rd Infantry. We saw some shit, that's for sure, compared to that it's really good to be back in the States, I can tell you that." My nerves were getting the best of me and I was talking fast trying to fill all the empty space in the car.

No response from the front seat, but the radio blasted static; at least someone was listening.

"I'm a machinist, well, at least I'm learning how to be a machinist, it's an apprenticeship, so I can't be late, you know. I probably should have slowed down. I guess I'll be more careful. I was just trying to make up a little time, you know, so I wouldn't be late."

Geez, I needed to shut up.

From the front seat, "If you'd been going any faster you'd have hit Warp Factor One."

I shut up. I was just making it worse. The trooper levered open his door and put his big fucking trooper boot out on the pavement. The trunk was about to become a formality. We still hadn't been passed by any other cars and only a few semis, although I was hopeful there wasn't much chance he'd get picked off by a passing car. The kid started to get out of the other side.

"All units, all units. 10-33. Vehicle emergency, car versus

semi-truck trailer rollover, milepost twenty-seven south-bound. All units respond." The radio blasted a lot louder than it needed to until I realized the trooper had switched it over to the rooftop speaker.

The trooper dropped back into his seat, gave a huge sigh, and thumbed the button on the microphone.

"This is one-two-one, I have a 10-26 still on board." (Detained subject)

"Multiple injuries, all speed. All units respond." Apparently the radio was in no mood for a debate.

The trooper dropped his boot back on the pavement and levered himself out of the car. Straightening up he adjusted his gun belt and with his hands on his hips he looked up and then down the road, took a deep breath, and then with a sigh he reached back and pulled open the rear door and beckoned me out with a twitch of his fingers. He made meaningful eye contact. It was the first time I'd seen his face. It wasn't a pretty face, it was a pissed-off face. I straightened up out of the cruiser. He was half a head taller than me.

"Hit the road, hippie, and work on the bullshit. It's weak."

Diary of Mick Casey, Tail Gunner

JANUARY 20, 1945

We're grounded today, bad weather. Heavy cloud cover here and apparently over our target area. I'm nervous. Tuesday was a different kind of mission and I want to get right back on the horse again before I let my nerves get the best of me. With the extra time, we got to go down the headquarters office complex and got showers. The water wasn't hot, but at least it wasn't ice cold either. Most of the guys seem like me—we want to go, we want the war to end, and we want to help make it end, but this isn't any fun.

It took almost a year of training to become a tight bomber crew. We know each other's jobs; we know pretty much how each one of us is going to react. We know we're good at our jobs. I'd say I trust these guys with my life, but that's what I do every day. I also know what happens when it's "Bombs Away." I know what happens down there, I see it. Riding backwards, watching where we've been, I watch as we finish our bomb run. I can see the flash of the hundred-pounders when they impact. I can even see the shock wave of the concussion as it expands out from the impact. The factories and railroads down there, those people are not soldiers, those people are just people. I see it, riding backwards, I know what it means to them. I found a passage in the Bible about it. "And I looked and behold a pale horse and the name that sat on him was Death, and Hell followed him." We ride the pale horse—*we go again tomorrow.*

Emmett 'Hole' Casey, machinist

March 1974
Elmhurst, Illinois

Ever since I had first gotten the job at Flick's and used his name, Andy Polanco had taken me under his wing. He was easy, a big man with a hearty laugh and had worked in the shop almost longer than anyone else both before and after he'd returned from the service. He was not a foreman, but he still called most of the shots. It was Andy who took me aside and gave me a little talk about working through my breaks when everyone else went to the lunchroom. In no uncertain terms he had explained how this was taboo. It made the other men nervous, and they didn't like it. So, I had stopped and spent the mandatory break time watching the young women through the glass as they worked at their desks inside the offices. I didn't go to the breakroom with the other guys. I wasn't here to make friends.

Every morning at precisely 9:00 Andy would stick his newspaper under his arm and leave the department for his morning "constitutional." He would be gone just as long as it took him to read the entire paper no matter how long it took him to finish his bowel movement. No one batted an eye at this obvious break in shop protocol, but I always puzzled about how he got away with it. It was after my six-month review that he explained it, right before he handed me his newspaper.

During my review the foreman made a production of explaining time standards. All operations in the shop had been studied very carefully by a time-study engineer. Once this person had observed the operation and machine operator, a standard was arrived at: this standard considered how long it took to set up a machine for the next job, and how long it took to make one piece, ten pieces, and a hundred pieces. This standard was then used as a yardstick to determine if the operator/machinist was efficient and also to gauge his wage determinations. I was pretty excited when he showed that my production was well above 100 percent of the time standards, and gave me a ten-cent-an-hour raise. That is, I was excited until Andy took me aside and gave me one of his talks.

Andy told me that I was a sprinter, and that the other guys in the department were long-distance runners. When I looked at him funny, he explained.

"Look, Hole, you're already bored. You'll never last here, you'll move on. You know it and I know it. At first, you'll move up and try a different, more difficult machine, sure, or a harder piece to make, but you'll run out of those pretty soon. Then you'll move on. I've seen it a hundred times. The rest of these guys," he said, waving his arm toward the shop, "they don't give two shits about job satisfaction, or whether it's fulfilling their inner needs."

He stopped and fished out a Pall Mall, lit it, and took a long drag. While he exhaled, he looked over at the busy shop and ran his hand across his tight crew cut. Turning back to me,

"Look. They want to punch the clock, get their paychecks and go home and grill on the patio. Guys like you turn it into a race, you make the standards, then you beat them, then the standards go up. Now these guys have to hit it harder just to make the rate. Pretty soon the job starts to really suck. These are guys that don't want to go anywhere; their imagination extends as far as next week's check and eventual retirement. They like it that way."

He pinched the ember off his smoke and stuck the butt in his shirt pocket and put his hands on his hips. Taking a deep breath in and out of his nose, he reached under his arm, grabbed his folded newspaper, and slapped me in the chest with it and then stuck it under my arm. "Think about it, okay?"

I did think about it. I thought about it as long as it took to read Andy's newspaper while I took a shit. I walked down to HR and checked the board. There was a position for a starting draftsman in the Engineering Department. I opened the door and went in.

Diary of Mick Casey, Tail Gunner

February 2, 1945

No flying today, too much cloud cover over the drop site again. I go out and run down the half mile of graded runway and then off into the fields beyond for another half mile to the end of our run-out, and back. I do it again and again. I get the rhythm going in my feet but it doesn't clear the visions out of my mind. I can't seem to exhaust it out of my body. My Pappy would have said that I was wound tighter than a two-dollar watch. Even in the winter cold I'm soaked with sweat and I can't stop the restlessness. I've already read the books that we have, and there aren't any newspapers here. I can't think of anyone else to write a letter to. I can't sleep all day, although I tried, it's too cold. I'm jumpy, we lost another plane yesterday. I saw their parachutes; then I saw the Nazi fighters come in and strafe them while they hung there. I can't think about anything else.

I went up to the HQ but the showers were off. One of the engineers told me it would be fixed in about thirty minutes. Over in one corner of the building there are a few dumb-bells and ropes that you could skip. Some of the guys had set up a makeshift ring for boxing. A couple of guys were hanging around on the ropes and there were a few officers smoking and talking against the wall on the other side. I didn't want to skip rope or lift weights but while I waited for the shower I just thought I'd watch them for a little while. Two guys had gloves on and were sparring. Nobody seemed to be any chattier than I wanted to be.

The sparring didn't seem very fair to me. The bigger of the two fellows could reach in and poke the other guy and the other guy couldn't seem to avoid it. After about five minutes he threw up his hands, signaled that he'd had enough, and came over to the ropes, where another guy was acting as some kind of referee. He helped him out of the gloves.

The big guy was still in the ring and looking around and asking who was next. Nobody wanted any part of him, but he seemed to take an interest in me for some reason. I was probably the only guy in there who he hadn't already beaten, I guess. He started to taunt me about coming in and having a round or two. He acted pretty confident about it, probably because he was a lot bigger than I was.

"I don't know anything about boxing."

"Well, time enough to learn—what'ya say, tail gunner?"

"I think it would be a nice thing for you to step in there and teach this young man a few manners."

I jerked around. Captain Brinker stood directly behind me with Lieutenant Holquist, our co-pilot.

"I don't box—sir."

"Casey, I've trained with you for over a year, and I've fought with you now. If there's one thing I know, you're one of the toughest sons-a-bitches I've ever met."

I looked back at the big guy. I thought I might have seen

him in the engine shop.

"I can't box that guy, Captain."

Holquist put an arm on my shoulder and turned me away from the ring. Reaching into the pocket of his bomber jacket, he produced a small pocket flask and handed it to me. I took a long swallow.

"This guy is a boxer for sure, Casey, so don't box him. Fight him!"

I looked at him and Brinker. Brinker's lips were in a tight line and he looked at me and gave me a curt nod. I took another drink out of the flask.

The gloves were heavier than I'd expected once I had them on, but I stepped through the ropes. Inside the ring seemed smaller than it looked from the outside and the guy seemed bigger. He came over and held out his gloves and I tapped them.

"I'm Mick Casey."

"Give a shit who you are, let's box."

He jabbed me in the forehead with his left hand and it rocked me back. I stepped back a few steps to shake the cobwebs out of my head, but he came on and really rocked me in the ribs with his right hand. I lost my breath and held my hands up for a break; instead he came on again and this time he nailed me right in the face—

"Mick, Mick, it's okay, Mick— stop now. MICK—STOP!"

Holquist appeared in my vision; someone else had me from behind holding my arms. My breath was roaring in and out of my lungs, and every muscle in my body was as tight as a banjo string.

"Jesus, Mick!"

The engine shop mechanic was lying on his back in front of me. His face looked like ground meat. His eyes were rolled up in his head. The unofficial referee was holding something under his nose, and another guy with a Red Cross armband was kneeling beside him.

"Jesus, Mick. You almost killed him." Holquist's face was white. "Jesus, I can't believe what I just saw. Jesus."

The grip on my arms eased and I dropped my hands. They suddenly felt like they each weighed a hundred pounds.

"Well, you were right, you sure can't box. That wasn't even fair." Lieutenant Holquist's voice was excited and tense. "I don't know what I just saw, but it sure wasn't boxing."

"Corporal, I think we'll just get those gloves off, and then get outside and cool off a little." Brinker, from behind me still gripping my elbows, his voice was rock steady.

Once I got the gloves off, I climbed out through the ropes and Holquist took my arm and steered me out the bay doors. Outside, the chilly spring air felt wonderful on my face. I took a deep breath of it. My mind was clear, the vision of the parachutes was gone, my body was unclenched—relaxed. I sighed and then looked up at my two flight officers.

Brinker spoke. "Here's twenty bucks, Casey. I had ten on you and it was three-to-one odds. I should have put down fifty."

"Should have been a hundred to one," Holquist added. "Jesus, I never would have believed it if I hadn't just watched it. I'm glad we've got you in the tail, Casey. You're worth your weight. I'm proud to fight beside you. By the way, here's another twenty. I had ten on you too." He handed me the flask. "Keep it."

R.E. Casey

Federal Criminal Courts Building
Chicago, Illinois, 1974

I always got a funny look from Human Resources at work when I told them that I had to go into the city for an Army thing, but they let me go. It was probably a good thing that I was good at my job, or they'd probably just fire me. I hated this, every bit of it. I couldn't stand that they kept me on a leash. Once a month, I called the number that I kept in my wallet. A man came on the phone with a voice that told me he couldn't give two shits about me or his job. I gave him my social security number and spelled my last name. I told him I was working and where. I told him my address hadn't changed and what it was. I could hear him write it down, the pen scraping across a paper on a hard desktop. He asked if I'd had any run-ins with authority, traffic tickets, and I told him no. We hung up.

Every two months I had to show up at the office in person just in case it wasn't really me on the phone. That was where I was, sitting in an office behind a closed door facing a desk with no one sitting at it. I'd been here awhile. I was pretty sure that whoever *Couldn't-give-two-shits* was not too bothered about making me wait. There was a window behind the desk with a spectacular view of a brick wall eight or ten feet away and just enough light filtering in from above so that you would think that it was just about to rain. When he did get here he'd rush in and drop my file in the middle of the desk from as high up as he could. That way it made a loud smack when it landed, somehow making it seem more significant. Then he'd throw his lard ass into the fake leather swivel chair and spin it toward the desk. Once he was facing me, he'd give me the long look and then break open the file. He would spend a solid five minutes reading my file, like he had never seen it before in his life. Then he'd ask to see my ID card and then he'd ask me the same stupid questions that he asked over the phone and then to see my paycheck stubs—to prove that I was working. Once he started asking questions, the interview would take about three minutes, but it would take me the whole day to get it done and cost me an arm and a leg for gas, parking, and lost wages.

When the door finally opened behind me, the probation officer didn't rush past. Instead the door closed. I could feel him behind me. The hair on the back of my neck rose. I don't like people behind me.

"You look a fair sight better than the last time I saw you, Mr. Casey. You need a haircut."

The chair didn't swivel, but I jerked around to see who it was. There was no mistaking the face, but I would never have recognized his voice. He gave me a good long look in the eye. We'd never exchanged more than a couple of dozen words collectively over the course of time, but you would never forget the face if you lived to be one hundred years old.

"You've been a busy boy, Casey." This time no "Mister" in front of it.

He was dressed in a suit and tie, a nice one, but even the clothes couldn't detract from the coolness that radiated off of him. The man I only knew as Dunn walked to the window and stood looking out with his hands in his pockets for a few moments. I could feel sweat break out under my arms and between my ass cheeks. Dunn had been the man who had pulled me out of the fire back in the service; if he was here it had to mean he had changed his mind.

It would have been enough that the man purely scared the hell out of me anyway; he just had that aura about him. Something was about to go terribly wrong. I had only seen Dunn at one other time in my life, and it had been one of the most frightening experiences that I had ever had. It still gave me cold sweats when I recalled it. But I had been able to feel him on the edges of other situations, always there but not there, and always it seemed when things were at their worst. He had to be here to finally drop the hammer on me. But why now?

Finally finished with his examination of the brick wall outside the window, he turned and sat in the fake leather swivel chair. Leaning back, he looked at me down his nose and over his prominent cheekbones.

"Nice to see you've put on a little weight. Prison chow didn't seem to agree with you."

I couldn't think of a thing to say, so I didn't.

He rocked forward.

"How's civilian life treating you?"

I couldn't imagine socializing with this guy, but he'd asked so I answered.

"S'okay."

"Like it—working I mean."

"S'okay."

"I'm not asking about your job at the shop. That's clear enough, but you've been moonlighting a little too, haven't you? There doesn't seem to be any mention of that in your file, I noticed."

My palms were damp and somehow the room was a lot warmer than it needed to be and the light seemed to have dimmed a little.

"I got just the one job."

"Hmm, that's not the way I hear it. It would seem that you've been taking the odd job on the side."

"Look, uh, Mister Dunn is it? Look, I'm staying clean, they make sure of that. I work, I go home, I mind my own business."

"It's Walter Dunn, but just call me Dunn. The last time we met I was with the Criminal Investigation Division, but I'm not CID anymore, or military either. I'm FBI now, and I'm with the SOG, Special Operations Group. That's a lot of alphabet soup, but it means I get paid to find people, watch them, and arrest them."

Well, shit!

"I've been on the road watching a particularly nasty prick. He's ended up here now, and I'm right behind him." He paused for effect and gave me another long look. "There are some tangent connections to military service, and he has local connections inside of this building somehow that he makes use of. I've been going through records and putting together a picture of his network and—well, what do you know?—guess who pops up on my radar?"

I took a deep breath. I was pretty sure I didn't know

anything or anybody inside of this building, and whenever possible I avoided nasty pricks.

"I'm just a working stiff now. I left that behind me, back in Stuttgart. Look, uh, Dunn," I held up my hands palms out, "look at my hands. I can't get them any cleaner than this anymore."

He didn't smile. Instead he gave me the scary face. The one I'd seen back in Seattle.

"Around here you are clean. Out a little west of here, I'm getting a different story. I didn't have to dig very hard to get it either. Especially once I had an idea of where to look."

How much could there be on that? He had to be fishing. I wasn't taking the bait. I tried to hold his gaze and I shut up. He continued, still leaning back feigning nonchalance and now looking up toward the ceiling.

"It would seem that when someone wants to, say, move something." He gestured with his hand in the air. "Something that they'd rather not move themselves, but that really needs to be moved, let's say." He circled his hand for emphasis. "They need a courier and there are a very few dependable ones that are, um, available. For a price, of course. Right now, in the western suburbs there seems to be one in particular that will do it regardless of the package involved, or, let's say, the neighborhood that it's going to. It would seem that this particular person is discreet, only works at night, and as far as I can tell has never dropped a package—yet."

Double shit.

"The FBI is a big operation. There isn't very much they can't find once you get them moving. I didn't even have to do the legwork. I'm not looking at you, Casey, but honest to God, you keep falling into my lap and I've got to say—every time you do, it always ends up being interesting." He leaned back in his chair and gave me another long down-his-nose look. After a sufficiently uncomfortable pause, he seemed to arrive at a decision because he took a deep breath and leaned forward, putting his arms on the desk, and adopted a more even tone.

"That business in Germany, they would have hung you out to dry just so it would look like they had cleaned up their mess. I'm not saying you weren't stupid; that would be a stretch. But in the end, I would not have gotten the whole thing sorted out before most of those guys had covered their tracks. In the end, we got the ones we needed to get. It took me an entire year to get inside that business in Seattle, and after you showed up I had it wrapped up in two weeks. You got off easy compared to what it could have been, mostly because you seem to know how to act stupid when it suits you, and smart when no one is looking."

That's as close to a complete explanation of the situation as I had ever gotten, but we still weren't where he was going. The room wasn't cooling off in the slightest.

"I went to bat for you back there because I'd seen how they cornered you. The same way they had you back at Lewis. By the time you could have had some way of protesting your way out, your hands were already dirty and you were in too deep. I'm not sentimental and I'm not a romantic, but I do have my own personal sense of justice, so I got it. Don't kid yourself for one minute, though, that it was because we are friends."

I was not about to consider him as a friend. The guy had an aura about him that just whispered, "Don't fuck with me." It bothered me a little that we were in the same area code.

"I'm not going to sit here and waste my time having a discussion about your extracurriculars. If you stay on the path you're on, you'll be caught soon enough—or dead. By now you've probably had plenty of lectures about making something better of yourself. It's your life and like I said I'm not looking at you—at this particular time. Please don't kid yourself either, you are much too small a fry for me to bother with you, but time is on my side and not yours."

This was an interesting albeit one-sided conversation, but I knew there was a point to it. He wouldn't be here otherwise. Even in his most benign posture, he still had a big hammer and he was just getting it ready. This part was just foreplay. Almost unconsciously the tension that had been building in my legs pushed my chair back an inch or two. I would so much rather have had the lard ass, "couldn't give two shits" pencil-pusher out for lunch and drinks. I fished out a cigarette, showed it to him, and he nodded, so I lit it and took a long drag on it. Well, fuck.

"Whether you straighten out your shit or someone else does it for you is only of marginal concern to me. I kind of like you, Casey. I've seen you do some fairly difficult things, and evidence of even more difficult things; you could go a long way or get put away for a long time. The path you're on is an unforgiving one. Once again though," he tapped his chest, "only marginal concern. Your interview with the PO is cancelled today, and when you leave here I will be leaving with you."

"You're arresting me!?"

"Don't flatter yourself. It's simply a favor for a favor."

Oh shit, oh shit, oh shit. I should have known from the beginning. This was not going to be a hammer; a locomotive was going to drop on me.

Dunn leaned forward and the tough voice was back.

"This nasty prick I'm looking for is in Chicago for now. He is, as they say, a businessman. The worst kind of businessman, drugs, prostitution, and worse. His latest enterprise is what is called human trafficking, and he has branched out into the slave trade. A sordid enterprise to say the least, but his specialty is abducting underage children, mostly girls. Once he has them he starts them on heroin to get them addicted, dependent, and docile, and then sells them to the highest bidder. He has already worn out his welcome in Detroit and Milwaukee and recently moved the operation into the western suburbs. Any young girls will do, but little white girls command the highest prices, and the suburbs have a lot of them. Once he crossed into Illinois he's mine, he's federal, and now I'm going to get him."

"Sounds like a real piece of shit."

"He would take that as a compliment. He is ruthless. We are aware of at least two former business partners who accidentally overdosed on heroin, and at least two girlfriends who somehow fell on very sharp knives across their throats."

This was just getting better and better.

"So, it sounds like your job's pretty interesting, quite the challenge, I'd say, but it sure doesn't have anything to do with me. I haven't heard anything about any of this going on out by me."

"I'm going to get this son of a bitch," somehow his voice got even tougher sounding, "but I don't have anyone on the ground here. I can't get into his operation—that takes a lot of time, years sometimes, and by that time a lot of kids are never going to grow up." He leaned forward and put his forearms on the desk and made hard eye contact. "That's where you come in, Casey. I need a little help from you for a change. You're going to be my catalyst, my 'boots on the ground.'" He brought his shoulders forward and leaned farther over the desk. Speaking through his clenched teeth, he dropped the hammer. "He's going to need a courier."

"Oh, FUCK NO!" He may have had me on some little things, and then only maybe, but there was no way I wanted to accidentally fall on a very sharp knife—with heroin on it.

His dark eyes held mine and narrowed. "Oh, fuck yes. Fortune is on my side for once. First of all, you have a knack for wrong place/wrong time, but that works in my favor here. Second of all, I think it might just work out, so I'm calling in a favor, a favor for a favor. If you won't or can't do it, I will certainly understand." He leaned back from the desk and swiveled back toward the brick wall outside the window. "But first I wonder if you know what the term implicit guilt means?"

I didn't even try to act like I didn't know, but he went on anyway.

"Let's say you show up for your probation interview, an SOG FBI agent arrives, shows his credentials, and tells your PO that you, Mr. Casey, are a 'person of interest' in an ongoing investigation of kidnapping and sex trafficking. The SOG tells the PO that he has jurisdiction in the case and will be interviewing you today, and you leave together. Suddenly you become far more interesting to your PO." Swiveling back from the window, he made eye contact again. "By sheer association, there becomes an implicit admission of some involvement in a criminal activity. You are still under the Uniform Code of

Military Justice, and the UCMJ is not the criminal justice system that civilians answer to. The UCMJ rules are very different when it comes to allegations of illicit activity." He rocked back in the chair and looked up at the ceiling. "I certainly wouldn't want to bet on the outcome of that hearing if I were a betting man."

My probation officer tracked us with his eyes all the way out of the office.

Diary of Mick Casey

March 24, 1944

Our luck so far has been good. We all figured it would probably change at some point and today was the day. Today the target was a big airfield, Budejovice, Czechoslovakia. Today we were carrying cluster bombs, five twenty-pound anti-personnel little bastards wired together and timed to go off before they hit the ground. They can disable airplanes and people. Lots of bombs, lots of clusters, and a lot of pins to pull when we hit the IP.

We hit the air and had just gotten pulled up tight to the squadron when we all smelled gas. We had developed a fuel leak. We were carrying tons of ordnance and thousands of gallons of high-octane. Without hesitation we got as far away as we could from the rest of the squadron before we became a fireball. The captain pulled her hard back and we dropped down and got off our oxygen. Captain Brinker alerted the field. I imagine that Captain was probably sweating as much as the rest of us. Chutes on for everyone. I was first in line at the back hatch; fuel leaks are bad. Landing with a fuel leak is bad enough, but the bomb shackles are made for take-off, not landing. If we hit hard enough…well, there it is and we were landing heavy.

Brinker and Holquist, our co-pilot, got her down pretty

easy. The crew chief and ground crew that had just gotten into their bunks swarmed onto the plane and found the leak in no time. No such luck that we might abort. Within fifteen minutes we were topped off and hit the runway again and it was a race to catch the squadron. They had a head start and the old girl roared after them. We caught up just before the IP. Thank God we didn't see any enemy fighters. I got my walking oxygen bottle hooked up and headed back to the bomb bay to help pull pins. That's when the real trouble started.

When I got there Taylor was already on the catwalk, looking at me. There's no intercom when we're in there, and we use hand signals we've practiced. It didn't take much to see what the problem was though. Taylor pointed down onto the doors. The shackles had busted loose when we landed back at the field, and the doors were covered with a pile of bombs lying on top of them, in a jumble of clusters, wires, and pins. Some of the pins weren't in the bombs anymore. He gave me a sign with his hand that he was going forward to tell the pilot and navigator. I climbed down. I'm the smallest guy and I lay out as best I could on the catwalk trying to clear the doors. When I looked up most of the crew was gathered at both ends of the bomb bay and talking. I wasn't hooked into the conversation though.

We had to abort the mission. I couldn't clear the mess before we got to the IP, and we were almost there already. The captain swung us out of the formation again and headed out to sea, the Adriatic. We would have to make it home on our own if we didn't get blown to kingdom come first.

Once we got over the water, we lined up on the catwalk. I had to take off my parachute, too bulky for the tight quarters, but I kept my oxygen on. The air was too cold and moving too fast to go without my goggles. I climbed down and stood right on the bomb bay doors. I looked up at Taylor; his eyes were big as dinner plates, but he gave me a thumbs-up. I took a deep breath and did the same. I cut the wires on the first cluster and handed him a twenty-pounder. He handed it to Janssen, who handed it to Spiegs, the navigator, who handed it to the next guy and then farther back. The last man dropped it out the rear hatch. I handed the next one up to Taylor. Today was supposed to be our ninth mission. We didn't get credit for it. We never made our run.

Emmett

A Shooting Gallery, Northside, Chicago, Illinois

They call these places shooting galleries. It was dark and cold, red low-watt lightbulbs randomly screwed into fixtures in the ceiling. A brick brownstone apartment building rose four floors above me from this basement apartment. There were people here and there, lying on old mattresses, or propped in corners. Their bodies were alive, breathing, twitching, but their eyes were not. An old woman lay spread-eagled on a mattress next to a man sitting with his back against the wall. Her dress is pulled up above her waist and the tie-off hangs loose around her upper thigh. His tie is loosened and the sleeve of his white business shirt is rolled up, the syringe still in his hand. Both of them stare at nothing, oblivious to each other. The air stinks of sweat, filth, and poppy. It is quiet, only wraiths live here. Low voices emanate from somewhere farther back. These people didn't come here for the conversation.

This was a new place to me. I'd been in ones like it before; they're all the same. In the service, these places were far off post and I was there to find one of the men before he got caught or robbed or worse. These days I was usually here to retrieve someone for someone else, a loved one gone too long, or a son or daughter gone astray. Tonight, I was here to meet someone. We were supposed to become friends.

The two burly men who stood out of sight in the darkened doorway had checked me out carefully and competently. They worked like a team, one in front, one behind, ex-military most likely, worth whatever they got paid. I had been expected but they were cautious just the same. I'd taken my new knife, thinking that they would expect me to. I'm not comfortable carrying a gun, so I left it in the car. This was supposed to be a business meeting. They took my knife They both pulled it out of its sheath and hefted it, then smiled at me and winked. One of them carried it with him when he brought me inside. I'd be wanting it back.

We stopped in the front room to let our eyes get used to the low light; there was no sense tripping over anyone. Then we went back in the direction of the voices. There were more rooms opening to the right and left as we walked down a hallway, each one with the same decorator. At the end of the hall was a closed door and bright light shone underneath it. The voices inside were now louder and clearer. The big guy knocked softly, two knocks, a pause, then one. The voices on the other side of the door stopped.

November 1958, Crandon, Wisconsin The Dew Drop Inn, Way Up North

The bar was rustic, smelling of woodsmoke, cedar, and stale beer. Mounted antlers and various furbearers decorated the walls between the Rhinelander Beer signs, and motionless cigarette smoke hung just below the ceiling. There were plenty of men already gathered, but in spite of them the place was quiet, subdued, everyone glad to be out of the frigid north woods winter and away from a nagging wife. Along the bar, patrons hunched over their drinks and debated quietly while smoking their cigarettes. The jukebox in the corner was silent.

The men walked in quietly, single file, deer hunters, here for the week up from down south. They all wore the descriptive winter clothing: red and black wool plaid coats and hats, earflaps pulled down over their ears. All but one was young, in their twenties or early thirties; the one other was in the lead and appeared to be maybe three times the age of the others. Six of them, hunters ready for a shot or two, and a beer after a long day of slogging through snow, tracking deer. They didn't look around but instead headed straight to the bar, where they wedged themselves into the available space of those already gathered. The eldest held up two hands, displaying six fingers, and then with his thumb and index finger he indicated short glasses.

The shots were poured, and the bottled beer arrived. Once again, the eldest turned and distributed the shot glasses and with a salute they downed them as one. The glasses hit the bar and then Little Mick stepped up and spun his finger, signaling another round. A burly local who had been crowded a little by the small posse turned to survey the group as a whole and then in a voice loud enough so that most nearby could hear him:

"Well, will you look here, the Irish potato farmers have arrived. Thought I smelled corned beef and cabbage."

The eldest of the group made eye contact with Mick, and then slowly shook his head side to side.

"Railroad must be layin' off if there's so many of you damn Micks got nothin' better to do."

One of the others in the little group straightened up and turned to the speaker, but once again the elder signaled with a shake of his head. Reaching for the newly poured glasses on the bar, he once again passed them out, but before he could raise his glass, the redneck spoke again.

"We don't like Catlicks like you up here. You boys better clear out or me and a couple of my guys will have to throw you back out in the snow."

Thomas Quinn, the elder, sighed, threw back his shot, and removed his hat and set it and the empty glass on the bar. He reached into his back pocket for his wallet and, opening it, he took out two twenty-dollar bills and placed them next to his hat on the bar. This time when he made eye contact with Mick, he nodded; just once. A feral grin spread across the young man's face, and brother Seamus turned and retraced his steps to the door, pausing only long enough to turn the deadbolt. Charlie, Danny, and Arthur joined Seamus and spread out behind Little Mick, and Thomas raised his refilled glass and took a seat on the nearest bar stool...and smiled.

Emmett

FOUR DAYS EARLIER, OLIVER'S MEDIEVAL BAR AND GRILL

As usual, these things start with a guy who knows a guy who knows a guy. The only catch this time was that way up the food chain somewhere, the guy who knew one of the first guys was a guy named Walter Dunn. Four days ago, I'd taken the booth in the back corner of Oliver's—a cavernous restaurant that had spared no expense on décor. Full suits of faux armor guarded the entrance, and torches fueled by natural gas burned in sconces everywhere. The inside of the place was all heavy timber, with monstrous laminated beams holding up the vaulted ceiling. A roaring fireplace festooned with shields, lances, and swords served as the centerpiece of the dining area, and the saloon featured a bar that was at least forty feet long. The place smelled like cooked meat and varnish. The menu was anything but Olde English, mostly burgers and anything that they could deep-fry, nothing you couldn't get somewhere else for a fraction of the cost. Which probably explained why it was almost completely empty.

I'd seen my guy when I'd come in. He was in the saloon chatting up an overdressed middle-aged woman with a laugh like a horse, four-inch heels, and a wedding ring big enough to finance my next car. He'd made eye contact with me over her shoulder, but he was in no hurry. Apparently, he thought there might be a blow job in his near future because while I worked my way through a pretty decent bowl of chili, the pile of money in front of him got smaller and smaller. I hadn't minded. Good luck to him, I figured, I was in no hurry. I much preferred the two-legged demons that I met at night over the ones waiting for me at home in my dreams.

When the waitress asked me if I needed anything from the bar, I ordered a shot of Jack neat and a bottle of beer with a short glass. She looked at me funny but wrote it down and left. My usual rule—no booze, no weed when you're working—would be put on hold tonight. Things were going to move at a snail's pace. The cocktail waitress brought the glass and set it on a cardboard coaster that featured an obscure coat of arms and then made a little gasp of surprise. I took a look at her again. She didn't look familiar, although she certainly deserved a second look. I should have noticed her before.

"I know you. You're the new guy in the drafting department. I noticed you when you were getting your nameplates and stuff down in Office Supply the other day."

"Um, yeah, you mean up in Bensenville? At Flick?"

"Yeah, I work there too. I'm in the order writing department. I saw you go by. You used to work out in the shop, didn't you?" Either she wasn't busy enough at her job, or she was seriously nosy. She cocked her hip a little and leaned the serving tray against it. "I noticed because you never went to lunch with everybody else. You always stay in the shop by the machine where you work. All the girls watch you guys through the glass, you know?"

"Yeah, um, the lunchroom's too bright for me, hurts my eyes."

"Is that why you wear those dark glasses?"

Good as anything else, I thought. "Yeah."

"I'm Angelica, people call me Angel. I work here nights 'cause I'm trying to pay off my car sooner."

She still hadn't put down my beer or the shot, so I fixed my gaze on the tray for a minute and then back at her. She got the message, and set them down, but she stayed next to the booth. The place was just about empty, so she wasn't in a hurry to leave. Apparently, she was waiting for me to chat, or give her a tip. I looked across at my guy. The woman was leaning close to him with one hand on his knee, speaking in a low voice. He was smiling and nodding his head.

"So…Angel, how's working here?"

"Weekends are great, especially if there's a big game on. Tips can be pretty good. Weeknights like this aren't so hot. I'll be lucky if I walk out of here with thirty bucks tonight."

"You stay until closing?"

"On weekends, yeah, but on weeknights they let me go after the bartender has his dinner break. No sense staying around. I still get paid a crappy hourly, so it's a waste of their money and my time if I stay. I don't think I've ever seen you in here before. I think I would've noticed. Pretty sure."

"Too pricey for my tastes, but now that I know that the waitresses are so pretty, I might be tempted to come back."

That got a shy smile and she dipped her knees a little and looked away.

"That's nice of you to say that." She was good-looking enough not to fall for stupid lines like that, so I figured she was just young. Something that isn't always measured in years. "So, what brings you here tonight."

"Well, the chili turns out is pretty good."

"Yeah, but you didn't know that before you ate it. Did you know I worked here? Some of the guys from the office come in after work." I guessed she was fishing for another compliment. From the way she looked I couldn't imagine that she didn't get her share as it was. The cocktail outfit was supposed to resemble a medieval wench, I guessed, and it sure didn't hide most of the merchandise. She appeared to be in robust health. Long, full black hair and dark eyes above fabulous cheekbones, nice teeth. Her body and fender work was spectacular. For a moment I let my thoughts stray to the more recreational possibilities. She did have a nice smile.

"No, that's true, but I'm glad I tried it just the same. Much better than what I'd be eating at home tonight."

"You live by yourself."

"Yep, can't find anyone that can stand me long enough to have a roommate."

"Listen to you. You gonna tell me you're some kind of bad boy?"

"Nope, just too lazy to make a lot of friends."

"Well, sometimes a roommate's a little overrated. Mine's really nice but we get on each other's nerves still sometimes."

The couple at the bar got up and started to shrug into their coats. My guy turned away from her while he fished for his keys or gloves and he used the pause to look my way and hold up one finger. "Back in a sec." was the message. I wasn't as nonchalant as I should have been because Angel noticed.

"You know those people?"

"Nope, but there aren't that many people in here, so when somebody moves, it catches your eye, I guess."

"Yeah, she's in here couple of nights a week. She likes the brothers, guys I guess, seems like she leaves with a different one all the time. Never seen him before." Then she had a thought and turned away. "I gotta go see if they left me a tip on the bar before Dickhead Dave picks it up. Let me know if you need anything." And she was off, the view just as nice from the rear.

Well, shit. Now that she'd marked me, I wouldn't be able to meet with the guy inside. Especially after I'd said I didn't know him. I was going to have to go out and catch up with him outside, maybe set up another talk site. I gave it a good five minutes, threw back my shot, finished my beer, and started to slide out of the booth. Angel was on me before I had both feet under me.

"I didn't put your drinks on the tab. Maybe you'll come back some other time?"

I dropped a twenty on the table and a five on her tray.

"Hey, thanks, Angel. Yeah, maybe some other time."

The parking lot, like the restaurant, was almost empty. It took me less than five seconds to spot the right car. A big white Lincoln Town Car, the windows fogged from the inside all the way around, and it was moving way too much for there to be a blow job in progress. I walked to my car and started it up. Flicking the heater to high, I tilted the seat back a little so I could relax and still watch the Lincoln. I hoped the heater would hurry up.

Ten more minutes and the rear door of the Lincoln swung open and Dwight unwound himself out onto the parking lot. He took the time to tuck his shirt back and zip up, then slammed the door and headed toward the front door of the restaurant. I flicked my headlights and he did a sharp right turn and hurried over, yanked open the passenger door, and popped down into the seat next to me.

"Mother fuck, is it cold."

"Looks like you weren't suffering to me."

"Man, sometimes that's hard work, you know." He paused as we watched the Lincoln reverse out of its parking space and with the headlights on roll smoothly out of the lot. "But she was very appreciative of the effort. Hey, maybe she would have a liked two boys for the price of one?"

"Jesus, that's all I need. Thank you, no. Besides, I got it on authority that she only likes guys with a black ass."

"None blacker than mine," he said with pride. "So…listen, Hole, there's a new job out on the street, and your name came up. That should tell you something right there, but, dude, this one sounds like a picky customer. I don't wanna tell you your business, but this one feels a little fucked to me. You been workin' steady, right?"

"I stay busy."

"I'm just ears on the street, man, but this ain't no dope deal. They're talking about serious bread, man. Real serious bread."

"I'm hip, I'm into serious bread. I need new tires on this piece of shit."

"The way I hear it, you'd be talking about a new ride, a brand-new ride if you work out."

"That much? That's pretty serious *dinero* for just one delivery. Must be a catch."

"Not one, man, that's the catch. They're looking for a crewman, regular, you dig?"

"I don't work with other people, Dwight, you know that. Shit, I don't even like working for other people. Sooner or later they fuck up, and then you're fucked up too."

"I don't know, man, anyway, I got the number and the address on this." He handed me a slip of paper. "Make sure you call, and you're supposed to tell them exactly when you gonna get there. They were very specific about that part. They'll talk you through once you're in."

"Sounds like a plan."

"Listen, Hole, watch your ass on this one. It smells funny to me."

Mr. Anthony Emmett

From behind me the big guy reached around me and turned the knob, then pushed the door slowly in. Bright florescent light spilled out into the hallway. He let the door swing all the way open while his hand came up and barred me from moving forward. We did not step into the room; instead we stood in the doorway waiting. There were five people in the room. Two of them had guns pointed at the doorway: one was a pump twelve-gauge shotgun with a pistol grip, the other one a Colt 1911. It took me a few seconds to notice anything else in the room.

The other inhabitants were an elderly man and two young women. One of the women stood in the center of the room and was entirely naked. Emaciated, with sharp, bony points sticking out everywhere, every joint in her body appeared more prominent than the skin that covered it. Her knees and elbows incredibly knobby, she shook all over and shifted from one foot to the other. Her breasts were shrunken and lay flat on her chest. Even if she'd been healthy, they would probably have been very small. Her filthy hair was sparse, her scalp showing clearly in places. Her eyes were sunken deep in their sockets, and her lips were thin and cracked, pulled back from her yellowed teeth, and she chewed on the lower one. Up and down her arms and legs ran a roadmap of tracks. She appeared to take no notice of us in the doorway.

The elderly gentleman stood looking at us with interest, a syringe poised in his right hand. He was dressed in an impeccable tie and white shirt with the sleeves rolled up. His well-creased pants appeared to be right off the hanger, and a matching jacket was draped around the shoulders of the last inhabitant in the room. She was hunched in the corner, sitting on the floor, pulling the coat around herself. It was not because it was cold in the room; she was trying to make herself as small as possible.

"You're the one they call Hole." Not a question.

"Yes."

"You should come in. We'll be finished in a few moments. William, you should stay as well. Charles can handle the front. We will need an extra hand in a moment."

I stepped into the room and walked to a corner where a capped gas pipe and the cracked linoleum evidenced a stove used to stand. Putting my hands in my pockets, I leaned against the wall. I was a little surprised they couldn't hear my heart pounding in my chest and ears, or my asshole clenching and unclenching. I tried to keep my high school coach's words in mind, *"Always act like you've been there before."*

From the corner I could see the girl on the floor and watch the proceedings. The girl on the floor was young, thirteen maybe fourteen years old, maybe not even that. She'd had a ponytail, but the tie had come loose and now her strawberry blonde hair was tangled up in it and all over the place. She was wearing stone-washed jeans and high-tops, and cheap nail polish. Her eyes were the size of saucers but puffy. She'd been crying, but the spectacle in front of her had fixed that. Now she was dumbfounded.

"Melinda, we cannot find a vein for you. Which one have you been using yourself?"

"Jeezus, Mr. Anthony, I'm dyin'. I got bugs and worms crawling out of my skin, c'mon, please, I can't hit nothin' anymore. I been skin-poppin' mostly. God! I itch all over. I can't stand it. I think I hit one between my toes yesterday though. I put one in my tongue the other day, but I don't think that worked too good."

The man with the twelve just kept watching me, and his finger never came out of the trigger guard. The one with the Colt spoke up, but his eyes never left me. "Christ, Mr. Anthony, she's all used up. You're wasting good product on her. She's not earning her keep anymore."

"Quiet, Willy, that will sort itself out in good time. William, please step up and hold Melinda still. I'm going to put this into a vein in her neck. I would just as soon she didn't flinch."

The burly guy who had accompanied me from the front door and was apparently named William stepped up and, grasping Melinda by the upper arms, simply picked her straight up off the floor. It didn't look like he expended any effort doing it. The syringe moved forward. Melinda did not flinch; Melinda didn't do anything. Instead, with a long sigh, her head lolled back and her eyes rolled up into her head so that nothing but whites showed. William deposited her on the floor exactly where she'd been standing, and she sagged like a pile of jackstraws. Turning, he walked to the door, where he paused with his hand on the knob and gave me a look, a combination of disgust and pity is what I got out of it. He dropped my knife on the old kitchen table, where there were a few other things, and went out the door. The young girl stared at the heap lying in front of her, just a pile of white and purple skin with bony corners sticking out in all directions. A puddle of urine began to seep out from underneath Melinda, spreading out in her direction. The smell just one more factor in this room already filled with horrors.

Mr. Anthony walked over to a small table and stowed his syringe, zipped the leather kit closed, then put the kit into a leather briefcase which he closed and set down near the door. Opening a bottle from the table, he poured some of the contents on his hands and scrubbed them, the smell of alcohol adding itself to the stench of the rest of the room. Shaking off the excess he held his hands up while they air dried and stood with his back to me, looking down at my knife on the table. Finally, he picked it up, unsheathed it, and turned it in the light, examining it closely, and then put it down. He turned back to me and gave me a long "up-down." The twelve-gauge had not wavered.

"You have an odd name." He stepped around the one called Willy. "I'm sure there's a story behind it."

My mind was starting to recover from the adrenaline-fueled fear and anxiety. The timing of the events in this room was too convenient to be coincidence; it had been calculated as a demonstration. If it had been meant to scare me, it had succeeded. *Act like you've been there before.*

I shrugged. "It works for me."

"You are ex-military, 173rd Airborne, a relatively elite unit, assigned to a reconnaissance squad. You received numerous decorations and were wounded, med-evacuated out of Vietnam with multiple injuries after an ambush and the subsequent fire-fight that included hand-to-hand combat. Only about half of your squad survived. You are rated expert both in rifle and pistol, and you also scored well in sniper fire. You carry a gun and a knife but apparently prefer to use your hands.

"You then served both stateside and then in Europe after that. You received an honorable discharge and separated with the rank of Specialist E-5, yet oddly remain on probation after your separation. You attend regular meetings with a probation officer, in spite of receiving an honorable discharge. A curious chain of events to be sure. Your record for much of your time in Germany has been redacted, however." He peered at me to see if I might offer a clue. I didn't. "Even though your record has been laundered, there are things that can always be discovered if one knows the correct passwords."

He paused and ran his finger down the barrel of the twelve that was still pointed at my chest.

"It would seem that you present a danger to people who work around you, Mr. Hole. It seems that you can be a rather bad man to get on the wrong side of. At least you were once." He paused and took another step in my direction. Making eye contact he added, "I am in need of someone who still is."

Most people who do the kinds of things that I do sort of expect employers to do a little background check, but Mr. Anthony had done some serious homework.

"I was concerned that the PO might present a conflict for you. I can't have someone with divided loyalties, you see. People who earn their way to a probation officer can often attempt to ingratiate themselves—do them little 'favors' in hopes of reducing their probationary restrictions—I wouldn't like that, I'm afraid." He raised an eyebrow, and Mr. Twelve-gauge nodded agreement. "But it turns out that your probation officer doesn't like you very much." He shrugged and made a small smile with only one side of his mouth. "I spoke to him personally, you see. I was impressed by how fast the color went out of his face. He is scared to death of you. Can you imagine that." He didn't say the last sentence like it was a question but instead looked me hard in the eye.

Score one for team Walter Dunn. He scared the shit out of me too. Apparently, he had had a little chat with Mr. Couldn't Give Two Shits.

The little girl still hadn't taken her eyes off Melinda but had moved her feet back to avoid the piss puddle.

"I believe the story may have outrun the reality."

"Anyone who fancies himself a 'bad man' can shoot someone," he looked down at the heap at his feet, "or poison them. It takes a different kind of man to kill someone with their hands. You see their death as you deliver it. It is intimate—personal. You, Mr. Hole, have done it more than once, and on more than one occasion. Most normal people cannot even conceive what it must take." Then with a half-smile, "Should I be afraid, I wonder." Again he did not word it like a question.

"Who's the kid?"

He looked me in the eye, a hard look.

"Which one? They're both kids." He looked down at the heap of bone and flesh. "This burned-out skank is Melinda; she just turned sixteen. For the evening, Melinda is the lesson. She is what happens to others when they don't want to behave the way we want them to. I'm afraid our Melinda is all used up and serves no other purpose to us anymore. The other is Megan. Megan is new—she just arrived today as a matter of fact. Little Megan has just had her first lesson, a hard one, I'll admit, but life is hard sometimes."

He casually put his hands into his expensive pants pockets and walked up to me, eye to eye.

"Megan is the package that I need delivered."

Diary of Mick Casey

March 13, 1944

We're shot to pieces. The fuselage has holes in it that I could put my head through. The flak was heavy today. Just when you thought it couldn't get thicker it did. They had the range down tight. Continuous flak through the entire bomb run. We were the middle of the last group through the run and it practically shook my teeth out of my head. There was so much damage that Taylor and Janssen started pulling loose sheet metal out of the way and cutting it off. It was flapping back and forth in the wind and was going to cut somebody's head off. There are so many holes in the plane that the sun is shining inside the bomb bay. The holes are anywhere from the size of saucers down to a dime; the smaller the hole, the more there are of them.

Once we cleared the flak, the fighters came back, and everybody got down to business. There was so much brass down on the floor by the waist guns that the footing was dangerous. My turret was getting a little crowded too. I was busy too; there was no place else to kick the brass out of the way. Usually we have to go short on ammo if we're going out too heavy, but we'd been pushing the ground crew and they'd been loading us all up. The last thing we need is to run out of bullets. We sure needed it today and it didn't look like we were going to take any home with us either.

I got cinched in good and tight again and right away I saw them coming around.

"Six o'clock a little low. You see 'em, Jans?"

"I see 'em, Mick. Take the right one."

I opened up the Brownings on them but they just kept coming. I could see their muzzle flashes and tracers; they bored right in. I knew they could see mine. I kept pouring lead at them, and they kept coming. They were going to pass under us but close. My glass took two hits. The shells couldn't penetrate the armor plate that I lean against, but I felt them hit it just the same. The glass cracked and spoiled my vision to the left. The ME-109 on the right coughed smoke, and part of his right wing came apart. The last thing I saw as he flashed underneath me was the pilot's goggles looking at me.

"You got him, Mick, score one, he's on fire."

Then Taylor said, "Two at eleven o'clock high, coming around. They're going to take us back to front. Now twelve o'clock coming to level. They mean business."

I set up on the one coming in down my right side and started giving him bursts, but he peeled away. The captain came on and asked the engineer, Reynolds, to check the number three. As soon as I heard that, I wanted to check it, and probably everyone else did too.

"Oil leak, you're blowing a lot of oil out of it, Captain. That last one got us. Better shut it down. Hold on, hold on. WE'VE GOT FIRE, CAPTAIN! SHUT HER DOWN, shut her down and feather the prop. Maybe it'll go out."

"This is Brinker—we've got fire in number three, boys. I've got to get out of the formation. We're going to pull away;

try and keep those Jerrys off of us. We're going to be a little busy for a while. Shoot straight. Casey, as soon as it looks clear enough, get up here and get your chute on."

The *Flying Ass* pulled hard to port, away from our friends, trailing smoke all the way. From where I was sitting it looked like a lot of smoke. She could fly on three engines, especially since we'd already unloaded, but she couldn't fly as fast. We would have to do it alone. Then we got more good news. With the number three shut down, we wouldn't have hydraulic power, and all of the wing and tail flaps had hydraulic assistance. The landing gear too. Brinker and Holquist would have to fight the ship all the way home. They started descending in case we lost oxygen too. I squeezed the trigger handles on the Brownings so hard my hands cramped.

The fire in number three went out.

The idea was to stay as low as we could without flying into the side of a mountain. That way if we passed over anybody trying to shoot up at us, we would be past them before they could get their guns up. The afternoon wore on; we weren't coming home in a straight line. I watched the sky, we all did. Ammo was already low; the wind sang through the plane. No one spoke. Reynolds, our engineer, discovered that the landing gear had taken a couple of bad flak hits, and he thought we could hand crank the left wheel down, but the right one was jammed and pretty torn up. I cranked the tail gear down from behind my turret, but I couldn't check it yet. The sky was a priority.

We were having a pretty wild ride. The guys were having a hard time keeping the throttles on the other engines even, so we yawed back and forth sometimes while they fought the flaps and rudder. It's hard to believe but we never saw another fighter, although they probably weren't looking for us at twelve thousand feet. Once we got over Italy, I was pretty relieved and hustled back and pulled on my chute. The sun went down behind the mountains and it got dark.

Brinker came on all business. "Listen now, boys, the airfield is alerted, but we're going to have to belly in. It's dark and so I won't be able to tell how close to the ground I am until we're on it, so it's probably going to be a little rough. Luckily looks like we're almost out of fuel, so once we run off the rest of any that's extra, I'm going to bring her in. When I say 'brace' get in your crash positions and get ready. Everybody got that?"

Each one of us confirmed, and then I found my spot and buckled in with my back to the bulkhead. I looked across the empty bomb bay at Taylor, he looked at me, and we made our peace with each other with just eye contact. Janssen too. We made a couple of long turns, and I could feel that we were getting lower and lower. We started another banking maneuver and then number two coughed, sputtered, and went dead.

"Okay, boys, we're losing fuel a little fast for some reason. I'm turning for home, but we may not make it. Get the rear hatch open. We may have to ditch, stand by."

The number four coughed and then the number one quit with it, and suddenly the sound of the wind in the flak holes was all we could hear. We were a dead stick, a flying brick. We started to drop fast. My headset was dead quiet. Then:

"BRACE! BRACE! BRACE!"

We hit hard. I was thrown against the harness. The bomb bay doors disappeared in a shower of sparks and screaming metal, and the plexiglass from the smashed ball turret hung suspended in the air of the bomb bay for a long time. The *Flying Ass* ground its way into the dirt, and then her nose came up and we were sliding…sliding forever, the fuselage screaming as she shredded her way.

At last she stopped—rocked forward, and then settled down on what was left of her belly.

"OUT, BALE OUT, EVERYBODY OUT! TAKE COVER!"

I cleared the door and took the side hatch on the fly. Taylor was right behind me. I hit the frozen ground and got up as fast as I could in my flight suit and we ran, but the sound of firewagons was what we could hear, not gunfire. We stopped and looked around. Captain Brinker had put us down in the dirt right alongside the runway—he had brought us home. I turned all the way around in a circle, looking back at our ship and then the wagons and ambulances bouncing over the field, I felt the tears in my eyes, I couldn't help it—Brinker had got us home.

R.E. Casey, 1974

Miramar Beach, Four Miles East of Destin, Florida

The car was a big smooth-rolling Chevy Caprice Classic with an excellent heater. The papers in the glove box said it was rented to James Clark, address; Winnetka, Illinois. William brought it around to the alley in back. In the alley I transferred extra blankets, my twelve-gauge, and both the Ruger and the Colt automatic—all fully loaded—to the Chevrolet. I stowed the Colt under the driver's front seat and stuck my knife under the pull-down armrest. The bulkier revolver I put in the glove box under the rental papers. William carried a Police Special in a shoulder holster. Once we had our gear loaded, the last thing to go in the car had been Megan. She rode in the backseat; unconscious.

After that William drove the big sedan and followed me while I drove the Buick to the airport and parked in the extended parking garage. The Chevy wouldn't be making the return trip; there would be another rental waiting at the other end for that. I would have preferred to fly back, but I had a lot of hardware to haul home.

The man called Mr. Anthony had filled me in—if all went well, I would be on my own in the future, but for the maiden trip, William would be a shotgun rider and performance analyst. After that Anthony pulled his suit coat off of Megan and shrugged into it. Willy held his overcoat for him and he pulled it on. Buttoning up the coat he turned and picked up his briefcase and signaled to Willy and the other guy, still holding the riot gun in one hand but which he now pointed at the floor, that he was ready. With one last sweep of the room with eyes that did not include Megan, he stepped out through the back door, the shotgun went out ahead of him, and Willy pushed it shut behind him and locked it. As soon as he left the room, the air seemed to freshen.

Willy stayed back but stowed his Colt in his belt. He was apparently the Number Two, at least for this operation, and was now in charge. The instructions were pretty clear. Megan was to be delivered completely clean. No dope, no smack, no sex. The customer had a particular taste, and only a particular sort of girl would do. He had insisted on a blonde girl between eleven and thirteen, a virgin, innocent, and malleable. There were no names to be exchanged; all he would tell me was that the customer was a Middle Eastern big-shot with more money than was necessary. The rendezvous site was predetermined, as was the time.

"Have you ever heard the term 'petrodollars,' Hole? It's oil money, from oil companies in the Middle East, Arabs, princes and sheiks. They got so much fuckin' money they take baths in it. Our U.S. president has put in effect an oil embargo in this country, and the oil barons are pissed off big-time. All oil sold around the world is traded for in American dollars. So, they call it petrodollars, and petrodollars are the new gold. Money talks and the ones with the most money get to buy whatever they like. They don't like it when someone screws with their money. But it doesn't stop them from spending it."

Willy went to the table and pulled open a drawer. He took out a few pieces of paperwork, a Mastercard credit card—I had never used one of them before, and he had to explain it to me—and two packs of money. He gave the smaller of the two to William, and the bigger one to me. "Half before, half when you get back." The denomination on the front bill was a twenty, and on the back of the packet was a hundred. It felt like it should have for half of fifteen grand. Then he handed me my knife back and started to put on his overcoat.

"William has a phone number to call when you make your rendezvous. Don't fuck this up and there could be steady work."

I looked at William and he looked at me, then shrugged. "You're on point, dude, you call the play."

I looked at Willy. I could tell he was trying to size me up. I looked down at the lump of a lost soul that represented Melinda, and then at Megan. Her eyes were as wide as dinner plates and they were looking right into mine. I looked around the room: There was an ancient Frigidaire that had plenty of anatomically correct graffiti scrawled on it but was humming loudly. Pulling it open I found a few bottles of soda, a couple of cans of beer, and what looked like a two-week-old dried-up, half-eaten pizza. I pulled out a bottle of Orange Crush and popped the cap on the opener screwed to the side of the refrigerator. Crossing to the table I turned my back to the room and crushed up a couple of Quaaludes from my pocket—they help me stay calm—and dropped them into the bottle.

I turned back to Megan and squatted down in front of her, careful to not intrude too far into her private space but close enough to hand her the bottle. I smiled at her and said,

"Hi, Megan, people call me R.E." I paused and let my gaze make a circuit of the room. "I think we should get out of here, what do you think?"

She gave me an enthusiastic nod, so I offered her the soda in as casual a manner as I could. I was surprised when she accepted it immediately and more surprised, she drank it, but she put it away like she had just walked out of the desert. Twenty minutes later, the money had been counted and I had gone over the map with Willy and worked out the route in my head. I only intended to stop for gas. Little Megan was out like a light. I felt a little guilty, but not a lot. The kid needed a break.

As soon as she had slumped over in the corner, I'd hoisted her up in my arms and carried her out to the sedan. She couldn't have weighed more than eighty or so pounds. I was glad that she had drunk the soda; otherwise, we probably would have had to force her. I figured she'd already had about a rough a day as anyone can. I also figured that even though she was almost catatonic with fear and disorientation, she'd probably overheard the discussion regarding her ultimate fate. Mostly what I figured was that there were people in the world who badly needed killing, and I had just met one. "A particularly nasty prick," Dunn had called him.

Twenty hours after leaving Chicago, we were sitting in the parking area, facing into the wind and watching the sand blowing across the dunes, and gazing into the narrow boardwalk that led through them to the beach. The drive had been long but quiet. Wherever possible I'd taken open interstate highways but avoided the toll roads. We had left on Friday, just before midnight. Other people don't drive when I'm in the car, so big burly William slouched in the passenger seat, changing position every hundred miles or so and farting every time he did. Now he was showing signs of some serious distress, sweating profusely. His stomach was making awful noises, and the shifting and farting were becoming increasingly frequent.

I reasoned that I deserved the noxious fumes, because after all they were my fault. Somewhere in southern Tennessee we had pulled off the highway for fuel and snacks. It was William's turn to stay with the car and I had gone in to pay the bill—I didn't trust the new credit card, so I used cash only—and pick up a few things. We couldn't afford to let Megan be seen, so I had led her out to pee between the two open doors of the sedan along the shoulder of the road farther back down the highway. She was pretty stoned and didn't put up a fuss about peeing on the side of the road. She was proving to be malleable, after all.

It was one of those new convenience stores with not just gas and oil, but also a little semi-grocery-style store complete with a soda fountain machine. The soda fountain provided three good-sized Cokes, and I picked up a couple bags of chips and a couple of day-old hot dogs off the little carousel that kept them hot and made them old before their time. I added a small bottle of eyedrops. In the restroom I crushed up two more Quaaludes for Megan's drink, and dropped a few drops from the eyedrop solution into William's. Four hours later, poor William was becoming seriously ill and he cursed eating both of the tainted hot dogs.

The parking lot was about three or four miles east of

Destin, Florida. The sign in the parking lot said Miramar Beach, and we were a little early—almost four hours early. I'd made good time. The temperature outside of the car seemed freezing to me even after leaving the sub-zero weather of the Midwest. Forty-five degrees in Florida seemed a lot colder to me than it should have. When I got out of the car to piss, I had started to shiver and hurried through the procedure more relieved to get back in the car than to empty my bladder. I checked my cigarette supply and was down to three, so passed on one for now and leaned my seat back. There were no other cars, no other people, it was winter, it was dark, it was cold. William had dozed on and off, and in the back Megan slept on—supplemented by Quaaludes. William could take the watch. I took a nap.

Diary of E. Mick Casey

April 19, 25th
Trento, Italy

Today was going to be different. The 3 a.m. briefing sounded pretty bad. The Germans are in full retreat; the war for them is lost. They're trying to get back to the Fatherland and they're marshalling all their weapons and manpower to defend against the Allies once they get back home. We can't let it happen, we have to cut off their retreat, so we're going to bomb the railroad tunnels out of Austria and Czechoslovakia. That way they'll be bottled up, right where the infantry boys can catch up to them. There is only one problem.

As the German troops pull back, they get more and more concentrated. More men and more artillery in a smaller space. More concentrated firepower. On top of that they can conceal their really big guns inside the tunnels, and only pull them out when they see us coming. The tunnels are dug into the mountainsides, so we can't aerial bomb them from five miles up; we wouldn't be able to do enough damage. We have to take them head-on. That means we have to come in at low altitude and fly straight into the 88s and 105s, and there will be a lot of them. Whatever is left of the Luftwaffe will be thrown at us too. They are desperate to get away. It is hard to get excited, knowing that they are in retreat, when you know that the mission and the one after that are probably suicide.

The padre closed the meeting with a prayer, and afterwards I made a good confession to him. I looked at my friends, and we all shook hands. Looks like I might not see twenty after all.

R.E. Casey

Miramar Beach, almost midnight

At 11:30 I woke up. William looked across at me, cocked up in the seat, and farted. His breath was puffing in and out, and sweat was beaded on his forehead. I had timed it pretty well, I figured. He was almost ready to blow. I pulled the cheap Radio Shack walkie-talkie radio from the floor of the backseat and turned it on; static and a loud hiss told me the battery was good. I shut it off. Reaching down I brought out the Ruger and flipped out the cylinder and checked the load. Dumping out the bullets, I reclosed the cylinder and dry fired a couple of times, then reloaded. The revolver had the added benefit of not ejecting the shell casing. They're hard to find in the dark if you need to clean up your brass. I was starting to get antsy. Almost showtime. *Act like you've been there before*—it was starting to feel like I had been.

I got out of the car and took another leak, then reached back in and lifted out the knife, unbuckled my belt, and threaded it through the sheath so that it hung down into my back pocket. Nice and stable, so that you could pull it without the sheath flopping or catching up on the blade. I put the Ruger in the back of my pants. A Colt 1911 is heavy, almost three pounds when fully loaded. I wasn't going to drag that around with me. I'd be busy enough. I loosened my belt one notch to accommodate the added diameter, just one of the reasons I don't like guns. They're hard to tote around, and clumsy to reach for. Especially if you're in a hurry. Knife is quicker, keep the gun for backup, that's my theory. I had William hand me the Colt and I field checked it too. I ejected the magazine and dry fired it, checked the action and thumbed out a round, then depressed the next one to make sure the spring feed was clear and then reloaded the round. I put it on the driver's seat with the butt facing out. Reaching back into the car, I took the walkie-talkie out and turned the volume on full. Even at full volume the hiss was barely audible with the wind howling in over the dunes. I could hear the surf crashing on the beach less than a hundred yards in front of us.

Next, I checked on Megan. She was nothing more than a pile of blankets in the corner of the backseat. I pulled the blankets back; her shadowed face reflected none of the horror she'd already witnessed. She looked young, and innocent. Her head was tilted back, her mouth slightly open. Her upper front teeth shone white in the darkness. Her breathing was quiet. Good enough. I quietly closed the door and walked to the front of the car and thumbed the squawk button on the radio. There was only the hiss in reply. I checked my watch, almost midnight. I lit a cigarette with my Zippo and leaned back next to the Chevrolet hood ornament and squinted into the wind.

Without warning the passenger door flew open and William erupted out in a stumbling run, wrestling with his belt. He got no more than a dozen good strides before he stopped and dragged them down, panting and groaning with panic and pain. Grabbing a handful of scrub grass for support, he squatted and gave birth to an incredibly pneumatic burst of shit.

"Oh my God, my guts are coming out," he yelled into the wind. "Fuck-ING hot dogs—" another shit blast—"FUCK, FUCK, oh Jesus, my head." He leaned forward and puked—hard and long, heaving until I was pretty sure we'd soon see his appendix. Duck walking sideways from the train wreck that used to be inside him, he dropped on his side in the sandy grass and curled into a fetal position.

I finished my cigarette and then hit the squawk button again; only the hiss responded. I put my hands into my coat pockets and eased over to William, careful to watch my step.

"Geez, man, that's disgusting. You gonna be okay?"

"Oh, man, I think I'm dyin'."

"Well, if you need help there, use your own gun, but not just yet. They're late according to my watch."

"Oh Jesus, I'm fucked up. I don't know if I'm gonna be any good to you." He paused long enough to retch into the sand. It was lucky he hadn't pulled up his pants, because the effort to puke was productive at both ends. "Can you handle it, Hole?"

I squatted down, at a safe distance, and took a look at his face in the dark. He looked pretty miserable.

"I'm used to working alone, but I was hoping I wouldn't have to get my boots wet. I'll do what I can, but listen, man, you better have my six, you know? If you hear it go down wrong, you better bring that Special on the double."

"I'll try, man, can't hear shit in this wind though. Surf's really gonna be up."

"I can hear it. It's a good thing it's the Gulf, not usually much surf on this side of Florida, but it's gonna be high enough for sure, but I've seen worse."

"Yeah, sure, I kinda doubt that—Hole."

The walkie-talkie squawked, then began beeping: long, short, long, short, pause, long, long, short. CQ! Universal Morse Code for all clear?—SHOWTIME!

Oh yes, I'd seen a lot worse stormy sea weather.

December 1971, HMS Leinster, The Irish Sea

I was starting to get warm. The shivering of my arms and legs had finally stopped, but my low back ached from the effort of trying to keep me warm. In the almost too warm saloon, I sat with hands underneath my butt and gazed at the cup of tea on the table in front of me while I tried to summon enough interest in it to drink. The level of the liquid constantly shifted from one side to the other, almost spilling over with each back-and-forth cycle. The cup itself, anchored to the table by a slotted bracket that the bottom of the cup nestled into to prevent it from sliding off of the table on the next cycle.

The saloon itself was empty—except for me—but the teapot was hot and the tender had not shown much interest in making anything else. It was past 1 a.m. and the weather outside was worsening; the deep bones of the ship quaked and shuddered with every massive breaker it encountered. The violence of the collision followed almost immediately by the deep boom of the impact and then shortly tens of thousands of gallons of seawater striking the ship and racing down the causeways on each side of the saloon. Anyone with any sense at all was below deck and riding out the storm in private misery. Which said a lot about why I was not joining them. I was getting ready to go back outside.

I don't know jack shit about ships, or the oceans, or winter storms on them, but I knew this one was a dandy. The ferry out of Liverpool had a bellyful of railroad cars, private cars, tour buses, and trucks. She rode the waves like a fishing bobber with a worm and heavy sinker on the end of the line. Outside on the forecastle deck, I had hung on to the rail below the bridge and stared ahead into the darkness and the teeth of wind. With a slight drop of the prow, the darkness ahead would get even darker and then with a tremendous shudder from the ship, everything in front of me would turn white as the fifteen foot swell would break over the bow and rise into the night above me. Hanging on for dear life, I would hunker down behind the rail while the tons of water struck the pilot house and everything else with a surface area. Then with water knee-deep rushing down the deck and out the scuppers, I had struggled to prevent myself from being washed down the deck and off the fantail at the rear. I had done this over and over for an hour as my legs began to tremble and ice began to form in my mustache. After an hour Ryan had relieved me, and I was making a puddle on the saloon floor. Ryan's hour was almost up—it was my turn again.

This had started out as one of those "what could possibly go wrong" episodes that occur in one's life from time to time. On Thursday last, the crew had been backed into the loading bay at Tech Supply; two trucks were heading out after lunch, one through Nelligan and on to the depot at Germersheim, the other bound for Army depots in K'town and Pirmasens. Lieutenant Kyle strode down the center aisle and, in his best Superman pose, paused, hands on hips, chest thrown with pride, watching as the loading progressed for a full minute before announcing:

"Specialist Casey and Specialist Ryan, First Sergeant wants to see you in the Orderly Room—ASAP."

I had looked at Ryan and he matched the look and shrugged. "Bullet Head" Sinclair only demanded audiences when he needed something, or when he handed out abuse; it was a crapshoot which one you'd get on any particular day. It was never a good thing either way. The L.T. gestured me aside and once we were out of earshot, he turned and made eye contact.

"Anything I need to know about Emmett?" Kyle was naïve, not stupid.

"Sorry, sir, I've no idea."

When we reported to the Orderly Room, Thompson, the company clerk, looked at both of us like it might be for the last time. He didn't hesitate but just waved us directly into Sinclair's office and then jumped up to shut the door behind us. Inside, Sinclair was in a state of complete agitation. I'd seen him upset before, but this was the first time I had seen him in a state of intense anxiety. His shiny head was sweating and he was wiping it with a handkerchief when we entered. Instead of the usual deep coral hue, his face was ashen. Without apparently thinking about it, he waved us both into chairs across from him—something was definitely wrong. Usually after this much time in front of him, one or the other of us had already picked up a fine.

"You two are going on a ten-day leave. Pack enough to get you there and back. You leave tonight, and don't report back here until a week from Sunday."

"First Sergeant?"

He dropped both hands on the desk, one with his handkerchief still in his hand, and took a deep breath. Then shaking his head, he pulled open the desk drawer, pulled out his smokes, and shook one out. Without lighting it he waved it in a state of dismissal. "Okay, okay—I'm getting a little ahead of myself—okay." He took a deep breath, shrugged his shoulder, and huffed it out and lit the cigarette. After a deep drag, we watched him become First Sergeant Sinclair again.

"There is a package that has to be delivered. It is not our package, but it is the package of one of the, uh—clients. There are reasons that we should do the job," he gave us his patented look, "and you don't need to know all of them." Then he relented. "The client is pushing back against us hard; he cannot handle the package, or doesn't want to. It needs to be delivered by hand, and it is fairly large."

So far so good.

"Ten days? Sorry, First Sergeant, but I've never gotten so much as a three-day pass. Why do we need ten days?" I asked.

"Because it's going to Ireland and it's a civilian job. You two are my best, goddamn it, and I hate to say that because you're also my two biggest fuck-ups. You're also both Irish and lucky. Listen, if you guys do this, it's gonna feather all of our nests, and there's five hundred bucks in it for you too."

"Five hundred bucks? Sounds dangerous all of a sudden. What are we supposed to be carrying?" Ryan was getting his feet under him.

"You'll find out anyway—" He looked over our heads, then the ceiling, then mashed his cigarette out in the ashtray. "Explosives."

"Jesus fuck me!" I couldn't believe it. "Explosives? What, like dynamite?"

"Some, and some other."

"How in holy hell are we supposed to move a case of high explosives from the middle of Germany across three different countries and two bodies of water without getting blown to kingdom come or, worse, arrested? Isn't there something called Interpol or something?"

"If you get arrested, you're acting as civilians; if you get blown up, well, one less headache for me. Listen, you guys, you do it or you don't." He gave us each a hard look. "You've done other shit already and you can't tell me that you two can't handle it. Both of you must have personal guardian angels if you ask me, but that doesn't mean I can't find somebody else." He shrugged and opened his desk and took out another cigarette, lit it, and then noticed the one smoking in the ashtray. Snapping the lighter shut he exploded, "I'm kind of sick of you two fucks around here anyway, so a couple of months up in Grafenwöhr, doing nothing but freezing your asses off on the Czech border, might do you both a lot of good."

"A thousand bucks." Ryan spoke quietly. I looked across at him with a newfound admiration.

Sinclair's eyes narrowed while his selfish little brain did the math. Ryan knew this wasn't just a favor. Sinclair was going to get a payday out of it too.

"Deal," he responded and started to roll back his chair.

"Apiece," I said, just as quietly.

Out came the handkerchief and he wiped his head furiously and then threw it at me.

"Fuck! Okay—apiece."

"In advance," added Ryan. "Just in case we get blown up."

"Don't press your luck, fuckhead." He dropped both hands palms down and looked down at the desk. "Thompson will pay you out; now get out and get ready."

Three days later we had crossed two frontiers and been waved through both. We drove an aging and rusted gray Volkswagen with green USA license plates which told anyone who might be interested that we were military personnel. No one was interested—at all. Now the VW was packed tight down in the belly of this ferry with a shitload of high explosives packed under the rear seat.

Just in case, Ryan had insisted on removing the battery from underneath the seat. We spliced new cable and rode with the battery between the passenger's feet in the front. I'd had to agree—it didn't seem like a good idea to have a spark from a loose connection in the same place as all that other stuff. With the battery removed we had a lot more room, so we also stashed enough hashish to get us through ten days.

The contact had been set in advance. We were to meet on the forecastle deck of the night ferry out of Liverpool sometime after midnight. No one had apparently thought to check the weather forecast. I waited to step out of the saloon until the next wash from the most recent shuddering crash had rushed past the door. Turning right I walked forward to below the forecastle—Ryan wasn't there. I wasn't too worried. I had been washed back down toward the stern once or twice during my watch; he might have gone by in the last rush of water and I hadn't noticed. Turning back astern I immediately saw three figures.

It was too dark to make out if one of them was Ryan, but no one else would be out here, so I carefully made my way down in that direction, bracing against the saloon windows because of the bucking deck. The deck was not afloat for a change, and when I got there, I could make out Ryan backed against the rail. Both men held handguns. Ryan had his hands on the rail behind him and facing them.

It was too dark to see features on faces, but Ryan apparently could make out my silhouette as I approached because he subtly began to shift to his right, forcing them to track left with their pistols.

"Stand still, Yank," the one on my left yelled above the howl of the wind.

"I'd rather get around the corner before the next wave hits, that's all," Ryan yelled back.

"Ya boys, ya ain't shite, ya know w'at?"

"Whaddya mean?" Ryan didn't sound too upset.

"We marked ya when you brought thet wee little bug on board, and we marked it where ya parked. We coulda took yer goods if we'd a wanted."

"Why didn't you then?"

"We need yer word that there ain't nae booby-traps wired to the car."

"There aren't any booby-traps."

"Easy to say, Yank. I think it's best if we hang you over the side and then wait on yer friend; once he gets the drift, he'll come clean with us."

"How 'bout we wait for him, then throw him over the side instead?"

"Yer in a lotta shit here, bugger, no jokin' now. Back down

the ladder and we'll walk to the stern to—"

He had to stop speaking for a moment because my Uncle Henry had just poked him below the ear from behind as my left arm came across and hooked him by the throat. His hands came up and Ryan took his gun, then relieved the other fellow of his, but only after he had righteously kicked him in the nuts.

"What say we take this conversation down below before the next wash takes us all over the side?" I put the knife back in my belt and took the revolver that Ryan handed me. The one held his neck, which was leaking a little, and the other was still trying to catch his breath, so they seemed agreeable.

"That is no way to treat a couple of good old Irish lads just on liberty to Dublin, boys," added Ryan.

The two rude Irish fellows spent the rest of the trip locked in the trunk of their own vehicle. We left the Volkswagen keys on the floor next to them. Ryan and I, with Sinclair's money burning a hole in our pockets, enjoyed five days in the City of Dublin, which included the Guinness tour—twice—several pubs, and the warm hospitality of two very pretty housemaids in a quaint bed-and-breakfast hotel just a few blocks from Dublin Castle.

On November 26, an explosion rocked the Burgh Quay and then on December 1, two more rocked Eden Quay outside of Clarey's Department Store: two men were killed outright and 131 Christmas shoppers and pedestrians were injured, many grievously.

We didn't trust Sinclair or his buddies to let us come all the way back the same way we'd gotten to Ireland. Ryan and I didn't report for duty to the CQ at exactly midnight on Sunday, December third; instead we hopped a BOAC to Switzerland and bought tickets to see Frank Zappa and the Mothers of Invention in Montreux.

Fuck, Sinclair, we'd earned it.

Diary of E.M. Casey

April 19, 1945, Trento, Italy

Once we lifted off we climbed up and joined the squadron. A full squadron today, everything we could get in the air. Three Combat Boxes of thirty-six in all; we'd meet up with more on the way to the IP. Today we were in the "low, low position" with two others; after that we were staggered out and stacked up in four layers. At twenty-five thousand feet we met up with another full group. I could see out of the nose turret far in the distance a full fighter escort. Their job to meet any enemy fighters head-on. We were bringing everything but the kitchen sinks. I'm not too proud to say that we were still an hour from the IP and I was already afraid.

I was not going to ride in the rear gun seat today. All the action was going to be in front of us, they said. I'd pull pins and arm the bombs in the bay and be backup for anyone that might get taken down in the front turrets. We were carrying cluster bombs and we were going in first. After us would come a wave of one-hundred-pounders, and after that another one. All ammunition was in the forward turrets and the waists. Our job would be to get them to take cover, maybe un-man some of the big guns. I cinched my flak vest extra tight and we checked each other's too; nobody was looking directly at each other.

After that we just tried to stay busy.

I dug out my lunch sack, orange marmalade again on white bread. Cruising at twenty-five thousand feet it only took a few minutes for it to freeze solid, the temperature up here is around forty below and the wind is blowing through the plane at over a hundred miles an hour. I dropped the sandwich on the deck to shatter it into bite-size pieces and sucked on them until they melted. Not because I was hungry but because it kept me from grinding my teeth together.

In order to make an effective run we would have to drop down to fourteen or fifteen thousand feet. It was the only way to drop our load where it would do any good. The target was a viaduct, their only escape route, but it was tucked up tight to the mountains. They wanted maximum accuracy, so they wanted us close to the target. The only problem was all of their antiaircraft guns were mounted on the mountains above the railhead. Some were as high as twelve thousand feet—this was the Alps, after all—so they'd be shooting straight across at us. We'd have to fly straight into their fire. We were going to be eyeball-to-eyeball and our pins were already pulled.

The fighters couldn't come into the flak with us; we left them behind with the next flight. The Kraut guns must have been tracking us all along. As soon as we reached our IP and banked for the run, the shooting started. Six miles from the target the sky started to blacken with the first shots. This was going to be like Vienna was—only worse. This time I was looking out through the nose turret. We could see the muzzle flashes of the howitzers; we were looking right down the barrels.

With the enemy pulling back and staging at the railheads, more and more big guns were starting to collect at these sites.

Instead of regular defenses we were getting a dose of everything that was left of the Wehrmacht, and it was a lot. Behind the Germans was the Brenner Pass out of Austria, and in front of them were the Americans. I bit down on a frozen bite of sandwich. The ride was already rough and we were still five miles out. The captain couldn't take any evasive maneuvers; the squadron was only spaced about fifty feet apart, and there wasn't any room for that. We had to go straight at them no matter what. The flak charges were set to explode at a certain distance. Flying straight into the fire, we hoped to close the distance between us faster than they could adjust their range, but that was just a theory—or a foolish hope.

"Eight-oh-six just lost their front turret and bombardier… whole nose is gone, she's still coming on though!" yelled Taylor from the waist into my headphones. I was braced up against the bulkhead up front of the radio shack, so I couldn't see what was going on except what was right in front of us. Just as I leaned forward to get a look, the ship got blasted sideways and I was thrown into the wall—the lights went out.

Emmett

Miramar Beach, Florida, Midnight

I grabbed my flashlight out from under the front seat and made my way out to the boardwalk with the wind whipping the sand away from my boots with each step. It was even stronger on the seaside of the dunes. The waves created a line of ghostly white as they broke still thirty feet offshore and poured themselves in toward the sand. With the noise from the wind in my ears and the roar of the surf, I reckoned that William wouldn't hear me if I had a bullhorn. I checked to make sure the Ruger was good and tight in my belt. As soon as I cleared the dunes, I blinked the light, first to the left, then straight ahead, then to the right. Nothing. The radio was silent.

I squatted down just to get out of as much wind as I could and repeated the flashes with the light, left, center, right. The only Morse Code I knew was SOS and CQ, so I thought my best bet was to stay with the light. The blackness of the sea in front of me was unbroken, and the sky was only slightly brighter. The surf continued to crash. I waited. It was too cold to sweat but I was still somehow managing it.

Then again, the radio beeped out CQ. I repeated the same two-letter code back by pressing the call button. Almost immediately a light blinked on and off, three flashes, far off to my right. I flashed the signal back and turned back toward the car, hurrying now.

William was a dark mass lying on his back ten yards from the Chevy. When I checked him his hands and legs were twitching and he was not fully conscious. Avoiding the dark stain directly behind his asshole, I heaved his bulk up on his side so he wouldn't drown in his own puke. It wasn't easy to do with his pants around his ankles. I made a mental note to reduce the dosage of the Visine the next time I might need it.

Back at the car I opened the rear door and began to bundle the blankets tightly around Megan. The air was already chilly and she was about to get wet.

"I'm hungry, Ahri." Instead of my initials R and E—R.E.—she spoke it like it was my one-word name.

I was sure she was. She hadn't eaten anything for at least twenty-four hours with the exception of a bottle of Orange Crush, a super-sized Coke, and an entire bag of Lay's potato chips—and a handful of downers.

"I know, Megan. You'll be getting something to eat real soon, I promise."

"Am I going home now?"

"We've got someplace else to go right now, Megan. Let's just see how it goes. I'm going to carry you for a little bit, okay? Can you help me and hang on to me? I want you to put your arms around my neck, okay?"

"I guess so. I don't like William, Ahri. He smells bad."

"Yes he does, Megan."

When I turned toward the boardwalk and the beach beyond, the wad of blankets with Megan inside them caught the wind as I walked, pushing me backward with each step. The wind taking over where my conscience left off, telling me not to go forward. With her hanging on tight I had to lean into it and push with my legs. When we reached the beach side of the dunes, I set her down twenty feet from the surf on the hard-packed sand. Even at that distance, the wind still blew sea spray over us as the waves broke out off the beach. I closed up the blankets over her. She spoke from inside, her voice muffled. "Are we at a beach?"

"Not one I'd ever want to go to."

I squatted down in front of her to keep most of the spray off her and flashed the light again. Immediately, the radio squawked CQ and the light blinked back, this time much closer than the first, still off to the right. I flashed again. For ten minutes the dance continued, a long pause followed by the light. Then after I had scanned the beach and what I could see behind me—my response. Each time the light from the darkness a little closer.

Suddenly directly out of the blackness a shape appeared, black against black, difficult to determine where one began and the other stopped, the sharp prow of a fast boat, black as night with no running lights, slowly gliding in on the incoming breakers. A big boat, completely silent, approaching carefully. It was going to be too big to beach. I was going to have to meet it, somewhere out where it was still afloat. Again, it flashed the light. I flashed once again and turned and hefted Megan into my arms.

"Okay, Megan, this is the part where you have to hold on tight."

Two thin arms appeared from among the folds and wrapped themselves around my neck and with surprising strength clutched onto me. Turning into the wind I traversed the final packed strip of beach sand and waded into the chilly surf. The first breaker hit me mid-thigh and shoved me back two or three feet. I hurried forward before the next one came in, aided by the small riptide that pushed at the back of my calves. I held the girl at head level when the next wave hit me in the chest, frigid and more violent, and again we lost another three feet of progress. I would not be able to hold her above the next wave; she was going to get wet. I held her as high as I could reach with the weight of the girl in my arms, but I was blinded by the bundle of blankets that blocked my vision. I could only keep pushing ahead into the water.

Before the next wave struck, strong hands grabbed the bundle and swept it up above my head and over the side of the now very close boat. With my vision restored I looked up as a hand appeared. I took it. Another pair of hands appeared and grabbed my other hand just as the next wave swept me under. I was hauled up and clambered over the side. The water was cold enough to take my breath away, and for a while I just stayed on my hands and knees gasping like a fish.

My first rational thought was for Megan. Inside the boat there was red low-level lighting running along the underside of the gunwales that helped as I raised my gaze to look for her, but my view was blocked by a pair of dark boots. Above them, dressed in black from head to toe, was a dark figure whose only discernable feature was a black camouflaged face. Even in this darkness I could see the face that looked down at me was not a friendly one.

"Good job—Casey. She's going to be just fine."

I was pretty sure that just fine was nowhere near what

Megan was going to be—for a long time. I spied her wrapped in another dark blanket and sitting up next to the helmsman, also dressed all in dark camo and face paint.

"She's hungry." I took another deep breath and started to shiver. "She's pretty tough for a kid."

"Yeah? How about you?"

"Um, me, nope, just freezing." Suddenly aware of something next to me, I turned my head. Next to me was another man, and he didn't look so good.

"Is this guy…?"

"Dead? Yeah, this is, I guess *was* his boat, he and his pal over there." He thumbed over his shoulder where another guy, also all in black but with a submachine gun in his hands, stood over another guy who was sitting on his hands against the opposite gunwale. "The boss is sitting out in international waters; the Coast Guard has an eye on him but they can't touch him out there. This schmuck didn't want to give us a ride in to the beach. He was surprisingly easy to convince to change his mind though."

I took another look at the dead man. Nothing ethnically special about him, regular clothing, regular face, about medium in most respects. I would not have thought twice about recognizing him in a crowd. Maybe not a drug runner but definitely a mercenary.

"You're going to have to shoot him by the way."

"What!?!"

"You need to shoot him. He's going to need to have a definite COD when they find him."

"COD? Isn't he already dead?"

"Yep, he's dead all right. COD, cause of death—I'd rather

they didn't look too hard for a different one. Besides, you'll need to show that it wasn't easy for you to do your job, right?"

"You know, Dunn, you are one sick fuck."

He leaned down close so he was eye to eye with me. "And don't you forget it."

Diary of Mick Casey

April 19, 1945, The End of Days

I must have been dazed when the ship was hit. It took me a few seconds before I recognized what I was looking at. I pulled myself up the side of the plane, struggling against the bulk of my flight suit, and looked out through the nose. The sky in front of us was almost dark as night, and it was hard to distinguish one flak explosion from the next. Brinker came over the headphones. "Target approaching. You got it, Nelson?"

I leaned into the front turret and nose section and looked to my left at Spiegs, who was leaning back at the navigation console, fumbling a tourniquet around his left leg. His flight suit was torn open and the fabric was turning dark. He looked at me through his goggles and then flicked his eyes to Nelson. Most of the side of the plane behind Spiegs was missing. What was still there was so full of holes it looked like a vegetable sieve. Forward of that, Nelson sat in the bombardier seat with his hands in front of him, not on the flight levers. I duck-walked up into the turret and took a look.

"Cap'n, this is Casey. We got trouble."

"Casey?"

"Spiegs is hit, looks bad. Cap'n—Nelson's got no hands, sir."

"Repeat."

"Nelson, sir, his hands, sir, they're shot to pieces, sir." I met Nelson's eyes—he already knew the score.

There was a pretty long pause on the intercom.

"Cap, this's Nelson, I got this, sir. Casey's gonna help me, sir, just give me the 'go.'" Turning to me, "Listen up, Case, I'm gonna do the sighting but you run the levers and pull the drops. Do it when I tell you, exactly when I tell you, clear?"

"Clear, but…"

"Ughhh…" He was having trouble getting his breath. "Ughhh…" two long, hard breaths, "do it exactly when I tell you. Roger?"

"Roger that."

The plane roared on. The wind howled through the hole in the side. The roar of the engines and the wind matched the one in my ears. My headphones were quiet, no one spoke, endless seconds. Finally:

"The plane is yours, Nelson."

"Roger, Cap'n. Casey, flip the left lever, then pull back on that one," he bobbed his head, "push forward on that one—now."

I tried to do exactly as he directed. Squatting next to the chair, the ship shook with each explosion around her. The flak no longer mattered; the shuddering of the ship as we bored in on the mountainside no longer mattered. Even the blood that poured out of the sleeves of his flight jacket no longer mattered. Only the buttons and levers, and the look in his eyes meant anything. For countless seconds he did not move. I barely dared to breathe. He closed his eyes and took another long breath and leaned forward to fasten his face to the bombsight.

"There's too much crosswind; pull back on the lower lever, slow—STOP—good, steady as she goes now."

Another crash, more cursing over the intercom. The ship roared on, the mountainsides the only thing ahead of us, somewhere beyond the smoke and flame of the flak.

Another shuddering breath. "Uhgg…that handle—now!"

I knew what that one did; it was the only thing that did matter. I slammed it with my palm.

"Bombs away!" He almost whispered it. He took another slow breath and turned toward to me again. "Now pull that one up and the other back."

I looked at him and he looked back.

"Switching control back to you, Cap'n. Throw that switch there, Case." He took another hard breath. "Be seein' you boys, uhgg—on the other side."

I unbuckled him and slid him out of the seat and back up against the radio shack bulkhead; the light was gone from him. Spiegs, one hand still pulling on his glove, was slumped over the chart table. The wind roared through the hole in the turret, almost drowning out the pitch of the engines.

"Casey here, we need first aid down in the nose, Lieutenant Holquist."

I duck-walked back into the turret and buckled into the front chair and got my feet set. I hit the booster motors on the guns and grabbed the trigger handles, because nothing else mattered now.

"Behold a pale horse and the name that sat on him was death, and hell followed with him," I whispered.

"Repeat? What was that last, Casey?"

The Waffle House

Greenville, Alabama

I was working my way through three of the greasiest eggs I'd eaten in a long time, plus a couple of soggy waffles, while I watched William. He was on the pay phone near the restrooms, hunched over and with his back turned to the room. All in all, his recovery was progressing well, he was now relatively coherent, and he had managed a glass of orange juice. He had turned a little green again when my eggs arrived so took the cue and went for the phone. It was William's job to make the call. He had the passwords that would unlock the offshore account to pass on. I didn't care how he painted the event or his role in it. The job was finished and that was what I had been there for.

He suddenly straightened up and turned and made eye contact with me. His eyes were as wide as they could get. He nodded a few more times, never breaking eye contact with me, then hung up. He looked at the phone for a minute, then at the restroom door, probably considering one more visit, then headed back to the corner table where I was. I was still making a puddle whenever I stopped moving and smelled of seawater, but there wasn't any doubt about who people noticed the most. William didn't smell very good.

"Was he happy?"

"Yeah, ecstatic." He gave me a serious frown and leaned

forward. “He said some jogger found a guy on Miramar Beach this morning. The guy had a bullet hole in his forehead. He doesn’t like complications like that.”

“The jogger had a bullet hole in his forehead? Geez, that’s awful.”

“Dammit, Hole!” He caught himself and looked around to see if anyone was listening. Then continued in a lower voice. “You shot a guy—in the face!? What the hell?”

“Me? No, man, I saw that guy last night, but he was already dead when I saw him.”

“Yeah, dead guys on the beach. Happens all the time, right? Jesus, why didn’t you say anything about that.”

“Maybe because I don’t know how some guy got croaked on the beach. I was a little busy doin’ my job—all by myself, I might add. Maybe it wasn’t even on the beach that he got croaked, coulda washed up—maybe.” I was careful not to make eye contact.

He had his elbows on the table and he was leaning forward with intensity. He was a big guy, so I squeezed a mouthful of greasy eggs out through my teeth while I smiled at him. He rocked back in disgust and nausea,

“Motherfucker!” He was too sick to be pissed off. “Well, Anthony’s impressed anyway, and that’s the guy that you gotta keep happy. Anthony said there’s a bonus due for you, and more work if you want.”

“I’m busy enough these days. How about I let him know. Meanwhile, we gotta get going. We’re supposed to switch out the Chevy in Montgomery, and I gotta find some dry clothes to get into. Then, man, I really gotta book for Chi-town.”

“Don’t you ever sleep?”

“Not if I can help it.”

Mick Casey

April 19, 1945, The Longest Day

I helped them carry Spiegs and Nelson out of the plane and then into the back of the meat wagon. The plane looked worse on the outside than it had from the turret. I stood on the grass next to her. I looked up at the busted-up glass on the front turret and the big hole in her left side. I turned and looked down the runway. I couldn't remember what I was supposed to do next.

"Casey! C'mon, you gotta get in the wagon!"

I turned back; the ambulance with its doors open sat at the rear hatch of the damaged bird. Taylor, Holmquist, and Brinker were all sitting on the tailgate having a smoke. Jansen, Reynolds, and Bonner were sitting on the ground in front of them. A couple medics were tying off a bandage around the captain's head. I just looked at them, not understanding. One of the medics separated from them and hurried over.

"C'mon, Casey, we gotta get you to the hospital. You guys are all gonna need some patching up."

I looked at him. I couldn't be sure if he was talking to me.

"Look, Casey." He pointed at my flight jacket. Looking down I saw the front of it was pretty ripped up. "You gotta come with us, okay, buddy? Captain Brinker's gonna need some patching, and the lieutenant's arm's busted I think. Don't make 'em wait, okay?"

I nodded at him and he took me by the elbow and led me to the truck. Taylor was braced against the inside of the truck; his pants were gone, and the medic was sticking plasters all over his leg where a flat piece of the fuselage was sticking out of the front. Blankets covered what was on the other two stretchers in the back. I sat down on the tailgate and set my hands down beside me. I looked down at my gloves where Nelson's blood had stained them. Taylor reached out a hand and put it on my shoulder; then Holmquist came over and put his on my other shoulder as he was climbing in and gave it a squeeze.

"Hell of a job, Casey, gotta tip my hat," Captain Brinker sighed from under his bandages, climbing in and lying down on the stretcher nearest the door. He pulled himself up and supported himself on his elbows. "That was number sixteen."

We won't go tomorrow.

Monday morning,
Flick's Engineering Department

I lit a cigarette and stared at my cup of coffee. It was cool enough to drink, but I wasn't sure I had the energy to pick it up. At 5:30 this morning I had left the Ford LTD rental parked in the spot that my Buick had been left in thirty-six hours before. After I wiped down every surface that I had touched, I swapped out the parking ticket in the Buick for the one just pulled from the attendant and left the old one in the Ford. I paid the seventy-five-cent parking fee for thirty minutes, the minimum, and headed home for a shower and to get dressed for work. They'd find the LTD eventually.

Two one-hour roadside naps coming from Alabama had cost me. You never wake up refreshed after sleeping behind the steering wheel, but it was still better than if the car had been moving. Usually I can go a couple of days without actual sleep, but this had been a stressful weekend and I had found myself unable to stay awake as I crossed into Kentucky and then again near Gary, Indiana. Now, even after a cold shower, I was a zombie, but I'd made it into work on time.

Since I was new in the department, only the routine, more vanilla projects were being spoon-fed to me. My in-box was empty this morning. I was hoping for an easy day of watching the other members of the department work and staring out through the glass at the poor bastards working out in the shop. If I watched long enough, Andy Polanco would look up and give me the finger, but it was usually with a smile.

I reached for the coffee cup and dared my first swallow and sighed. This sucked, this life of not belonging with the type of people who surrounded me here and disgusted by the people I was comfortable with. I took another swallow of coffee; it was weak and lukewarm already. I thought back to how my father rarely got to drink a hot cup of coffee, always drawn away to some minor crisis only to return and hurry through the room temperature coffee hopefully before something else captured his attention.

My father was a lot of things—some I admired and some I resented. But one of those things was that he was a man of impeccable integrity and honesty. He served as a constant rebuke of the life I was leading currently. He was also a penitent man and used it as reinforcement of his "straight and narrow" ways. Every month without fail he attended confession on a Saturday night. When I was younger confession was a family event, and he went last after making sure that we knelt at the communion rail and said our assigned penances. Once he entered the confessional, he would be in there for what seemed forever and puzzled all of us. We knew he wasn't a sinner. I couldn't imagine any transgression that he could have engaged in that would require a ten- to fifteen-minute audience with the priest.

I still went to church on Sunday albeit sporadically, driven by habit and guilt, but I would never hazard a trip to the confessional at the back of the church. I drank the tepid coffee and imagined that encounter.

"Bless me, Father, for I have sinned; it has been one month since my last confession. These are my sins: I passively watched the attempted murder and brutal assault of a sixteen-year-old girl, one time. I facilitated and participated in the sale of a fourteen-year-old girl into slavery in a foreign country, one time. Oh, and I also shot a dead man in the head, um, also recently.

"Yes, Father, all in the last month."

I didn't think there were enough *Our Fathers* and *Hail Mary's* to absolve those sins, and there was a good chance that I might do them all again anyway. They were also the most recent in what was a lengthening line of mortal sins. I thought about penance and the difference between that and repentance. To repent meant to turn around. Maybe what I needed was repentance. I knew that Walter Dunn was most likely correct, that sooner or later this was not going to end well. I could feel it coming.

"You look like you had a rough weekend." Angel looked like she'd just stepped out of a beauty parlor, and she smelled like Ivory soap.

"Me? Naw, I spent the weekend just sitting on my butt. Relaxin'."

"Well, your tie isn't straight."

"I was kind of in a hurry this morning, and besides, I don't like wearing a tie."

"It's the dress code. They just started letting us girls wear pants to work, you know. That was a pretty big deal around here. They're pretty strict."

"Well, they keep hinting that I need to shave off my beard too."

She made of kind of *harrumph* sound, then, "Well, don't if you can help it, K?" She did a quick 180 with her head and added, "Look, I'll get into trouble if I stop and talk, so I brought this stuff from Office Supply that you ordered, even though it's not my job." She stopped long enough to gather up her nerve and added, "There's a bunch of us getting together after work on Friday at the Thirsty Whale. It's gonna be Becky's last day. I already took the night off from Oliver's, so I'm going. I thought it might be a way for you to meet some of the other people."

"I sometimes work on Friday night. Which one's Becky?"

"She's the one with the pageboy haircut. You know, she's married and her husband got transferred to Ohio, so she's gonna leave."

I didn't have anything to say to that, so I just looked at my coffee again. It would have been rude to look at what I wanted to look at.

"Well, I was just letting you know...you know, in case."

"Yeah, I think I know where it is. On Grand Avenue over in Franklin Park, right? Friday's a long way off though, so I'll have to see."

I left that there, and after she had shifted her weight from one hip to the other, a couple of times she drifted back up the aisle, smiling and greeting the other guys, who, not surprisingly, were very happy to see her. She was an eyeful, that was for sure. I took a swallow of coffee. *Dammit, cold already*. Maybe a little repentance wouldn't be a bad idea after all.

Emmett Casey

Springtime 1971, Nuremburg, Germany

My grandfather always said that it wasn't really springtime until the oak leaves were the size of a squirrel's ear. Back in Wisconsin, I had seen it snow on Memorial Day, so springtime's arrival had no specific date or timeline. Which made oak leaves as accurate an indicator as any media weatherman. Grandpa Quinn had quite a few of those silly axioms that he spouted from time to time. In my short time as an adult, I had realized that most of them were fairly accurate, and not surprisingly, I began to quote them myself.

In Sud Bayern (Southern Bavaria), all of the seasons seemed to arrive ahead of schedule. Last fall the temperature had begun to drop below freezing in mid-September. Snow began in early October. First Sergeant Sinclair had addressed a full company assembly to inform us that the heat would not be turned on until October 15th, and until then we were not "authorized" to be cold. None of us had seen the humor in this statement, and I was fairly certain that he had not intended it to be funny. Now spring had come early and quickly as well. The days were warm and pleasant, the nights chilly and damp, and we had begun to sleep outside of our sleeping bags.

In Nuremburg, there were no sounds of frogs croaking and

crickets awaking, only the constant buzz of city noise, auto and street-car traffic, horns and industry. It was not the kind of spring that I would have preferred, but it was a change from the biting wind and bitter snows, frostbitten toes and fingers, of only a few weeks before. Almost none of the trucks we drove were equipped with heaters.

It was Wednesday morning, and the weather was perfect. The sun, which never touched the inside of the quadrangle, was bright on the south-facing walls and mediated the chill and damp of the large paved square space. The quadrangle was one of two huge barracks facilities. Standing five stories high and with more than one sub-basement level, it made up the bulk of what was known now as Merrill Barracks. In a past life Merrill Barracks had housed the headquarters of the Nazi SS. Connecting the two massive brick quadrangles was an equally imposing building that straddled an archway and tunnel and provided the only entrance into the complex. The chapel that we used for church services on Sunday was previously been the office of the SS Commandant, and overlooked the archway facing the street. The entire front of the building was still splintered and pockmarked with evidence of the firefight that took place decades ago when it was captured by the allies at the end of World War II.

From above it would appear like two square balloons connected by a stick or bar in the middle. Occasionally, at night and on weekends, with a careful eye on the various sentries and armed with flashlights, we would sneak out onto the parade ground and pick a likely manhole cover, lift it, and descend into the lower levels to explore the cavernous spaces. We had never inquired as to whether it was off-limits, but also knew better than to ask. We discovered secret ways into the gymnasium and the various workshops on the compound and we discovered the mother lode as well, a secret way into the mess hall. We were never short on rations after that.

The quadrangle was a vast, paved, empty space, fully 150 feet, or more, square. It was rarely occupied by any objects other than foot traffic and a couple of dumpsters. The dumpsters were a central point of interest. On most Friday nights, and most especially on payday, they provided a special form of entertainment when someone would set them on fire. This would bring the local Kraut fire department roaring in through the tunnel on the south wall, and we would all assemble on the roof to watch their efficient, almost weekly routine. As a result, the dumpsters were guarded almost better than the motor pools, and that served to add a more sporting aspect to the arson efforts.

Today the dumpsters took a backseat to the spectacle in front of them. Assembled in the quadrangle today were the entire 182nd Light Equipment Maintenance Company (LEM) and the personnel of the 303rd Maintenance Battalion. The 42nd and the 66th Heavy Equipment Maintenance companies had been exempted due to the distance geographically of their installations, but even so, representatives from their two companies were represented by one full squad each. It was a formal formation and all squads stood in tight order, each soldier warned to wear their best fatigues, starched and polished. The group spanned the entire breadth of the enclosed space. In spite of the number of men assembled, there was no sound from the throng, all eyes fixed on the small group that faced them.

In the center of the quadrangle stood the reason for the

assembly. There a cadre of officers in full dress uniform stood at the ready. Lieutenant Kyle stood ramrod straight, beaming with pride, and next to him our CO, Captain Grissom, solemn and, for a change, engaged. On the far left, First Sergeant Sinclair, resplendent in a uniform that threatened to cut off his breathing at any minute. It must have been the uniform making him uncomfortable because he was having trouble controlling a frown that kept dragging down the sides of his brilliantly crimson face. In front of these three stood our battalion commander, Colonel Parks, his XO, Major Barksdale, and next to him, General Somebody, a one-star all the way from 7th Corps, down in Stuttgart. A Command Sergeant Major, also from Corps, rounded out the assembly.

We faced each other over half the quadrangle apart, and for a long time there was no movement or speech. Finally, the CSM from Corps coughed quietly into his fist and then in a loud voice that echoed back from the bricks, "Battalion—Attention!"

There was the general stamp of all feet striking the pavement in absolute unison. We were, after all, soldiers.

"Specialist Robert E. Casey, front and center!"

It was inevitable, no good deed goes unpunished. Even when the deed was not so good. I stepped forward from my position as a squad leader in the Tech Supply Platoon and right-faced in a perfect military imitation. Upon reaching the center of the formation, I left-faced and marched straight up to the center of the little delegation directly in front of General Somebody, snapped my heels together, and threw a salute that stopped just short of taking the top of my head off. Lieutenant Kyle stepped up along with Colonel Parks and flanked the CSM. The general returned my salute, and then taking an embossed folder from Parks opened it and addressed the entire group.

"On the evening of July 18, 1970, Private First-Class Robert Emmett Casey was a member of a reconnaissance squad from Company B, 503 Infantry, 173rd Airborne Division performing operations out of Firebase Storm in the Central Highlands of the Republic of South Vietnam. During a patrol along the Ho Chi Minh Trail, their squad was ambushed by a force of North Vietnamese Regular Army and Viet Cong guerrillas in superior numbers. The squad became pinned down in a drainage ditch, returned fire, and defended their position. Over the course of the next fourteen hours, throughout the night and into the early hours of July 19, they held their position. In the early hours of July 19, their position was overrun, yet they stood over their fallen comrades, preventing them from being defiled by the enemy. They continued to defend this position with small arms and eventually hand-to-hand combat when their ammunition ran out. As a result of this uncommon bravery and..."

He continued to read from the document in his hands, but I wasn't listening anymore. I was listening to Hitchcock screaming like a demon from hell. I was smelling cordite and copper, the smell of blood, flashes of bright light in the total darkness. The blood roared in my ears and I remembered the red mist that caused it to do so. I hadn't realized how warm the morning had become as sweat poured down my forehead and stained my armpits.

I understood the purpose of the event—it proved to the drones and technicians that soldiers still fought and that there was purpose in their mission—but to me it spoke of futility and loss, shame and guilt. My feet wanted to run away, but instead I stood rooted at full attention while the torture dragged on. Finally, the general stepped forward and pinned a medal on the left side of my dress green's jacket, below the blue-and-silver Combat Infantry Badge and Purple Heart. "Specialist, ABOUT FACE!" I spun on my heel and faced the final humiliation as the entire congregation saluted.

After the formation split up, my mates and others crowded around to look and admire. They all wanted to touch the medal and feel the weight of it—far heavier to me than to any of them.

"Shit man! You're a fuckin' hero Hole." Exclaimed Anderson. "Who knew?"

"Nah, you can't be a hero if you didn't die." Ryan was closer to the truth.

It was a pretty thing, with a bright red ribbon and a blue stripe, and the bright bronze star that hung beneath catching the sunlight. The box that it had come in was also a beautiful thing, with a rich, soft cover and a felt lining, well made and useful for a number of things. I slid it into my pocket and turned to go back to work with the rest of the company.

I tossed the medal into the dumpster as I passed.

Mick Casey

April 20, 1945, Trento, Italy

My new ship is the *Irish Lassie*. She's got history and a lot of air miles and it shows. I met my new crewmates today and we went over her from top to bottom. It felt good to be busy. I broke down and cleaned the Brownings and checked the boosters. The bolts holding the armor plate I'll kneel behind were loose and I tightened them up. The plate has some pretty good dents in it. We are a new crew made up of men from other crews—we are the survivors. We shook hands and got to work. We didn't show each other pictures from home or tell each other about our girlfriends. There wasn't any joking or poking fun. We don't want to get to know each other—we've all learned our lesson.

Conscience and Forgiveness
Emmett Casey

Friday night arrived like they all did: too soon if you dreaded them, too late if you hated what you did with your life the rest of the week. For me it was both and neither. Friday was just Friday, no different than Thursday, Tuesday, or Sunday—just Friday. It had been a cruel week. Work hadn't been busy enough to preoccupy my thoughts. I no longer had the feverish pace of the machine shop to match my need for distraction. Instead I had smoked packs of cigarettes, drunk cup after cup of bad coffee, and wrestled with my own personal taskmaster—conscience. I already knew that although I could be granted forgiveness, I would not and could not forgive myself.

I would soon turn twenty-two. I had spent my twenty-first birthday in prison. Before that and since then there was a lot of water under my bridge. I thought about penance and how much or what kind of penance would qualify as repentance. I thought about what things were benefitted by penance and what things were beyond the ability of penance. It was a revolving mental discussion that always came back to square one—no forgiveness, no redemption.

After each workday I drove out into the country, taking random turns until I would finally become lost in the darkness as night fell. Parking along the side of unnamed roads, I got out and I walked. I walked until my calves ached because I still had on my dress shoes. I pushed my pace until I could hear my heart in my ears and my breath became ragged. Only then would I stop to squat down along the shoulder with my forearms on my knees and let my head hang between my arms, my eyes closed. There I let myself cool and listened to the sweat drip from my forehead into the mud, slush and gravel between my feet.

The images hung there in my mind, my waking nightmare.

Dunn's face only inches from mine. "And don't you forget it."

The prick Anthony as he stepped over the crumpled body of little used-up Melinda, "It seems that you can be a rather bad man to get on the wrong side of. At least you were once. I am in need of someone who still is."

I thought back to SFC Franks. "…you survived a situation that by all accounts you should not have."

Father Lamb's kind face and voice. "How far is far enough when you are running from yourself?"

This last phrase echoed over and over in every empty space that allowed itself into my mind. "How far, how far, how far is far enough…"

Penance—this was penance without the Our Fathers or Hail Marys—or the forgiveness. Dunn wasn't about to disappear, Anthony still walked the earth, and by all accounts I should not have survived, and I knew it. The bridge up ahead on the road to my future was out and the train was picking up speed. Repentance or penance, I needed to turn around. I needed to find a new road, one with a future. But I didn't know how to get off the road I was already on.

Now it was Friday, and on this Friday night I was going to go to the Thirsty Whale. I was going to have fun, or whatever passed for it these days. I was almost as afraid of what that might be, or might turn out not to be, as I was of Dunn or Anthony.

Different is almost never good.

The First Step in Repentance—Turn Around, Emmett Casey

I came awake suddenly, the back of my head and neck aching from sleeping with my head kinked into the armrest of the sofa. I slept on the couch frequently, but this time it was uncomfortable; mostly because it wasn't my couch. I didn't have to open my eyes to know there was someone else in the room with me. Whoever was in the room with me was being very quiet, but their presence was unmistakable. I didn't sense a threat, but there was someone there nonetheless. Even with my eyes closed, I could feel that the room was filled with sunshine; open windows breezed fresh early summer air, and the sound of songbirds and weekend activities streamed in with it. Involuntarily, I took a deep breath and sighed it out.

"Well, this is new and different."

The voice was female, confident, but not one I knew. I stopped the pretense of sleep and opened my eyes; lying flat on my back, the view was of the sun-bright ceiling. The kind that you sprayed up and then painted. I turned my head, and she returned my look without any sign of being ill at ease. She was sitting across the room curled into an impossibly large easy chair. Wearing a Chicago Bears jersey that looked to be at least three sizes too large and not much else, she dunked a teabag into her cup and held my gaze.

"Different is almost never good," I said, because in my life that was usually true.

"Hmm," with the help of her spoon she unhurriedly squeezed the last breath out of the teabag and dropped it onto a saucer on the side table next to her, "then I guess I should assume the worst."

I sat up into the corner of the couch and dropped my hands onto my knees and looked around, trying to get my bearings. I hadn't sized the place up much when I came in last night, and I had turned on a minimum of lights. It was cozy—comfortable furniture, tasteful pictures and wall hangings, plants everywhere and they all seemed pretty healthy-looking. Looking back at her I knew I'd never seen her before. I definitely would have remembered her—incredibly long bare legs were tucked up underneath her. Even in the football jersey she appeared long and thin; she would be tall when she stood. Thick blonde hair was neatly parted in the middle and braided into two thick pigtails that hung down onto her chest. Her face was neither classic nor stunning, instead perfect, a well-shaped chin, high cheekbones, and wide-set eyes. Her eyes, pale blue behind the glasses she wore, were bright and intelligent.

"You're the roommate." I addressed the wall below the black-and-white drawing of two women embracing on the opposite wall. I didn't have to ask. It was obvious that she was in her own surroundings.

She nodded to me over the lip of her teacup as she breathed across the top of it.

"Angel sometimes brings them back here, and sometimes they take her home with them. When she goes home with them it doesn't seem to end well. I usually have to go and rescue her once she's locked herself in his bathroom."

"So, I'm the other one then."

"Nope, not the other one either."

It was discomfiting to be sitting in front of her, in her place, and not even been introduced. Although she didn't seem uncomfortable, she also didn't seem to be ready to offer any hospitality either. She simply sipped her tea and idly petted the nearest plant with her free hand. Her eyes alternated between giving me the once-over and looking out through the double patio door windows.

To break the tension, I was beginning to feel, I got up and wandered into the kitchen. Searching through cabinets, I found a glass and filled it at the sink. She seemed cool enough so I didn't ask permission. Everything in there was clean and tidy, the kitchen was bright with the sunshine, and the glass in my hand gleamed. I drank the whole thing in one breath and it finished waking me up. Once I was awake, bladder issues became immediately urgent. When I came back into the living room, she watched me with interest and not a hint of embarrassment.

"Is all of that you under that shirt?"

I looked down at the rumpled shirt that I'd just slept in.

"I guess. May I use your bathroom please?"

"You can use the one in the hallway; mine is through the bedroom and that one you may not. There's a couple of new toothbrushes in the medicine cabinet, so you can brush your teeth if you want. We sit down when we pee in this house, so don't piss on the seat."

Well, that certainly was clear. After I finished the immediate necessity, I washed my hands and face and broke open one of the new toothbrushes and used it with the available toothpaste in the cabinet. After that I took a moment to regard the asshole in the mirror. He didn't look different to me. After that I did the best I could with my hair and beard and exited out into the living room again. The door to Angie's room was closed.

"I just checked in the mirror; can't say I see anything different."

She took a good look again across the top of her teacup while she sipped it.

"I wouldn't have known what you looked like before, so how could that be different?"

"Well, you started the conversation, so what's different? You wouldn't have any coffee, would you, by the way?"

"The teapot is hot, teabags above the stove; I don't make coffee unless it's a workday."

I decided it wouldn't do me any good to pout, beggars can't be choosers, so I wandered back to the kitchen and found a cup in the cabinets next to the one with the glasses in it. When I opened the door above the stove there were half a dozen different tins of tea with names that all sounded ridiculous and unappetizing, but near the back I discovered a jar of Sanka.

"Well, hello, old friend, where you been?"

"What was that?"

"Nothing, I was just talking to myself."

Sanka acquired I returned to the couch and braced the hot cup on my knee. I appreciated that she hadn't tried to talk to me while I was in the other room. She was patient and I was apparently her morning entertainment.

"What's different is that you're on the wrong side of that

closed bedroom door, or maybe not on the wrong side." She waved the cup toward the hallway. "Also, I just gotta ask, I've never seen it before, so do you always sleep like you're laid out in a coffin? That's the damnedest thing I've seen in a while, flat on your back, hands folded on your chest. I had to get really close just to make sure you weren't dead."

"I'm not in the other room because that would have been the wrong thing to do."

"Well, that's different right there. Since when do boys turn down a piece of ass when it's free?"

"I'm no boy."

"Just sayin', I bet she offered though."

"When I got her here she was barely conscious; she didn't offer anything. I actually had to carry her over my shoulder from the parking lot. I would have turned down anything she offered. I'm no *pendejo*." I looked over my shoulder toward the hallway and added, "I've never seen a girl puke that much in my life."

"If you're gonna spend time with Angie, you better get used to holding her hair up out of the toilet. That kid likes to party, but she doesn't seem to be learning how. So, you didn't fuck her?"

I pointed at my chest. "Again, no pendejo."

"I don't know what that is. I speak English, Swedish, German, and some Polish, but no Spanish."

"It means idiot, but most people use it to mean stupid asshole."

"You speak Spanish?"

"No, but enough people have called me that so I finally had to ask someone."

"Okay then, not an asshole according to you—then what is your name?"

Well, this was a dilemma. "Emmett."

"Ang won't surface until sometime this afternoon, so I'm gonna rustle up some grub…pancakes and bacon or sausage? I'm Gail and you can call me," she paused and looked up at the ceiling, then took a deep breath, "—Gail." She unfolded herself up and out of the chair and rose to an impossible height. Turning back, she bent to retrieve her saucer, teacup, and spoon. From my vantage point the view did not get worse. Then on her way to the kitchen she paused and looked down at me. "But you're the one they call Hole."

The Thirsty Whale
Emmett Casey

In my naiveté I arrived at the bar far too early for the party crowd. There were plenty of twenty-somethings with their ties loosened and shirtsleeves rolled up, drinking two-for-one tap beers and talking too loudly. This apparently in hope of being overheard by the few women sitting at elevated table tops along the walls. The women for their part laughed too loudly while their hands stroked the base of their neck and stole glances over the shoulders of their friends at the room, and boys, beyond. I took one of the empty seats at the end of the bar farthest from the door and which apparently was a dead zone of activity. I ordered a shot and a beer. The bartender made eye contact, smiled, and waved off my five-dollar bill.

"Don't worry, dude, there's enough cash on the bar from all these guys to cover your real drink. Happy hour, Friday night, you know?" He winked.

When happy hour ended at six, not surprisingly, so did the bar crowd's interest. By six thirty the bartender and I were practically the only ones left in the room. The ones who still remained were intent on getting sloppy drunk. Once empty, the place appeared stark, lifeless, and smelled like ashtrays, stale beer, with a hint of Hai Karate aftershave. The bartender leaned on the bar across from me, and I ordered another shot. When it came I slid it back across to him; he threw it back and nodded his appreciation. I ordered two more.

"You been in here before?"

"Nope, not my kind of bar."

"Well, if you stick around you're in for a real shit-show by the time bar time rolls around."

"Gets crazy?"

"Chicks like you can't imagine, all on a mission, you know, and enough guys trolling for tail so it's wild. From back where I stand it's like watching a tragic comedy. Jesus, I'll tell ya I'm glad I don't have to swim in that pool anymore."

"I'm supposed to be here for a going away party."

"Shit, there's one of those in here every Friday night, you know, just an excuse to outdo each other. Half the time I think you need a scorecard to tell who's on what team."

"Same crowd as just left?"

"Oh yeah, mostly regulars, and party girls, but yeah, about the same. Right now, they gotta go home and get changed. The guys put on those godawful leisure suits and the girls squeeze into some crazy tight-as-shit stuff so that there's nothing left to the imagination. Mind you, I'm not complaining."

"Great." I looked down at my freshly ironed oxford cotton shirt, blue jeans, and boots hooked on the bar stool. "Oh well."

"Geez, man, you're the first normal-looking guy in here in about a week. Please don't leave me now." He quickly poured another beer for me and I dropped a ten on the bar. He saluted and threw back the shot.

By eight thirty we were getting to be pretty good friends and the hopefuls were starting to arrive. By nine the bouncers at the door were at it full time, checking IDs and turning back doomed hopefuls. There were plenty who made it through the gauntlet anyway.

The initial arrivals were almost all males who hurried to preferred positions and staked their spots, leisure suits remarkable in their sameness. Females arrived later and in groups of three or four, sticking closely together. Their slacks and jeans so tight that there was no doubt they were all anatomically correct. These groups almost universally consisted of one physically exceptional one, and two or three others less gifted in the same way. These companions appeared to be in hot pursuit of their aspiration to become an overweight middle-aged housewife.

Happy hour long over, the males opted for bottled beer now, and the girls ordered different-colored drinks in tall, curvy glasses filled with fruit. Without exception, both drank while their eyes wandered over the tops of their drinks, their heads on a swivel. My bartender friend was working up a good sweat keeping up, and occasionally rolled his eyes at me. The music, impossibly, got louder. I was working on a very pleasant buzz, and my seat was perfectly positioned as a vantage point. I saw Angie's group as soon as they cleared the second bouncer. So did all the boys in the place.

I swear it was like the lights in the room dimmed except for what surrounded her. Because of my vantage point the bar blocked my view of her from the waist down, but that's where everyone else's eyes tracked immediately. There was nothing wrong with the waist-up view either. Five other girls arrived with her; one had a pageboy haircut. Even the married one did a complete three-sixty of the room, and when she spotted me, she poked Angie and whispered into her ear. Angie's eyes got wider and she smiled a bright smile at me just as her first drink was delivered—by the first of many hopeful leisure suits. She wasn't going to get to me even if she wanted to. I poked a finger in the air at the bartender, and we both threw back another shot. I dropped a twenty on the bar. I was going to need to pace myself.

By eleven thirty the music was on its second time around, the room had become hot and crowded, the air close. Jade East cologne vied with Heaven Sent perfume to overcome the dense cloud of cigarette smoke, beer, and sweat. Desperation was starting to tighten some of the men's faces, and the girls were starting to sag at the knees when they laughed. I had had a brief "hello, see you later?" with Angie when she passed on the way to the restroom. She continued to make occasional eye contact, but I was enjoying the shit-show just as the bartender had said I would.

I did not see him come in, but then he was there, and his posture told a completely different story than any of the other boys in the room. His flowered shirt and leisure suit were perfect in every detail. He was on a mission and the mission appeared to be Angie; and he was angry. He was standing too close to her for comfort, and although I couldn't hear the words, it was obvious that they were loud and aggressive. He would only pause in his diatribe long enough to sweep his carefully styled hair off his forehead with a wave of his hand and a flip of his head. He was at least a full head taller than Angel and he was leaning down over her, speaking firmly and waving his arms. His face was set in an angry scowl. Angie's posture changed too; instead of standing tall with her head up to survey the room, she had slumped and now stared down into her drink, and her hair had fallen forward, hiding her face.

Whenever he stopped speaking and dropped his arms to his side, she would shrug her shoulders or shake her head back and forth. This seemed to make him even more agitated, and he would fire up all over again. It went on for a full five minutes before her head came up and a different Angie appeared from out of her drink. She was mad and there was fire in her eyes. She spoke what must have been hard words while her mascara streaked down her cheeks and her perfect eyebrows pulled down with the heat of her words. Immediately his hand came up in a classic face-slap position.

It never landed. Instead his hand ended up somewhere between his shoulder blades, and his knees buckled.

"I think your car is on fire," I whispered in his ear so only he could hear.

He tried to turn his head to see who it was, but we were in a hurry to get to the front door and he needed to concentrate on keeping his feet underneath himself. The bouncers, quick to sense trouble, both turned and started our way, but a shout from the bartender got their attention. They looked at him and then back at me, then stepped to the side and let us pass. In the parking lot I let the little rooster loose, and he whirled around flexing his shoulder and rubbing it with his other hand. Then he got himself back together and jumped back into his dipshit persona and rocked up onto his toes.

"What the fuck, who the fuck do you think you are? I should call the cops."

"I'm Mr. None-of-your-business and you should get lost, punk."

"You can't talk that way to me, motherfucker."

I said nothing.

"I'm gonna kick your ass, asshole."

I knew I didn't have anything to worry about from him; he was seriously too full of himself. I wanted to see how far he'd push his luck before he came to his senses.

"You know...people say that to me a lot, and a few have actually done it. Maybe you should give it a try. Jump on up if you're feeling froggy." I was just drunk enough myself that the idea didn't sound entirely unappealing. Men who hit women pissed me off on a whole new level.

I waited for him and watched. The longer I waited the more he started to take stock of the situation. A small group had rushed out through the front doors following the excitement, along with the two bouncers. He looked at them, then at me. I'm not a big guy, but I'm not little either, and this little fucker wasn't entirely stupid. My posture was relaxed. I hadn't adopted a fighting posture. I was obviously comfortable, which made him less so by the moment. You could see the realization dawn on him that I wasn't another run-of-the-mill leisure suit.

He dropped his shoulders and sagged a little.

"You're lucky, motherfucker. I've got better things to do or else I'd clean your clock."

I let him save a little face and said nothing. He began to back up, and finally turned and headed across the parking lot.

"But I'll see you again, bastard fucknuts."

"It was nice meeting you," I called after him. Without turning around, he waved his middle finger at me and disappeared between the parked cars.

"After that Angie was on a mission. She was two-fisting drinks the rest of the night, none of which she bought herself, of course. Apparently, this Todd guy was an ex-boyfriend of hers; he'd co-signed her car loan—he took the car when he left. By the time they made last call Angie could barely stand up. There were a few guys who had stayed so they could drive her home, but I thought it would just be best if I did it. They understood—eventually."

I finished my wrap-up of the previous evening's events while I ate my way through three eggs, several pancakes, and a half-pound of bacon. Gail matched me bite for bite and remained quiet for the entire story.

"Well then," she said as she set her fork down, "this was something different after all. For all of us. Todd's not a new problem." And for the first time, she smiled. "I think I'm gonna make some coffee. Reach that ashtray off the counter behind you, will you? I hope you have a cigarette you can spare. I'm thinking I'd like one."

She got up and danced around the kitchen, every move graceful. While she busied herself scooping coffee into the coffeepot, she added over her shoulder,

"By the way, people call me Dutch."

Diary of Mick Casey

May 2, 1945,
Nuremburg, Germany

We're going every day now. There are no more enemy fighters, there's not much flak, they can't fight back anymore. According to the CO we are Maximum Effort and we're throwing everything into the air that will fly. Today our target was Nuremburg, and we had hundreds of bombers in the flight. We were supposed to target the railyard and the south of town and not hit the castle on the north end and to definitely not hit the cathedral in the city center. When we got there, it looked like those were the only two things still standing. We dropped incendiaries.

The war seems to be over, we'll go home soon. Those poor bastards won't have one to go home to. We've seen to that. We got our second Presidential Unit Citation when we got back to the airfield.

She Rises
Emmett

A pot of coffee and a half pack of cigarettes later, Dutch was turning out to be an excellent conversationalist. She currently worked as a stewardess for Lufthansa but modeled on the side. She hoped to make the modeling a career, her ticket to fame, and wanted to get into commercials. She had seen someone named Shelley Long at Second City Comedy Club and now Ms. Long was appearing in Alberto VO5 commercials, "and probably making the big bucks." Dutch maintained that she had more talent in her little finger than Ms. Shelley Long. She was a rabid Chicago Cubs fan and was planning on watching the game as soon as it started, which didn't hurt my impression of her either. I told her I was thinking about going back to college.

Eventually we heard the bedroom door open and feet shuffle into the bathroom. The door closed, Dutch gave me a meaningful look, and soon the toilet flushed and the faucet blasted water. I suddenly realized that I should probably have been long gone by now to prevent one of those uncomfortable morning-after encounters, but the morning had taken an unexpected turn for the better.

Angie exited the bathroom and shuffled out into the

living room area with her eyes only halfway open. Gone was the sexy Angie, replaced by a messy girl in a hobo costume that looked as if it had been dragged through a knothole. Without hesitation she climbed up into Dutch's lap and snuggled her head down under her chin. Dutch set her coffee cup down on the side table and petted her hair.

"Rough night, darling?"

"Uh huh..."

"Well, honey, you need to get in the shower. You smell like death—and puke."

"I'm sorry, Dutchie."

"It's okay, sweetie. Hole saved me from having to come and get you, so I'm not really upset."

"He was amazing, Dutchie, he was going to kick Todd's ass right in front of everyone. It was like it was no big deal for him either. Becky and the other girls said he's scary."

"Hmm...he left that part of the story out." She made eye contact with me over Angie's rat's nest of hair. "But, sweetie—he's still here."

She jerked up and looked across the room. The look on her face went through a kaleidoscope of surprise to amazement to shame, and finally her eyes and head dropped and through her cascade of hair she said, "Hi, Emmett; thanks for last night."

"Go get in the shower. Jesus, you stink to high heaven, Angel!" Dutch ordered as she shoved Angie off her lap. Angie staggered to her feet and took a moment getting her balance, then gave me a shy little smile from under the wild mop of hair and shuffled back to the bathroom.

"I'm going to have to fix something that she'll be able to keep down." She unwound herself from the chair again and started for the kitchen, then stopped and looked down at me. "She is an innocent child, you know, but I'm so glad she found me. I truly do love her."

I took a drink from my coffee and returned her gaze.

"She is very special. Like a kid, you know, precious and innocent. And she needs me." She started for the kitchen again and added, "I think we need each other."

I raised my cup in her direction and nodded. I understood that need. Pushing up out of the couch, I knew it was time to leave. She stopped just inside the door and looked back at me, waiting to see if I'd respond.

"Then I guess you're the lucky one too, aren't you?"

I started dating Angie; sometimes we'd go out, sometimes Dutch went with us.

Repentance My Way
Emmett

My life consisted of arising from the recliner every morning and waking up in the shower. In the morning I dreaded getting dressed and going to work. In the evening I dreaded leaving work and going home. The wheel went around every twenty-four hours, never getting worse, never getting better. Every day mind-numbingly ordinary, every night interminably long.

The apartment water heater allowed ample time for reflection and escalating dread while I scrubbed my skin awake. Reflection that was painful because it came from remembrances. Remembrances that fostered internal arguments of what might have been, could have been, and the wrong turn involved in each outcome. During these internal *woulda-shoulda-coulda* moments, I never seemed to win the argument. Then as the hot water ran out, I would resolve to be smarter and more energetic. I would towel myself off with reminders to watch for the harbingers of disaster with a more practiced eye. I would comb my hair and adjust my tie with a degree of hopefulness I knew would dissolve as soon as I arrived in the parking lot.

I traded in the Buick for a shiny car. Polanco and everyone

at work liked it better than I did. I decided it was the car's fault, so I traded it for a windowless panel van so I could customize it into a party van. But then that sounded like too much work and I didn't have any friends to party with anyway, so I traded the van for a pickup truck. All in about eight weeks. I had paid cash for the first one and lost money on each one after that. I should have kept the Buick.

Instead of providing sanctuary, the apartment started to feel restrictive. Instead of climbing into the recliner every evening, I paced the caged space and stole peeks out through the closed drapes. The apartment suddenly became responsible for my mood. Weekends became a series of aimless drives to nowhere, cruising neighborhoods or driving toward a compass point until the fuel tank was exhausted so I could escape the cage as long as possible. One Saturday I passed a billboard for a new apartment complex that seemed very modern and had a golf course wrapped around it. A banner had been added that shouted, "Now accepting new applications!"

I parked in the tree-lined lot and followed the winding pendant-lined walk to the Open House model. An attractive female associate met me with enthusiasm and walked me through the one-bedroom example. It was spacious, smelled of new paint, had expensive furniture, and screamed possibilities of a different and exciting lifestyle. The complex encouraged an active social life and featured a swimming pool, a health club, and a young adult clientele. I signed a lease. It took longer for me to rehang the privacy drapes than it did for me to move my shit possessions to their new home. What didn't go in the truck went in the dumpster next to it.

The new apartment had a large sliding double glass door

and a tiny eight-by-eight-foot walk-out concrete slab the brochure called a patio. The patio had a view of the pool. At the hardware store I bought a folding lawn chair and some hooks to hang artwork on just in case I ever got some. The manicured shrubbery in front of my new patio provided sufficient camouflage so I could sit comfortably shielded and watch the more socially active young adults having fun in the pool. They seemed to enjoy themselves.

But all apartments look the same once you close your eyes. It took less than forty-eight hours before the nightmare found my new hiding place.

I bought a motorcycle—it was new, loud, and very fast. It scared me when it went fast, so I did it a lot. It wasn't as much fun when it rained though and it made an oil spot on the shag carpet in the living room. I thought about getting a dog, then decided I wouldn't be good company. I thought about Angie—and Dutch. I got the dog. Every name I came up with for it had a negative association in my memory, so I just called it "Dog." It didn't seem to mind. At night it twitched and whimpered in its sleep. I let it sleep on my lap. That seemed to help it.

The following Monday I got arrested at work.

R. Emmett Casey
Well Hello Officer

The office model at Flick's was one of a wide-open space fully three hundred feet from end to end. Each department commanded two or three rows of orderly desks lined in militarily straight lines, eight in a row, sixteen in a squad, then a dividing aisle and repeat. From the Office Supply Department, with its shelves and cubbyholes of staplers and manila folders, you could look out across a sea of diligent pencil-pushers all the way to the far wall where the engineers and elevated drafting tables presented the only break in the landscape.

One side of this immense office space separating the office and its staff from the machine shop and its worker bees was thick double-pane glass. The glass served two purposes: It was thick to muffle the intense din of the metal lathes and hydraulic presses. It was clear so that the two worlds could look into the other's and each feel a part of a larger thing.

It was common, even encouraged, for the two sides to intermarry, and there were numerous postings of wedding receptions and save-the-date notices on the bulletin board in the lunch line. It guaranteed Flick's employee longevity if your wife or husband worked just on the other side of the glass. I had appreciated the view when I worked in the shop, and now enjoyed flipping my former workmates off as they passed by on their scheduled breaks.

On the opposite side was the hallway, which was the only way to cross from one department to the next, and it, too, was glass lined. You had to walk up your aisle to the hallway, then down the hallway before you could access the proper aisle of interest. The hallway was a major highway with constant coming and going, a constant merging and exiting expressway.

In spite of all of the traffic flow, I spotted them as soon as they turned the corner at Office Supply. With my drafting table right up against the far wall, I tracked them all the way. As they passed each successive aisle, heads came up from their labors and followed the entourage. Just their appearance probably puckered a few buttholes, but they were here for a different reason today and it showed. With each aisle passed it became evident where they were headed. It was confirmed as soon as the necktie that accompanied them from Human Resources looked right at me, nodded, and spoke to the cop in the middle. Just in case the cop was deaf, he also pointed right at me. There was an audible rustle as two hundred office chairs swiveled in unison.

When the three reached my particular aisle, they left the pencil neck in the hallway and turned in. The uniform on the left stopped at the hallway entrance; the one on the right walked right past me without a look but stopped and turned to face back up the aisle as soon as he'd gotten to the far end. The suit in the middle stopped right in my twelve o'clock.

"Are you Robert E. Casey?" Apparently, a friendly good morning was too personal.

I already knew where this conversation was heading. The

uniforms had me bracketed so the only possible escape would be to run across everyone's desktop. Their presence spoke volumes about the seriousness of the visit, but I had been racking my brain ever since I'd seen them. I knew they were coming for me, but why they were coming, I had nothing. I thought I was pretty clean—for a change. That being said, there was no way I was leaving without saving a little face with the audience. That's just the way I am. I can always find a way to make it a little worse.

Still sitting in my high drafting chair, I opted for the smart-ass approach. "I'm sorry; who wants to know?"

He drew a long-suffering sigh but pointed to the badge hanging in his breast pocket of his suit coat. The badge was the most distinctive thing about him and his outfit.

"Federal Investigator Janes, Federal Bureau of Investigation. Are you not Robert Casey?"

Well, that was different. SOG Walter Dunn must have gotten tired of me at last, and after all I'd done for him too. That kind of pissed me off. I leaned over and carefully examined the badge. I took my time. I kept my voice even. "It doesn't say that on your badge."

Another long-suffering sigh, but he reached into his pocket and flipped out the badge. It was in a leather case; the other side had an ID with his picture behind a little plastic window. Federal Investigator Janes didn't take very good pictures, but the long-suffering scowl matched up pretty well with the one in front of me. Underneath the picture, JANES, Phillip, M. and Federal Bureau of Investigation above it. It didn't say anything about the SOG though, and that was good, I thought.

I straightened up and looked at him. Janes was middle-aged,

in pretty good shape, and probably good at his job. He was also up on his toes a little. His hands weren't in his pockets. He was expecting me to run. I looked at the cops at each end of the aisle, and they weren't checking their fingernails or lounging against the wall either. They were alert; ready. This wasn't about overdue parking tickets. This was serious. I reassessed my attitude and adjusted it—down a notch.

"Nobody calls me Robert."

"May I see some identification please."

"I have a blood donor's card; will that be okay?"

"Not unless you're planning on leaving some on your desk in about twenty seconds."

"Goodness, Agent Janes, we're a bit testy this morning. No coffee? May I ask what this is about?"

"Identification please."

"It's in my desk drawer behind me," I hooked my thumb up over my shoulder, "next to the explosives."

I was amazed how fast the son of a bitch really was—even when I'd been expecting it. My drafting pencil almost put my eye out when my face hit the table. After that, the three of them spent a little time deciding who got to Mirandize me, who got to squeeze the handcuffs too tight, and which one got to frog-march me out of the building. From my vantage point with the right side of my face mashed into the blueprint I'd been working on, I used my one good left eye to look out through the glass into the shop, where every face had the same O where their mouth used to be. All except for one. When Andy Polanco saw that he'd caught my eye, he raised his right fist in defiance and then struck it hard over his heart.

Hoorah, brother—Semper Fi.

Another Interrogation, Another Disappointment
Emmett

It was nice to know that there are some constants in life where so many things had changed. The interrogation room was a carbon copy of other ones that I'd logged time in. The mirror in the wall had gotten bigger, but the No Smoking, No Spitting sign was still next to it. They'd added another sign that was probably not as effective as the No Smoking sign: "If you know something, tell someone," with a smiling cop face next to it. I was in luck there because I didn't know anything, so I couldn't tell someone, even the smiling little cop in the picture.

The walls were painted a flat cigarette smoke gray with scattered tears in the drywall fabric and black scuffmarks above the gray plastic floor trim. The gunmetal gray table was now big enough to allow two chairs on each side of it but still bolted to the floor. The chairs were still the basic standard-issue uncomfortable ones. The ring in the floor was still there and nicely accommodated the chain attached to my wrist cuffs.

The chain wasn't really heavy, but it carried a different kind of weight. If I sat with my knees apart and my elbows rested on them, it helped ease the weight on my wrists while

I waited. Anchored in one spot, I could only face in one direction; the only view forward was the mirror in front of me or the floor between my feet. The floor tile was the usual asphalt one-foot square in a speckled gray pattern that needed a good mopping. In order to rein in my angst, I counted the number of black spots in one square of tile, then mentally did the math on the number of spots possible on all the tiles in the room. I lost my place during the equations several times and had to start over again. I still had plenty of time to finish the calculation. I'd been waiting a long time. There was no sound from behind the mirror, but I knew it was because it had excellent sound-deadening acoustics. They were standing behind it. They were just being quiet about it.

The lengthy wait could mean they were having a hard time getting me a public defender, or it could mean they were executing the search warrant on my apartment. Sometimes, if there were witnesses, they stood behind the mirror and identified the perpetrator, but I hadn't done anything I could think of, so most likely it meant they were just fucking with me. The longer I sat, the more likely I would be more forthcoming when they finally decided to have a chat. For once I was looking forward to the chat. Up to this point everything had been absolutely professional, every 'I' had been dotted, every 'T' had been crossed, no room for error, but I still didn't know why I was here. The level of professional energy expended didn't look good to me. I wanted to know how deep the shit pile I was standing in was.

I had been processed in, and they'd taken my belt, my shoes, and my new butane lighter with the fake tortoiseshell embossing. I'd been given a thorough pat-down. So far, I hadn't been given my one phone call; that would come after the little chat. I'd been placed in this room that featured no door knob on the inside. They'd only lingered long enough to run the cuffs through the steel ring anchored in the floor. Then they'd left me here, to perform intermediate algebra on the floor tiles. As a change I practiced holding my breath while I tried to count to sixty to pass the time. I needed to quit smoking. I could only manage a forty-two count. After that I started on the gray spots in the tile.

For most I imagine the phone call is a relief and comfort. For me it's just another source of anxiety. I don't have friends—no close business associates, no trusted confederates. I didn't have anyone to call, unless it would be my father, and that just made the call even harder. Da had gotten that call before, he would understand, he didn't have any friends either, but I hated having to admit that I needed him—again. I rolled around any other possibilities in my head in between the math problems and decided that no phone call would be the best option.

One million fifty-five thousand seven hundred and twelve little gray spots on the linoleum, give or take. I might have misplaced the comma. The door finally opened and Inspector Janes entered, all business but in no apparent hurry to get to the point. His tie was straight, his jacket was buttoned. He took a seat across the table from me and set a manila folder on the table in front of him. He squared his shoulders and opened the folder. His posture was composed and the boredom he had previously expressed was no longer present. It made me wonder who was behind the mirror. I knew that the people still behind the mirror would be watching my face as he asked me questions. I wasn't unwilling to cooperate, I simply didn't know how to yet.

Careful so that I couldn't see the rest of its contents, he slid out three large color photographs. He took a good look at each one before reversing it and sliding it across the table toward me.

"Is this your vehicle?"

The photograph was of a Chevy C10 van, bright burnt orange, late model with mag wheels and opera windows cut into the otherwise windowless exterior. The poor thing had been treated badly. The photo showed the van resting at the bottom of a deep culvert. The front third was submerged in muddy water, the driver's side door was open, and the water and mud were level with the floor pedals. There was crime scene tape festooned around the outer border of the photo.

"It sure looks like mine but it's not."

"How do you know that it's not yours?"

I looked over his right shoulder directly at the mirror. "I don't own it anymore. I sold it about four weeks ago. Besides, this one's got Indiana plates on it."

"The license plates were stolen. The serial numbers of this van match the one registered with the Illinois Department of Motor Vehicles in your name."

"I sold my van to a guy for cash and a pickup."

"Did you get a bill of sale for the transaction?"

"No, it was cash and title. We just traded."

"How much cash?"

"He gave me twelve hundred and the truck."

"You recently registered a 1968 Chevrolet C-10 style side pickup with the state. Is that the vehicle you say you traded the

1973 Chevrolet van for?"

"Yes sir, that's correct."

He reached into the folder again and pulled out two envelope-size pieces of paper, looked at them both, and then slid them across toward me faceup. In my position, with my elbows on my knees, I scooted close enough to look directly down on them without using my hands. They were two paycheck stubs, both in my name, both from last month's payrolls.

"These were in the glove compartment of the van in the picture. Are you the Robert E. Casey referred to on them?"

"It looks like it. I have to keep them so I can show them to my probation officer during my interviews. I wouldn't have put them in the glove compartment though. Nobody does that, do they?"

This was starting to look like he was walking me down a blind alley. I was starting to sweat.

"Can you verify where you were last Saturday morning? At nine thirty? Or same day at eleven?"

"Um, I'm usually home, doing laundry or something if it's Saturday."

"Can anyone vouch for you during that time?"

"I live alone. I did see a girl in the laundry room, but I don't know who she is. I'd never seen her before." That was no lie. I didn't know anyone in the building.

"You only recently moved into your present apartment?"

"Um, yeah, only last month. How'd you know that?"

"The on-site manager was aggravated when he discovered your motorcycle parked on the living room carpet." You could just make out the twitch in the corner of his mouth. He was enjoying himself a little.

"You guys were in my apartment?" Well, shit and double shit. I was not particularly careful about putting my toys away when I was home. There were more than a few things to find there that would be separate problems all on their own.

"In all fairness, I'm trying to cooperate, and I'm not trying to be a pain, but what is this all about, please?"

"This van was the vehicle employed during two daylight armed bank robberies that took place last Saturday. It is registered to you. The person you say you sold the van to, if indeed you did, never re-registered it with the State of Illinois. The plates on the vehicle when it was discovered were stolen last year in Gary, Indiana. There were two paycheck receipts in the vehicle when it was discovered, both with your name and social security number on them, both quite recently issued. Your fingerprints are in our files already due to your history, and this vehicle has your fingerprints all over it. Two bank branches were robbed, and in both incidents the perpetrator brandished a handgun, threatening bodily harm. An as yet undisclosed amount of cash was taken. That is an enormous amount of circumstantial evidence and more than enough to put you at both of the crime scenes. You are a prime suspect in both crimes as a result. Any statements you make I would advise you to do so with care."

"Hold on! You seriously can't think I'd rob a bank? Two banks! Wait a minute...just a minute."

I was going to need my brain to do more than algebra now. This looked really bad, and for the first time in my life, it looked really bad and I'd had almost nothing to do with it. This was karma in its most incredibly unique expression. I tried to get my spinning head to synch back into balance. *What am I supposed to do?* I looked up at Janes, who was sitting passively, his wrists resting on the edge of the table; his jacket was now unbuttoned, he was relaxed. I stole a glance over his shoulder at the mirror.

"Should I ask you for a lawyer?" I posed my question to the mirror, but Janes answered.

"That would be an option—if charges are going to be pressed, and it's likely they will be, you'll be arraigned in federal court and there'll be a bail hearing. Lawyers do that usually."

I'd been in tight spots before, and this one qualified as one of the tighter ones. I had learned a few things from those other ones. One thing was always clear. Keep your wits about you, and you might walk away. Lose your cool and you were more likely to catch a bullet, sometimes figuratively and sometimes literally. If I stepped back a little and thought about it, I could usually see my way to an exit. I tried not to think about Janes or the mirror. I started fitting different pieces from different puzzles together. I looked down at my wrists, at the chain that ran down through the ring on the floor. Well, fuck this.

"I want to speak to Special Agent Walter Dunn."

Little Mick Casey

Back in the U.S., Christmas Eve, 1946

I mustered out in Milwaukee. Seamus and Charlie weren't out yet. There are more Army grunts than airmen, and it takes a while with that many. It took until the third train going to Madison before there was enough room and I could get on one and headed for home. I wanted to see Ma. It had taken a lot longer than I thought it would to get home. We spent three months getting ships and crews together and breaking down the airfield. Army engineers did most of the work; we just carried things where they told us to carry things.

Once they were ready, we flew the birds back to Morocco with a fuel stop in Sicily. The citizens were happy to see us; we were the first wave of homebound troops, and they made us feel welcome. Most of the women were darkies, but some of them were pretty good-looking. The planes were gone over again from one end to the other—every screw was tightened and every bolt given one more yank. The next jump was the Atlantic to Brazil. We didn't want to have to ditch in the drink because some bolt worked itself loose.

I was back with Brinker, Jansen, Reynolds, and Bonner. Lieutenant Holmquist had gone home earlier. We had other guys filling the other vacancies. Nobody said it but we didn't want to have come all this way just to ditch and drown on the way home. I was pretty jumpy. I didn't think I'd get over it until I was back in the good old USA either. Captain Brinker told me to find a gymnasium somewhere and work it off. I stay as far away from those places as I can get nowadays.

We spent almost three weeks in Africa. There wasn't enough fuel on hand to fill up the entire 301st Bombardment Group. We went to the beach, and I tasted the salty water. At night we slept under the planes. When the call came up, we went with the first squadron. Each squadron was given a long head start before the next one jumped. Just in case the weather turned foul. We didn't have any idea what the weather over the horizon would be like. We needed to go in as straight a line as we could because there wouldn't be any extra fuel to fly around bad weather. Good or bad we were going to fly straight through it. They broke up the squadrons so they didn't lose all of us in one freak storm.

Brazil was just hot. We were told to stay out of town. There had been some fights and the citizens were getting tired of getting their asses handed to them. Bonner bought a monkey. It bit him, so from then on, the monkey slept with me. Ugly little guy but he was really smart. I taught him how to grin at Bonner when we were eating. It drove Bonner crazy, so he killed the monkey. After that Bonner ate using a straw for a week. I dressed the little guy in a shirt and pinned my Air Medal on it, then I dropped him out the rear hatch when we got back out over the water. I'd never given him a name.

Emmett

Interrogation Room, Elmhurst, Illinois

When I'd mentioned Dunn's name, Agent Janes hadn't even blinked. He just picked up his manila folder and put the photographs and check stubs into it, then stood up, straightened his tie and buttoned the second button on his suit jacket, turned to the mirror and shrugged, and the door opened and he went out. I started counting holes in the acoustical tile on the ceiling. There were quite a few, but I had plenty of time to get them counted, twice. The second count was 236 more than the first time, so I started over. Then the door opened again.

Walter Dunn came in alone, dressed in a Ban-Lon golf shirt with a little alligator on the front of it and neatly pressed khaki pants. I didn't want to look him in the eye when he sat down across from me, so I looked at his slip-on loafers with little leather tassels on them. I kind of liked them. I'd never have pegged him as a stylish kind of guy, but it looked like he was Joe Suburban lifestyle. Then I looked him in the face, and immediately his wardrobe was out the window. His eyebrows were drawn down and his eyes were boring right into my brain from close range.

"We've got ourselves a little bit of a dilemma."

I'd been expecting a different tone. From this opening

statement Dunn sounded more deferential. It knocked me off balance.

"This has all the usual earmarks of Emmett Casey stepping on his dick once again, but there's something else afoot here. It's a frame for sure, but it's a good one."

"What are you talking about?"

"First of all, dumbass, what the hell is with that apartment of yours. At least half an ounce of hashish in your sock drawer, way more than an ounce of weed in the freezer, and another ounce or so in your pillowcase already rolled into joints; six buttons of peyote in a baggie behind the toilet tank, forty-seven hits of downers, Quaaludes no less. Jesus, don't you even try to be careful?"

"I have trouble sleeping."

"What a surprise. Honest to God, Casey, I wasn't even surprised by the fucking Harley in the living room after the bathroom and bedroom turned up all that shit, but then I looked behind the refrigerator."

Shit and double-shit.

"I guess I'm not as surprised as I am impressed. Moonlighting pays better than it used to, thirteen thousand three hundred and eighty dollars in multiple denominations. Then the closet turned up an illegal sawed-off twelve-gauge shotgun and another eight grand in a shoebox, also in multiple denominations."

"What? I don't own a sawed-off! And I don't know anything about any money in a shoebox."

"That's it?You take exception to those two things but nothing else? Jesus, Casey, you could at least try and act a little more innocent than you look."

"If you guys found all that shit in the apartment, it's not going to really matter if I robbed a bank or not, is it?"

"I found all that shit—not them. Do you honest to God think I dress like this on purpose." He gave me the patented Dunn stare-down. "I got the morning brief across my desk this morning about the time they were picking you up at Flick's. By the way, it was kind of silly for you to resist arrest in that situation."

I just did a fish face at that statement.

"I left the office immediately. I'd swept your apartment a full hour before they got the approval for a search warrant. By the way, it wouldn't hurt to wash a few dishes once in a while either."

"So, you got my stuff out before they got there? Thanks, man! But why, why'd you do that?"

"The fucking motorcycle wasn't going anywhere, and it being there just speaks to your general level of stupidity, so I left it there. The other stuff I took out. Except for the Ruger in your underwear drawer and the eight grand. Oh, and I walked the dog. Nice dog."

"What? What the fuck, Dunn? You mean you took some of the shit, but left the other shit?"

"Yep."

"Geezus, Dunn, why? Why'd you bother at all? That's the stuff that's not mine. Swear to God, Dunn, it's not mine. Now I'm screwed on a whole new different level."

"Slow down, take a deep breath, lean back, and look at me."

I looked at him first. He held his hand up palm out as a stop sign.

"Let's just take this apart. You're one of the smartest dumbasses I've ever met, deep breaths and think a minute."

Now I was confused—and stressed. I looked hard at Dunn. He dropped his head just a fraction and drew his eyebrows even lower, making eye contact. Think, I needed to think. I looked at the mirror, looked up at the 57,680 holes in the acoustical tile, and then I said, "I'm being set up."

A little nod from Dunn. "And?"

"Those check stubs were from my file at the PO's office?"

"And?"

"That prick Anthony has access to my file. He's fucking me over!"

"I wouldn't bet on that one."

"He's gonna fuck me himself?"

"He's got an end game in mind, I'm sure of that. When was the last contact?"

"I've had a couple of tickles, but I didn't follow up. I don't want any of that shit anymore. I do my own stupid, not somebody else's. Anthony—he's the closest thing to the devil I've ever met. He's mainlinin' pure evil. I'm a lot of things, Dunn, but I got a meter in me somewhere and it tells me to avoid him. Big time!"

"He's got something that he needs you for, I'm guessing, but this seems a little over the top to me, even for him. Think, Casey, when was that last 'tickle'?"

"It was a few weeks ago. There's a brother on the street that he contacts me through. Name's Dwight Thomas, he's hooked in. Something out of state, but that's a hassle for me, leavin' the state. I'm not sure what the PO would have to say about me going out of state, so I respectfully declined."

"No details?"

"Didn't ask."

"That's why I left the stuff in your apartment. I knew what was probably yours and I pretty much knew what probably wasn't. We need to see how he plays his hand, so you're on the hook for the cash that you can't explain." After a slight pause, "And being a dumbass."

"How'd you know what was mine and what wasn't?"

Another long look down his nose.

"Son of a bitch! You've been in my apartment before, you fucking fucker."

He just lidded his eyes and waited.

"So, you mean to say, I'm going down on a bank robbery, armed bank robbery no less, and weapons, and you're gonna let me—just for shits and giggles?"

"Watch your six and keep your eyes and ears open." He leaned forward ever so slightly. "I'm curious about the idea behind all of this, and I don't get why you're so valuable all of a sudden, or maybe so suddenly expendable. You're in for a bumpy ride for a little bit. But you've been there before, I gather. I've got every confidence you'll handle it. I'll be watching."

"So…you don't really give a shit except if it helps you get the guy you're after. As far as I go, tough shit?"

"Pretty much. Let's face it, the evidence is pretty substantial. I can't just make that disappear. Janes is good at his job, and this is a fresh scent, so let him figure it out on his own. He'll get there."

I sincerely hoped Janes was fucking amazing at his job.

"In the meantime, I'll have a chat with him…see if I can

get you some chow, maybe your smokes. You're gonna have a bail hearing, my guess around twenty-five thousand. Can you come up with ten percent of that?"

"You took all the money I had, so yes, if you're gonna post it."

"Nope, not a chance. If someone is interested I need to be far away from any dealings with you."

"So I'm out the money—and fucked in the ass."

"Life catches up with everybody, Casey, but that might come later, the ass fucking, that is. But no, I don't want your money or the other shit either. Is there someone you can trust with it? A friend, a relative maybe?"

"I don't have any friends."

"What about those two girls you've been friendly with? They look a little above your pay grade."

"Geezus, Dunn, don't you have a life? What kind of guy are you? Do you honestly follow me around constantly?"

"I don't have to. I've got people for that."

E. Michael Casey

Madison, Wisconsin, 1947

Everybody's glad to see me. When I go out to the clubs, I get asked to dance a lot by the girls. Dancing's something I'd never thought I'd do, but I try it, mostly for the girls. These girls are something different from what I remember from before. They're not afraid of asking for what they want. It seems mostly what they want is in my pants. I'm not complaining. I guess the war changed them too.

I was one of the first guys back to town, so I got a job right away at the Oscar Mayer plant out by Truax Field. It's the very same plant where my Pappy was killed a long lifetime ago. I'm working on the kill floor, swinging the stun hammer. It'll pay for what I need for now. On my breaks I walk over to the spot where I think my Pappy died. I try to feel if he's still there. I don't know if it's my imagination or possible, but I feel something there.

I take what they're offering, the girls that is. I keep wondering if this is what love is supposed to feel like. I ask myself the same thing when I'm with Mary Evelyn and Ma. I even asked Thomas while we had a beer up at Willy's, and he just looked me in the eye with that long look you get sometimes. I like spending time at Willy's and it's always better when Thomas is there, but I wouldn't mind it if I was alone. I feel like I'm pretty much alone most of the time anyway. Lizzy is pregnant.

Interrogation, R. Emmett Casey

"Don't make a mess with those." Janes dropped my cigarettes, an ashtray, and a book of paper matches on the table. From his other hand he handed me an ice-cold egg salad sandwich that probably came out of an automated deli machine, and a can of Royal Crown Cola. Egg salad was always the last one to go out of those vending machines. Ditto for the RC.

"This figures, didn't you guys ever hear of Coca-Cola?" Nevertheless I cracked open both the sandwich and soda and dove right in. The handcuffs made it a little difficult.

"Geezus, Casey, give it a rest."

"Sorry, my ass is killing me, and I'm hungry."

Janes twiddled the matchbook while I finished the sandwich and half the RC.

"So, when do I have to appear?"

"You don't."

"I don't what?"

"You don't have to go before the magistrate; we're not charging you."

I looked at him like he'd just told me he was really a girl.

"No fucking shit!?! What, are you kidding? After all of this you can't be just letting me out of here. What gives?"

"All you need to know is that you aren't being charged—at this time. I'll bring you your property bag in a few minutes." He kept twiddling the matches, looking down at them like they were the most interesting thing he'd ever seen. Finally, he looked up and gave me a half smile and a deep sigh before his eyes wandered off to the corner of the ceiling. "It's your lucky day."

E. Mick Casey

A Wedding, 1947

The wedding was nice. The women decorated the pews along the aisle with daffodils from the backyards in our neighborhood. Father Dempsey was in a jolly mood and passed a flask around the sacristy while Charlie and I waited with the two altar boys. One of the boys almost choked when he took a snort, and we all had a good laugh. I stood in the doorway and looked up at the ceiling, thinking about the steeple up there. Thomas Quinn had come to Madison to rebuild it when the steeple burned after a lightning strike. If that lightning had picked something else to hit, I wondered about who I'd be marrying instead of Lizzy.

When it was time I took my place with Charlie out in front of the altar. I bought a new suit with my Oscar Mayer paycheck, but Charlie only had his dress Army uniform. I thought he looked pretty good, lots of lettuce on his chest. It didn't sound like he wanted to talk about it though, and I was plenty okay with that.

In the back, Mary Evelyn looked really nice in a gray three-piece suit; she was the maid of honor. Thomas looked ready to bust, hopping from one foot to the other. I'd never seen him in a tie, and his collar was a couple sizes too big around his thin neck. The suit he wore made you notice how big his ears were.

When Ma saw me standing in the doorway, she flashed me a V for victory sign and smiled. She was wearing the lavender suit that she wore for Andy and Martha's wedding, with a big orchid corsage. She'd refused to sit in the wheelchair coming up the aisle. Instead she stood behind it, gripping the handles, and shuffled her way up the aisle to her seat of honor. She's still tough as nails.

When Lizzy appeared, I almost choked up. She had on the most beautiful dress I'd ever seen. Her belly wasn't showing yet. She looked good. Somebody stayed up all night working on that dress.

I guess I didn't really know what to expect when I got back home. There was no real plan, no briefing by some flight officer. I was just going through the motions, get a job, buy some clothes, maybe get a car then find someone to settle down with and have some kids. I guess that's how it goes, I watched the whole wedding from somewhere else, maybe the choir loft, a vantage point somewhere removed from me. It didn't seem real as I listened to myself recite the vows, till death do ye part? I guess that's how it goes.

R. Emmett Casey

Back on the Street

They gave me back my shoelaces and belt, wallet, and thirty-seven cents. I put the belt on and re-laced my shoes after they unlocked the handcuffs. I got my new butane lighter with the fake tortoiseshell laminate back and pocketed my cigarettes.

"Where's my keys?"

"Your truck is impounded for now. Here's the rest of your keys."

"How long will the truck be in the impound? Geez, I thought you guys were done fucking with me."

"The truck is important in sewing up the robberies, and we know you can't be leaving town, so when it's processed, we'll probably still keep it until after the trial and conviction, maybe longer. Nobody said that we're done fucking with you either."

"So basically, I won't be seeing it again for a while?"

"Basically."

"I'll need to use a phone."

"It's almost midnight. Who you gonna call at this time of night?"

"None of your business."

Normally my go-to for a phone call like this would be

Kate, but he was right—it was late and Kate had her own life now. She'd married a good guy, had a kid, and lived out west in one of the more up-and-coming 'burbs. I couldn't call her with a clear conscience. She would pick me up and start a conversation about weather or garbage pickup times, like we were going to lunch. It would never occur to her to ask what this was all about.

I could call my father, but it was a weird concession to make. Unlike Kate, Da would arrive and have a prescient awareness of everything that was going on. He wouldn't need to ask questions about it because he already would somehow know. He would reach across and pull up the door lock on the passenger side, then drop his hands in his lap until I was in the car gazing out through the windshield. With a glance in my direction he'd then drive on without a hello, howdy, or what the hell is this all about. The ride to anywhere would be in silence while my shame hung in the air like a cloud of cigarette smoke. When we arrived at wherever we were going, he would again drop his hands in his lap and again gaze out the windshield until I was deposited on the curb.

Being late to my father didn't matter. As long as I'd known him, he hardly ever seemed to sleep. Instead, he sat in the dark, smoking and drinking his shots and beers as the night passed. Off to work the next morning before I would rise. It was his unspoken acceptance of the situation without apparent judgment that rankled with me. Catholic upbringing had taught me guilt and shame, so I couldn't handle his acceptance.

I called Angie.

"Oh God, I was so scared! They were so mean to you; how could they be like that? Are you all right?" She covered the phone but I still heard her say, "It's Emmett." To me she said, "My dad knows a lawyer. I could call my dad if you want."

"No, Angie, I'm okay. Please don't call your dad. Geez, that's all I need right now." I'd met her father.

"Okay, sorry, Emmett, but what are you going to do?"

"Angie baby, I'm out. They're letting me go; it was just a case of mistaken identity. No big deal. But they're keeping my truck, so I could use a ride, if you don't mind?"

"A ride? Sure, but Todd's still got my car, so I'll have to get Dutchie up. Is that okay?"

"Sure, sure, but tell her I'm sorry, okay?"

Again, she covered the phone and whispered, "He says he's sorry."

I told her where I was and figured by the time she woke up Dutch and drove over here, it would be the better part of an hour and a half. I had been sitting on my ass for more than twelve hours, and it and the rest of me could use some air. Looking out the windows, I thought it seemed like a pretty nice night, so I decided to get the cop smell off of me and wait outside. Once outside I took a deep breath of the cool, damp night air and shivered off the bad vibes I'd picked up inside. It's never quiet in the city, but there is a peace that settles in the middle of the night where even the cars and planes try to tone down the noise so people can sleep.

The brightly lit parking lot was almost empty, making me feel conspicuous; exposed. Toward the far end of the lot, trees lined the property line and shaded the light poles with their branches. I walked down the building to where the service driveway went around behind it, and it was a little darker. I lit a cigarette and leaned against the sign telling everyone it was a service driveway.

On my second drag, a car in the lot started up and the lights came on. Switching into gear the car started forward, but instead of turning toward the exit, it turned my direction and eased up toward me. It was a big car, white or cream-colored, what they might call a saloon in England. When it got close it pulled up into the mouth of the service driveway next to me, and the passenger window buzzed down. Willy, Anthony's left nut, bent down over the steering wheel and said, "Get in the back."

"No thanks, Willy, I've got a ride coming."

He popped his door and stepped out far enough to show the 1911 in his belt.

"Well, okay then." I pulled up the door latch, opened the door, and took a look in before I entered. Sitting behind the driver was the ugliest woman I had ever set eyes on. She was smoking a small cigarillo, looking out the opposite window. She was long and lean, dressed in a long, shiny dress that looked expensive and with a slit on the side to show about half her thigh. What could have passed for circuitous designs on her hose were in fact bright blue varicose veins that ran up and down her calves and the parts of her thigh that I could see. I hesitated another second, but she turned to me and crooked a finger in my direction. Climbing in to the seat I left the door open just in case. Lately I'd been in a lot of backseats that didn't have a door handle on the inside, and I thought I might need a quick exit.

"Close the door please, it makes the inside light stay on if it's open." Her voice sounded like she ate gravel for breakfast. I shut the door. "You've had a bit of a hectic day, Mr. Casey."

She was even uglier in the dark. Her black African face was all angles and planes that the shadows sharpened and hid her deep-set eyes. She had an enormous nose and mouth; the nose looked like it had been broken. Maybe more than once. Her earlobes had suffered jewelry that was far too heavy for far too long, and they hung low, sagging under the weight almost to her neck. The dangling earrings that sparkled in the light and matched the incredible amount of jewelry she wore on both hands, wrists, and around her neck helped to distract from the otherwise unattractive face. Just above the broach she wore at her throat, a gigantic Adam's apple bobbed when she inhaled her cigarillo. Her hands were big, with long fingers and knobby knuckles that featured long, painted nails filed to a sharp point.

"I've had worse ones."

"I know." Another drag on the small cigar, another long exhale out over the driver's seat. "Tell me what they know. Or what they think they know."

"I don't have a clue what they think or know."

"They didn't say anything to you about who they are really looking at?"

"Not to me. Should they have?"

"No, they wouldn't have, I suppose. So, you are free to go…how odd. Don't you think?"

"There is nothing about this day that hasn't been—odd."

"Well, you can be assured that you won't have anything to worry about, at least on this score anyway. They know who they want, and they know it's not you."

"Why is that?" I looked out the windshield at Willy leaning on the hood of the big sedan with his hand resting on the big hood ornament, his back to us, taking in the night air.

"This one is put to rest, but you have to admit it didn't look good there for a while." Another drag on the cigar. "Wouldn't you say?"

"I would say."

"Pretty easy to put someone in a box when or if you need to, isn't it?"

"I guess…so is this some kind of hazing ritual that you people do?"

"I should be insulted—but I'm not of course." She gave me a small smile and put her cigar out in the already full ashtray and immediately fished out another one from a leatherette case. "You've blown through a few of my stop signs. I don't especially care for free thinkers. Free thinkers try to do things their way, change plans, ad lib the game plan, and they gum up the works. I sent you a message; you didn't respond. Suddenly your luck took a turn for the worse. That's what happens to free thinkers. I can make their luck change."

"So, you work for Anthony then." I wasn't asking.

"Good lord! Alexander Anthony is a psychopath, or a sociopath—or both. Heavens no. Anthony works for me. I just don't like to be near him, so Willy there," pointing the unlit end of the cigarillo out the windshield, "takes care of the in-between."

"So, you sent me a message, two messages." I much preferred the first one.

"I have a need of your delivery services, nothing quite as glamorous as the last job, but it requires discretion and timing. You don't like to sleep very much according to what I've been told, and the distance between the two contacts is great, and the timing is on a razor's edge. Thanks to your bullheadedness, you forced me to put you in a bind, so now you need the work, and the money."

"How much money?"

"Not as much as it would have been if you'd taken the job outright, but generous."

"How much is generous?" The amount would betray the risk value.

"Twenty Gs."

"Geezus! What's the package, a dead body?"

"You mean like the one on the beach in Florida?" She gave me a squint-eyed look. "Powder burns all over his face and a through-and-through from a thirty-eight. Odd choice of weapon for an execution killing—wouldn't you say?"

"I told William that the guy was dead when I first saw him. Didn't he tell you that?"

"He did tell me that. He also told me that he thinks you poisoned him."

"How could I do that? We were never out of each other's sight!" William was someone I didn't want to get crossways with. He seemed formidable. "Sounds like he's just trying to make his part of the job sound more interesting."

"I wouldn't turn my back on William anytime soon, Casey. I'll be sending you word once everything is in place, it will take some time but be ready to move when you get it. Once everything is arranged, you'll have to go at a moment's notice. I don't think you'll need to take the time off of work now though—will you?"

Nope, the possibility of me ever setting foot on Flick's property again was slim to none.

"Don't fuck me over, or the next time you might not walk, literally or figuratively."

Headlights flashed across the parking lot and a small compact car pulled into the lot and up to the front door. Dutch in the driver's seat, Angie in the back but leaning forward between the two front seats. They both leaned forward and peered at the front doors of the building.

"That's your ride?" She lit the cigarillo and purred the words without making eye contact.

"Yep." I reached for the door handle, but she put her hand on my leg.

"It's good to have friends that you can count on when things go wrong. Keep that in mind, Casey."

There was no way I could get out of the car without the girls seeing me do it, and no way I could do it fast enough to suit me, so I just got on with it. As soon as the door cracked open, their eyes swiveled to me and widened. I tried not to hurry, but the daughter from hell behind me had scared me shitless enough that I wanted as much distance as I could muster. As I approached, Dutch unwound herself from behind the steering wheel and walked to the other side of the car.

"You drive. I can't wait to hear this one."

It's a Girl
E. Mick Casey

She was born this morning, the same day that used to be my Pappy's birthday. Mary Katherine. Old Doc Braun came out to the waiting room to tell me. He said she's healthy and that Lizzy did fine. I wasn't sure how I was supposed to react; mostly it just didn't seem real, another person, a little person, my responsibility, someone that I had actually made.

I went to the nursery, where a smiling nurse in a white uniform and starched hat held up a bundle of pink blankets with a tiny face in the middle of it. All of the other babies were screaming their heads off, but this one wasn't crying at all. I looked at her face; her eyes were wide open and she just looked out through the glass at me with big dark eyes. Eyes that were just like mine. Her gaze never left me, like she knew me, right off, like she knew the score. She looked wise and smart. It made my throat tighten up and I had to look away. I guess that's the way it goes.

I'm going to need a better job.

Starting Over
Emmett

When the two girls heard that my apartment had been searched by the FBI, they couldn't wait to see what it looked like. I was less enthusiastic. When we got to the apartment complex, they piled out of the car even before I even had turned off the ignition. After I let them in through the front security door, they hurried ahead of me past the mailboxes and around the corner to my apartment, where there was a loud "Uh-oh" cried in unison. When I got to the apartment, the door didn't look any different than it usually did except for the eviction notice taped to it. The notice was a standard boilerplate legalese notice with information regarding the landlord's right to evict if said tenant violated certain aspects defined by the lease agreement. There wasn't any sense in reading it carefully; it was probably a sound and defensible document. What was worthy of note was at the bottom, below the signature of the manager, an additional addendum, this one written in red felt-tipped pen: "By Friday!!!!"

Inside the apartment was a different story from the outside of the door. There apparently had been a tornado. What little furniture I owned had been pulled out into the middle of the rooms, and the dresser drawers in the bedroom were stacked on the bed, empty with their previous contents dumped next to them. The bed clothes were piled in a heap on the floor. I couldn't remember if I'd made the bed the previous morning or not. The dresser faced sideways and was on its side. All of the hanging closet clothes were on the bed too, along with boots and sneakers. The closet was completely empty. Throughout all the rooms the strong scent of dog shit added to the overall ambience of the situation. The pup was glad to see us, but ashamed that he'd ruined his good record.

In the kitchen, all of the cabinets were empty, their previous contents spread across all of the available counter space, and the stove and refrigerator were not quite all the way back against the wall. The living room carpet had been lifted up around the edges and not put back entirely down, and the hanging sconce lamp was taken down and lying on the floor disassembled. The Harley had been moved out of the living room altogether and stood outside the sliding glass door on the tiny patio. It was easy to see because the blackout drapes were lying in a heap in the corner. All in all, a definite no-stone-unturned search, and a mess to clean up.

"Oh my God!" was Angie's response.

"Wow" was Dutch's. She put her hand on my shoulder and added, "Geez, Emmett, I'm so sorry."

"Fuck me to hell and back," was mine.

"Well, grab some of your stuff—you sure can't stay here tonight. You'll have to come to our place."

"Are you sure?"

"Oh Emmett, you stay over some nights already. Just get your shit together and let's go. It's way too late to try to be intelligent tonight." Dutch was just being practical. "Tomorrow you'll need to find a new place to live and get packed up, but for now let's just try to get some sleep. Your tomorrow is gonna be busy."

Time to Go

My telephone number was tied to my apartment, and without the apartment I didn't know how I could be contacted in the next few days by the ugly woman with no name, or one of her people. With only the motorcycle to get around on, I cruised some of the local spots, stopping just long enough to be seen, and then moving on. Mostly I was looking for Dwight Thomas, but I wanted to quash any rumors that I might be in jail too. Word on the street is faster than any telephone more often than not.

Cleaning out the apartment had proved to be every bit of the hassle it had promised to be. Without the truck I had to borrow Dutch's car to move my things. She had left for a week's worth of flights to Europe and the Middle East and wouldn't return until the weekend. She said she didn't mind if I used the car while she was out of town, but I hated having to ask. Borrowing anything was taboo in my family. My father would rather have taken a whipping than owe someone his gratitude, and I had learned at the knee of the master.

Dutch's car was a model that had captured my imagination while I was in Europe, and she knew I loved to get behind the wheel of it. It was a little beauty, and fun to drive. A 1971 powder-blue Mercury Capri manufactured by Ford but in Europe. They had been a popular car with the young GIs who were eager to spend their re-enlistment bonuses while in Germany. I loved the lines of the body style, and even though it was a little underpowered, it was quick off the line.

The downside of the car was that it had almost no trunk space and the backseat was tiny. Even though I had downsized just a month before, I still had plenty of crap to move and some of it was too big to move with the Capri. I also didn't have anywhere to move it to. I didn't have another apartment in mind, and no money to put down for a deposit. I knew I couldn't stay at Angie's forever, but for now I was going to have to store the furniture at least.

By Wednesday I knew I was going to have to call my father. Calling him without an explanation of the circumstances was out of the question. Little Mick had a "bullshit detector" that never failed him, so trying to invent a plausible story that painted me in a better light was unlikely. Outright evasion sometimes worked, but only if he really wasn't interested in the story to begin with. Most of the time, it was better to tell the truth and then watch his lips tighten into a thin line, followed by a long, discretionary silence. Unquestionably, he would assist—diligently—to work me through whatever was needed but always in silence. Which made asking him for help that much more difficult, because he always knew the real score.

1966, A Little Run-in with the Cops Little Mick and Emmett

Working at JCPenney's in the evenings and on weekends provided me with more spending money than I needed to get into trouble, but it was also placid. The work was strenuous and filled the hours but wasn't very mentally stimulating. Most of the men I worked with were working-class stiffs who moonlighted after their regular jobs. They had stepped into family life, marrying, fathering children, and given up their youth in pursuit of the American dream. A split-level house in the suburbs with a postage stamp-sized yard and a barbecue grill outside the back door. They didn't want mental stimulation, but they wouldn't turn down prurient entertainment, so we worked out an agreement.

In exchange for details of events, I was availed any amount of liquor that I could distribute. This assured me invitations to most of the high school post-pubescent parties that were held at homes where parents were absent, or tolerant. It guaranteed the invitation and accompanying admiration but not necessarily the approval of my peer group, which I was perfectly happy with. The income supplied by this side job more than covered the cost of supplies and bolstered my popularity with my coworkers.

The little Opel Rekord station wagon that I drove had a storage compartment under the rear seat. When you flipped up the seat, you could fit an entire case of beer on each side of the drive shaft hump in the center and the seat would still fold back down. There was still plenty of room for the occasional half pint or two wedged between the cases. Even though the car had no functional door locks, I never worried about theft or police search because unless you were familiar with the car, you would never suspect that the compartment was there, or at least I was pretty sure of that.

One evening, long after curfew, I was aimlessly driving the streets of town because I had nothing better to do. It was a beautiful summer night, the temperature was perfect, the humidity tolerable. I cruised houses where people I thought would be worth getting to know, girls mostly, lived and the darkened Root Beer Drive-In lost in thought.

While I cruised, I smoked cigarettes that I bought myself even though I was underage and nursed a can of beer nestled between my legs on the seat. I did this often enough that I gave no thought to the negative possibilities associated with it. That is until the police cruiser and I arrived at the four-way stop sign simultaneously.

The squad car was going in the opposite direction I was. It was no reason to panic; what I was doing was illegal but not visible. Just the same I decided to turn right and create a little distance. As I started to accelerate into the turn, the speaker on the top of the squad blared out,

"Out a little late, aren't you, Mr. Casey?"

Shit! My car was unique in appearance, the only one I'd ever seen on the streets. In addition to multiple cancerous rust holes over the fender wells, its faded blue paint had multiple splotches of dried raw egg that had fried themselves to the enamel over time. The fried eggs were a story for another time, but definitely enhanced the overall unique viewing experience. If you knew me from Penney's or high school, you knew the car, and if you saw the car, you knew I'd be the only person willing to drive it. The cop had to be someone from work, and he would know that I was out after curfew. I hung a right turn and accelerated the little piece of shit away from the intersection and up the only hill in town, trying to appear as law-abiding as possible. In the rearview mirror the police car was still sitting at the stop sign as I crested the small rise a block away. As soon as the squad disappeared behind the hill, I dropped my smoke in the beer can and threw them both out the passenger window as hard as I could.

I still had the backseat lifted up out of position so I could reach for another beer when I wanted one. Driving with one hand I turned in the seat and flipped the seat down, giving it a good shove to push it firmly in place. In response to the good shove, my left hand jerked to the right on the steering wheel and the car swerved to the right and jumped the curb just in time to take out the STOP sign on the corner of the next intersection. With the violence of the curb jump and the crash of the signpost, I jerked back eyes front and almost went cross-eyed as a No Parking sign also disappeared under the left front of the little Opel, also with a thunderous bang. The little son of a bitch was a runaway at this point, and she left her muffler on the No Parking sign post as a calling card.

I blasted along for another hundred feet in order to avoid the trees planted along the parkway up and now straddling the sidewalk. I took aim at the driveway that exited back out on the street up ahead without reducing my speed. As I hit the driveway and roared the now un-muffled car back out into the street, I glanced right and into the open doors of the local fire station. Several firemen stood frozen in various poses of surprise, staring at the spectacle blasting by and up the street into the night, making enough noise to wake the dead.

Feeling like the fugitive from justice that I had actually just become, I zigzagged through town, attempting an elusive route designed to get me home and seemingly innocent. I had no idea what I would do once I got there, but rationalizing action and outcome wasn't part of my current playbook. It took less than five minutes for me to learn that you can't outrun a police radio.

Small towns are the same the world over. Car chases where gunfire is exchanged and tires squeal around corners, while exciting, just don't happen very often on the late weeknight streets of small towns. There is nothing to keep the silent streetlights company except the soft summer breezes. Porch lights go off at ten o'clock, and upstairs lights go out moments later. Even so, when I rounded the corner off of Princeton onto Charles Road, the roadblock in the middle of our main street with two of our three police cars cross-ways in the street and officers shielded behind open doors might have been a bit of an over-the-top response. As soon as I saw them, any intention of continuing the chase was quashed when the third and final squad raced up behind me with lights and sirens blaring. Within seconds of stopping the car, my face was mashed into one of the dried-out starburst fried eggs splattered across the hood of the Opel and I was being handcuffed by my old friend

Larry "the Asshole" Johnson.

"Geezus, Emmett, this may be the dumbest thing you've done yet, and knowing you that's sayin' something. We've been listening to you coming for over five minutes. You have the right to remain silent. Anything you say can and may be held…"

I'd been in the cell before. The last time had something to do with a six-foot tall dick sculpture made out of snow and right in front of the high school. That time most of the cops thought it was as funny as I did. Larry Johnson hadn't. This time they took my shoelaces when they took my belt. I let them call my Da this time.

My father had refined his going to the police station outfit when he was called to retrieve one of his children. Over time, the list had grown from just me to a few of my brothers, and even a sister. The outfit he appeared in never varied by all accounts, and I had corroborated this with my siblings. The outfit had its own personality. Baggy blue jeans cinched tight around his tiny waist so that it bloused his tucked-in pajama shirt. The shirt unbuttoned at the neck to reveal stray chest hair under the same canvas duck hunting jacket winter or summer. This always capped with his matching canvas duck brown hunting cap, turned up on the sides and back and pulled down over his forehead in front. From the time that the call went out, the time it took him to arrive was exactly whatever the drive time was. It was as if he was poised in the driveway just waiting, and there was never a delay. The effect of his arrival also had never seemingly changed. So far at least.

From down the hall in my cell, I could hear the front door open and slam shut. There were murmured words of greeting, then a short conversation, then a few hard words spoken in my Da's voice. Then more quiet conversation, and finally, in this case, the angry, loud voice of Larry the Asshole. Eventually I was released into my Da's custody. Throughout the exchange my father betrayed no emotion, and simply facilitated. His hands wouldn't have left his pockets, his briar pipe would have been perched in his shirt pocket, and his voice would never have fluctuated more than a few decibels. Outside the station, he handed me my car keys and with his eyes fixed out into the parking lot deadpanned, "You okay, R.E.?

"Feel a little stupid, but yeah." By now, I had come to understand that the episode between him and me ended when the police station door closed behind us. I could wait until the sound of the trumpets, but he would never mention it again. My mother was a different matter, however.

"Follow me home then, and then get that liquor out from under your backseat. Next time they might look for it—idiot."

Somehow, Little Mick was always quietly a step ahead of everyone else. How he did it and seemed to be completely uninterested at the same time was profound. We were Caseys, and Caseys took care of each other. How that played in the outside world was no one's business but ours. My Da saw to the Casey business and that was that.

The two signposts ended up costing me fifty bucks apiece. I didn't even get a traffic ticket, evidence of the magic that surrounded my father. The front end of the Opel now featured two deep V-shaped dents in its solid steel bumper under the left headlight. They were still there when one of my brothers sold it years later after it had been passed down a few more times.

New Digs, Old Emmett

Emptying my apartment had taken Da and me less than three hours, two trips with his station wagon. All of it fit easily into the far corner of his garage, which he covered with an old green canvas tarp that he still had from his Army days. The smell of the old canvas was so strong that I was pretty sure I'd never have to worry about mice getting into anything. After that we stood in the driveway looking down the street together, both of us with our hands jammed into our pants pockets. He with his pipe clamped in his teeth and me wishing I had a cigarette. The dog finished with his running around came over and lay down, putting his head on Da's foot. He bent down and scratched his ears. I was glad that they seemed to like each other. Just another thing to feel bad about since I was going to have to leave the dog with him too. That they liked each other made it a little easier.

The silence spread out in front of us. Finally, he pulled out his pipe, lifted his foot, and tapped it out on the heel of his boot.

"So? You aren't staying here?"

"No, Da, over in Addison with a couple of friends for now."

"Good friends or something else? Only askin' because, you know—your mother; she worries."

"They've been good friends for me, Da. I'm dating one of them."

"You've got a girlfriend? Since when?" He caught himself expressing interest and covered it by pulling out his pipe again and starting to repack it. "Cuz your mother will want to know."

"A little while now. I'll bring her around one of these days if that'd be okay?"

"Suit yourself. Make sure you tell your mother though. You know how she can be if you spring somethin' on her. Doesn't end well."

Angie had moved into Dutch's room with her. Dutch had a queen-sized bed. Angie's was a twin and the room was small. Just the right size for me. A week had turned into two, then four, then six. After the first four weeks Dutch asked me for rent and we settled into a roommate routine and I stopped looking for another apartment, for now.

Angie still slept with me but not every night. On the nights that she didn't, I heard her and Dutch engage in their own nocturnal activities. It was at first disturbing, after a while it was exciting, and now it just kept me awake. Someone had once told me you can get used to hanging if you hang long enough. I was getting used to hanging.

Angie had brought my personal effects from Flick's. A call from their Personnel Department secretary had officially ended my employment there, and my final paycheck had generously included no severance pay. I started to work for a temp agency. I kept two changes of clothes in the saddlebags of the motorcycle. One change, a dress shirt, tie, and good shoes, the other a denim work shirt, jeans, and boots that were in addition to the outfit I left the apartment wearing every morning. I could do almost any job that the agency might have, but with multiple options of dress I could take any one of them immediately.

So far, I'd bound books, collated magazine pages, and even worked a week as a key punch operator in my white shirt and tie. I'd also sand-blasted burned-out buildings, shoveled shit out of horse stalls, re-roofed a couple houses, and crewed a moving crew hauling tons of furniture and filing cabinets out of an office complex and into another two miles away. The office work had occurred during pleasant weather; the muscle jobs seemed to happen only when the temperature inside the trucks was above ninety degrees and seventy percent humidity. I was making enough to pay rent and some groceries and keeping gas in the bike. Sooner or later I was going to have to get a regular job, but I worried about the reference I was going to get from Flick's, so I was procrastinating. I was going to need a vehicle before the snow flew, and the temp money wasn't going to get me there. The clock was ticking.

Near the temporary employment agency was a large cemetery. Near its back fence a large family plot featured a massive obelisk marker with the family members' individual stones spread out across its base. The obelisk provided privacy for me to change from one work outfit to the other if I followed the gravel drive around behind it. Which I did, sometimes twice a day as I jumped from one workplace to the next. I opted for the cemetery because it was significantly cleaner and roomier than gas station restrooms, and more private. By evening both outfits usually needed a round of washing and ironing for the next day.

In the third week of temp agency work, I had pulled into the cemetery. After checking for surveillance—I didn't want to get rousted for possible vagrancy—I pulled off my dress shirt and reached into the motorcycle saddlebag for the work shirt. When I pulled my shirt out of the saddlebag and shook the wrinkles out of it, a thick bundle flew free of the wadded mess. It landed with a thump at the base of the potted roses near Andrew James Martin, husband and father, 1909–1957. The bundle was wrapped in brown butcher paper and gray duct tape. Using my Uncle Henry, I cut the paper away. Inside, a thick wad of paper currency, and a note. My heart dropped into the pit of my stomach as I recognized the handwriting.

"I believe this belongs to you; don't expect to get the other things back. Your man will be at Oliver's tonight, 8 p.m. Dunn."

The Package
Emmet

I had spent extra time in the mirror getting ready. Dutch and Angie stood in the doorway and offered multiple comments, none of which seemed to help. Finally, they crowded in and took over. Dutch gave me an impromptu hair trim, then pulled it tight into a ponytail that hung between my shoulder blades. Angie made me stand in the bathtub, where I stood embarrassed in my boxers in front of Dutch as Angie hacked my beard into a much trimmer and neater shadow of its former self. I had met Dwight Thomas the night before and over shots he'd given me the address and the time for tonight's meeting. He'd also voiced his fears.

"Man, don't go in there without some kind of backup plan. There's some shit coming down, and they're plenty pissed at you. I been looking for you for a week, man."

"I've been busy, got pulled in back a while ago. I'm tryin' to watch my six."

"No shit, man, I heard about it. Also heard they got the guy they were after. You hear about that?"

"No, man, I didn't. Who was it?"

"Three-time loser, strung out on smack, guy named Marks. He did kind of look like you—if you stopped showering for a month. He's up for life now, but he's one of those guys what's happier on the inside than he is on the street. You know, a lifer. Stupid fucker turned himself in."

"No thanks, overnight's bad enough for me."

"I dig that, man. So, listen, Hole, I mean it, they're serious as shit about making sure you show up. Stay out in the open, man, you know, in public, you dig?"

"I dig, man. Where'm I supposed to be? And when?"

"It's a nice place, way the fuck over in Oak Park, Slicker Sam's. You know it?"

"I know it. That's a nice place, all right. Shit, I'm gonna have to get all gussied up."

"No jokes, man. Just watch it."

I ordered another round of shots, Jack Daniel's for me, Courvoisier for Dwight. After we saluted and threw them back, I leaned in.

"Need a favor, dude."

"I ain't givin' you no fuckin' bread, Hole. You might not be around long enough to pay me back."

"Fuck you, Dwight! No, man, I need some dope. The Feds cleaned me out and I can't sleep."

"Shit, ain't no big thing, Hole. C'mon outside, I'll hook you up. You'll sleep like a motherfuckin' baby tonight."

Slicker Sam's had a reputation for the best king crab legs anywhere. It had Old Italian charm with checkered table cloths and wine bottles crusted with the wax of countless candle burnings on every table. The lighting was subdued, the tables widely separated, both to allow ample room for the huge platters the waitstaff carried and to allow plenty of private conversation. Rumor was that the mob ran the restaurant, and used it as a place to meet without prying eyes, and to launder money from other enterprises.

To me it was just a great place to eat and one I hadn't thought about for a while. It was currently too pricey for my present income. Its claim to fame was its spectacular all-you-can-eat king crab legs along with as much salad as you could put away. The rest of the menu was primarily authentic Italian cuisine that would blow you away with its spicy palate of tomato, cheese, basil, and garlic. The menu was expensive but worth it and compensated for the fact that the table turnover was slow as diners lingered over a last glass of chianti or the fabulous tiramisu and espresso.

I didn't know the protocol for a fancy restaurant, but when I gave the maître d' my name, she looked me up and down and said that my party was waiting. I didn't like the sound of that, and when she directed me to a table in the far corner of the room, I liked it even less. The table was large, half again as big as the others in the room. Only one chair of the six chairs around the table was unoccupied and it was in the back against the wall. No one stood when I arrived, but everyone stopped what they were doing, and their silence spoke volumes instead. I was the odd man out.

Willy finally stood and scooted his chair forward far enough for me to get around to the empty seat. Directly across from him William took up enough room for two people but was crammed into one space. To his right and two seats over next to Willy's seat sat Charles, the other half of the security detail outside of the front door of the shooting gallery downtown where I had first met these charming people. Directly opposite the empty seat my ugly friend from the night outside the jail sat. She was smoking another cigar and swirling a stemmed glass of what looked like champagne in her other hand. She held my eye as I slid past Willy, an amused expression on her face. On the other side of the empty chair sat the malevolent Alexander Anthony. The gang was all present and accounted for.

Charles and William must have been told to play nice, because they both made eye contact and nodded once. Willy sucked in his gut and belched in my ear as I passed in front of him. I did my best to appear relaxed, but it was going to take a few days for my asshole to unpucker thanks to the two across from me. Almost immediately after my ass hit the seat, a waiter glided up to the table and asked for my drink order. I ordered a Coke with no ice. I didn't want to let myself get too relaxed. He didn't bat an eye and glided away.

"Dinner is already ordered. We'll eat somewhat family style tonight. Crab legs, salad, and spaghetti. The boys will do their best to bankrupt the restaurant. We'll talk after dinner." She still sounded like she'd been eating gravel.

Dinner was slow and steady. The salad arrived in a monstrous bowl that only she and I ate from. After that, mountains of crab legs arrived and trays of exoskeletal remains left. The spaghetti was a side dish, but there were numerous servings of it required as well. Willy, Charles, and William performed diligently. Anthony touched nothing but busied himself instead with numerous cups of coffee and cigarettes. In spite of my nervousness, it was hard to pass up the food, which was delicious. There was no small talk around the table.

Once after-dinner drinks and coffee were served, the

boys all leaned back and relaxed. Neither of them, it seemed, smoked. Maleficent lit another small cigar, and Anthony had never stopped smoking.

"We have a shipment that we are going to be moving into Chicago. It is large and it is expensive. The product has been brokered already, and the delivery arranged."

I let that sit there without trying to react. William and Charles leaned forward.

"The three of you are flying to Miami tomorrow morning. Once you're there, you will rent a truck and drive it to Key West. The pickup will be tomorrow night, Tuesday. You need to be back in Chicago no later than Thursday morning at the crack of dawn."

"That's a lot of driving in a short period of time."

"That's why we wanted you."

"What kind of truck?" The size of the truck might give me a clue of the type of shipment.

"You'll need something big enough but not too big," this from Anthony, "ten to fifteen feet. Something that will hold the shipment but not attract attention. A U-Haul most likely."

"Why is it always Florida? Can't you guys go somewhere else once in a while?" There was a universal frown that seemed contagious and a few glances at the ugly woman, so I changed my tack. "What's in Key West that needs to come to Chicago?"

"Careful, Mr. Casey, not so fast. Alexander, fill him in on the particulars." She signaled a passing waiter and waved her champagne flute at him.

"It's really quite simple. Key West is the farthest west of all of the Florida Keys. That makes it the most remote site for products that might be of questionable legality to be brought into the country by sea. Things coming from Cuba, Mexico, Central America," he nodded toward the woman, "and Haiti. Deliveries are brought into the beaches at night and dropped in the surf, where they float ashore or are picked up by the locals. Then they're either warehoused or immediately trucked to the mainland and distributed."

"Isn't there only one road in and out of the Keys? Don't the Feds watch it?"

"Yes, and yes. The Overseas Highway connects all of the little islands back to South Florida; it's the only way in and the only way out. There's roughly a hundred miles from Key West to the mainland, so the Feds watch all the traffic and they're getting pretty good at intercepting some of the contraband. That's why we've worked out a different plan that we think will work."

"So federal enforcement on the only road out, and enough contraband to warrant a fifteen-foot-long truck. Sounds like a walk in the park."

"Not for some, but we think you'll handle it." She leaned back and French-inhaled her cigar smoke, cradling the freshened champagne stem in the other hand.

"Why three of us?" I didn't like working with people I might have to depend upon, especially if one of them didn't like me.

"Charles and William are going along to help load and unload. It's going to be hot, and there's going to be a lot of things to load. Your job is to proctor the deal and make the call. We'll transfer the funds once the count is verified. Then you'll make the final drive. When you get back to Miami, one of those two will catch a flight back and wait for you to arrive in Chicago with the truck."

"What makes you think I'll do that? I could just as easily sell it to the highest bidder, or just ditch it and disappear."

"That's why we need you." Anthony waved his cigarette toward me. "First of all, only an idiot would bring that up if he was thinking about doing it. You've proved your head's screwed on right and that you'll handle any bumps that might crop up. Second of all, that's why we need a new courier—the last one had ideas of becoming his own kind of entrepreneur. Willy had to discourage him from those kinds of thoughts. Didn't you, Willy?"

Willy grunted and then grinned at me. "Yeah, he didn't change his mind so easy either."

"Additionally," Anthony went on, "it would be pretty hard for you to just dump fifty kilos of marijuana and cocaine on the market without us or the authorities noticing."

"Fifty kilos! You're shitting me! That's half a ton! How are we going to get that from here to there without someone catching us? Holy shit, what if the truck breaks down on the way here?"

"You should pray that doesn't happen. I can give you a thumbnail, but the details are going to be up to you. We've rented a small condominium in Homestead, Florida—that's on the mainland. The truck will be used to pick up a load of assorted furniture in Key West that we've systematically moved to a warehouse there on the Key. Then you haul it to Homestead and dump it. You'll make a few trips. At first, you'll probably be searched diligently every time you leave the Key or shortly thereafter. After that you should be looked over but waved through once they've seen you often enough. The address in Homestead will make it look real if they ask you for proof of destination. Make several trips. Once that happens we'll give you the mother lode. William and Charles will also supply the appearance of a moving crew."

"That's a lot of back-and-forth in only a little more than forty-eight hours. We'll need more time."

The woman leaned forward and spoke up. "That we don't have. We have to time the tide surge for the drop-off, and the other end in Chicago is critical. You don't need to know the reasons for that."

"I need to go sooner then. We gotta go tonight. If we need to be finished by Thursday morning, we have to be in Key West by tomorrow sunup."

"As good as done. Willy will give you enough cash to operate with. Go to O'Hare and catch the next flight out if you like. William and Charles will follow as soon as possible."

I took a look around the table. William and Charles were leaning back, pros, relaxed and ready. The woman, who had never told me her name, was watching me intently, leaning slightly forward, her lips a tight line, both hands on the edge of the table waiting to see which side of the fence I was coming down on. This was the important moment for her. Alexander Anthony, with his dead eyes, was smiling a toothy grin at me—like sharks do. Willy was drinking his coffee, but his hand was shaking; excited—or nervous.

"I'm gonna need a ride to the airport."

Emmett

Tuesday morning, Key West, Florida

The U-Haul truck was a late-model rolling crate built on a Dodge chassis with a Dodge van front end and a fifteen-foot aluminum and steel box on the back. The big engine provided plenty of power, zero acceleration, and featured plenty of "top heavy" sway when it changed lanes. U-Haul had started to offer some of their trucks with air-conditioning—this wasn't one of them. It did have an automatic transmission. I had made the arrangements for the rental by phone once I'd gotten to O'Hare, so the truck was ready for me as soon as I got to the agency. I used the credit card they had given me to pay for it. Mr. Michael D. Nelson of LaPorte, Indiana, was in for a big surprise next month when he got his monthly statement.

The rental office was open even in the wee hours of Tuesday morning surprisingly. The rental agent in Miami, who I'd probably woken up, had been pleased when I told him it was a one-way rental to Biloxi. He wasted five of my minutes explaining that the trucks were hauling down snowbirds from the Midwest faster than they could get trucks back up north. No one was moving back to the Midwest once they were down here, and the trucks were piling up. U-Haul was having to pay drivers to return some of the trucks back up north. Biloxi was better than nothing.

I told him I was going to Biloxi because that was the first city name that came to mind when he asked me where I was heading. I didn't want to take any chances that someone down the road might ask him if he remembered me or where I was going. He didn't seem to care anyway, but I felt better with the lie. Once I had the truck I swung back through the Arrivals line and picked up Charles and William. The three of us were a tight fit in the truck cab, and there wasn't enough room for their knapsacks that they had carried on the plane, so we threw them in the back of the truck. The automatic transmission seemed like a genius move now. The thought of shifting gears with the floor-mounted gear shift lever between Charles' knees for the next twenty-four hours wasn't appetizing in the least. By the time we were rolling into Key West, the sky was bright in the rearview mirrors behind us.

We wasted another thirty minutes looking for the warehouse and our furniture connection. Once we'd done an initial drive-by, we drove out to the little harbor on the north end of the island and found a greasy spoon restaurant that was already open and competing with the smell of fish guts and saltwater. It wasn't winning the battle but it had excellent coffee and a limited menu of mostly sandwiches. We each ate two of everything while we occupied three of the four stools at the counter and took up all of the available space. We were here to work and hopefully stay out of jail; we didn't engage in light conversation while we ate. It had already been a long day, and the rest of it was going to be a hot one.

Time to Saddle Up
Emmett

By nine o'clock the temperature reached an even ninety degrees according to the big thermometer hanging on a mailbox post directly across the street from the open warehouse doorway. The thermometer had a big happy sun who seemed quite amused by our labors as we stuffed the U-Haul truck full of sofas, end tables, mattresses, and chairs. In a manner of minutes everything I had on was soaked with sweat and my eyes were stinging from it running out of my scalp. Finally, I took off my shirt and fashioned a turban around my head to stop the flow of moisture.

Not surprisingly, both Charles and William carried furniture like it was all made of balsa wood and climbed around the inside of the truck like they were monkeys. They appeared to be unfazed by the heat and humidity. The only telltale sign was the moisture that appeared in the armpits of their T-shirts and the copious amounts of water they put away. The first load was crammed into the back end of the truck in forty-five minutes. William grabbed the overhead door strap and jumped down off the back of the truck, bringing down the door with him. Charles threw the latch and they both turned to me.

"Hot." It was a statement from William, not a complaint.

"Fuckin' A, I'm lathered up like a fuckin' horse." If this heat kept up I was going to have some seriously chafed inner thighs by the end of the day. "You guys ready?"

"Ready as we're gonna be. I didn't see any Feds coming in."

"I thought you were sleeping all the way in."

"Sleepin' and restin' are two different things. We won't have any trouble first time anyway. Right?"

"I figure we could drive back and forth all day long and not see a thing and then get nailed when it matters."That had been my private thought since I'd left the restaurant. "Or we could pull this off without a hitch. I'm too pretty to go to prison, you know."

"Five minutes with the wrong guy and you won't think so anymore."

"I've already met that guy. He's not as good-lookin' as he used to be."

"Fuck you say…"

"I did some time, couple of times now. It's all fun and games—till the lights go out."

"Fuck you say. Didn't know—sorry, man."

"Yeah, well, I'm not plannin' on doing it again anytime soon, so let's be cool and try and get through this without steppin' on our dicks."

"Roger that."This from Charles. "So I gotta ask, you Green Beret or something over there?"

"Nope, 173rd Airborne, Recon, Central Highlands. You?"

"101st, Dac To, after that the Tet. William was Marines, Mekong Delta. Silver Star."

"Shit, I only got a Bronze, Jesus." I looked at William again. "No fuckin' shit?"

"Yeah, they just had 'em layin' around, I guess. Didn't want to have to pack 'em up and send them back, so they just gave the fuckers away—I guess." I looked at him, William was embarrassed.

"You wounded?" Charles was looking down at my forearms.

"Yeah, got the cluster."

They gave you a Purple Heart if you were wounded. It came with a cluster if you got wounded more than once. It saved on hardware cost. "Willy Peter, bayonet."

"Jesus fucking Christ! Peter? That's some serious bad shit. I wondered about the scars, shit, Willy Peter." He looked across the street at the sundial thermometer. "Bayonet, that's getting personal."

"Yep."

"Geezus, I got the cluster too, William too."

So here we were. Three war heroes who fought hard for our country and no one gave one ounce of a rat's ass about. All three of us with our own walking and dreaming nightmares. All three of us walking down the wrong side of the law for reasons that probably didn't make any sense if we'd taken the time to think about it. As we stood and looked down the street, we were just looking for the next danger point so we could feel a little alive again—even if it was only for a few minutes.

Running Drugs
Emmett

The Feds' traffic stop was east of Islamorada. It was set up in a long parking lot that used to be a strip mall. All the storefronts were empty and the windows were soaped up to discourage nosy inspections. The parking lot was set up in two lanes, passenger vehicles on the left nearest the road, trucks, vans, and larger vehicles to the right. There were two dark sedans pulled up to the curb, both with their engines running and the windows rolled up. At the entrance and exit a couple of Monroe County police cruisers directed traffic off and back on the highway. Across the street, two more county cruisers and another dark Crown Victoria sedan were idling.

The left lane moved right along, but the right one hardly at all. With the three of us jammed into the cab, it was too hot to stay in the truck if it wasn't moving, so we piled out and stood beside the open doors waiting our turn. The cracked blacktop reflected the heat up through the soles of our boots, and the idling engines of the vehicles ramped that heat up another ten degrees. By the time they got to us, another thirty minutes had ticked off the clock.

"Afternoon." He flashed his badge toward the three of us. "I'm Agent Bolton. May I see your license and rental agreement, sir?" From the look of him, he was about to melt into the pavement.

"Yes, sir." I gave him my license and the paperwork for the truck. The license listed my name as Michael Dennis Nelson, and would only pass inspection if he didn't spend too much time examining it, with an Indiana address that matched the rental agreement.

"Do you have anything in the back of the truck, sir?"

"Yep, a load of furniture. My aunt's movin' from the Keys back to the mainland. She's payin' us to haul her things for her."

"Do you have the name of the owner?"

"Yep, and her address. She's rich as hell, so her stuff's pretty nice."

"Would you please open the back of the van?"

Charles threw the latch and flipped the rolling overhead door up and caught one of the chairs as it fell out of the back as if he was expecting it.

"All right. We're going to want to look at the load. Would you please step over to the building and wait?"

"In this heat? Geez, how long do you think you're going to be, sir? Maybe we could walk over and get a Coke somewhere while you're doing it? Get out of the sun for a few minutes?"

"No, sir, we will require you to stay with the vehicle. As a precaution. Is there any reason that you might not want us to look at the load?"

"No, except that we have a few more to do. We shoulda got a bigger truck, but my aunt said it was just a few things. I shoulda known. She thinks she's only got a few pairs of shoes too. Needs a whole closet just for shoes, swear to god. We were hoping to maybe get one or two more today. This kinda throws a monkey wrench into the works for us."

"I understand. We will try and not delay you any longer than is necessary. Please step away from the vehicle, sir."

William and Charles did exactly what they were told to do and headed to the buildings. With the sun directly overhead, there wasn't any shade to be found. The storefronts were too hot to lean against, so they both sat down on the curb and got ready to wait. I wasn't about to fall into that. By the time they finished fishing through the truck, my brain would be boiled to flat-out useless. Instead I put myself right over the Fed's right shoulder and started working him. Normally I diligently avoid authority figures with clipboards, but I wanted to leave an impression on him.

"Yeah, we're moving all this shit up from the Keys for my crazy aunt. She's my mom's sister, you know, but younger. Not a lot younger, you know, but younger than my mom."

He shrugged and looked back over his shoulder. "Please step over to the curb, Mister…um…Nelson."

"Yeah, you know the type, right? Married an older guy with money, then fucked him to death."

That got a reaction. "This is your aunt you're talking about?"

"Yeah, my mom's sister. Good-lookin' too, still got it goin' on, if you know what I mean."

Now he was trying to look at the clipboard, but he was also listening.

"Yeah, I took the week off to get this done and thought I'd come down and enjoy Florida, but geez, so far this fuckin' heat and the cockroaches seem to be the only thing worth talkin' about."

I was losing him. He actually pulled a pen out of his shirt pocket and started writing things down.

"She's got one of those blonde hairdos, you know, the bee-hive thing. Thinks it makes her look younger, as if she didn't look good enough already. Fucks like a rabbit. If you know what I mean."

Both of his eyebrows popped up on their own. He put the pen back in his pocket.

"Your aunt?"

"Yeah, like I said she's still got it goin' on, you know, if you know what I mean." I gave him a little nudge with my elbow and winked.

"Your mother's sister you say?"

"Yeah, our black sheep—every family's got one of them, right?"

He was trying to show that he wasn't interested, but his head was cocked in my direction. The two guys climbing in and out of the truck were listening too, both with smiles on their faces. I wiped the sweat off my forehead and out of my eyes, and pushed on.

"Yep, black sheep or not, she's the one with the dough-re-mi now. Rest of us, pickin' shit with the chickens, know what I mean, poor as church mice, but her, man, she can buy and sell every one of us, if she wanted to. Tell you what, if she wants something, she ain't afraid to ask for—and pay—for it." I paused and made eye contact with the younger guy in the back of the truck. "She just uses a different kind of currency, if you know what I mean."

The two boys in the truck were working slower already so they wouldn't get out of earshot.

"Yep, she used to be a dancer, got legs that must take a week to shave."

Federal Officer Clipboard pushed his clipboard up under his left arm and leaned up against the side of the truck.

"You don't sound too put off by your dear sweet aunt's behavior." He gave me a sideways sardonic smile.

"Shit you say, after all this time we're kinda used to it, you know. 'Sides, in this world you get the advantage you take it, right?" I stuffed my hands into my back pockets and made eye contact with the other guy in the truck. "She's got the real estate, and there's lots of people interested in plowing that ground. Might as well make it pay. Right?"

The Feds first tried to climb into the truck to inspect the load, and then conceded that it was too haphazardly loaded for their own safety and carefully unloaded every stick of furniture out onto the pavement. They paid particular attention to the sofa cushions and mattress and box spring. We watched with no small amount of amusement while one of the officers took his shoes off and carefully walked over every square inch of the mattress to feel for parcels that might have been concealed within it apparently.

"Your mother's sister?" Agent Bolton sounded marginally interested now.

"Yep, she's the baby of the family, my aunt Esther; my mom's next up the line. Yep, she got the looks, that's for sure. She's got a front shelf on her, geez, you'd think she'd need running lights after dark."

"Lives in Homestead now, your aunt?"

"Well, not yet, that's what we're doing. Once her stuff gets moved in, she'll come in and tell us where to set all this shit up. She's on a yacht somewhere out by Bimini, wherever the hell that is…never heard of it myself. Some guy took her for a two-week cruise. He'll be lucky if he can still walk by the time he gets back on dry land. If you catch my drift."

"She does that a lot, does she?"

"Oh no, she's always sayin' how much she's wantin' somebody to settle down with, you know, down-to-earth, good guy. Now she can afford it, maybe she'll find somebody and get happy. Be a relief for the rest of the family, that's for sure."

"But she's sleeping with all these men in the meantime?"

"Well, not just men, if you know what I mean. She's got sort of an open mind about things like that."

Both the men in the truck had stopped working altogether now.

"She likes all kinds of guys though. Shit, I was lucky to get Billy there." I pointed over at William with my thumb. "She took a particular likin' to him. Likes big guys, I guess, if you know what I mean."

William looked up and gave them all a thumbs-up.

"Big guys with little peckers seem to be the ticket these days," I added.

William flipped the thumb over and gave me the finger, but he and Charles were both smiling.

"Your aunt was sleeping with one of these guys?"

"Well, yeah, that's what I said. Billy there kinda got her attention when he took his shirt off last week, while we were doing some painting at the new place. Didn't get any more work out of him for three days. I mighta saved his life just by gettin' him outta there for a while."

"But you said she was on a cruise."

"She wasn't going to go for a while there, said she wanted to get to know Charlie there too, but you know, we had to get the furniture moved. I only got so much vacation."

"So, she's going to be back in Homestead soon?"

"Well, yeah, that's what I said, 'cept she's gonna have that friend of hers staying with her for a while."

"Oh? She has a friend that she's bringing home with her?" He sounded genuinely disappointed.

"Yep. Aunt Esther, she's got her faults, but that friend of hers, Marcia, she's a real something else. I swear she's gotta have callouses on her back, she spends so much time on it, if you know what I mean."

"Marcia?"

"Yeah, she and Marcia, they got kind of a thing. They like to go at it together with a guy; they say it's twice the fun. Kind of crazy if you ask me, but Aunt Esther, she's always been a little different."

Both the guys who were supposed to be inspecting the truck were now on the pavement and standing with their hands in their pockets.

"No shit, this rich old lady just takes guys in and screws them?" the one on the right asked.

"Well, first of all, she ain't that old, just older than me by maybe fifteen years or so, could be like thirty-five, I guess. She has some preferences, but yeah, pretty much. But that's my aunt, see, so I feel a little guilty telling you guys about it. Especially, you know, cuz you guys are gonna know where she's livin'. But you guys are like okay, right, you know, bein' the law and all?"

"Preferences? What kind of preferences?" The one on the left.

"You know, young, athletes, and she really likes sailors, or Army guys, pretty much guys in uniform."

"And firemen!" William was getting into the swing of things.

"She really went for that cop, the one that fixed her ticket for her, don't forget." Charles was warming up too.

"She goes for young guys?" The one on the right was hooked.

"She likes younger guys for fun and, you know, company, but she likes older guys for…um…profit."

The young guy turned to Agent Clipboard. "Nothin' in there, I'd say, Bolton."

"Good enough for me. You boys gonna make a few trips, you say?"

"As many as we can today, should be a couple more."

"We'll be here until this afternoon when we get relieved. So, I guess we'll be seeing you again in a few hours."

"Say, you guys got enough water? Need us to pick up something for you? Maybe some conch fritters or somethin'?"

I thought William's eyes were going to pop out of his head for a minute.

"Naw, but thanks. We've got lunch ordered, and plenty to drink."

"You guys should be wearin' hats out in this sun, you know."

"Good idea…we've got some in the cruiser."

We stood baking in the sun for another two minutes while Agent Bolton wrote down my "aunt's" address and gave us back our paperwork. All three of them turned and started down the line to the beat-up pickup truck that was next in line, shoulder to shoulder, looking down at the clipboard. They left our furniture sitting on the boiling asphalt right where they'd dropped it. Halfway there, Bolton turned and gave us a thumbs-up and walked on. All three of us gave his retreating back the finger in unison.

"What the fuck, Hole?" Charles hissed in a whisper. "Now they're gonna remember us big time!" The heat was making Charles irritable, I guess.

"I sure hope so. Next trip's the last one."

No Guts, No Glory
Emmett

I wasn't going to be able to go much further without a break. Florida had come and gone, we were burning through the third tank of gas on the piece of shit U-Haul truck, and I had no conscious recollection of driving the last two or three hundred miles. Truckers call it white line fever, highway hypnosis, driving on autopilot while your mind is somewhere else. The trouble was that my mind was mostly thinking about closing my eyes. Charles dead asleep in the shotgun seat wasn't helping either; he was contagious, preoccupying, like riding with the Sandman.

I needed to rest somewhere and soon. The excitement of the last thirty hours had long since worn off, replaced by the monotony of the last seven hundred miles of strictly adhering to the speed limit. The mind-crushing sameness of the Eisenhower Interstate System offering no stimulus hour after hour. I like to drive, and I like to think, but I was approaching my physical limits; they were getting stretched thin now. Valdosta was in the rearview mirror and I'd stopped watching for trouble behind us. Ahead of us was still a different story, and I needed to get my wits about me.

The round trip back to Key West and back to the traffic

inspection point had been the last danger point—so far. The rendezvous with the payload had gone well. Once the count was clear and the product tested out, I'd made the call. Willy was surprised that we were going to make the money run ahead of the schedule we'd discussed, but he confirmed just the same. He'd sounded tense and there had been conversation at his end while he held his hand over the receiver for a long minute. When he came back he was his old self again.

"What's your planned route once you're on the mainland?"

"None of your business. Better if nobody knows what I'm thinkin'."

"Don't give me any of your shit, Casey. This is a big deal and you better not be fuckin' with us."

"Should'na sent me then if you were thinking that. I'm taking Charles with me. William will be on the flight sometime tonight. If we clear the checkpoint, that is."

"They've got a checkpoint set up!?! Shit!" The hand went back over the receiver for a few more long seconds. This time the voices were a little louder, but still unintelligible.

"Shit, Casey, you can't go in daylight."

"No, we need to go now, time's too short, and they'll look harder if we get there after dark. We need to get through before they change their shift; the new crew will be fresh. I don't want anybody that's thinking about diligence." I stopped and waited a tick before I took the next step. "But I need a favor."

"What kind of favor?"

"I need a phone number down here, same area code as down here at least. And I need a seriously sexy voice on the other end of it."

"Geezus, Casey, what the fuck is wrong with you?"

"I need it for the Feds, man, just get it and give it to me." After I'd told him the situation, he told me to call him back in fifteen minutes.

The second load had to be managed differently than the first one. Just loading the truck so it looked full wasn't the point this time; the weed and dope had to be placed so that a haphazard table or chair leg wouldn't puncture the packages. There is no mistaking the smell of strong, fresh weed. In the heat of the back of the truck, the smallest hole in the canvas and plastic wrap would give us away if the back of the truck was opened at any inspection point. It wasn't just a matter of having it out of sight; it had to be hard to get at and airtight too. I placed every piece carefully as the other two men handed them up. This time we'd tied everything down to the rings that were strategically arranged along the inside walls, and I used a lot of rope for it. It wasn't going to fall over, and it wasn't going to come out very easily if someone might want to take it out. It was slow, hot work and we were tired when we started. By the time it was done right, a full ninety minutes had passed and we were all risking serious dehydration. I called Willy back and he had the number. I wrote it down.

"William doesn't want to ride with you anymore, huh?"

"Goddam truck doesn't have air; it's hotter than balls down here. William says he's not eating any more gas station food, ever. So, it's Charles' turn. I'll see you tomorrow night. I'll call this number, right? Don't forget, her name's Esther, and her friend is Marcia, got it?"

"Right. Swear to god, Casey, this is bigger than you or me. Don't fuck up."

"I got that. See you in Chi'town—or hell—whichever comes first."

On the road north, I pulled into Marathon and did some shopping. Once back on the road east, it was only a matter of half an hour before, sure enough, the checkpoint was still in place, and there was still a line of trucks in the right lane. It was quitting time for most people, and most of the trucks were pickups, repairman or handyman trucks heading back home to the mainland, at the end of a workday fixing wealthy people's shit. A big brown UPS truck was right in front of us and we were next.

Bolton was working the truck now, and one of the younger guys was doing a shift on the clipboard, and the three of them looked much less energetic this time around. As we pulled up, two of them picked up the cartons and boxes in the back of the UPS truck and gave each one a shake, but with not much enthusiasm.

I didn't wait for them to approach. Instead, I jumped out and went to the back of the truck and threw up the rear door. Reaching in I pulled out the five-gallon cooler I'd picked up in Marathon and carried it to the front of the truck. Popping the lid, I pulled out a two-stick Popsicle and gave it to William and another one to Charles. I took a red one. We stood clear of the hot engine of the truck but still in front of it. Bolton almost hit the ground running, and the clipboard guy waved the UPS driver through and turned to us as well.

"I thought you guys might like something to cool off a little. There's a place back away that had dry ice, so these are nice and cold. That is, if you want one?"

Bolton smiled and gratefully took an orange one out of the cooler and handed one each to the other two fellows. There was a collective sigh, and other gratifying sounds of pleasure.

"I can't believe you guys haven't been spelled on this detail. Geez, even in the service they wouldn't leave us out there all fuckin' day."

"Oh, we got a good long break right after you left last time. But one of the guys got sick, too much sun probably, so they took him up to Miami, and the evening crew won't be here for another hour or so. Traffic's been pretty light, so we're taking turns sitting in the car with the AC on."

"Oh geez, sorry, guys. I thought you might like these though and I wanted one too. I brought some of those raised donuts too if you guys are interested?" They were cops after all, I'd thought.

"Naw, it's too hot for doughnuts." Bolton dropped the first Popsicle stick on the ground and started in on the next one.

"Speak for yourself, Frank." The young guy reached in the cooler and pulled out the bag with a dozen yeast-raised donuts, chilled to perfection.

"Hey, guys, we're gonna try and get one more trip in tonight, so I'm hoping we can get through this pretty quick. I already got the back open, if you don't mind, I mean."

"Let's take a look."

They'd slow-walked to the back of the truck. The sun was starting to angle toward the west, but it was still intense and it was shining right into the back end of the truck.

"Shit, you've got even more in there than you did on the last trip."

"Yeah, I told you she said it wasn't much stuff, but if we

don't pack it pretty tight, it's gonna take two more trips, not just one. She's got a lot of shit."

"Your aunt, what was her name again?" He was either checking my story out or he was still thinking about Aunt Esther in a different sort of way.

"Esther, Aunt Esther, c'mon, you remember."

"Oh yeah, Esther."

"Well, who's up on the truck this time?"

"It's still your turn, Bolton."

"Hey, before I forget—shit this heat, my head's as slow as molasses—I called her, my aunt Esther, when we were down at her old place. The phone's still hooked up down there, so I gave her a ring. So, I was telling her about how we got stopped and they went through her stuff and all. She thought it was soooo exciting. She's kinda nuts, you know? Anyway, she told me that I could give you her phone number if you needed it. You know, in case you might need to have another look, like later or something."

"Her phone number?"

"Yeah, I could write it down for you, but you guys gotta have better things to do than just make her life more exciting. I told her that you wouldn't be needing it, but you know, like I said, she likes, you know, she likes to think things are more exciting than they really are or something."

"No, no, that's okay. Maybe we should make a note of it, just in case, you never know. Right?"

"Really? You guys are too cool. Sure, I'll get it for you, no big deal to me. I don't remember it cuz it's a new one, so I got it up in the cab. Wrote it down, you know. Hey, maybe you guys could give her a call and, you know, um, give her a little scare or something. Man, it'd be the only thing she talks about for the next six months."

"Okay then, we'll take a look at the load. We'll get you out of here as quickly as we can." He turned to the other two guys, both of them with a donut in each hand, and frosting on their faces. "Geezus Christ, you guys, that's stuff is gonna sit in your stomachs like a ten-pound rock. Chambers, get up there and check the load."

By the time I had gotten back from pretending to write down poor old Aunt Esther's phone number, the one called Chambers was pulling down the door as he jumped down from the truck. He was still holding a donut in his other hand.

Macon Trouble
Emmett

According to the map Macon was going to be coming up on the horizon pretty soon. On the map it looked like a crossroads of a couple major highways, some going east and west, and the one we were on continuing north toward Chattanooga. I was hopeful we'd hit a truck stop, or at least a busy place where we could fuel up and get out on our feet for a while. The air hadn't cooled off at all; it remained thick and hot. Even as we rolled along at sixty-five miles an hour, the wind pounding in through the vent windows didn't give any relief. I was starting to think that my ass had melted to the cheap vinyl seat of the truck. Charles said he didn't care how bad he smelled. But if there was a truck stop, there was a good chance I could get a quick shower, change my shirt, stretch my legs, and we could both get some grub.

Traffic started to pick up as the glow in the sky ahead of us got closer. It had begun to cloud over again and the lights from ahead reflected off the underside of them across the horizon. It was going to rain again. As the glow in the sky grew, all the semis that we came up on stopped pulling out to pass each other like they usually did. Instead they hung to the right, which gave me a good feeling about the next few exits, and sure enough, at the second one a monstrous truck stop oasis appeared with enough parking lot wattage to need its own power plant for electricity. Billboards called out amenities every hundred yards along the roadside: Home Cooking, Diesel Repair, Tire Service, Truck/Trailer Wash, and right down in the corner of one of them, Hot Showers. I tucked in behind the trucks as they filed down the ramp, and veered into whatever available space they could find under the intense lights of the parking area. It was three o'clock in the morning, but the place was busy. The truckers were mostly looking for a place to crawl into the back of their truck cabs and sleep. I was going to get cleaned up. Charles just grunted and put his head on the open windowsill as I slammed the driver's side door and headed for the gift shop and lobby.

Fifteen minutes and ten dollars later, my hair was dripping down the back of a new Harley-Davidson T-shirt and I was wearing a new pair of socks while I sat in one of the restaurant booths staring into a seriously good cup of coffee as I waited for an order of French toast, bacon, eggs, hush puppies, and some corned beef hash. A tiny tap on the window to my left made me glance up. Just beyond the window Charles stood with his right shoulder up against the glass looking down at me. I lifted my hands in a *what gives* gesture. In answer, he nodded toward the rear of the building, dropped his hands into his pockets, hunched his shoulders, and started walking toward the semi rigs parked behind the complex. It was then that I noticed the flashing lights on the walls and ceiling of the room. I took the longest drink of the still too hot coffee that I dared, dropped a five-dollar bill on the table, and headed back out to the showers again.

Bumping out past a few sleepy truckers who were waiting in line for the shower stalls, I pushed open the steel fire door and stepped out next to the dumpsters. Charles was waiting.

"Cops."

"Shit. County or state?"

"One's a regular squad car, but the other two are unmarked."

"Man, somebody's rolled over on us. Son of a bitch. You're sure they're eyeballing for us?"

"I went in to take a piss and grab a Snickers bar. I was at the counter payin' when the first one rolled up. Two more right behind 'em."

I squatted down and untied the flap on my backpack and pulled my Uncle Henry out. I stood up and pulled my belt out far enough to thread the sheath through so that it fit into my back pocket. I took out the rest of the money Willy'd given me and split it evenly and handed half to Charles. For once I was glad I wasn't carrying a gun.

"Hole?"

"Relax, dude, around here you're more suspicious if you're not carrying a knife than if you are. You did your job, I can't cover the rest, but use this if you can."

"There sitting on the U-Haul. Shit, never thought a fuckin' candy bar woulda saved my ass."

"We gotta move out."

"I'm hip with that. No time to plan. Listen, Hole, you watch your ass. You're okay, man, nobody can say you didn't do your job. Shit, I gotta tell you, I've never seen somebody throw so much bullshit into one bucket before. You are one of the coolest motherfuckers I've ever worked with, I gotta tell you. I'll shotgun for you anytime. Try and get clear; maybe they don't know who they're lookin' for yet."

"Trust me, man, if they know about the truck, they're already lookin' for us."

Charles looked out into the parking area. The entire fringe was guarded by mature pine growth and scrub brush. It might have been ten miles deep or it might be only a hundred yards; it wouldn't be dependable to hide out in. I scanned the lot. The semi rigs were shoulder to shoulder, all with their engines idling, blasting their air-conditioning into the sleeper cabs. Anyone in them wouldn't hear a thing no matter what went down out here. Unless they were already alert to the police lights and watching already.

"I'm gonna get on one of these rigs if I can, and book. I got a CDL. I can convince the driver that he'd like me to ride along. How 'bout you? We need to split up," he said.

"Yeah, that too. Looks like the woods is out for sure. If they want to take the trouble to put dogs on us, they'll have us in no time." I checked the corners of the building; still no police presence on this side anyway. "You don't think we can save the load?"

"Shit, man, they were all over it before I made the corner of the building. They know what's what."

"Okay, but somebody owes me a payday."

"Fuck that, man, it won't matter if you're someplace you can't spend it. Get goin', man."

"Roger that. Like my old man says, Charles, watch your six. You go ahead. I'll give you time to get clear before I move out."

"Fuckin' A there." He turned and walked slowly away; ten steps away he turned back. "Oorah!"

"Oorah!" And just like that it started to rain.

Then he moved out to the rigs in the back and around behind them. He was okay in my book. No way he'd had time to drop a dime and have the heat there so quick; he deserved to get clean away. I wasn't so sure about me though. I went back around the restaurant the way Charles had come. From where he'd gotten my attention at the window I could watch the parking lot by looking through the side windows, then through the restaurant and out through the front windows. The cops were around the U-Haul, but they were waiting. One was taking flash pictures of the truck; the rest were leaning on their car fenders. Not all of them were wearing uniforms. There were three cruisers with their gumballs rotating on the roof positioned in front and behind the U-Haul so that it couldn't be moved. The other two vehicles were dark Ford Crown Vics parked in the lane behind the others. Eight or ten onlookers were standing near the building watching the excitement from under the protection of the roof overhang. It was a real downpour.

I couldn't figure out why they were not moving. Then it dawned on me: they needed a search warrant to open the truck, and they were waiting on the warrant. I had a little time, not much, but a little. I walked to the opposite side of the building and stepped out into the parking lot toward where the big truck rigs were fueling. The smell of diesel oil and grease filling the muggy air. I didn't look around. I walked directly to the pumps where a big red Peterbilt with an enormous sleeper cab was just topping off. The trucker pulled the fuel hose and nodded to me. I nodded back and took the nozzle out of his hand and holstered it back to the pump. Reaching into the wash bucket I grabbed the long-handled windshield brush and started on the right side of his windshield, while I turned to him and adopted my idea of a Georgia cracker accent.

"Y'all can go on inside and settle up. I'll get these windscreens shined up for ya."

He countered back in a perfect Midwestern dialect.

"Hey, thanks, pal. I'll be back in a flash."

"No sweat, sir. It'll be spotless when you get back. You headed north, I reckon?"

"Nope, south. Runnin' into Naples, Florida. Should be there around noon."

"Long run. Watch out for them four-wheelers. Florida's got all them old ladies driving, ya know. They so short ya can't see 'em, and they can't see you."

"Yep, and they all drive big ol' Buicks and they don't want to see me."

"Well, good luck to y'all. Them ol' ladies, man, they got more money than God."

He handed me a dollar and left to go pay for his fuel. Once he'd gone, I put the brush back in the bucket and walked around to the other side of his rig. Putting it between the cops and myself, I walked straight into the woods at the back of the lot.

Twenty yards into the trees, the brush thinned out underneath them and I turned around to get a look. From this vantage point I could see both the front and back of the entire property and not be seen. Only the rear of the U-Haul was visible from where I stood, and both sides of it were parked in by semi-rigs, a police cruiser with its roof lights flashing behind it. The rear door was still in the down position, but it wouldn't be long before all of poor Aunt Esther's furniture was stacked out in the rain on the parking lot. I figured I would go from being a person of interest to fugitive. We had worn gloves most of the day while we worked, but it had been too hot to keep them on all the time. I thought I'd only taken them off when I wasn't touching anything truck related. There were going to be fingerprints to find, and some of them were going to be mine, probably.

Behind the cruiser was a blue sedan also with a small gumball light spinning on the roof. There were a couple of uniforms moving from one tractor cab to the next, checking inside and questioning the drivers. I didn't see any sign of Charles, and hoped that I wouldn't. If he'd gotten in one of the tractors, they were going to find him if it didn't move out soon. If he'd slipped into the trailer somehow, there was a chance he'd get away.

The choice for me seemed to be walk back out into the open and turn myself in or turn around and wait for them to catch up to me. I had had more experience with the latter choice, and my feet wanted to go in that direction. But outright fleeing the scene seemed counterintuitive. It is always better to hide in plain sight, but hide nonetheless.

When in doubt turn right. I turned that way and made as straight a line as I could manage in the dark just inside the tree line but at ninety degrees from my exit point of the parking lot. As the edge of the cleared property approached, the ground tilted sharply downward and the trees ended at a property fence and a drainage canal directly on the other side. The stink and sheer number of mosquitos attested to the amount of stagnant water in the ditch. The fence was in good shape—strong hog wire and recently stretched. The canal was a good twenty feet wide and a solid concrete construct six to eight feet deep and made to move a lot of water when necessary. It looked like it had a foot of water in the bottom as far as I could tell in the low light that reached it from the parking lot.

I went farther back into the trees before I climbed the fence and dropped down into the culvert. I don't like snakes, and every southern boy I'd ever known had warned me about cottonmouths, rattlesnakes, and copperheads. Essentially, I'm a city boy with a little north country farm in my blood. Snakes give me the willies, and ones that can kill you, they make my sphincter spasm. I was absolutely sure that the snake population vastly outnumbered the number of fugitives in the culvert. I didn't like the ditch at all, but I could now walk in the open without being seen and just barely stay out of the water. The concrete sides were about even with the top of my head. Turning right, I started away from the truck stop and watched my step. I'd much rather have been arrested than snake-bitten.

Within a hundred yards the drainage ditch turned into a wide corrugated culvert as it dove under the interstate. There hadn't seemed any current in what little water there was in it, but I couldn't be sure if the culvert drained the median of the highway only or if it went all the way through to the other side. Either way the way it was raining I had no idea how fast the water level was going to rise in there. I don't swim well, and swimming with snakes in the dark seemed a good argument against going in there. If it did go through it meant another one hundred yards at least of pitch black, or a dead end in the middle. I was absolutely sure that every snake on this side of Macon, Georgia, lived in that culvert, but I needed to get the highway between me and pursuit. I opted for no snakes.

I climbed out of the culvert and up the embankment. Squatting down behind the guardrail, I checked traffic, which was almost nonexistent. The sight of a grown man running across four lanes of high-speed traffic was something a driver was sure to remember, so I waited until I couldn't see any sign of oncoming headlights and vaulted the rail and ran. As fast as I was running, there were still headlights approaching fast by the time I cleared the guardrail on the other side and slid down the opposite embankment to where the culvert exited from under the road.

In front of me was another hog-wire fence and then a frontage road, and beyond that another much smaller truck stop, with a flashing Good Food sign in the window. This parking lot wasn't lit up like a small city at least. Directly in front of the restaurant was a big blue-and-gray Greyhound bus. I cleared the fence and hurried across the lot, went around to the back of the building, and came in through the trucker's entry. Walking straight through I bought a bag of potato chips, a box of donuts, and a quart of milk, then walked out to the bus.

The driver, a large black man in a gray Greyhound uniform and hat, was stretching out in front of the bus, leaning back with his hands on the small of his back and looking up into the rain. I walked over to him and got a look at the marquee above the windshield. He was headed to Jackson, Mississippi.

"Ticket to Jackson?"

"Got any luggage?"

"Just this and some groceries. How many stops between here and there?"

"Oh, quite a few. This is kinda a local run, Columbus,

Montgomery, Selma, Demopolis, York, and a couple in Mississippi too, but we'll have ya there in plenty time for tommorah. I only go as far as Meridian. Get a different driver after that."

I lit a cigarette and looked out into the rain with him for a while. People started to come out of the truck stop and climb back onto the bus.

"It'll be eighteen dollars and fifty-seven cents from here." He was still talking to the clouds.

"All I got's a twenty. Shoot, keep the change. I'm so tired I don't think I can count it anyway, and I gotta be to work by tomorrow night in Jackson." I thought for a beat; it might be better if I didn't leave any more tracks than I had to. "Better yet, I'll give ya the twenty and you don't sell me the ticket, how's that sound?"

I pulled out a twenty from my wallet. There weren't that many left. He looked at the twenty, then took a longer look at me. His eyes went to the truck stop, and then looked through the windshield at the sleepy passengers finding their seats again. He looked back at me, then at the twenty, then back at the rain.

"Much obliged. Not too many riders tonight. You can probably stretch out across the backseat and get some rest if you like."

Reaching sideways he took the twenty and pushed it into his shirt pocket. I turned and boarded the bus and went all the way to the back. No one even looked up as I passed them. This bus was a local and thankfully had no restroom back there with the stink of the chemical toilet and constant foot traffic. Instead there was a full bench seat across the back of the bus.

I broke open the donuts and cracked the jug of milk and got my feet up.

I'd be getting off at Meridian. And I was going to need some help this time.

Emmett

Meridian, Mississippi, Daybreak

I got off the bus in Meridian when it made its regular stop. There were quite a few people waiting to board, and there was a new driver. When he got in the driver's seat and started going over the manifest with the driver who knew me, I made eye contact and stuck my thumb up over my shoulder. He gave a slight nod and then a wink. He was a good man.

The bus stop in Meridian was another gas station with a little mom-and-pop restaurant that was just starting up for the morning rush of laborers heading in for ham and eggs and grits. The town started at the edge of the parking lot, and a pay phone stood watch over the traffic. I picked up the receiver and was glad I got a tone right away. Feeding a quarter into the slot, I dialed O and waited for the clicks as it went through the connections, and finally a ring.

"Operator, how may I assist you."

"I would like to make a collect call to Addison, Illinois. I do not have the number but the name is Gail DeBoer, D-small e-capital B-o-e-r, on Birch Street."

"One moment, sir." I waited a full minute, feeling like I was standing on a pedestal with a spotlight trained on me. There was no reason to think that anyone would be interested in me here in Meridian, but my paranoia radar was on full volume. Someone had tipped the police off about the load. We had been in the clear, and should have been good. It could be anyone in the inner circle. William was a definite possibility, but not likely. When I made it back home, if I made it back, he and I were going to have a little talk, that was for sure. There was a rat in the woodpile, and there was a reason the rat had wanted me involved.

Finally, the operator came back on. “I can connect you now, sir. Who may I say is calling?”

“Bobby Casey.”

The phone rang and it was answered before it finished the first time.

“Hello? Emmett, is that you? I’m so worried. Where’ve you been?” Just Angie, being Angie.

“I have a collect call from Bobby Casey; will you accept the charges?”

“Bobby Casey? I don’t know anybody named Bobby Casey!”

There was the sound of a muffled exchange, a slight struggle with the rustling of what might have been bed clothes.

“Hello?” Dutch this time.

“I have a collect call from Bobby Casey; are you willing to accept the charges?”

“Yes.”

“Hey, Dutch.”

“You better have a good excuse for calling at this time of the day, Hole.” There was a brief pause and then she connected the dots.

“Don’t tell me, you’ve put your foot in it. What’s going on?” Then to Angie, “It’s okay, Angie, it’s Emmett.”

"Up to my ass. I'm sorry, Dutchie, I think I'm in trouble."

"Angie, settle down, he's all right—for now." She covered the receiver and there was an extended discussion that I could hear nothing of. When she uncovered the mouthpiece, the sound of hysterics was clear in the background.

She took a long breath and let it out. "How much trouble?"

"A lot."

"The police?"

"Them too."

"Those others then." She was a quick study. "Why are you calling us? I'm not interested in getting in to any kind of mess with either one of those. Geezus, Emmett!"

"I'm sorry, Dutch. I just need a little assist. I promise it won't come back to you, I promise."

There was a long pause. I could hear her moving around, maybe sitting up onto the side of the bed.

"What is a 'little assist'?"

"I'm moving. So far, I'm out ahead, but I can't do it for long and I'm almost out of bread."

"You need money? Where the heck are you even?"

"Yes, I'm gonna need money, but I have money, just not here. I need to get it here."

"Again, where is here?"

"I'm in Mississippi, but not for long. Listen, in my underwear drawer, rolled up in a pair of socks is my cash. I need to get it wired to me somehow."

"Hold on." She dropped the phone with a clunk. It didn't sit there for more than three ticks.

"Emmett!?! What's going on? Are you hurt? Oh my god, Emmett, I'm so scared." Angie was just getting revved up.

"I'm okay, Ang, just need a little money so I can get home."

In the background I heard Dutch tell Angie to give her the phone again. Another brief struggle ensued.

"I'll say some prayers for you, Emmett. Don't worry, Dutchie will help you. I love you."

The last sentence dropped on me like a sack of wet leather. Well shit, that's just what I needed.

"Holy shit, Emmett! What the fucking hell are you doing with this much money in your goddam sock drawer?"

"That's a longer story. Listen, Dutch, if I can get back to Chicago, I can get started on straightening this thing out. If I get caught out here, I don't like my chances. I gotta get enough to travel, and I've gotta get there as soon as possible."

"Is there a Western Union where you are? I can wire it."

"No, there isn't. 'Sides, I can't stay here and wait for it. I've got to get up the road and away from here before they start looking in this direction."

"Well, then what?"

"Listen, Dutch, I hate that you guys are involved in this. I don't want you doing anything. I don't want you guys in any possible trouble."

"Well, then what?"

"Have you got a pen and paper?"

I took a long, deep look into my past and then a deeper breath; the push had come to the shove.

"I need you to call my Da."

Time to Save My Boy
Little Mick Casey

When the phone rings in the middle of the night, it can only mean one thing. Someone has died, there's been an accident, or someone's in trouble. If you're a Casey, it's usually the third thing.

Trouble only came in a few forms for me these days, and most usually it was one of the boys, or lately one of the girls. They were Caseys too after all. The call tonight was more of the same, and less of the same. A woman, nice voice, and all business. It was Emmett and according to her, this time it was bad. Not that it usually wasn't, but most of the time it was just boys being boys. Emmett's troubles had always been different. Kate said he has a restless spirit. Maybe that's why he'd always been special to me. He was as tough as nails and as soft as bar soap, but he always takes the long way around. God only knew what he'd already been through in his young life; a lesser man would have just knuckled under, but Emmett always leaned into the wind just a little harder than he did before.

The woman told me her name was Gail, and she said Emmett called her from someplace way down south and needed help. She was one of those two women Emmett had been living with since he got evicted from his last place. I met the other one, a dago Italian girl, dumber than a sack of doorknobs, but a real looker. This was the other one, and she sounded like she had some brains. She gave me the thumbnail of what he'd said on the phone. There was too much detail and I was afraid to raise my voice and disturb anyone trying to sleep. I needed her to repeat it a couple of times. Finally, she said she would drive over here and give it to me straight. I gave her the directions.

I poured another whiskey and put my boots on, while I thought about Emmett. Upstairs I closed the bedroom door to his mother's room. I went into the children's rooms and looked down at them sleeping quietly, the rooms muggy with their warm bodies wrapped in too many blankets. Little Seamus, sound asleep only half on the bed and half on the floor. I took a few moments to gently urge him back in and covered him again. He didn't awaken. It was still a few years before he'd start getting into Casey trouble for me to deal with.

Back in my own little room tucked up under the eaves, I got my Colt down from the shelf in the closet and threw some socks and clean underwear in a knapsack. I grabbed a full box of cartridges out of the sock drawer. I got my skinning knife out of the lower drawer and unsheathed it and ran it up the outside of my left forearm, shaving off the dark hair to check the edge for sharpness. It went in the knapsack with the rest of it. I filled my tobacco pouch and made sure I had spare matches.

Trouble comes and trouble goes, but Casey trouble is our trouble. We handle our own shit.

There was no sense in waking the house with the sound of a strange voice. I went out and sat in the hot early morning air on the front steps to wait for the girl named Gail. I lit my pipe and listened to the crickets and the trains off in the distance. The sky was brightening in the east. Another long night thankfully gone; today would be a different kind of day.

Time to go and get my boy.

Heading North
Emmett

I'd done something that I hated doing almost more than anything else. I'd asked for help and admitted that I needed it. The shame burned in my throat and the guilt fueled my footsteps. After hanging up the pay phone, I went back in the restaurant and got a solid meal of grits, gravy, chicken-fried steak, and coffee. I had them pack me a to-go lunch of sourdough bread with meat loaf and a quart of sweet tea. Now I was walking north. I wanted distance, and I needed to work out some things in my head so I didn't try to hitchhike. It was early and already hot—looked like more rain would be coming before mid-morning. The humidity was already oppressive.

I knew Dutch would deliver the message and I had no doubt that Little Mick would respond. That alone made me feel worse. The constant disappointment that I must be for him was like a boat anchor that I dragged behind me with every step of my life. Little Mick by his very being made everyone around him recognize their own shortcomings. He was only about five foot six and I outweighed him by at least eighty pounds, but he was a bigger man than I was in almost every way.

I needed to get to Memphis now. That's where I'd told Dutch I'd head for. I'd never been there before, but it looked pretty good sized on the map. Dutch had been to the airport there and said that was the place to go; it would be busy and it was not likely that I'd be looked at too carefully. If I could get to the city, I could call again. She'd given me the name of a place that she thought was safe. It was going to take me most of the day and by then she'd be able to tell me how it had gone with Da.

If he'd finally decided enough was enough and cut me loose, that would be as far as I could probably get. I'd have to get by on my own, and it would take a lot longer to get back to Chicago. By then someone would have covered their tracks. I needed to get there quickly.

I slowed my pace. I'd been walking fast trying to burn off some nervous energy and I'd worked up a good sweat. It was going to be a long day again, and I'd only slept about three hours. I couldn't walk to Memphis and although this was a fairly good-sized highway, it was going to be hard to get a ride all the way. I'd seen two cars in the almost an hour that I'd been walking and they were both going the wrong direction. At the speed I'd been walking, I figured I'd probably put about five miles behind me out of Meridian. At a bridge over a small river, I stopped and sat down on a guardrail post to take a breather and have a smoke. I didn't want to sit too long; it would just make it that much harder to get back up.

In the shimmering morning sunlight, a vehicle appeared coming from Meridian. I shouldered my backpack and turned away. I didn't want to be just sitting with a post up my ass if whoever it was proved to be overly curious. It didn't take long before a faded and rusty Ford pickup chugged up next to me and slowed down to match my pace. The windows were rolled down, and when I looked up an elderly black woman with gaudy rhinestone glasses smiled a perfectly bright white smile and said without a hint of suspicion, "Mornin' suh."

"Good morning to you, ma'am."

"Plenty hot already, gonna be a scorcher fu'shure."

"Plenty hot." I kept walking.

"You going someplace up ahead, suh? You shudna be out walkin' in the Miss'ippi sun thout you gotta hat on, suh."

"Yes, ma'am."

The truck brakes squealed as it pulled to a stop. I stopped walking and turned to face the woman.

"You can ride with us shud ya want."

"That would be much appreciated, ma'am. I've got a ways to go."

The driver shut the engine off and the driver's door screeched as he shoved it open. I wasn't expecting him to get out, and I dropped my backpack and set my feet.

"You can drive my truck, suh. I'll climb up in the back."

"What?"

"Suh, I can't no way drive past no white man thout axin him he needs a ride. But ain' no way I can give him a ride and haf him sittin' in the back o' my truck. Folks round here, well, they'd hang me from the nearest tree fuh sure."

The woman added, "Yo ain' from these parts, tell that from your speechin'. Things different roun' here. Go on, you know how to drive, right?"

"Yes, ma'am, I know how to drive."

"Well then, get up in here, if'n you don' mind riding with an uppity nigger woman. Lester don't mind gettin' in the back. We're goin' up t'other side of Philadephee, gotta see to my sick mammy. That'll save ya some forty, fifty mile if you is goin' that way."

"Ma'am, I'm obliged."

"Well, it's too hot to sit and jaw then. Let's go. Lester, you get y'self sitiated. My name Maybelle, you?"

"Some call me R.E."

"Arie it is? That sounds like a good name." She smiled a satisfied smile and nodded her head.

The old truck ran hot and the heat coming through the floorboards was much worse than the heat out in the sun. Lester probably was glad to be riding in the back with the breeze. The old exhaust system produced too much noise to make any conversation possible, and the steering pulled hard to the left, keeping me busy staying on my side of the road. For her part, Maybelle sat shoulders back and looking straight ahead—a huge floral print purse on her lap under her folded hands and a large casserole pinned between her feet on the floor.

An hour later the old truck chugged into Noxapater, Mississippi. I pulled into a grungy filling station on the edge of town and up to the single set of pumps that the old woman pointed me into. Switching off the key, I heard the engine knock and miss and finally backfire itself into silence while steam oozed out from under the hood. Two old black men sat on a bench out of the sun in front and watched without expression until Lester climbed down over the tailgate and gave them a healthy "Good mornin'."

Between the two men sat a paper bag with the neck of a bottle sticking out of the top. Lester shuffled over and picked up the bag, gave it a shake, and then took a long pull off the bottle. "Plenty warm."

"Plenty hot, you mean; it's even hot here in tha shade, boy. You comin' to see Maybelle's momma this day?"

"Yeah we is, she made one of her hot dishes to get her through to Sunday."

"I heared she not doing too well, but maybe she was rallyin' of late."

"That'd be good news to Maybelle."

"Lester, you put that bottle down now, we gots too long a day ahead foh you to be startin' that behavior so early." Maybelle spoke from the truck, and immediately the bottle clunked back down on the bench.

"You need some watah for that steam engine of yourn, Lester?"

"That too." He looked back over his shoulder at me, and I took my cue and shoved the creaking door open and stepped out into the dust. "Maybe some little gas too?"

Both of the men jumped to their feet, and the older of the two headed toward the truck.

"Sorry, mistah, saw you was in the truck but didn't mean to make yah wait. Lester, he my cousin and we was just catchin' up a bit."

I walked around to where Lester was standing and pointed up the road into town. When he turned to look at where I was pointing, I handed him three five-dollar bills.

"Suh?"

"Least I can do is buy you folks a little gas for the trouble."

"Suh?"

"This way you pay for your own gas, but I've got a clear

conscience. I appreciate this more than you know."

"Well shoot, mistah, that's ten dollar more'n it take to fill this thing."

"Just the same, my thanks."

"Well, you wait right here, suh."

I walked around the old fellow holding the gas pump hose.

"Mr. Lester here was nice enough to offer me a ride out of the heat." I handed him a five-dollar bill. "Would you check the oil too please?"

The old man looked at Lester, whose jaw muscles were working overtime.

"Suh, yes, I will do that, suh."

He pumped the gas and checked the oil. Heaving up the huge hood, he pushed on a big leather blacksmith glove and twisted open the radiator cap. While the steam blasted ten feet in the air, he puttered around the engine, checking the oil and the brake fluid reservoir, then refilled the radiator. After that he got out a squeegee and cleaned the cracked windshield all in about five minutes. Maybelle never flinched and never seemed to move from her soldier straight posture.

Lester snuck a few more hits off the bottle and then went into the back of the shop. In a few minutes he came out with another black man.

"This here my cousin Mose. Mose' goin' north with a load of steers this afternoon. Goin' all the way to Oxford. Where you say you goin'?"

I decided there was no use trying to be cagey with this most excellent man.

"I need to get to Memphis."

"Memphis! Well, that's a whole nother thing. Away up

there!?" He walked around to the other side of the truck. "Ma, he say he goin' all up to Memphis." He handed her the five-dollar bills.

"Memphis! That is somethin', I'll say. Memphis, that's a big place, big for its britches Memphis is. My brutha Sammy, he work in Memphis, makes some fair good money, but it cost some money in dat big place. Lester, you go and you call Sammy." She leaned forward and spoke across from the other side of the truck to me. "You sit tight, Mistah Arie."

"Please don't call me Mister, ma'am, R.E.'s just fine." Less than an hour with these folks and I was already developing an accent.

"Well, Mister Arie, you sit tight fo' five minutes, and we gone get you a ride clean all the way to Memphis city. And get you a hat too." She flashed those perfect teeth at me again. "How's 'bout that?"

"Sounds really great, Maybelle."

"My brotha Sammy, he work in Memphis washin' dishes at one o' dem fancy rest-o-rants from Thursdee to Sunday. He sleep on my cousin's sofa when he up dere, but he come home on Sunday so's he can go to church. He got a nice car. You gonna ride in style all de way up to Memphis city, Mistah Arie, and won't dat be nice."

"Can I ask you a question?"

"Yes, Mistah Arie, what you need?"

I looked down at my shadow in the dirt and the dust on my boots.

"Is there a place in town I can get a haircut?"

Her lips tightened and she leaned across the inside of the truck and put her hand on my arm.

"It's that way, is it? Well, you just come on to my mammy's. We gonna get you cleaned up good and proper." And then she showed me a completely different smile from the ones I'd already seen. It came with a little wink.

Little Mick Casey

The Peabody, Memphis

I saw him as soon as he came around the corner onto Union Avenue. Even with the shimmering air of the late afternoon heat pouring down onto the concrete buildings and pavement, the sidewalk was busy. People leaving their office jobs heading home or out for a drink. Cars were stacked up outside of the hotel entrance puking fancy overnight guests while the bellhops hurried to keep up with the excessive luggage that came out of the trunks. Even if I hadn't been looking for him, he would have caught my attention. The way he held his shoulders and walked with a long-legged, loose-kneed walk that looked casual but wasn't. The knapsack on his left shoulder and a brown slouch hat hid most of his features. He was on my side of the street opposite the hotel, checking shop windows, looking up at the building across the street. He was being careful; his right hand was empty for a reason. He came up opposite the front entrance but kept right on walking. I would have done the same thing. At Second Street he crossed the street and then crossed Union and headed south where I lost sight of him. I waited and watched. I wanted to see if he was followed. He wasn't—that I could tell.

The girl across from me was nervously nibbling on a bread stick, and kept watching out the window. She'd missed him.

"It's getting late. I was hoping he'd make it before dark." She was anxious but didn't seem nervous.

"He's already here." I reached for my wallet and stood up.

"How do you know that?" She dropped the bread stick and swiveled her head in a complete one-eighty.

"He just checked the front entrance, then went around the block behind the building. Did you leave him the message at the front desk?" I'd asked her this at least five times before, but I wanted to break the tension and I don't usually need someone else's help, so I didn't completely trust her.

"Did you see him? How do you know that?"

"Couldn't miss him if he was in a crowd of a thousand. We better get in there; he's already at the front counter by now."

"You said he went by the front entrance."

"Lots of ways to go inside a hotel…front door's not always the best way."

I left a couple of bucks on the table of the coffee shop, and she grabbed her purse. Outside we crossed Third Street and then crossed Union and came in through the eastern-most door to avoid the doorman and bellhops. He was standing near the huge fountain in the lobby looking at the ducks swimming in it, seemingly transfixed by the sight. I eased up behind him, not sure how I should greet him.

"What's she doing here?"

He didn't even turn around. He could feel me standing there.

"She insisted."

He turned slow, but his anger got there ahead of his face. He'd shaved his beard off and cut his hair. He looked so much like his mother as I looked up into his face, I was surprised I hadn't seen it before.

"Goddamn, Dutch!" he hissed. "What the fuck are you trying to get yourself into?"

"Your dad said he hated airplanes and wanted to drive. I thought that would take too long to get to Memphis. Your dad didn't know how to get a ticket for a flight, so I had to go to the airport with him anyway. I got a free hop in the jump seat. Honestly, Emmett, you should be happy. I brought your dad, didn't I?"

Emmett's shoulders were still tight, but the bright color was draining out of his face a little. He looked tired and tight.

"I saw you two in the coffee shop." Of course, he did. "How long ago d'you get here?"

She ignored the question; instead she just breezed ahead.

"I've done layovers here when I was first stew'ing. This old hotel is so cool, with the ducks in the fountain. I thought if you could get here we could be safe long enough to work out something. Do you know they actually have a thing where they march the ducks in and out of the lobby twice a day?"

I had to admit, this woman was smart. She was taller than Emmett in her high heels. A good dresser too. Creepy eyes, ice blue, like you wouldn't know what she's thinking behind them. I'd probably think twice about crossing her. I was beginning to like her. She'd shown up at my house fully dressed and already packed. She handed me almost twelve thousand dollars, and told me the plan. She'd worked it out driving to my house. I'd told her that she wasn't going along, and she just gave me those eyes and crossed her arms. We were in Memphis before 2 p.m.

We ushered Emmett into one of the elevators. The old black operator recognized Dutch from when we'd checked in and didn't need to ask the floor number. I got the feeling she was used to that sort of thing. We had a big two-bedroom place up on the fourteenth floor. I'd never seen a place like it before. There was an ice bucket and fresh flowers in a vase on a table in the entrance. Dutch breezed in and picked up the telephone while she was still swinging the room key in one hand.

"Room service? Yes, I will need a bottle of that good Tennessee Jack Daniel's whiskey, and some ice-cold Schlitz, a dozen. We'll need three T-bone steaks, yes, medium rare, yes, baked potatoes, yes, and yams, and a couple of side salads. Yes, that's right…no, send the liquor up right away, don't wait for the food, and two packs of Marlboro cigarettes please."

She hung up the receiver and turned to us. We were still standing in the doorway with the door open.

"Emmett, get in the shower, geezus, you stink! I can't believe they let you in the hotel. Dinner will be here when you get done. I packed you a bag; you'll find clothes on the bed."

She looked at me. "Okay, Mick?"

"Okay, Dutch."

The Winds of Change
Emmett

Later I woke up as she climbed into the bed next to me. She started to slide up against me, and I turned to meet her gaze in the darkened room. There was no way to deny that she was naked.

"Well, I can't actually sleep with your dad, now can I?"

I still held her eyes.

"Don't look at me that way. This has been a pretty tough day or two for you. I don't know how to show you how sorry I am about that. I can see how bad you feel—on the inside."

"Dutch?"

"I've never slept with a man before—well, once, but that was a long, bad time ago—so don't make fun of me, Emmett. Please?"

"I don't understand. What do you mean?"

She reached down under the blankets and ran her hand down my lower stomach.

"Emmett, dear Emmett. You're a good man and you work so hard trying to be a bad man. Anyone that can see anything can see that. Why not for one night stop apologizing for giving a shit about it. At least let the good man out and let someone just be nice without having to prove that it doesn't mean anything to you."

Her hand had never stop exploring.

"I like sex, you know, and I like men. I just don't like sex with men. I don't think. At least the ones I've known so far. Please, Emmett, I know you won't hurt me. I know you'd never let that happen?"

Afterward I paused one more time, poised above her, and looked down into her eyes.

"I'm sure, Emmett, you need this…I need this."

Sometime later the nightmare came back. I jerked and fought my way back to the surface, panting in my own sweat. She wrapped me in her arms and threw her leg over me.

"Shhh, Emmett, it's all right, I'm right here."

The Night Train

Friday, I slept until almost noon. I'd missed my delivery rendezvous, more than enough time for more people than just cops to start looking for me. I felt the dread and fear of the situation descend on me before I even opened my eyes. From now on the hounds would be looking for me under every rock, and if they found me, there would be no bullshitting my way out of it.

It had been one of the hardest things I'd ever done last night. While we ate dinner and after a few shots of whiskey, I'd come clean with my Da. I'd told him the entire story and I had done it without trying to fancy it up. I gave the facts, the circumstances, and I gave him the whys and the wherefores. For her part, Dutch had done her best to keep quiet, but by the time I was done there was no color in her cheeks. Da on the other hand never broke stride with his fork, listening but making no comment.

When I'd finished, he poured a couple of fingers of Jack Daniel's into three glasses and passed them around. Without waiting for us he raised his glass and threw it back, then looked me in the eye.

"This is going to be a hard fight to get clear of. We're going to need a plan."

Dutch tried her best and managed half of the whiskey in her

glass before her throat said no more. Between coughs and with tears running down her face from the effort, she wheezed out, "Seriously? You're not going to turn yourself in? Mr. Casey? This is a bad idea—you've got to get him to turn himself in."

"Doesn't sound like that would be a very good idea to me." Mick was miles ahead already. "First, they frame him for armed robbery, and then somehow they don't. Then they fix it so he loses his job and can't find another one. They threaten harm to either his friends or his family if he doesn't play ball. He plays ball, but the game was rigged from the beginning. He's the perfect patsy."

"That's what you got out of this? Seriously?"

"Worse than that. Somebody's on the inside with the cops, pulling the strings. If they take him, he'll go down for the whole deal, and the investigation will be over, no one else gets touched. He's expendable."

"You mean he was set up from the beginning?"

"My bet is that the truck got stopped and searched in Macon, but I'd put serious money on it that what they found was just enough to put Emmett in trouble. I'm guessing that the bulk of the shipment never makes it into any evidence locker, anywhere. Like I said, they've got a patsy with a history, and enough evidence to convict, and the crime disappears as a major news story, because there wasn't enough to warrant a second look."

I looked at Dutch. "That's my take too. The fix was in, somebody's lookin' at a major payday, and somebody's going to take it up the ass. I'm just the excuse to look someplace else."

Dutch finished the whiskey.

"Who do you think is the rat?"

"My bet would be Anthony. He thinks he's the big fish. I don't imagine he likes working for anyone else. It's gonna be almost impossible to explain to whoever put the dough up for that big of a buy if the product just disappears. Madame Nightmare is probably in some pretty deep shit right about now, but Anthony would be in the clear. That's my guess."

"I'd say that sounds about right. What about this Dunn guy? Can you trust him?"

"I'd say you can trust him to follow the bread crumbs, but he's not going to be interested in playing any games, with us or anyone else. He's a straight-ahead policeman, but he's got integrity, so if we can lay the bread crumbs to the right front door, I think he'd take it from there."

"You can't be serious, Emmett, this is too big. These people could try and kill you for the kind of money that's involved." Dutch was not getting into the spirit of the evening at all.

"I'd say that they probably are already thinking that way. He's a loose end that needs to be tied up," Little Mick's lips were in a tight line, "but that door swings both ways, missy."

When I came out of the bedroom, Da was sitting on the sofa watching the noon news on television. There was no sign of Dutch.

"Nothing about it on the news today so far. If they'd have got that much in the sting, you'd think it would be on the front page."

"I'm thinking you might have been right last night. Where's Dutch?"

"Left this morning at daylight. Took a cab to the airport. Didn't have much to say."

"Well, shit."

"You got something you're gonna need to apologize for?"

"The list is endless."

"The lady downstairs told me that the night train for Chicago leaves at 8:20 tonight. We'll have to stay here until then…had to pay for another night though. We can be at Randolph Street Station tomorrow morning, first thing."

It had been a lifetime ago that Little Mick and I had last visited Randolph Street Station together, and things hadn't changed all that much in the meantime between us. Only this time we were going toward the trouble instead of away from it.

"I'm gonna need to get my hands on a good can bat."

"What's a can bat?"

"It's for hittin' cans."

"Cans?"

"Yep, Puerto Ri-Cans, Mexi-Cans, Afri-Cans," he gave me the stink-eye and then he winked, "and this time some good old Ameri-Cans."

"I'm sorry, Da, really I am. If there had been any other way, I wouldn't have called you. I hope you know that?"

"If there had been any other way? I'd like to hope that I was your first choice. I called Charlie this morning. He and Seamus will meet us in Chicago."

Brothers in Arms

Although still painted the trademark brown and orange of the Illinois Central rail cars, they appeared sleek and polished on the outside. To me they had gotten smaller both in appearance and importance. Maybe the seats seemed a little more tattered, the conductor a little less personable and engaging. We'd bought our tickets at the station window and waited until we could hear the engine bell start to toll that it was intending to leave before we rushed out and boarded the last car. We found the seats as far to the back of the train as we could and sat across the aisle from each other, our backs to the bulkhead, our eyes on the forward compartment doors.

As the train began rattling its way out of the switchyard, I looked at the window across from me but watched him in the reflection, just as I once had. There were new lines on his face, and his hair had grayed more to almost silver. He was only forty-five years old, but life is not always measured in years. The last time we'd ridden together, I'd looked into his face and wondered what he thought about in the long silences of his life. Today he'd sat forward, eyes darting about, alert and capable. This was a different man from the laid-back and slow-moving one I witnessed on any other day. He was excited, animated, and ready. It rattled me that although it had been so near, I had never seen it before.

The ride was uneventful. Long, smooth rides followed by intensely long layovers. First in Dyersburg, then Fulton in Kentucky. Once in Illinois, eight more stops beginning in Carbondale and ending at Randolph Street. We had packed enough food and drinks for the trip, warm beer and sandwiches. We left our seats only to piss off of the back of the train. Neither of us dozed at the same time. I was fairly certain that we wouldn't have any trouble at least until we got to the city, but we were both on high alert and it didn't hurt to practice. There was no point in conversation; we'd discussed what we wanted to do and how we would try to do it. We'd never been much for small talk between each other, so I'd settled in for the ride, but an hour into it he broke his silence.

"You know, it's a hard thing. Watching someone die."

I jerked like I'd been shocked with electricity.

"'Scuse me?"

"Watching someone die, right in front of you. Not something you can get used to."

I chewed on that for a full minute. Not only was I not expecting him to talk to me, I really wasn't expecting the choice of topic he'd landed on.

"You mean like a family member or some such?"

"No. Well, yes, that's hard but different. Sometimes those can be a blessing."

He was warming up but true to form, he was choosing his words carefully.

"Watching someone die who wasn't expecting it, wasn't ready for it, that's what I meant."

"Well, really, is anybody ready for it?"

"Some are, but there's only a few of those."

He took a long time filling his pipe and lighting it. His eyes never wavered from looking up the aisle over the few heads that occupied the car with us. Using a match, he puffed it up, then repacked the tobacco down tighter and then lit another match and relit it. Finally, he had it going to his satisfaction and pointed the stem at me.

"This conversation isn't going to get very far if you keep dodging it with clever questions."

He was serious about where he wanted to go with this, so I took a breath and answered honestly.

"Yes, it is, Da. It stays with you."

"So then, you've seen it." He nodded and took another puff on the pipe, took it out, and looked into the bowl like it was the most interesting thing he'd seen in a while. When he spoke again he addressed the pipe bowl. "I'd thought as much. Shows, you know, marks you."

"Not my favorite day, or my favorite memories."

"Mine either."

I looked at him from across the aisle. The pipe was clamped in his teeth now and his jaw muscles were tight. His gaze was directed far up the aisle, but he wasn't focusing on anything in the train car.

"I was a tail gunner you know. B-17s, Flying Fortresses. Tail gunners, they didn't live very long usually. They were tough planes but they weren't bulletproof. Lost some good men, a lot of good men—just not me."

I'd never heard him utter a single word about this. I felt a flush of heat in my face, and my palms immediately began to sweat. If he went where I thought he was going to go, I was suddenly afraid of it.

"Killed a lot of people we did. A lot of people."

"I'm sorry, Da. I've killed some people too."

"I know you did. We killed them with bombs, we fought our way in to do it, and we fought our way back out when we turned and ran. You did it on the ground, with your hands, like your uncle Charlie. It's a hard thing killing—a real hard thing—hard from a distance, harder close up, I imagine."

I looked up the aisle. I couldn't argue with him. It is/was a hard thing.

"They haunt me at night." He took a long pull on the pipe, and there was sadness in his voice. "They come back, all of them, the men and women, and the children—especially the children, the lives we took. They come back at night to accuse me."

I turned my head as slowly as I could. I didn't want to break the spell.

"They can't rest, you know, so they make sure that I can't either."

I decided that this was a conversation that was way overdue.

"It's not fair, you know, Da."

"I heard you last night. The shouting, the nightmare. I heard you." He paused and took another puff, then nodded. "Who makes the decision? Which one dies, which one lives."

I lit a cigarette and looked up the aisle. "I don't understand. I've tried, you know, to understand. I know who I am and what I've done, and somehow, I got to live, but the kid right next to me, a good kid, a smart kid who loves his parents and got straight A's in school, he doesn't get to live. Who decides?"

"There's no fairness in it." His pipe had gone out. "I can't believe that it's just a random selection, like some ugly lottery."

Both of us were filling the back of the train car with smoke as we puffed our anxiety out through the only avenue we had.

"It's not fair that's for sure why he killed Vega and Spencer and didn't kill me. Or why I killed those others. I was right there too, why them, why not me? I don't believe God's got some crazy plan for me to do something that will make sense twenty years from now."

"If that was the case, then you'd be my twenty years later."

Well, shit. I hadn't thought of it that way before. So many times in the past I had wanted to have this conversation with someone, anyone—just not my father.

"Well then, why, Da? Why won't it rest? How is it that I'm still here, and what's his plan? Why do I feel so guilty about it? It twists inside of me, even when I'm not trying to sleep."

"I know."

"It makes me angry, makes me want to look for another fight, Da."

"Thomas calls it the 'darkness,' that evil thing that is inside us all, that makes us fighters—survivors. That thing that we are afraid will wake up and make us monsters."

"I've talked to Thomas about that too. I'm afraid that I'm already the monster, Da."

"No, son, you're not, but just for now, I'm thinking that it's time to wake that thing up. Looks like we got a fight comin'."

At the station we waited until the other passengers had debarked the train and the queue on the walkway outside had slowed to a trickle before we got off the train. To the left of us the switching yard was bathed in the morning sunlight, and to the right the roofed railheads were swathed in shaded twilight.

Both directions looked clear; there was no sign of anyone who might be looking for us that we could see. We opened a space between the two of us, Little Mick with his hands clutching his knapsack and his head on a swivel, me with my bag over my left shoulder and my hat pulled down over my eyes. We adopted a brisk, purposeful gait and headed for the stairs that would take us up to street level.

At the doors to the station proper, a dapper Seamus was leaned back propped against the bricks watching behind us, casually smoking a cigarette, tweed jacket and tie, and his tweed newsboy cap covering his bright red hair, tipped back on his head, the newspaper tucked under his arm seemed perfectly placed. He fell into step behind us. At the foot of the stairs, Charlie sat reading a paper while a shoeshine boy buffed his heavy boots, his heavily muscled upper body making him look top-heavy. By the time we reached street level, he had flanked Seamus.

"Take a cab to the Palmer House. We'll catch up there."

"It's only a few blocks, Seamus."

"Take a cab, we'll be right behind you."

At the Palmer House, Da and I went to the restaurant and gawked at the outrageous prices on the menu while we tried not to look like we were loitering. Five minutes later, Seamus and Charlie came in and walked up.

"Let's go. We were going to stay here but now we can't. Someone came out after you got in the cab and wrote down its number then he hurried back inside. I think he might have dropped a dime. It won't take long for them to find out you came to the Palmer House if they check with the cab company. Seamus' car's parked in the Underground; we're going to need to get out of the city. They wouldn't have missed you either, Mick."

"That's not good then." Mick was a full head shorter than either of the two of them.

"It was all we could do to keep Thomas from coming."

"What? Why'd you tell him about this?" Mick looked ready to take them both on.

"I had to let him know that Lizzy and the kids would be coming to stay for a few days."

"What? Why's Ma going to Madison?" All three of them looked at me for a second. "Oh."

"Man, if that's all the sharper you are, you're gonna need to get some more sleep." Charlie looked a little worried as he rattled the coins in his pockets. "C'mon, let's go, we'll go out through the back just in case."

"Let's go, we'll talk in the car." Seamus was used to being in charge. "We dropped Mary Evelyn at your place, Mick. She'll take them home in the station wagon. Lizzy's in for a rough couple a days, and she's gonna need to be around Thomas."

Seamus' car was just the type of car that you would expect a successful medical doctor to drive. Soft leather that smelled wonderful and enhancements that not only increased the comfort of the ride but also muffled most of the outside road noise. With Seamus at the wheel, Charlie and Da took the backseat. For my part I was grateful that I would be in the passenger seat and facing the windshield instead of these three men of integrity.

As soon as we got on the Eisenhower Expressway and passed under the old U.S. Post Office, Charlie spoke from the backseat.

"Okay, Emmett, start from the beginning and don't leave anything out."

I tried to start at the beginning, but Seamus stopped me.

"It started way long before that, Emmett; start again, and hold the bullshit."

I went back in my mind and thought about it. It had started before that. It started so long ago that I couldn't replay the whole thing. It had started back with my behavior in school, and in the Army; it had started before the first time I was detained by the police as an eight-year-old boy, but I knew that's not what they wanted to hear. So, I started where the past and present started to fuck with my future. It had started when my deeply instilled Catholic sense of guilt had finally found the justification to begin my own personal route to self-destruction. It started when another man took my place and died instead of me. It started when I killed a man.

I used that as the beginning point, and I talked to the windshield. I talked about the guilt and the shame, and then I admitted for the first time that, at the same time, the joyful rage that I'd experienced scared me half to death. I talked about the simmering anger I felt for being in that situation in the first place and how I kept it deep inside of me. I talked about my inability to reconcile my anger, guilt, and shame where there was no forgiveness, or redemption, and then I talked about how I wanted to die so I wouldn't be angry or sad or incorrigible anymore.

When I was finished I was exhausted. I hadn't realized that I was leaning hard into the seat belt, and I slumped back into the leather upholstery. After an extended silence, Charlie spoke up.

"Well, that's all well and good, but now if you don't mind, Emmett." He blew a lungful of smoke into the front seat. "I think by start at the beginning Seamus meant, what are we doing in this car, and where are we going from here."

Da started. He gave the background of the late-night call from Dutch. He filled them in on who she was and what her involvement was. He gave her all the credit, not taking any for himself, and he told about the race to Memphis, and the rendezvous at the Peabody Hotel. He told it in under a minute and only in a matter-of-fact tone.

"So, this is the girl that you're pokin' these days?"

"Geezus, Charlie! Focus, for Christ's sake." Seamus didn't want any diversions to muddy the water.

Then it was my turn. I couldn't put myself in the current situation without giving them the reason for it, so I began with my late-night activities when sleep wouldn't come and my slide into my questionable courier forays, and went on from there. Whenever I tried to shave the edges of my guilt off a little, Seamus would stop me with a look, and I would retrace my steps. By the time I finished the whole sordid tale with the ride I'd gotten from Maybelle's son, Sammy, into Memphis, we were parked in front of a motel well out of the city and at the distant edges of the western suburbs.

"Well, that'll pull the rag off the bush for sure." Charlie had a gift of understatement even if most of his musings didn't make sense to anyone but himself.

Seamus tipped the rearview mirror down and looked into the backseat.

"Well, what do you know? We got ourselves an honest-to-god Casey on our hands here, eh, Mick?"

"I don't act in any way like this dumb shit acts."

"Oh really? Guess we won't be needing to go up north deer hunting anymore then."

“This isn’t the same thing. This is honest-to-god life and death, this is.”

“Let me get us a couple of rooms. Geezus, this is a god-forsaken hole-in-the-wall. Then we’ll get some food. Emmett, would you object too much if I gave you something to sleep? I think we’re going to need you hitting on all eight cylinders pretty soon.”

Where to from here?

When I woke up the room was empty and it was late afternoon. Darkness had fallen. At first, the foreign surroundings were confusing and I was uncertain where I was and groggy from whatever it was Seamus had given me. I stumbled to the window and peeked out through the drapes. Outside in the parking lot Seamus' car was nosed up to the curb right outside. It didn't help me feel any better that it was still here. I sat down on the edge of the bed while I waited for sanity and consciousness to merge. For some reason the damp, musty air of the seedy motel room made my situation seem ten times worse than it had earlier. I hated myself for getting my father involved and even more for bringing my two uncles into it as well. The thought of putting my boots on and sneaking away occurred to me but only in a fleeting way because in all honesty to myself, I really needed them. Finally, I stood up and knocked on the connecting door to the next room and then turned the knob.

The three of them were lounging around the room. Charlie and Mick in their sleeveless T-shirts, Seamus with his sleeves rolled to the elbow, pipe in hand. Charlie was lying on the bed, Seamus was sitting in the lone chair next to the tiny table that served as a desk in the room, and my father sat on the foot of the other bed. They were doing their best to watch a black-and-white television with a terrible picture that between static was airing a college football game. I walked around between the beds and sat down behind Da, too sleep stupid to think of anything else.

None of them looked up, but Charlie waved his hand at the little table where a half-full fifth of Jameson sat. On the floor under the table was an ice chest with several bottle necks protruding up out of a bed of shaved ice.

"Dinner is served."

Seamus began.

"You'll need to bunk here for a bit. We're going out, to try and get some information. I'd like to know how 'hot' you are, and who thinks so. Where's the best place to look?"

I took a swallow straight out of the bottle. The Jameson burned all the way down, but I felt the heat spread into my brain, and my mind started to become slightly more functional. I'd had almost three days of trying to figure out what I didn't know and what I needed to know. I'd run the different scenarios through different pursuits and outcomes, and still didn't know where to start. I had a strong idea of why it had happened and I had a good feel for who the players might have been, but how to resolve them to an outcome that helped me had not yet become clear.

"If I was free to move around, I'd try and find Dwight Thomas. He's on the street and his business is knowing what goes down. He deals a little, but mostly he sells information. If this has come back as far as him though, he'll be layin' low. I don't know where I'd look first beyond him."

"What about that shooting gallery where you first met these guys?"

"I don't know about that one—they might be still in business, or they may have shut it down by now. I don't know who actually ran that gig, maybe Anthony, maybe Madame, I think I heard her last name was something like DuBois, maybe the mob. If they're looking for me, that's not a good place to be asking questions, would be my guess."

Charlie's eyes never left the television screen. "What about the nigger then?"

"Geez, Charlie, we don't call them niggers anymore. Christ, you spend too much time on that farm. You gotta get out more." I'd never heard my Da say anything even remotely close to such an informed statement.

"Okay then! What about him?"

"Dwight's always a little paranoid. If you guys start asking around, he's not going to surface."

I finished another long swallow of Jameson and started working down a bottle of beer. The football game was impossible to concentrate on.

There was a sudden subtle knock on the door, two knocks, a pause, and two more.

Seamus jumped to his feet and positioned himself behind the door. Mick pulled his big Colt revolver out from under the edge of the bed and stood next to him against the wall. Charlie was off the bed and shouldered me up and into the bathroom. Shutting the door, he leaned against the inside of it, a .45 automatic in his hand. He put his finger to his lips. "Shhh."

I heard the outside door open, and then there was a rustle of activity, then silence. I held my breath.

"It's okay, Charlie." Da's voice was right outside the bathroom door.

Charlie snapped the safety on the .45, and opened the door. On the other side stood Kate.

"Kate?! Oh my God! What are you doing here!?!"

Her answer was to step forward and slap me across the face as hard as she'd ever hit me in my life. Then she took another step and wrapped her arms around me and put her head on my chest.

"Emmett, how could I not be here?"

She smelled like baby shampoo and flowers, and I felt the genuine and embarrassing warmth of her. The sweetness of her presence stirred something deep in my guts, and I felt honest tears spring into my eyes. I looked over her head into the room where the men all stood with looks of concern and embarrassment on their faces.

"Why'd you call Kate? She can't be involved in any of this! Whose idea was this?"

"I called her." Da was unapologetic. "She needed to know what was going on; by now she's been talking to your mother, or Thomas. I needed to let her know that we're okay and that you're still stupid as always."

"But why's she here? Oh my god, this is too much! Kate, you can't be here!" I pushed her away and put my hands on her shoulders. In truth, I didn't want to let her go completely. "These guys, well, shit…this is too much. Kate, you've got to go. What's Jim got to say about this?"

"Jim's okay; he's watching the boys. He's not a Casey, Emmett, but he gets it. Besides, all I did was do a little shopping and brought you some clean outfits and some hot food. That's not really doing anything."

I looked a hard scowl at Da, and he gave me an equally hard look back.

Charlie walked to the little table in the room and started to paw through the large picnic-type basket now sitting on it. “Saints be praised, you brought one of your pies, Kate! And fried chicken, and I smell fresh bread! Damned if I’m not hungry enough to eat the ass out of a skunk.”

Seamus walked up and looked over his shoulder.

“Fresh bread? Kate, you are an angel from heaven.” He reached in and pulled out a drumstick. “Let’s get some food in our bellies and have a little chat. Then we’ll get Kate out of here. Emmett, you go change out of those clothes, take a shower, if there’s any hot water in the god-forsaken excuse for a motel room, and see if Kate got the sizes right. We’ll save you something to eat if you hurry. That stuff you’re wearing has had just about enough of you.” Seamus was all business, as usual.

Thankfully there had been hot water, and plenty of it. The tiny bar of motel soap was long gone before the water started to cool off—before I’d finished my internal argument. Physically comforted but emotionally disturbed, I was ashamed for involving my family. I couldn’t think of anything else that I could have done. I hadn’t taken the next logical step of where I could take the situation from here, and I couldn’t think of a way to go forward on my own. The chance that my uncles and father would just step away was nonexistent and the risks that they faced through their involvement could be devastating. Through it all, a cloud of fear and dread colored my thoughts. I knew that there were now some people who would find my continued existence inconvenient.

I had already been in situations where my life was in danger. At those times, the choice had been clear, and the circumstance dictated my response. In a fight, defend yourself. I had been lucky enough to do just that, but there had been only one enemy. This time, the thought that someone would want to kill me because it was just business was unsettling and frightened me in an entirely different way.

The new blue jeans and shirt fit perfectly—thank you, Kate. I cut the tags off and put on my boots. I was ready to do something, but didn't know what the something would be. Instead I sat on the side of the bed and stared at the wall. Well, shit.

The other room had been quiet for a long time. I couldn't delay going back in any longer. Now that I was clean and dressed in new clothes, my guilt was turning to shame as I considered the sacrifice the ones in the next room were willing to make on my behalf. I opened the door and went in. No one greeted me.

I sat on the side of the bed and ate directly out of Kate's food basket. She had already gone. The football game had either ended or the three men had given up on the god-forsaken television because the room was silent. A second bottle of Jameson had appeared, and the three sat each with a bottle of beer in one hand and a cigarette in the other, two staring at different walls, and Charlie lying flat on his back, staring at the ceiling.

Seamus

"I was at a battalion aid station," Seamus broke the silence, "7th Army, Operation Overlord. The army had pushed to the Vosges Mountains but stalled there. We couldn't get supplies fast enough, overextended. The Germans were dug in and reinforced. Their supply lines were probably better than ours, shorter too. They pushed back—hard. It was September or October; not sure I remember which—or knew even. The casualties were coming in so fast that we kept needing to move closer and closer to the action. Like I said, there weren't many supplies, and we were working around the clock; we were sleeping standing up. We were so close to the action that we could feel the concussion from the shells.

"One morning the Germans mounted a counterattack and started shelling. The aid station took a couple of direct hits. One of the tents that we were holding the wounded in was taken out in the blink of an eye, and all the souls in it were lost. It was pandemonium; our boys were falling back. The retreat came directly across our bivouac, and the bullets were flying right in through the tent canvas. There was smoke everywhere; one of the ambulance jeeps was burning. The aid station is supposed to be protected by the Geneva Convention, as a non-combatant, but there was so much confusion, smoke, and noise that I couldn't be sure the men would be safe.

"We had a couple of squads of soldiers that were detailed to us. They drove the ambulances and managed the heavy lifting, but they were soldiers and I ordered them to take their weapons and form a fire line on the east side of the area—they immediately took fire. I was busy, moving the wounded men that we had from cots to stretchers on the ground to help them avoid as much of the incoming as possible. Some of them started crawling toward the pile where we'd stashed their weapons when they came in so they could join back in the fight.

One of them started to get up even though he'd been badly wounded in the legs. I was busy with someone else and I ordered him to stay put. When I looked back at him, he was lying down on his side on his cot. He'd been shot in the head. His name was James. He was from Cedar Rapids, Iowa."

He paused and pulled out his tobacco pouch and packed it carefully, then struck a wooden match down the wall next to him and puffed it to life. He took a long pull from the bottle of beer in his hand and continued.

"That's when I got hit—the first time."

He reached for the whiskey bottle and took a good swallow.

"It was a flesh wound, as they say, passed through my arm halfway between my elbow and shoulder. Bled pretty hard, but I was able to tie it off and went back to business. Our perimeter guards were pushed back and surrounded the tent we were working in. We weren't supposed to be fighters; we were non-combatants, so ammunition and weapons were in short supply. I had my service piece but never wore it because it was too heavy, and I thought it was a pain in my ass anyway.

I knew where it was though, and once the boys were as safe as they could be, I fetched it out of my footlocker and went to see about helping the boys on the fire line. I felt I owed it to those wounded boys.

"One of the Army officers that was trying to manage the retreat came through and saw our situation. He rallied his boys and told them to dig in and fight. We had sandbagged some, but like I said, we were constantly moving, so it wasn't much. We took cover where we could. The officer told us to only shoot at targets we could see in order to preserve ammunition. By noon, we could see plenty and we were taking heavy casualties. I was working like I'd never worked before in my entire life. But the line held, and we held them at bay for the entire morning and into the afternoon.

VII Army reinforcements came up from behind, and the fight turned in our favor for a while. They slowly advanced away from our encampment, and although they were still close and the gunfire was intense, we had a moment. I rallied my men and sent them to care for the wounded. I grabbed a medic kit and headed forward with them. The air was cold and a light rain had started to fall; if we didn't get to them right away, the hypothermia would take them.

"There were plenty of wounded. Most of ours were gathered near the tents, so I wasn't surprised when we came upon three German soldiers. One was already dead, but the other two seemed to be breathing. I called for one of the medics to check one of them, and I knelt down to check on the other. Something moved in my peripheral vision, and I glanced over at the other soldier just as he reached up and grabbed the front of the medic's shirt and pulled him down close and stabbed him in the belly with a knife.

"I couldn't save him; he bled to death in a matter of moments. He was a medic with a red cross armband and on his helmet, but he died just like any other man."

He stopped and looked at his pipe, which had gone out. He looked at it like it had betrayed him, then set it down on the table.

"I jumped to my feet and stood over the German soldier who had done such a cowardly thing and pulled my service pistol out. Until then I had not fired it, but I snapped off the safety. When he saw my weapon, he went white and said, '*Nein, bitte, nein! Meine arme mutter*.' No, please, no. My poor mother. I shot him right between the eyes.

"I turned back to the second soldier, and that's when God's vengeance for my act was swift. He shot me just as I turned toward him. I was still shooting him when I blacked out. I will burn in the fires of hell for all eternity—as well I should."

My shower had only been ten minutes ago, but I was bathed in sweat. Without my noticing Charlie had sat up and was sitting on the edge of the bed behind my father. Da was clenching and unclenching his fists. He got up and went to the table and took the whiskey bottle and took a long drink, then handed it to Seamus and put his hand on his shoulder.

"Show him."

Seamus stood and unbuttoned his shirt and shrugged out of it. His upper right arm was wasted with no visible muscle, and there was a ragged hole in the middle of it. Just below his last rib on the left side was a dimple that I could have put my middle finger into. The area around it was discolored and blackened. I looked a question at him and he said, "Powder burns, from the muzzle blast. He was close."

I couldn't speak because there was too much to say, and no words could say them. In the matter of these ten minutes in this crappy, cold, and damp motel room, my vision of this stalwart pillar of our family had changed completely. Seamus had walked into the darkness.

"Charlie? Your turn." Seamus was embarrassed by the attention and wanted to redirect it.

Charlie

Charlie got up and walked to the table and picked up the whiskey bottle.

"Slainte."

"Slainte," we all said in unison.

He went back to the bedside but took the bottle with him. He rifled through his cigarette pack and fished one out, then lit it with the Zippo lighter from his pocket. He took a long drag and blew the smoke out. When he spoke, he talked to the wall above the headboard.

"Well, I wasn't some glamour boy hospital doc. I was just a grunt soldier, just like a hundred thousand other grunts. We walked from Anzio to the Rhine, and there wasn't an inch of it that we didn't pay for. You know me though, I'm a big guy and so I got pretty tired of being asked to carry everyone else's shit, so I started loading myself down with my own ammunition and grenades and such so there wasn't any room for nothin' else. You know, so that way if I got pinned down somewhere, I'd be prepared.

"Well, the rifle they give you, it's a good rifle and all, but now that BAR, that was a rifle. There's a lot to be said for semiautomatic when you need it, so's first chance I got I upgraded. The guy who'd had it first didn't need it anymore, you know what I mean. Well, that went pretty good for a while, but then

I got a hankering for one of them Springfield '03s, with the scope on 'em. For the sharpshooters, first chance I got I picked one of them up so then I had that BAR and I was also carryin' the Springfield. That Springfield, geez, you could pound nails with that thing from a hundred yards. It was accurate as hell, had a five-cartridge magazine too. I hated to let that BAR go, but the two of 'em were just too much to tote together.

"Pretty soon, I'm the company sharpshooter, you know, the sniper. I'm moving pretty far forward from the advance, hunkerin' down, and my job is to shoot what I can see. It's war, you know, all's fair in love and war, they say. Well, tell that to your friend who just gave himself away by lighting his cigarette. I was good, I was damn good."

He stubbed out the cigarette he'd been smoking and lit another one. Once he blew out the smoke in a huff, he continued.

"Anyway, so one rainy morning I got my head down and I'm inching forward, checking the wind, lookin' around to just see what I can see, and I must've moved right past their sentries, because when I do get a good view, I'm inside of a hundred yards of where they've set up. A tank company, Panzers, thank god, not Tigers anyway, but they're moving around and running up the engines, and smokin' and jokin'. It's too good to be true, and it's a nightmare all at the same time. I've got my pick of targets, but if I take one there's no escape.

Just the same, my guys are just over the hill behind me, and if they come up against a company of Panzers, it ain't gonna end well, you know. So, I take my Springfield out from under my coat, cuz it's been raining all morning, windy too, and I start looking for a good shot. Right away I see an officer standing in the turret of one of the tanks, giving directions. It was a good shot. He dropped right down into the tank.

"I didn't wait to see what the response was. I started to move back and to my right. I don't know if they saw my muzzle flash or just got lucky, but the shooting started right up and they really focused on where I'd been. I was moving as quick as I could, but I had to be quiet and the cover wasn't the best, so most of what I was doing was rolling and crawling. Then one of the tank guns went off and it was close. I took a couple of fragments, but I couldn't check to see how bad. I was really scrambling.

"I got up against a downed log and covered up with leaves, everything but my face, and tried to wait it out. I could feel that I was bleeding. Pretty soon the shooting stopped, and then the hunt really began. I couldn't see them, but I could feel them getting closer. They were looking for me—hunting."

Charlie got up and started to pace the room, waving his cigarette while he collected his thoughts. He stopped at the whiskey bottle and took a long pull. Eventually, he ended up back where he'd started and sat back down. It was a while before he began again.

"I was pretty sure I was camouflaged by the leaves. The only thing I'd left uncovered were my eyes, but I could only look in one direction without turning my head, so I remained still. My side started to hurt and I felt like I couldn't take a full breath, but I stayed still. All that morning I never moved while they hunted for me, but they didn't find me. That is until they did.

"I'd started to think I was in the clear when I heard footsteps. They were close and coming closer. All of a sudden, a big black boot comes down right next to my face. The soldier had stepped over the log I was up against. The other boot followed, and then stopped. He gave a sigh and then sat down on the log. His rifle butt came down next to the left boot as he leaned it up against the log, taking a break. There was no way he'd miss me if he sat there for another minute."

Charlie stopped for full minute.

"I decided that it was now or never. As fast as I could manage after lying there so long, I pulled my bayonet out and stabbed him in the foot. I was lucky, I caught him by surprise. Before he could yell, I was up and shoved the bayonet under his chin as hard as I could. I didn't stop until it came out the top of his head.

"I looked around and there were others coming. Not close yet but getting nearer, so I hopped over the log and set up my spot. I figured I was a dead man—so I made up my mind not to die alone."

The room was dead quiet.

"I pulled out my spare magazines and set them next to me. After that I picked my targets as soon as they moved. They weren't as good a shot as I was, and the Springfield was a hell of an equalizer. All the hullabaloo got my guys' attention, and they came up behind me. Pretty soon, they gave me enough cover and I skedaddled. Spent the next two weeks back in a field hospital, smoking cigarettes and drinking coffee."

"How many, Charlie?" Seamus almost whispered it.

"That day? Sixteen. May God forgive me."

"Jesus...!" I couldn't help myself. I said it before it occurred to me that I shouldn't.

No one spoke for a long time after that.

The phone on the bedside table rang. The claxon sound electrified us all back to reality as we jumped in unison. Charlie picked it up on the second ring.

"Yes."

He snapped his fingers at Seamus and pointed at his pocket. Seamus lifted out his pen and tossed it to him.

"Yes, I'm ready." He listened for a few seconds. "Yep. Yep." This time he listened for almost a minute while he wrote on the bedside pad. "No, but Mick will. Okay. Thanks."

He cradled the receiver and looked up.

"Time to go. Emmett, you stay here. We'll be back."

All three were moving and geared up in a matter of seconds and whisked out the door. I hadn't even had the presence of mind to protest. The dank room was immediately and oppressively quiet. I looked over at the whiskey bottle where Charlie had left it on the nightstand, but it didn't seem like a good idea to me. After rummaging through the food basket one last time, I ate the half of the pumpkin pie that Kate had baked and was still left over, then lay down on the bed and stared at the ceiling. What the fuck was I supposed to do now, I thought. When in doubt, eat when you can, sleep when you can. I went back into the other room, lay down on the bed, and went to sleep.

Time for Some Intel

I woke up when I heard the key fumbling in the lock of the door of the other room. I hadn't shut the intervening one, and I quickly jumped up and shut it, turning the lock. I plastered my ear to the door, but all I could hear was people moving into the room, the key dropping onto the table, and then;

"Oh, man! Hey, man, please, please, don't kill me, man! Don't cut my nuts off. Man, I'm beggin' ya!"

I knew the voice but it took a minute before I placed it. Opening the door, I stepped into the room. Dwight Thomas was sitting in the chair that Seamus had previously occupied. He was fully decked out in a tan polyester leisure suit and paisley print shirt with enormous collar tabs. Big chunky shoes completed the ensemble. Wherever they had found him, he had been ready to boogie dance the night away, that was for sure.

Charlie was behind him with his big hands pressing down on his shoulders. Da stood in front of him with his big Colt pointed right at his chest. Seamus was lighting his pipe. Dwight's eyes got as big as pumpkins when he finally recognized who I was. For Dwight, this particular evening had gone from probably okay to pretty awful, and the sight of me just about made him pass out.

"What the fuck!?! How'd you find him so quick?" I couldn't

believe my eyes.

"Hey, Hole, what the fuck, man, you're hot as a pistol. I can't talk to you. Oh fuck! It's you, I can't fuckin' believe it. How are you still walkin' around?"

I looked at Dwight, then looked at Seamus. He smiled and took a pull on his pipe while he looked at Dwight.

"We didn't find him, Emmett. Kate did. As soon as this raggedy piece of shit heard about some red-headed Irish married woman asking for him, he showed up in no time. Charlie is an excellent persuader."

"He ain't no kind of that. The son of a bitch nearly broke my arm! That red-headed bitch punched me in the face!"

"Listen, Mr. Thomas, is it? We need to ask you some questions, but first, just so you know where you stand right now. That pretty girl you were sniffing after is my niece, and she is this man's niece too. More importantly, she is this man's daughter, and this idiot's sister. I would hate to imagine what you might have had in mind for such a nice young lady.

"As it happens, I am also a licensed surgeon, so removing your testicles would be a fairly routine procedure for me. I suspect it would improve the culture wherever you are after that. That being said, now that you understand our mood, may we ask you some questions?"

"You can righteously go fuck yourself! Motherfucker!"

"Listen, Dwight," I decided that maybe a different tack might work better, "I'm pretty screwed right now. There's no way to clear this mess up if I don't try and get to the bottom of it myself. I don't know where to look," and I added, "I don't know who the bad guys are either."

"They're all bad, Hole, man, I told you to watch your ass.

I told you it stank to hell and back, but no, now you're in the shit! I told you, man!" He spread his hands in a pleading gesture. "I told you."

He shrugged his shoulders out from under Charlie's big hands.

"Everybody's lookin' for you, man. Some mean motherfuckers a couple of 'em. And cops, a couple of them too. They all looked me up, can't hide from those people; if you do, when they find you, then they don't feel like just askin' questions anymore. If you catch my drift."

"Cops?"

"Yeah, they were cops—don't matter how they dress, cops are cops."

"What'd they look like, the cops?"

"One guy, like he just come out of the showroom, wasn't the nicest cop I've ever talked to. But the other guy, geezus, he was like walking death or something, dark-like, you know, he didn't say nothin' at all, just stood there."

"Face like an eagle?"

"Yeah, sharp edges all around. Yeah, you run into him before?"

"I've had the pleasure. What about the others?"

"Two of 'em, big, asking if I'd seen you or heard from you. They weren't interested in small talk, but let me know how the bear goes through the buckwheat for sure. They told me that if I hear from you, that I'm supposed to tell you to find some guy named Willy. Said you know where to look. Told me not to even think about not telling them if I seen you."

"Shit!"

"Shit what?" Da looked over his shoulder at me.

"Fucking Willy, a professional son of a bitch if there ever was one. If he's looking for me, it means he's got an assignment, and it's probably me. Double-shit!"

"You know where he is?"

"Pretty sure, but it'll be a shitfest."

"Well then, we best go have a chat with this Willy guy. Sooner the better." Da was all business.

"Okay, Mr. Thomas," Seamus tapped his pipe out against his palm and dropped the ash in the wastebasket, "we'll drop you off where we picked you up. Thank you by the way for your help, but perhaps it would be best if you didn't mention this little visit. Hmm?"

"That's it? Geezus, Hole, I thought you were a one-of-a-kind motherfucker, but holy shit, you come from a whole line of 'em."

"You can still ride back in the trunk if you like," Charlie added in a grim voice.

Dwight cranked his head around and looked up at him. Charlie's face wasn't a friendly one.

"No, man, I meant it as a sorta compliment, sorry, man. Listen, Hole, when you get there—if you get there, I'm s'posed to tell you the password is Diego. They may be lookin' for you, but I don't think they'd recognize you with the new look and all."

Squad of Brothers

This time Charlie and I switched places. With me behind Seamus I could direct but still be inconspicuous. Once in the city we made a right off of Fullerton south onto Central Park, and three blocks later we passed the brownstone on the left. The streetlight near the alley entrance was out. In the half-light of the one up at the corner of Lyndale, I could make out the figure standing just inside the doorway as we drove past. We didn't slow down but instead went down another block and circled back. Turning north one block east on Drake, Seamus slowed enough at the end of the alley for Charlie and Da to get out. Once they were out, we made a left onto Belden and were lucky enough to find an empty parking spot halfway down the block.

"You stay back of me a good fifty, sixty steps, Emmett."

Seamus got out and headed off back to the brownstone apartment building. When he disappeared around the corner, I got out of the car and locked it. As soon as Seamus was out of sight, my blood pressure started to ramp up and I could feel it pumping in my throat. I knew I couldn't hurry, but I hated not being able to see him. Instead I compromised and hurried to the corner but hung back there and peeked around it.

It was after 1 a.m., and there were no other pedestrians that I could see. The windows of the small homes across

Central Park were all dark as people slept their nights away like they should. In spite of the empty sidewalk and the late hour, Seamus' silhouette took its time as it approached the alley, walking with a slight reel. At one point he staggered off the sidewalk, the perfect imitation of a middle-aged fellow who had stayed at the pub a little too long. Righting himself he continued but then stopped and fished in his jacket for a cigarette. As he strolled on he made several attempts to light it as he walked, burning one match after another, throwing each one away in disgust when it failed to do the job. At the alley, he stepped into the dark opening for a moment and struck a match that finally worked, took a long pull, looked up at the sky, then up the alley, and then stepped back up onto the sidewalk and continued.

When he got to the apartment doorway, he seemed to recoil in surprise that there was someone there, then turned toward the man standing there. The silhouette of his hand reached out as if in a greeting; then with a sudden burst of movement, there were two silhouettes on the sidewalk as one was swung in a wide arc and collided with the brick wall of the apartment. Before he could begin to slump to the ground, Seamus closed on him, and the sound of a fist on flesh carried loudly to my ears, twice. I was moving toward them before he hit the ground. By the time I walked the half block, Seamus was moving the unconscious man into the entry and examining him with a small penlight from his pocket.

"No skull fracture, hmm, but when he regains consciousness, he's not going to be any good to anyone for a few days."

I was a little shaken by the efficiency that I'd just seen on display and the contained savagery in my uncle, who I'd never even seen strike his children.

"Okay, Emmett, your turn. I'm the new door guard."

Like the last time the front door of the apartment stood slightly ajar, but unlike the first time the rooms were empty. All of the scattered mattresses were empty of clientele, and only the pervasive odors of urine and sweat hung in the air as a memory of their visits. The subdued lighting that had been on previously was gone; instead the rooms were dark with dim light entering from the outside through the windows to light my way. I moved back in the apartment through memory and feel. In the hallway the floor was lit by the light that appeared from under the doorway at the end. So far, I hadn't made a sound and hadn't heard one. When I reached the door, I slowly took a deep breath and let it out silently. I loosened my knife in the scabbard and listened for anything or anyone on the other side. I put my hand on the knob and slowly started to turn it.

Suddenly there was the sound of an enormous fart from the other side of the door, followed by a deeply satisfied "Ahh…"

I shoved the door open hard, slamming it against the wall behind it, and stepped into the room. I wasn't surprised to see Willy sitting at the table. I *was* surprised to see William. Willy was in the middle of finishing a large take-out pizza that he was eating out of the delivery box, and he rocked back in surprise. His .45 was lying on the table but under the raised lid of the box. Apparently, he needed the extra room in his belt that it was taking up after the pizza. The gun was on my side of the table, but I left it there for a moment and watched his eyes. It took a moment but then he made a quick glance at the box lid.

"I don't think you're as fast as I am, Willy. Wanna try and see?" I lifted my knife out and held it nice and loose in my hand up against my leg.

He opted for negotiation. His beady eyes looked like they were trying to think.

"I don't have your cut. You have to get that from the boss."

I swept up the automatic and snapped off the safety and pointed it at his forehead as his hands came up to shoulder level. I took a look at William.

William was sitting against the other wall, leaning against the rattling refrigerator in a pool of blood. His massive neck had been cut from ear to ear, and he still had a look of surprise on his face. I felt my rage rise up in my throat as the bile choked me. To have come all this way and survived countless trials, he had not deserved this.

As I turned my focus back on to Willy, the back door burst in with an explosion of noise and splinters as the deadbolt tore its way through the door frame and the door slammed into the wall of the kitchen. In an instant, Charlie and Da were in the room. Da's revolver was already out and he sidled up to me and took over covering Willy. With his spare hand he reached over and chucked me in the shoulder with his fist. No other words were necessary.

"Charlie, can you go up front and get Seamus? I don't think he can do anything, but I want him to have a look."

Charlie looked at William, then at fat Willy and went down the hallway. Within seconds they were both back in the room.

"We locked the front door and bolted it. No more visitors tonight."

Seamus was a quick study. He grabbed the pizza box off the table and dumped the remaining pizza crusts in Willy's lap, turned it over, and laid it on the floor next to William. Carefully avoiding the pool of blood, he stepped onto the cardboard and squatted next to the dead man.

"Exsanguinated, he bled out, but he was probably dead almost instantly. Took a while for his heart to stop. Carotid shock, possibly an air embolus to the brain. Been dead less than an hour. Razor cut, from behind, too sharp and deep for a knife."

He stood up and turned back to the room.

"Poor bastard."

Charlie produced a roll of duct tape and proceeded to wrap Willy into the kitchenette chair. When his chest was secure he taped both ankles to the legs of the chair, but left his hands and arms free. Up to this point Willy had still held some cards in his hand, but with the duct tape being applied, his face changed to one of apprehension. The sweat had started to run down his fat face, and I could smell him above the copper odor of the blood.

"I don't have to ask if you did this, you miserable piece of shit," I said.

Willy smiled up at me and opted for bravado. "He was a loose end, just like you."

"Why didn't you just pay him and send him on his way?"

"Wow, I gotta say, Hole," there wasn't even a hint of respect in his voice when he said my name, "you impressed the shit outta me; they'd never have gotten through those inspection points without you. That must've been a true performance. All that but still not all that smart."

"This guy was loyal; he wasn't a fucking loose end. Just some piece of garbage that you throw away."

"Just like you? Tell me you're here with your little posse so that you can tell me you're still on the team."

"I'm here because you made it so that I had to be."

He smiled and folded his arms and belched.

"What are you gonna do? Torture me?"

"I just want the story, and the name of the person that I need to talk to next."

"You're fucking crazy, Hole. You're just small change—nobody the fuck cares what you want."

"I am not crazy, Willy, I'm just goal-oriented, and I don't fucking care what you think. I need to know, and I think you're proud enough of who you think you are, so you're gonna want to tell me all about how smart you think you are."

"Go fuck yourself."

"That's a distinct possibility, but maybe later. How about it?"

"I ain't gonna tell you nothin', asswipe. I give two shits what you and these old fuckers think you can do." His face was smug, but sweat was running out of his scalp and down his forehead.

Seamus spoke up.

"Hold on a minute. I think I've got just what we need out in the trunk. I'll be right back."

He went out through the shattered kitchen door, and Charlie stepped over and leaned against it to hold it shut. The space in the room was reduced by almost half in order to avoid stepping in William's pool of blood. I leaned against the wall, ironically where I had the first time I had visited. Da hunkered down into a squat and patted his pockets, then turned to me and said, "Gotta smoke?"

He'd never asked me for a cigarette before. I was surprised

for a minute, then pulled out a Marlboro, and since he was still holding the big Colt, I lit it and passed it down to him. Willy couldn't help but notice that we were not nervous or fidgety, so he started. He already couldn't sweat any more than he already was.

"So what's he gonna get outta the trunk? A tire iron?"

"My uncle is a doctor, a surgeon actually, and a good one. He's much too refined and intelligent to use a tire iron. I can't wait to see what he brings back."

"Me neither." Charlie sounded excited about the prospects.

"So, Hole, I gotta know, how'd you get clear of the bust at the truck stop. You didn't just walk away from there, couldn't have—there was probably an APB out within fifteen minutes. Your fingerprints had to be all over the inside of that U-Haul, but here you are. How the fuck does that happen. Shit, you shouldn't even be a loose end; you shoulda been wrapped up in Georgia." He licked his lips, and after looking up at Charlie one more time, "C'mon, spill."

"As a matter of fact, I did just walk away, and by the way, I never took my gloves off the entire time I was anywhere near that truck. So, unless they catch up with Charles, and I trust him to hold his peace, or you, they shouldn't be looking for me." I gave him my best hard look. "That makes you *my* loose end."

Willy hadn't considered that angle until just then, and it showed in his face.

We didn't have to wait very long to find out. In less than ten minutes a tap on the door signaled Seamus' return, and Charlie stepped back from the door. Seamus entered along with a breath of fresh air from the outside and strode up to

Willy. Reaching into his inside jacket pocket, he pulled out a small hypodermic syringe and held it up to the light. The syringe appeared to be filled with a light yellowish fluid.

"Charlie, would you hold his arms still for me?"

"What? You gonna inject me with truth serum? I ain't gonna tell you nothin', so you're wastin' your time."

"Truth serum? You mean sodium pentothal? No sir, that stuff is really hard to get hold of, and illegal. Besides, I'm fairly certain that you can't tell the difference between truth and a lie, so it would be a waste as you say."

He pulled the protective tip off the needle and pushed the plunger until a small drop appeared at the end of the needle.

"So then what's that shit then?"

"Battery acid. That's why I was gone so long, had to draw it off the car battery."

"You shittin' me!"

I had to admit, I was surprised myself.

"No, sir. When this is injected into the body, it causes incredible pain. Sets the nerves on fire. Death is within an hour or so, but it can be the worst hour in a person's entire life. The trick, you see, is to inject just the tiniest amount so that you can watch the fun for as long as possible. If you stop before it's too late, sometimes the person can survive, but it takes a steady hand." He nodded at Charlie, who swung Willy's chair ninety degrees. With his large hands he gripped Willy by the forearms and pressed them down onto the table. The cords in Willy's fat neck appeared as he began to struggle against him.

"Hold still now, fucker, you don't want the doctor here to miss, do ya?"

"You guys are fuckin' nuts! I don't know what you want."

"I want to know who's pulling the strings, and I want to know who's in and who's out." I spoke from the corner.

"You're out, that's for fucking sure. I told Anthony you were gonna be a pain in our ass. You're just a fuckin' smartass who's gotten lucky so far."

"So, because I'm too smart, I'm not lying over there next to William. Score one for me." From my vantage point behind him, I saw my father nod his head. "Since it won't do me any good one way or the other, how 'bout I tell you what I think is going on, and then you just tell me if I'm right? How 'bout that? That way you didn't really tell me anything at all."

"Go fuck yourself and the horse you rode in on."

"Uncle Seamus?"

"Hold him still, Charlie. They say that at the end, the brain tissue liquifies and actually runs out of their ears and nostrils. Pain must be incredible."

Willy's eyes bulged out and his forearms bunched as he tried to lift them against Charlie's grip and weight.

"Guess we'll see." He stepped forward and without any preamble grabbed Willy's bicep muscle and stabbed the needle up into one of the veins that was bulging on his forearm above Charlie's hand and pushed the plunger halfway in.

"Shit!"

"Now, Mr. Willy," Seamus addressed the terrified face of the newly dead man, "you have about one hour to live, give or take. There is a fairly simple antidote available in almost any hospital emergency room, but time is of the essence. Should we leave you taped to this chair, or should we let you see if you can win the race?"

"Shit! It burns, god, it's burning all the way up my arm.

Oh my god, you fuckin' crazy son-of-a-Irish-fucking-bitch, you fuckin' killed me! I'm dyin'!"

"Not yet you're not, but the clock is ticking."

"Okay, okay, yeah, it was a set-up, okay? Anthony wanted that fuckin' voodoo witch queen outta the picture. Nobody had the kind of money that it took to make that big a buy, but she had some connections with Joey Doves' boys. You know, the guy that took over for Sam Giancona. Anyway, the syndicate guys put up the dough. I don't know how much, but they agreed to sixty-five percent of profit plus the vig. As soon as the shipment went down, they thought they smelled a rat, and Madame Creeps-Me-Out disappears. I don't know, maybe for now, maybe she's at the bottom of the lake, I don't give a shit."

Now that the dam was open, Willy was talking fast.

"In the meantime, we manage to keep about three-quarters of some pretty high-quality shit out of an evidence locker, and got it tucked away down in Georgia. Anthony's set up now pretty comfy, and so he can move down to Atlanta, you know, set up his own operation, not have to work for assholes who only think of themselves. So, I'm just hanging back a little to tie up the loose ends. Honest to god, Hole, it's just business, you know? I didn't mean anythin' personal by it."

"Where's Anthony now?"

"Fuck! You gotta let me go. I gotta get to a hospital. My whole arm is on fire. I can feel it pumping in my neck! I told you enough—let me outta here!"

"Where's Anthony."

"I don't know, probably up at his place, packin'. I gotta get outta here, man!"

"Address?"

"Then you'll let me go, right?"

"Address?"

Back in the car we turned toward the city. The walk back to the car had been in stunned silence. None of us had witnessed that kind of stone-cold violence on another human before. Seamus started to laugh, shocking us all with incredulity. Finally, Charlie couldn't hold it anymore and spoke up.

"By god, that's the coldest thing I've ever seen, Seamus! You killed him in cold blood, for Christ's sake. Not that he didn't deserve it, but just the same..."

"Well, you're right there, that man is lower than snake shit, but unless he has a terrible car accident racing to the hospital, he'll be just fine by tomorrow morning. That's when the trouble should start for him in earnest though."

"What are you talkin' about?" Da and I were all ears. "Didn't you shoot him full of battery acid?"

"Jesus, Mick, what kind of a monster do you take me for? Of course, I didn't."

"What the hell was in that hypo then?"

"A mixture that I made out in the car, two-thirds alcohol and one-third urine. Won't kill him, might make him nauseous for a while, screw up his blood alcohol levels too, but no, he's not even close to dying. The alcohol burns when it's introduced. I needed that to sell the battery acid lie."

"Well, if that don't pull the rag off the bush," Charlie was impressed, "maybe even colder than killin' him outright. They're gonna want to know whose blood is all over his pants' legs once they figure out that he's not dyin'; just drunk."

"Exactly, and they'll know for sure it's not his. Should be

an interesting conversation with the cops. I hope he forgets to take that razor out of his pocket. That would be the frosting on the cake."

"The piss was a nice addition. I bet your little pecker just fit inside that needle too, huh?" After he'd recovered Mick was back in the spirit of things.

"Yeah, well, isn't that why we call you Little Mick? That's why you sit down to piss, isn't it, Mick?"

From where I sat in the rear seat, I looked at the three men in awe. They were miles ahead of me in almost every respect. These guys were tough guys. Capable, self-assured, and tough in ways that the street feared, quiet until the storm broke. Shoulder to shoulder they emanated strength and calm, fiercely and frighteningly loyal, but only to each other. They were the heroes that I had walked the entire continent to find, and all along, they had been only an arm's length away from me.

While they all smoked, joked, and chuckled with each other, I was humbled to just be in the same car with them. In all my years, I'd looked at them as just what they looked like. I'd never looked any deeper than the surface. They were deeper and wider in every respect than I'd ever imagined. Somewhere in the back of my mind, I was realizing that more than anything in the world, I wanted to be one of them, and maybe—might have always been.

Thirty minutes later we were just a little bit north of the Chicago Loop and cruised past the renovated early twentieth-century condo building where Anthony supposedly lived. It was one of the architecturally reclaimed structures from back in the mid- or early century. Lots of ornamental brick with cornices on the faux pillars and arched stone with keystone caps above the windows. The double front doors were stained leaded glass. The stonework was dingy and needed sandblasting. It looked expensive. It was after three o'clock in the morning, but we could still make out the distorted image of the security guard sitting at the desk in the entryway beyond the leaded glass doors.

"Nice place. How do we get past the security guard?" Charlie said. "Assuming that the fuck-stick is actually here."

"I'm pretty sure old Mister Willy was being honest. He was too preoccupied to be creative, and he seemed to know the address pretty well, like it was right at the top of his memory."

"I'll get us past the guard; you guys take the car around to the back, find the alley or whatever they use for deliveries, and I'll open the back door for you once I'm in. Give me five minutes; if I'm not out there by then, come in after me."

"I'm going in by myself." I couldn't let them get in any further, and it was my mess.

"Roger that. We'll watch the rear door and wait for you there." Da was already checking his revolver, and there was almost no emotion in his voice.

At the corner traffic light, Seamus nosed the car over to the curb and put it in park. He stepped out and then walked around and opened the trunk. Lifting out his medical bag, he came back to the open door. "Five minutes, no more."

"See you there." Charlie slid across the bench seat and then readjusted it.

Seamus crossed the street and turned back toward Anthony's building, walking with purpose. Charlie eased the car out and made a left turn out of the right-hand lane. There wasn't any traffic moving anywhere on the street. Most of the traffic lights were flashing yellow instead of cycling through their color sequence. It was too late at night, or too early in the morning to be concerned about traffic gridlock.

In half a block an alleyway opened on the left side that was big enough to drive down; even this far downtown rats scurried to get out of the headlight beams. Charlie eased the big sedan down the alley and passed the back doors of the condo building, its street address number stenciled in white on the dark steel double doors. In another twenty yards he stopped and shut off the engine and doused the lights.

"I'm on the car. Mick, you've got the door. Emmett, you're with Seamus, at least until the plan has to change."

"Okay…and thank you, Uncle Charlie. I mean it, thanks."

"If I hadn't helped you out, Bridget would never let me hear the end of it. I'd have to move out to the barn. Just make sure you tell your aunt how amazing I am, got it?"

"If I get out the other end of this, I'll never stop telling her."

"Hey, a little's good, a lot's not. Just a little, okay? Oh, and you buy the beer."

I got out and stretched, my nerves singing in my ears. The city is never really quiet, but I could hear my heartbeat bumping at a high rate in my ears too. Da walked around and stood next to me.

"Steady, boy, don't stumble now. If he's in there, he's gonna be one surprised son of a bitch."

"Do you think the back door's alarmed?"

"Seamus will figure it out. He's a devious guy."

Suddenly, we heard the crunch and creak of the door latches being thrown from the inside, and the rear door down the street cracked open.

"Let's get it. This is your IP, Emmett, time to pull the pins."

"What? I don't know what that means."

"Someday maybe. You're up to bat."

We came up from behind the door and I peeked around it. Seamus smiled and winked. We stepped inside and Mick leaned over and dropped a wooden wedge, placed on the floor for just that purpose, in the doorjamb to keep it ajar. We both looked a question at Seamus.

"How'd you get past the guard?"

"Oh, come on. It's three thirty in the morning, and he's been on the clock since eleven last night. It's been years since anything interesting has happened in this building. I told him I was Doctor Mo Grobstein just in from Miami and they'd lost my bags again. The airlines promised to send them over as soon as they found them, so I asked him to have them brought up to my brother-in-law's place up on fourteen. He was glad to make my acquaintance, especially when I slapped a twenty on him. They probably pay the poor bastard shit money, for his shit job. Shit, he's my new best friend, so let's make sure we don't do anything that will get him in trouble. Okay?"

"Who's Mo Grobstein?"

"Apparently, he's Jacob Melmann's brother-in-law, who lives in 1408."

"What the fuck, Seamus?"

"There was outgoing mail on the counter."

We took the elevator to the sixth floor. When the doors opened, the sign on the opposite wall showed that the apartment numbers descended to the left, toward downtown, and up to the right. We turned right. Anthony's was the second one from the end facing east toward the lake. He wouldn't have a view of it though; the sixth floor was too low to see past the buildings in between. Lakeview apartments were much more expensive, and much higher up.

Standing outside the door, I checked the knob. There was no dead bolt, supposedly not necessary because of the security guard downstairs. This was going to be easier than I'd expected.

"Do you have a credit card, Uncle Seamus?"

"Yeah, but what for?"

"Could I borrow it for a minute?"

He gave me that patented one-eyebrow Casey look, but reached into his inside jacket pocket. "Let's see. I've got American Express, and the new Mastercard."

"I don't care which one, just about any one will do."

He handed me the little green AMEX card. Turning it on end I leaned against the door and pushed it hard. With the card in my right hand, I ran it into the doorjamb right at the knob's level. There was a little resistance, and I wiggled it a little; then the lock released and I eased the door open past the jamb. I handed the card back to Seamus. He looked at the card, turning it over, inspecting it for damage, then flipped his wallet open and put it back inside.

"Well, aren't you just full of surprises."

"You should stay here, Seamus." He made a face. "Please?"

"I'll give you a few minutes, but if it's too long, I'm coming in."

"Ten minutes max."

The foyer just inside the apartment door was dark. I made a quick move to get on the other side of the door and avoid too much light from the hallway coming in. Once on the other side,

I unlocked the door, turned the lock tumbler, and closed the door as quietly as I could. The foyer wasn't totally dark; there was light entering from beyond and to the right, and there was also ample ambient light that filtered in from the street below through the six-foot windows directly ahead of me. Even so, I waited until my eyes adjusted enough to avoid furniture, and started moving into the room. The space smelled of cooked meat, leather, stale tobacco smoke, and cigarillos.

It was a big space, with high ceilings and lots of dark woodwork. I didn't have to look far to find what I was there for. Light from what appeared to be the kitchen spilled out into the living room. Just off the entryway, two suitcases with a hanging suit bag draped over them sat on the thick carpeting. Two large and thick wingback chairs that appeared to be leather were arranged facing the room from under the windows with a wooden side table between them. A long leather sofa faced the two chairs across a long coffee table. In the chair on the left, Mr. Alexander Anthony was sitting with his feet up on a leather hassock. He appeared to be looking directly at me, but made no indication that he'd seen me. His entire body looked rigid.

He still had his shoes on, and in the half-light, he appeared to have his eyes open, but otherwise might have been asleep. Next to him on the table sat a liquor bottle, a shiny ice bucket, and a half-full rocks glass. A full ashtray added its aroma to the general scent of the room, and a small table lamp with a low-wattage bulb added its meager illumination to the area.

Moving to the table, I looked down on him. His eyes were wide open, but he stared at nothing; as I stared at him his chest rose and fell slowly. At least he wasn't dead.

Now that he was right in front of me, I wasn't exactly sure what I should do. I had intended to confront him, scare him, maybe even kill him, but now while I stood over him, I was confused about my options. I didn't fool myself into thinking that he wouldn't take advantage of the situation if the situation was reversed. I knew that he was a cold-blooded opportunist who had risen to the top because his level of ruthlessness was worse than anyone he had climbed over to get where he was.

I looked down at the small table. Maybe just to take a bit longer to think about those options. The bottle looked unusual and I turned it so that I could read the label: Absinthe. What the hell? I took a whiff from the bottle, and it smelled like licorice. This was a new one for me. I'd never heard of it before. It certainly wasn't anything that remotely tempted me to put it in my mouth.

If there had been ice in the glass, it had melted. The stuff looked like slightly green-colored water, but smelled awful. I picked up the glass and held it under my nose to give it a good whiff.

"You should not take a drink from that glass." The voice behind me scared the shit out of me, and I dropped the glass. The carpet was so thick that the glass bounced but did not break, and the newly spilled contents splashed onto my boots. I spun around, my knife out in my hand.

In the opening of the darkened hallway stood a shadowy figure, hard to make out in the deeper shadow. There was no mistaking the voice though, gravelly and deep—creepy.

"I am unarmed, Mr. Hole. I am no danger to you."

"What the hell!" I also didn't believe her.

"You should ask your companion to come in. He will draw

attention in the hallway if he stands out there much longer."

If I did anything at all, it would be to tell Seamus to make a run for it. There was no reason to wonder why she was here or how she had gotten in. She had just as much right to be here as I did. The darkened specter of her in the hallway didn't do anything to enhance her impression on me though. She'd scared me shitless from the very first moment I'd met her, and now she seemed determined to raise the bar to a whole new level.

"I heard you whispering in the hallway. It gave me a moment to step out of the light. He is still out there, I can feel him."

"You can feel him?"

"Yes," a match flared and as it moved up, it lit her face in the glow, "I can feel him standing there. He is not afraid." She hissed out a lungful of smoke.

"Maybe I should just go."

"No, I think we should talk, your friend too. This is a complex situation."

"Can you please step out into the light?"

When she stepped out into the half-light of the room, it didn't do a thing to improve her looks. She was dressed in a long, flowing caftan; the sleeves were tapered at the end, extending well beyond her fingertips, and the hem ended just above her feet. It appeared to be floral with countless gauzy folds, perhaps multicolored, but in this light it was varying shades of gray. It was probably expensive. The entire image along with the darkened sockets of her sunken eyes reinforced the impression of the specter of death. I still hadn't moved from Anthony's chair; the knife was still in my hand.

"Did you come to kill him?"

I again looked down at him. "Maybe."

"He is already a dead man."

"What, he's dead!?! Did you kill him?"

"Ask your companion to come in please."

She raised her hand and directed it toward the front entry. Her cigar was dangling from the corner of her mouth, but her left hand was concealed in the folds of the outfit. I couldn't tell if she had a weapon or not. I went to the door and opened it slowly. Seamus was leaning against the opposite wall.

"You need to come in, Uncle Seamus."

He was immediately alert and on his toes to the implied danger in my voice. He looked the question and I shrugged. When we re-entered the living room, Madame DuBois had taken the other leather chair. The small table light didn't do anything to improve her craggy looks. She was arranging the folds of her dress, seemingly unperturbed by the situation. A small Beretta had appeared on the table next to the ice bucket.

We stood just inside the doorway, and she gestured us to the matching couch that faced the two chairs.

"Please?"

With some hesitation we took a seat. I was trying to check Anthony to see if he was still breathing.

"You said he's dead."

"No, I said he is a dead man."

"There is a difference?"

"Decidedly."

Seamus was out of his element, but he was also used to taking charge.

"So? This man is dead, but not dead?"

"Yes."

"How is that possible."

She waved her cigar in the air to take in us and then the still form of Anthony.

"I am from the islands. As a young girl I learned the methods of inducing a type of sleep. Almost untraceable during an autopsy. It is a sleep but it is not a sleep; it is more like a shallow death. My former friend Alexander is fully conscious, his mind is active, and he can even see. He is currently in incredible pain but cannot cry out, as he has been deprived of the ability to move a single muscle. He is a spectator at his own trial but cannot utter a word in his defense." She drew on her cigar. "As if there could be one."

She took another drag of the cigar, rose, and turned to the ashtray on the table next to Anthony. Before she stubbed out the cigar, she dumped the entire contents onto the carpeting, then put her smoke out in the now empty ashtray. Setting it down on her side of the table, she once again arranged the folds of her dress, moving with some grace in spite of her angular appearance, and continued.

"This pig has succeeded in single-handedly ruining my life. Something that many have tried before; to their detriment. I must leave here soon and disappear or my life will be forfeit. I cannot leave though until he has learned the error of his ways. For now, he sleeps the death sleep, but eventually the rigor will cause his heart to fail, and then he will truly be a dead man. By that time, he will have wished that he could have died a hundred times, for he will suffer pain like he could not imagine until now. I will take my time. Of course, I might be able to revive him from his current state, but that would spoil the party."

Her gravelly voice never changed pitch, she had spoken without emotion, but I felt that the temperature in the room had dropped twenty degrees in a matter of seconds. The cold delivery of her words left the both of us speechless. It spoke volumes instead that I didn't doubt a word of it. In the next few moments I was about to find out if I was going in the same direction as Anthony or if there was an exit available.

"I have not had the pleasure of an explanation of how my life has come to take such a disastrous turn. You, Hole, played the pivotal role, no doubt. You would not be here now if Alexander had not also worked his wicked magic on your fate as well, or am I mistaken?"

I didn't speak but I met her gaze.

"Yes. If you please, can you recount the events of the last few days, from where you witnessed them?" She arched her eyebrows to emphasize her request. "Please feel free to add your conclusions or thoughts. I would truly like to know what transpired. To this point, I only know that the shipment was intercepted but not recovered, and that I am now a fugitive from my recent business partners. With a typical lack of compassion, they have placed a contract upon me. I am only certain that Alexander orchestrated this fiasco. But, and for once he has now extended his reach beyond his grasp. If you would? Please, I am merely curious."

I looked at Seamus and he nodded, so I started at the checkpoint inspection in Florida. In short order I was able to recount the entire episode, ending with our recent encounter with Fat Willy. I didn't need to add any of my own thoughts—the evidence was more than sufficient for her to make the appropriate conclusions. When I finished, she brought another cigar out from under the gauzy film of her outfit and lit it. Leaning back in her chair, she directed the smoke toward the high ceiling for a full minute.

"I couldn't have done a better job of fucking someone over. So simple, just the right connections, almost elegant." She took a long drag and exhaled again, then dropped her gaze to look me in the eye across the space.

"No honor among thieves, so they say," she rasped. "You, however, are something special, the ultimate wild card. He didn't count on you being as smart as you were made out to be. Of course, Alexander never believed anyone could be as smart as he was. You not only did your job, you wiggled off of his hook. That makes you the worst kind of loose end. A smart one, with a sense of honor, dangerous and unpredictable."

"Why is that?"

"Just the fact that you are here instead of running as far away as you can proves that. You are here to exact your revenge, full of righteous indignation; your poor little sense of integrity has been violated. Pity, I would have enjoyed working with you, I believe. You're in for an excellent career."

"No, he is not, ma'am." Seamus' voice was firm.

Her dark eyebrows rose and she looked at him. "And who may you be, his father perhaps?"

"He's my uncle. My father is downstairs guarding the elevator."

"There are more of you? All built this same way? On the inside? That there are more like you is a little unsettling. You came prepared."

"Yes, we did, and we plan to walk right back out of here." Seamus' voice was hard.

"I mean you no harm, sir. I was very surprised to see Hole. Partially because I thought he was involved with Anthony and Fat Willy, as you call him. Now I understand. But I am sorry to disappoint you. Alexander is mine. Your nephew's desire for vengeance would be justified, but in this instance—mine trumps yours.

"In the morning, a limousine will arrive to pick us up. I am known to the security personnel, so that would not be considered unusual. Mr. Anthony will appear to have taken ill, and we will be taking him for medical attention. We will leave this place and go to one more suitable for what I have in mind."

"We can go then?" I was relieved but there was no way I was going to turn my back on her either.

"You always could have left. In this present circumstance we are both trespassers here, both with the same goal in mind. I have no hold on you. I hope you prosper in whatever life and the gods have in mind for you, Hole."

The report of the gun was impossibly loud in the closed space. The bullet struck her in the right shoulder, passed through her, the chair, and buried itself into the plaster between the two multi-paned windows. Dark droplets spattered across Anthony's white shirt in the half-light of the small table lamp. I jumped to my left involuntarily and jerked my head to the right. The revolver's barrel trailed a faint trail of smoke as it held steady on the woman. Seamus' hand was dead still. Madame DuBois' eyes bulged out of their sockets and she stared at him across the space. Then she looked down as the folds of her outfit blossomed a dark stain that spread down toward her lap. With her right hand she tried to reach for the Beretta, but her hand didn't seem to be responding to her desire.

Taking a deep breath, she gave a wet cough and tried to turn so she could reach the gun with her left hand. My ears had been deafened by the blast from the revolver, but not my senses. I jumped to my feet, skirted the coffee table, and beat her to the little automatic. She looked up at me. There was no question in her eyes; instead she smiled and coughed again.

Taking a shallow breath she whispered, "Ah, self-righteous to the end."

Seamus stood and moved to Anthony. "He's going to have to finish the job."

"What?"

"Here, put this in his hand." He handed me Da's big Colt Python. "He'll need to have gunshot residue on his hand and arm." Immediately I understood. Seamus added, "Do you know if he's right- or left-handed."

I went back to the vision of the hypodermic needle going into the neck of poor Melinda.

I picked up Anthony's inert right hand and arm. Taking the Colt, I put it into the palm of his right hand and pushed his finger into the trigger guard. Cocking the hammer, I raised the gun and pointed it at the woman. Her eyes tracked the barrel. Using Anthony's finger, I pulled the trigger. The bullet eventually buried itself into the plaster of the outside wall with the first one.

I moved to her side, and using the flowing sleeve of her caftan, I wiped the Beretta down, then put it in her right hand. I fired one shot into the wall over Anthony's head and dropped it next to the chair.

"Everyone in the building will have heard those shots, Seamus. That fuckin' gun of Da's makes a hell of a bang."

Seamus had his handkerchief in his hand and was wiping down the glass I'd handled. "Maybe…the walls in these old buildings are pretty thick, soundproof, but you're probably right. We need to go."

"We need to rearrange him a little so that the angles match."

The security guard was asleep behind the counter when we stepped out of the elevator and peeked around the corner to check. At the rear of the building, Da was squatting on his haunches at the back door, alert to our approaching footsteps.

"Sorry, Mick, I seem to have lost your gun," Seamus said quietly.

"WHAT?" My ears were still ringing.

An Ending, a Beginning
Emmett

I stood in the driveway of Da's house. The sun was just asserting its light over the darkness of a long night. Bright sunshine made the scattered cloud cover glow as the sun lit it from underneath. Seamus' car sat idling in the driveway, while we four stood together but apart in front of it. The old percolator, almost full with fresh coffee, was perched and vibrating on the hood of the running car, slowly migrating toward the front edge. Charlie reset it farther back on the hood and turned back to the three of us. Each of us held a steaming cup of coffee in one hand and a cigarette in the other.

"This shit ends here, Emmett," Charlie stated flatly. "Whatever is left to clean up is up to you, but this shit ends right fuckin' here."

Seamus was not as subtle. He stepped forward and stood chest to chest to me, causing me to lean back on my heels.

"That is not a request, Emmett; we aren't asking, we're telling you."

Charlie opted for subtlety. "If something like this happens again, I will personally kick you into a bloody pulp and then feed your body to the pigs. Clear? No fuckin' joke."

Da stood a little to the side, smoking and staring down the driveway, seemingly a million miles away.

"No bullshit, Uncle Charlie, I'm out—really!"

Charlie bull-rushed me and pinned me to the grill of the big car. The coffeepot tipped and rolled off onto the gravel. The coffee cup I'd been holding flew out onto the lawn.

"No bullshit!?! Really!?!" He mimicked my voice. "Right now, we should be plannin' your wake. Instead you get to go past GO at least one more time."

"Grown-up games aren't like the sophomoric crap you're used to pulling, Emmett." Charlie had me bent backward over the hood of the car, and Seamus leaned over my face. "We've all watched as you've pulled one fancy rabbit out of your hat after another. This was one too many. This time it would have probably been your last. No rabbit, no hat. It's time you reached down and grabbed hold of those balls of yours and decided to be a man. A Casey."

In my peripheral vision to my right, Little Mick maintained his distant gaze and continued smoking his cigarette. He gave no indication that he was a part of the conversation.

"I'm sorry I dragged you into this, Uncle Seamus, and you too, Uncle Charlie. I don't really know what I would have done if it hadn't been for you guys."

"Save it." Charlie wasn't about to be mollified; he had a full head of steam going. "We're family, and I for one would have been pretty pissed if I'd heard you didn't call us."

"You actually did the right thing for a change." Mick finally weighed in. "But you've got a long haul to get clear yet, and for that, you're on your own. However they take what happened tonight, you'll answer for it alone. We can't be involved."

"We weren't even here." Charlie looked me in the eye. Then he offered his calloused hand and pulled me up off the hood of the car with the other. Once I was standing, he didn't release his grip on my shirt; instead he looked me in the eye and then shook my hand.

Seamus stepped up and offered his as well. He met my eye. "You're every bit a Casey, Emmett, and it's time you embraced it. We cannot bring the dead back to life and we cannot take their place. Find a way to stop letting your sense of guilt turn into shame. That's a lonely road and it leads into darkness."

Charlie put his hand on my shoulder and smiled. "Now get your shit together, and this fall come to deer camp with Mick."

Step One, Turn Around

I awoke to the sound of soft voices rising up through the heat vent in the floor of the upstairs bedroom. It was stuffy and I was too warm swaddled in the sheets and blankets, still fully dressed. The room was dark with only ambient light filtering in through the curtained window. I knew where I was, my old bedroom tucked in the eaves of my father's house. I had woken up in this room for years upon years, but not recently. The outside darkness meant that I had slept the day away. The luminous dial of the clock on the nightstand was no help, telling me it was about half past three. No doubt it had been unplugged to save electricity in a room that no longer had a resident. Struggling out of the bedclothes, I swung my feet out and put them on the floor. Immediately my stomach began to growl. It had been more than twenty-four hours since I'd eaten out of Kate's picnic basket. The voices downstairs continued, both male and female, soft and continuous. I stood up, and immediately the floor in the old house creaked. The voices from below stopped.

In spite of the familiar surroundings, I was slightly disoriented. As I made my way down the narrow hallway to the stairs, I bounced off of walls, not quite fully awake and not sure that I wanted to be.

The last five days had been a lot to digest. If I'd opened a book and read about it, I would have stopped reading, disgusted by the overblown drama and hyperbole, an unbelievable narrative. The last twenty-four hours had been a walk into the darkness again, and again I had found a place inside of me that was capable of dispassionate violence. My next visit in front of the mirror promised to be difficult for both of us.

I creaked my way down the unlit old oak staircase toward the lighted living room at the bottom, apprehensive about who and what was waiting in silence for my arrival. The first person I saw as my head cleared the ceiling was Dutch and sitting next to her Angie. Three empty plates, bowls, and glasses sat on the coffee table in front of them. Unable to contain herself Angie jumped to her feet and rushed around the table. Throwing herself into my arms, she began to sob. I met Dutch's eyes across the top of her head. I thought I knew what the look on her face meant. Well, shit.

Sitting on the edge of his chair in the corner sat Little Mick. A cloud of smoke filled that corner of the room as he regarded me without expression. His hand casually cradled his pipe in the corner of his mouth. I didn't need to ask whether or not he had slept.

"Oh, Emmett! I've been worried sick." Angie hiccupped. "Are you okay? What did they do to you? How could they be so cruel?"

I looked at Da, who just shrugged.

"Angie, baby, it's okay. It's gonna be okay. Promise."

"You can come home now—right?"

"Not just yet I think, honey." That comment drew Dutch's eyebrows down.

"Why not? We want you to come home with us." Angie huffed.

I looked at Mick. "I still haven't finished what I've got to do. Once I do that, I promise, I'll come home. Okay?"

"What? I thought you were already finished."

"I have to see some people, and I have to do it right away."

"Come home tonight, you can do it first thing in the morning. You can sleep in your own bed and get a good night's sleep."

"This won't wait—I think." Dutch looked at me to see if she'd gotten it right.

I nodded. "This won't wait. I really wish it could."

Da snorted and relit his pipe. "I bet."

"I called your father to see if you were both safe. He said we could come over. We've both been on pins and needles."

"Thank you, Dutch. I didn't get a chance…" She stopped me, drawing her hand across her throat. The universal gesture to shut up. I looked at her, confused. She raised her eyebrows and bobbed her head. *Think about it*, the expression said. It took me a second to realize she hadn't told Angie about her trip to Memphis. When that dawned on me, it must have shown on my face because she nodded.

"Angie, there are a few things that I have to do. I'm hoping to have them wrapped up pretty quick, but I might be awhile."

"Awhile? How long is awhile?" She huffed and snuggled her head under my chin. "I miss you, Emmett."

"Awhile is however long it takes. You'll be the first to know, I promise."

Dutch rose to her feet. "Thanks for letting us come over and make sure he's still alive, Mr. Casey. Apparently, it was too difficult for him to pick up the phone. C'mon, Ang, we'll hear from him pretty quick, I bet." She made eye contact with me.

"Yeah, I promise." I looked her in the eye.

Dutch stepped up and peeled the still sobbing Angie off of me; turning back she gave me a long, tight hug that lasted longer than I'd expected. When she pushed herself away, she reached up and put her hand on the back of my head and gave it a shake.

"Finish it—then come home."

Two Cats

In the kitchen a substantial pot of chili simmered on the stove, next to it a sleeve of saltine crackers and an empty bowl. I filled the bowl and carried it and with the sleeve of crackers under my arm made my way back to the living room. I sat down across from him in the spot where the two girls had been. He was still holding his pipe while he puffed up another cloud of Amphora smoke, but now he was leaning back, looking at me through the vapor. He never moved until I had put away the chili and half the crackers.

"Gonna be more than one thing you'll be clearing up in the next little while."

"Why, what else?"

"You got two cats in the same gunny sack."

"What? Two cats?"

"That girl Angie, she's as innocent as the day's long, but that Dutch, now that girl…" He took a long, considered pull on the pipe. "That girl, she's gonna be a handful, and she's setting her cap for you, that's certain."

"I know, I didn't mean for that to happen. That's gonna be a problem."

"Good problem to have and the worst kind of problem to have. All at the same time."

"No, Da, it's not a good thing."

"You ever hear what happens if you were to tie two cats together by the tail? They won't just end up hating you; they're gonna tear each other apart too."

"Maybe by the time I get outta jail, they'll have moved on? Maybe." I was trying to lighten up the conversation, but that outcome was distinctly possible.

"Maybe." No help from Da.

The Push Comes to the Shove

I opened the heavy glass door and walked into the office. Just like always, it was too hot inside; the air was stale and smelled like bureaucratic paperwork. The vinyl padded steel chairs that lined the inside wall were all full, full of social reprobates, but with no vacancy left for my sorry ass. I walked to the long Formica counter and took one of the numbered cards that hung under a sign that read, TAKE A NUMBER. I was number fifteen. I did a quick count of the full chairs; there were fourteen.

Since there weren't any seats, I leaned against the wall at the end of the counter. From there I could see the desks beyond the counter. All were occupied, and all the occupants were busy. They were busy talking to each other, drinking coffee, clipping their fingernails, or eating pastries. They were just not busy taking people back for interviews.

I located my P.O. across the sea of desks. He was hunched over his desk, stuffing a jelly Bismarck into his face, a cup of coffee in his other hand. Something told him to look up, and when he did he looked me right in the eye and I gave him a little Boy Scout salute. He spilled his coffee putting it down, and his first stab for the telephone on his desk knocked it on the floor. Everyone turned to look at the racket as he recovered it and started dialing while still holding it. I sighed a deep breath. So much for the hoped-for warm reception.

In less than a minute, the first U.S. Marshal came through the door. Well, that's not exactly correct. His weapon came through the door ahead of him. With the gun still the only thing in the doorway, he shouted,

"U.S. Marshals Service!"

Almost upon the appearance of the weapon, every one of the fourteen chairs emptied and everyone hit the linoleum, face down, hands behind their heads. This was not their first rodeo, it appeared. I was only a little slower than the rest of them.

There was a shuffling of feet, a lot of feet.

"No one moves!?!"

"That's him, that's the son of a bitch, him right there—down on the end!"

"Subject, state your name!" I was prodded by the toe of someone's shoe.

"Casey, Robert Emmett. I'm here to see my probation officer."

"He's not here to see me. He doesn't have an appointment. He's a fugitive. There's a BOLO out for him from the FBI."

I was immediately handcuffed and hauled to my feet. The space in front of the counter was crowded with men in white shirts, dark ties, and guns. They were having trouble not stepping on anyone.

"Honestly, Officer, I'd like to turn myself in, but I didn't know the best place. That's why I came here. I thought my probation officer could assist me."

"Hmmph." I'd never seen my probation officer show this much interest in me before. He had Bismarck jelly all over the front of his shirt.

The ride downstairs was cordial. They put me in a holding cell in the bowels of the building. The floor was cold on my stockinged feet, as they'd taken my boots, belt, wallet, and earring. I guessed they wanted to avoid the possibility that the earring might be a cyanide capsule. There was a bench anchored to the wall and a toilet/sink in the corner where the two cement walls came together. The bars went from the floor to the ceiling and looked like they'd been installed just for Eliot Ness. I settled down to wait. I figured it would be awhile, I didn't know how long, but I was pretty sure that I did know who was going to show up.

I was wrong on both counts.

It couldn't have been more than thirty minutes before there was activity down the hall. I had just started to get chilled in the damp air. There wasn't any conversation, but there were a lot of feet coming. After the pause the entourage trooped down to the cell.

"Step to the rear wall, place your hands apart on the wall, and lean on them. Place your feet shoulder length apart."

I did as I was instructed. I'd had plenty of practice. This time I was both handcuffed and shackled. Surrounded by six suited authority figures, I was shuffled down the hallway in the opposite direction that they'd arrived. After another security desk, the door in front of us clicked and an alarm rang. We stepped out the door onto a loading dock. A white-and-blue Chicago Police Department paddy wagon sat idling at the end of the ramp. In the sunlight beyond it, two black Chevy Suburban's stood with their doors open, drivers behind the wheel.

When the heavy steel door behind me closed, the officer stationed at the back of the wagon pulled open the large rear door and stood back. I knew what to do next and started down the ramp and headed toward the wagon. At least I had plenty of protection, wherever I was going.

There weren't windows in the back of the wagon, and I didn't have anything else to do, so I counted the turns and the time between stoplights. Where I was going was two right turns, five stoplights, one left turn, and up a short ramp. We'd gone uptown, that much I knew, but how far was anyone's guess.

When the rear door opened again, the ramp and the décor looked like we hadn't left the probation officer's building. The only difference was that there were an awful lot of Chicago Police officers standing around. They took over the detail and assisted me down out of the wagon. Walking with shackles isn't the easiest thing to do, the chain is long enough to carry in your hands, but you have to keep your feet apart to keep from tripping. I had one officer holding each elbow as we went up the ramp and through the back door.

Once inside, we headed down a long concrete block wall, made one turn, and then directly into a large glass-walled room that had long tables and chairs facing each other. There were other chairs along the glass, and all of them looked comfortable, except for one. They directed me to that one, sat me down, and locked my shackles to the ring in the floor between my feet. Then they all left. I watched them as they filed down the hall outside the glass windows. Just as the last one disappeared from sight, another group appeared from the same direction. They were dressed mostly in suits and ties and one police uniform. The first one was Federal Investigator Phillip M. Janes. I stopped looking at the rest of them. Janes was looking right at me.

Opening the door, Janes moved directly to the center chair of the table facing across from me, while the others filed in and took random seating. The police uniform took a position to his right. From the other direction, another suit approached; it was Walter Dunn, and he was alone. Once he entered, Janes moved one chair to the left and Dunn took the middle seat. Janes opened his brown manila folder and they all sat.

"Mr. Casey, as you know, my name is Federal Investigator Phillip Janes, to my far right is Detective Andrew Morrison of the Chicago Police Department Homicide Division, and on my immediate right is Special Agent Walter Dunn of the FBI. The others in the room represent other members of these departments and tangential involvement. I have asked them to sit in with us for the initial discussions. Do you have any objections to their presence?"

I couldn't see that it made any difference one way or the other, and I said so.

"This interview will be recorded in its entirety. It can and will be used as legally admissible evidence in a court of law. As a result, we will conduct this as we would any court proceeding. If you are asked a question, you should speak your response; do not nod or shake your head. That would not be an acceptable answer. Do you understand, Mr. Casey?"

I nodded my head just for fun, which got the expected scowl. I smiled at them and said, "Yes, I understand. Do I have the right to plead the Fifth to any questions?"

"You always have that right, Mr. Casey; however, we might

then consider you a hostile witness."

"Do I have the right to representation?"

"You may request that an attorney be present throughout the proceedings if you wish. That is also your right under the law."

"Am I a suspect in a crime?"

"We believe you are a primary witness in a number of crimes, Mr. Casey. We are in the process of determining which ones you are a central figure in, and which ones you are only tangentially involved in. We would like to ask you some questions of clarification. Should you be willing to cooperate, we would consider offering some type of plea-bargaining agreement in any crimes that we deem your involvement in should that information prove useful. ONLY if the information should prove useful, and that would be something for you to discuss with a qualified legal counselor."

"I'm sorry, but I'm not sure why I'm here at all. Except that you personally seem to have a thing for arresting and detaining me for no apparent reason, Inspector."

"We will find out about that soon enough, Mr. Casey." Janes was all official business, and I wasn't going to be able to budge him. I was here to clear up my life, not entertain myself, so I said, "I'm here to cooperate if I can. I'll answer your questions as best I can, but I am not about to admit guilt where I have none."

"Understood. You were already Mirandized at the time of your arrest, is that correct?"

"Yes."

"Then we will begin. The first questions will be from Detective Morrison. Detective?"

Morrison spent a few moments looking tough and making meaningful eye contact.

"Mr. Casey, do you know a woman by the name of Marianna DeBovier?"

"I can honestly say I don't know anyone by that name. No sir, I don't."

"Do you know anyone who may have gone by that name at all?"

"On Halloween maybe; otherwise, I don't think I could guess of anyone else. Is she a part of this?"

"We ask the questions, Mr. Casey." Janes was holding court.

"Do you know anyone by the name or alias of William Benson?"

"No sir." I looked at Dunn. He was leaning back in his chair, arms folded. His eyes were boring a hole in the back of my head. He gave a slight shake of his head.

"How about Fat Willy?"

"No, sir."

"He says he knows you. He says you tried to kill him."

"I'm sorry, uh, Detective, why would I try to kill someone I don't know? I don't think I could ever actually kill someone at all."

"Mr. Casey, there are three newly deceased people this afternoon in Chicago. There seems to be a connection between each one of them and yourself. Each seems to have some association with your activities, and we are trying to determine the link between their deaths and also explain the nature of their deaths. All three are violent homicides, and we have reason to believe that you were at least at the site of these crimes."

"Wow! Three? Somebody's been busy. I'm sorry, but when

did these occur? Recently, you say?"

"The preliminary reports say in the last twenty-four hours, so yes, recently."

"Well, I was playing poker for about the last sixteen or eighteen, with my uncles. They'll be glad to vouch for that. Then I heard that people were looking for me, so I immediately reported to my probation officer in order to see what it was about."

"These uncles, you say, they wouldn't also have made the acquaintance of Mr. William Benson?"

"Not unless he was playing cards at my dad's last night."

"That is your final answer, you do not know, or have ever known these people?"

"Not that I recall, no, sir."

The detective gave a long, disgusted look at Janes, then looked at Dunn, who shrugged.

"Mr. Janes?"

"He's not going anywhere, Detective. You'll get another crack at him down the road."

"I certainly hope so."

With that he pushed his chair back and rose to leave. Half the other suits got up with him. Once they were out the door, Dunn spoke.

"Now that the formalities are concluded…" He waved his hand at the ceiling and waited for the doorkeeper to nod.

"Casey, we're off the record now. No recordings are being made, we can speak frankly. It was important to let the Chicago P.D. have their interview first. They've got a couple of very hot crime scenes and an uncooperative suspect in custody. I have informed Investigator Janes and his task force of your willing but reluctant undercover work at my behest, and we now would like to conduct a debriefing. Feel free with your information; it will not go any further than this room, providing that you have not willingly participated in a major crime, or worse. Have you?"

"Certainly not, sir."

"I will be making notes." Janes wanted to still maintain some authority.

"No sir, you won't. We will have a formal statement once we sort out what questions we want to record. As you said before, he's not going anywhere for now."

Janes put down his pen. The others in the room turned their chairs in my direction. Dunn leaned back and crossed his arms. With a wave of his right hand he beckoned.

"Start at the beginning, all of it. Don't sugar-coat, don't fib. Before you start, what we do know is that you were in Florida, and then eluded capture in Macon, Georgia, during a major drug bust in which police received an anonymous tip. Late last evening, Mr. William Forst was murdered in a drug den on the west side; your fingertip partial was found on the kitchen doorknob of that site. We do not have any way of knowing how recent that print was set. It was also found on the front doorknob of an upscale condominium on the near north-side where there were two individuals, both deceased, both violently. The circumstantial evidence of your attendance is clear, but thin—so far. They will continue to sift through evidence, and if they find more that points at you, you're going to need a good story. As far as protecting you somewhat, that can only go as far as we know that you have acted in good faith and are not responsible for committing any of the acts. With that in mind, begin please."

I looked him in the eye as squarely as I could. He nodded. I looked at Janes, who was angry, but curious. If I made one misstep, he was going to have me for lunch. I'd showed him up twice, and he wasn't going to take that easily. So, I started right from the beginning, and the talk with Dunn in the probation office. I talked for the better part of an hour by my internal clock. When I finished, one of the spectators got up and got me a glass of water from the cooler behind me. There was general silence in the room. Dunn was looking at the ceiling, steepling his fingers on his chest. Janes was staring at the table top in front of him. No one was looking directly at me.

"What size shoes do you wear?" Janes was first to speak up.

"Um, ten. Why?"

"Footprint impressions were taken at the site of Mr. Forst's murder; they were on a pizza box near the victim."

"What size were they?"

"Eleven and a half. Wingtips, distinctive soles."

"I only wear boots."

"So, when you arrived at the address on Central Park, Mr. Forst had already been killed, presumably by William Benson?"

"That's my take."

"So, Mr. Benson arrived in the Emergency Room at Presbyterian St. Luke's raving about being injected with battery acid by two giants with red hair. Did you see anyone like that at the scene?"

"Two giants with red hair? I'm pretty sure that would have been in my story. No, when I arrived, Willy was in a pretty weird state, like crazy, Mr. Forst was definitely dead in the corner; the amount of blood was incredible."

"And you have no idea where the shoe prints came from?"

"No, sir. I did see the pizza box though. It was on the floor next to William, um, Mr. Forst."

"So, then you questioned Mr. Benson?"

"As best as I could. He was kinda nuts."

"And he told you where to find Mr. Anthony?"

"Correct. Well, eventually."

"And you went to see Mr. Anthony, only to find both he and Marianna Debovier had apparently murdered each other?"

"Correct." I looked him directly in the eye. "I was never told what her real name was."

"And at no time did you consider calling the police?"

"I was reasonably sure that the police would be more interested in me than in anything I could offer those people. They were dead already. I'm going to have a whole new set of nightmares just from the one night."

"How did you get past the security guard at the condominium? Didn't he have to buzz you in?"

"He came outside to smoke a cigarette, and when he did, he left the door braced open and took a stroll down the street. I just went in. When I left, he was asleep with his head on the counter."

"The preliminary autopsy on Mr. Anthony showed severe petechial hemorrhages in his eyes and tongue, as if he had been choked, but no sign of bruising of the skin on his neck. Can you explain that?"

"I walked in, saw two dead people, knew them both, didn't like either one of them, and I wasn't sorry that they were dead, but I didn't spend any time checking them out, at all. I was maybe a little disappointed to be totally truthful. I really had wanted to confront Anthony. I wasn't expecting to find Madame What's-her-name there. Sorry."

Dunn leaned forward. Up until now he hadn't been appearing to pay any attention.

"They've got Benson for the murder of Forst. What about the other guy, Charles?"

"In the wind is my guess. Probably a quality guy, but definitely a taste for the other side of the street. If I had to pick a place to look for him, I'd look in Atlanta."

"Atlanta?"

"Somebody had to be on that shipment from the beginning to the end. Otherwise, how would they figure out to catch us in Macon? Fat Willy didn't know the route I'd chosen. I sent William back because I didn't trust him. It's hard to walk away from a police stake-out for one person, but two of us did it, and I was lucky. That takes some doing, and I never saw him leave the truck stop. My guess, he was eyes on the truck all the time, and is waiting for Anthony to show up down there so they can get back to work."

Dunn nodded his understanding.

"And Fat Willy is the connection?"

"Fat Willy is where you'll find the drugs, and maybe Charles."

"Well, Casey, you never disappoint, I'll say that for you." Dunn was ready to move on but Janes wasn't.

"Mr. Casey, you will be detained for a period of time—for questioning—by us. At this time we are not processing you as an arrest. The Chicago Police Department will probably need at least one or two more interviews with you, once we decide what information we can share and what information we cannot. I believe it would be safe to say that there are people right now that are looking quite diligently to find you, so I think you would be well served to remain under our surveillance for now. I repeat you are not being arrested, but you will be in police custody. You will, in most likelihood, be detained for a period of time, during which I will speak to the U.S. district attorney to see if there are any charges that would be appropriate to level at you. Until then, at least, we know that you will be staying out of trouble. After that, well, we'll see if you deserve to be re-released back into society. I suspect you know my feelings about that already."

"I'm sorry Mr., uh, Investigator Janes, but I would like to say something else—as long as we're off the record?"

"By all means."

"Okay, um," I thought back to the look in Uncle Charlie's eye and Uncle Seamus' words, when they told me that it was time for me to become a Casey, "well, you see, um, I get the impression that you think I'm some sort of smartass."

That got a fairly strong eye roll from Janes, but Dunn leaned forward, intent.

"The honest-to-god truth is that I'm pretty sure that I'm not. The real truth is that I'm scared to death. All this time. I've been making it up as I go along, I've done what I needed to do, but really it wasn't because I was trying to do a good job for Mr. Dunn, or anybody else. I was just trying to get through it. Trying to survive, without getting my throat cut or ending up in a landfill somewhere. It's just my way, sir, it's how I get through. If I'm a smartass, you know, if I act that way, I'm hoping you won't see that I'm scared shitless. All the time—every day."

Janes had made solid eye contact while I blurted this out, almost in one breath. He didn't respond, or blink, or flinch.

Dunn leaned back in his chair and gave a nod.

"We're all making this up as we go along, Casey. Some are more experienced and some are just lucky. You're somewhere in the middle, lucky, and starting to pick up experience. Don't forget our conversation earlier on." He tapped his chest. "Only marginal interest."

He said it matter-of-factly, but then he smiled and gave me a little nod. It actually looked genuine.

Two Cats, One Bag
Emmett

Little Mick stopped the car in the parking lot of the apartment building. I was on the building side and looked at the patio doors of the apartment. Evening was progressing into night and lights were on, but no occupants were visible. I was in no hurry to get out of the car.

Da reached across the car seat and nudged my shoulder. When I looked at him, he jerked his head at the door, signaling me to get out. For once he looked at me instead of out the windshield. I took a breath and reached for the door handle, but before I could he lifted a manila envelope out from under his seat and handed it to me. I didn't have to open it to know that it was the money that Dutch had given him. I also didn't have to count it to know that he hadn't touched a penny of it. He would have sooner died. Once on the pavement I bent down to look across at him, maybe tell him thanks for the thousandth time over the years. He beat me to it. He nodded at me, raised his fist. "Neart, mo mhac." (Courage, my son.)

I had a key, but I thought it might be better if I rang the bell. It was a long time before I heard the deadbolt and door being unlocked. When it opened Dutch stood inside dressed in a robe; her long blonde hair was wet and appeared dark in the evenings half-light. She opened the door slowly until she saw it was me and then she stepped back. I couldn't wait any longer. Stepping inside I shut the door behind me and wrapped my arms around her. She hugged me back. She was still damp from the shower and smelled like heaven. She felt like it too. Something in my guts changed places, and my blood rushed into my ears. She was here for me and it meant something to the something inside of me.

"Is it finished?" she whispered to my chest.

"Yeah, well, mostly—there's more to do, but I think I'm gonna be clear. I'm still gonna be their bitch for a while." I coughed and it almost brought me to my knees.

"What's wrong? Are you hurt?"

"Pretty much. I need to sit down."

I sat down on the hassock. It was the closest thing.

"What's wrong with you—are you sick?"

"No, just kinda bruised."

"Bruised? What from."

"Some Chicago policemen have some pretty creative interrogation skills. I've never been punched in the stomach so many times in my life."

"Policemen don't do that.'

"These policemen did." Just taking a breath hurt, and the very thought that I might ever have to sneeze made me weak in the knees. I took another breath, afraid that I might cough. "I'm pretty sure their interests weren't purely law enforcement related."

"That can't be true." She crossed her arms and arched her eyebrows. "You're making this up. Why would they do that?"

"They were detailed to get the information that the FBI

was withholding from the PD. There's a half ton of drugs that went where it wasn't supposed to go. People want to find it, lots of people. Some of them are not law-abiding citizens." I took a couple of deep breaths. "Some of them are not very nice people," I adjusted myself on the hassock, "not very nice at all."

"Angie went to her mother's for dinner. She won't be home for a while."

"How's she been?"

"A basket case. Her folks are none too happy about her choice of boyfriends either these days."

"Me neither." The hassock wasn't as comfortable as I'd hoped. I tried to get up but my stomach muscles refused the effort.

"You need to get in the tub. Let's get you in a hot bath so you can have a soak."

"I'm going to need a hand getting up, Dutch."

The tub was nice and hot. Dutch had put some weird bath salts in the water that made it slippery. It felt wonderful. Dutch, still in her robe, sat on the floor, resting her chin on one hand, and with the other she gently stirred the water with a finger. My entire abdomen was black and blue; there was no way to see where one bruise ended and the next one began. Neither of us had spoken for long minutes. I was starting to doze when the sound of the front door opening roused us both from our individual reveries. A set of keys dropped on the table near the door, and then;

"Dutchy?"

"In here, sweetie."

Angie appeared in the door, and there was a quick intake of breath.

"Oh, Emmett!"

The bathroom wasn't a big one and suddenly it got a lot smaller. Angie, still in her coat, pushed her way in and knelt down behind Dutch and leaned into the tub and threw her arms around me. The pain that shot through me almost made me pass out.

"Jesus Christ, Angie! He's hurt, get off of him!"

"What? Oh God, what happened? Are those bruises? Oh God, oh my God, oh, I'm so sorry, Emmett. What happened? Are you okay?"

"He's obviously not okay, Angie. Get out of the tub! Go get your coat off; you're flooding the whole bathroom floor. Then come and help me get him out."

Angie jerked back from over the tub. Her soaking wet coat sleeves started raining on the floor—and Dutch. She suddenly realized where she was and what the situation was. Her face showed confusion, but her brain started to do the math. She looked at Dutch, whose robe had fallen open, then down at me. She was never a quick study, but she got there fast enough anyway.

"Oh..."

Consequences and Common Sense

It is said that consequences are the things that common sense is made of. If that is true, then over the last weeks I hoped that I was accumulating a lot of common sense. I had been back into the city regularly for more questioning. By and large, the Chicago police officers that I'd spoken with more recently had been much more polite than that one evening visit I'd experienced in my cell. They were polite but not cordial. At best I was a stool pigeon; at worst I was an accomplished liar, smuggler, and murder accomplice. So, they didn't waste a lot of time with jovial conversation.

Conversely, the FBI seemed to have moved on. Their interest seemed diffident, distant, and centered more on traffic moving in from Florida and through Atlanta. They still insisted that I stay where they could find me, but their interest in all things Chicago had certainly dimmed. I spoke with Janes on a few occasions briefly. Dunn had vanished over the horizon.

In the meantime, I started learning a different lifestyle. In an agreement that didn't include my input, the two women moved me to the larger bedroom with the queen-sized bed. Angie couldn't do enough to ingratiate herself. She bought me jewelry, she cooked and did my laundry. She seemed starved for physical contact. Throwing her arms around me spontaneously, holding me too tight, and having temper tantrums when I ignored her. Dutch remained aloof, containing her daytime contacts in soft touches to the back of my neck as she passed behind me, or touching my arm while she spoke. She commandeered my wardrobe, replacing most of it, my checkbook, and my social calendar.

I still did stupid things. Sometimes I even pissed myself off with my behavior. I knew diplomacy, but I'd never needed to practice it twenty-four hours a day. It was as if I couldn't let things go smoothly, and when they were both angry with me, I got the twin bed. When they weren't mad at me, it was almost comedic. Angie still took the lion's share of the time in the queen bed, but Dutch took turns when she was in town. Occasionally, they both stayed together in the twin bed, and occasionally they sandwiched me on the queen bed.

But the sex was tinged with performance anxiety. I did my best to please. I had been trained to perform at a high standard. And in this case, it was the only way I knew how to apologize for what was inevitably to come because I knew better.

I knew that this all could not end well and I knew that it was me who would have to put a stop to it—but I couldn't. Angie was delightfully enthusiastic in all aspects of her life. She was beautiful. She embraced every experience without thought of consequences, reveling in the pure and simple enjoyment it provided and let tomorrow take care of itself. Emotionally selfish and immature, when she hugged or snuggled, it was because she needed it. Dutch was thoughtful, warm, and deep, and each step was carefully mapped before taken. She was smart and funny. She was also stunningly beautiful. They were as different as night and day, but were two halves of a whole.

I was always slightly off-balance whenever we were together. Uncomfortable, because of the guilt I felt by my participation. Too Catholic to enjoy it completely. It was too good to be true and a mistake from the very beginning. The guilt would eventually evolve into shame, but I was not there yet. I couldn't explain it to myself and I couldn't make it stop. When we were all together, we laughed, probably drank too much, and smoked a lot of weed. We focused on avoiding the eight-hundred-pound gorilla in the room, but we all knew it was there. We had become a three-legged stool. We couldn't stand without the other two, but we weren't comfortable.

With my status as a wartime veteran, I was able to get a job as a night watchman for a large steel and iron fabrication company that had vast outside storage for their raw materials. The job was mind-numbing and only required that from eleven at night until seven in the morning I had to walk through the yards and plant, punching a hand-held time clock every hour. Otherwise, I sat at the front desk and read books. It didn't pay for shit, but it was a job. With those hours it also relieved me of what was becoming an increasing awkwardness of being home at night and wondering what my sleeping arrangements for the evening were going to end up being. As a result, some of the tension went out of our living arrangements.

The company was in the throes of trying to incorporate a computerized inventory system. The infancy of computer technology was burgeoning, and fax machines were the newest thing. Companies bought time on mainframe computer hardware owned by Xerox at a central location. The data was entered at a workstation on keypunched cards, and then the deck of cards was hand delivered to the computer site, processed, and reports were generated and delivered back to the company.

An incredible amount of data had to be punched in every night at the end of the workday. As a result, while I worked there was always one guy diligently punching away at a keypunch machine in the building. Since I didn't have anything else to do most of the time, I would often hang around him and watch the process. He was horrible at it, slow and clumsy—and frustrated. It would take him hours each night while he ruined card after card run, trying to get it right.

The U.S. Army had graciously taught me how to keypunch like a pro, so to spell him and relieve my boredom, I often took the chair and showed him shortcuts on the machine. Eventually, he sat and drank can after can of soda while I did his job. It was better than staring at the time clock waiting for my rounds, and he was usually done more than an hour before he had previously been. On one occasion, the plant manager returned to the building to retrieve something he'd forgotten and caught us red-handed.

I was hired as the new company keypunch operator. I got quite a pay bump, a desk, and a respectable job. Unfortunately, the former operator had to find a new place to drink soda. I had to start wearing a tie again.

The first time Dutch saw me getting ready to leave for work, she gushed, "Wow! You going to a funeral? Look at you, all grown up! I've never seen you get all gussied up before."

"Dutch, just because I don't doesn't mean I can't."

"You look kinda good. I can see I need to go shopping again."

"This time I'm going with you."

"Deal. But only if it includes dinner and drinks."

"Done. See you Friday?"

"Friday."

Angie watched the whole exchange from the corner of the couch. Her eyes were big but her mouth was turned down at the corners.

Different Is Almost Never Good

In spite of her childlike enthusiasm for all life had to offer, Angie hated the motorcycle. She refused to ride on it, and she constantly hinted that I get rid of it. Dutch, on the other hand, in spite of her usual conservatism, reveled in it. She was always up for a ride to anywhere. The grocery store wasn't too short a trip, and she avidly searched the road maps for long rides in the country. Weather was not a factor—rain or shine, too hot or too cool, she didn't seem to mind.

The summer had given over to fall, and the leaves were bright in the trees. The air was warm and dry, and the sunlight was intoxicating. Whenever Dutch was in town on a layover, she wanted to go for a ride. She would even work in overnight trips, rides to Galena or Wisconsin Dells with an overnight and a ride home by a different route. It was the first time I'd seen her experience and express joy outright. Sometimes while we rode, she would burst out in giggles of delight, releasing her hold on me and throwing her arms in the air with the pure joy of freedom.

She became increasingly comfortable with sex. She never spoke of the one other time she had slept with a man, but every indication pointed to the experience not being a good one. As she eased into it, she began to broaden her scope and expand her horizons. She unabashedly initiated spontaneous encounters, both at home and in public. She seemed excited by the prospect of being seen or caught in the act of any lewd or lascivious act. She became insatiable, and I became ever more addicted to her.

With the shift, first to the middle and then more away from her, Angie became moodier. She pouted and flounced about the apartment aimlessly. She bought me more jewelry, hats, socks, and silly underwear. She tried too hard in bed. And she pressed me for a commitment.

I decided she needed to get her car back, and Dutch agreed.

Her car was still in the custody of the ex-boyfriend Todd, as far as she knew. In the almost three months since he had taken it, Angie had studiously kept up the payments, saying that she couldn't be sure that Todd would. In my opinion, she was the rightful owner and should have it. When I told her we were going to go and get it, she burst into tears and locked herself in the bathroom for over an hour. Through the door, between sobs, she railed about how she couldn't face him, that he was a "psycho," and that he would find some way to damage the car, or her. She admitted that he often waited in the parking lot after work, trying to talk to her. He apparently drove by the apartment and, when she was home alone, came to the door or called. This was all news to Dutch and me. Had I known we would have made the trip a lot sooner.

Dutch stood outside of the door and attempted to reason with Angie until she finally lost her temper and ordered her to open the door, which she reluctantly did. Dutch pulled her close and stroked her hair, telling her to change into something sexy, put on her makeup, and get ready. She told her that we were a family, and that we were going to get her car—together.

Dutch looked at me over Angie's head, and for the first time I recognized rage in her eyes.

Angie spent ninety minutes getting ready, and when she emerged the finished product was stunning. Flanked by an equally dolled-up Dutch, they were an unrelenting heartbreak on heels. Todd was going to have a hernia.

Todd lived in an apartment with two other boys. The International Village was billed as an upscale apartment expanse, numerous units each individually with sixteen apartments. The outside décor spoke of alpine design with stucco facades and dark wooden accents. Inside, it was every other apartment in every other suburb near a large urban population center. International Village targeted the younger, college-educated and as yet unmarried population segment that commuted to work in the city and spent their paychecks on Friday night. It was essentially an upscale college dormitory setting, with more spending money.

Cars in the parking lot ran the range of rusted-out shitboxes to spanking new sportscars. Cruising the lots, we spied Angie's baby blue '74 Monte Carlo parked near the back. Over the time period of its stay, it had accumulated dust, leaves, and bird shit, and one of the front tires was low. It had apparently not been driven since it arrived. Todd's car was parked in front of his building unit. A snappy little Datsun 240Z, black, with custom wire wheels and not a spot of dust on it, and it meant he was home.

We bypassed the mailboxes inside the entrance door, each with their individual buttons underneath them that would ring a bell inside the designated apartments, and headed directly upstairs. Angie knew which one we were going to; she'd been there before. With each step her body language showed increasing hesitation. She was afraid of the upcoming encounter. I was afraid if she started to cry, her face would be a mess by the time she got to the right door. As we neared the apartment she stopped and leaned back against the wall hyperventilating, her eyes as big as saucers.

"Ang! Sooner or later we've got to get this done. C'mon, honey, a little spunk now, okay?" Dutch was whispering, but all business.

Angie looked at me. "Can't you just talk to him, Emmett? You know, like you did the last time." She was trying to whisper too, but the emotions were making her voice squeak.

"Angie, baby, really there are a lot of reasons why I shouldn't. Most importantly, Todd could just call the police on me. My name's not on the title of the car; yours is."

"Oh geez."

I hung back in the hallway as they moved to the apartment door, and without hesitation Dutch knocked. There was a long pause of silence and then the door swung open.

"Hey, Angie! Wow, it's good to see you, c'mon in. Hey, Todd, Angie's here!"

That brought other activity, and then Todd.

"Hey, Ang, where you been? C'mon in."

Angie found her voice at last, but it came out small and quiet. "No, it's better if I don't."

"Aw, honey, I'm so glad to see you. I've been wanting to talk to you in forever. C'mon in and have a beer. The game's just coming on."

"No, Todd. I came to get my car."

"What? Why?"

"It's my car. I'm making the payments, and I need my car."

"It's my car too, you know."

She looked down at the floor. "I want my car, Todd."

"Just give her the keys, Todd." Dutch wasn't having any trouble with her voice.

"So, what? You had to bring your dyke friend with you? For what, protection from me? Big mean old Todd?"

"Shut up, Todd, Dutchie's my friend."

"She's a fuckin' lesbo; she's just tryin' to turn you into one too."

"That's enough, Todd, just give her the keys and we'll leave you to your football game." Dutch was pissed.

"What's the prob out here, Todd? Tell Angie to come in and watch the game with us."

"She says she's not stayin'. She's got a date with her lesbo girlfriend."

Dutch pulled Angie out of the way by her shoulder and stepped into the apartment doorway.

"You've got three minutes to get those keys, motherfucker."

There was a resounding slap.

There aren't very many things that make me snap instantly or that I can't abide. Hitting a woman is one of them though.

I double-timed down the hallway and pushed past Angie. She backed up to the opposite wall and fell against it. Inside the entranceway Todd was still holding one hand up high in the aftermath of a full-on round-house slap. Dutch was holding the side of her face, but she was still staring straight into Todd's eyes. His eyes got a lot bigger when I stepped through the doorway.

"Hello, Todd."

"What the fuck!?! You brought this troglodyte from the bar for backup?"

"This is my boyfriend," Angie yelled from out in the hallway.

"What—the—fuck, Angie?"

"What's going on?" The two roommates crowded into the other end of the hallway from the living room. All three of the wannabes were decked out in polyester track suits, with zippered jackets and matching pants that featured a white stripe down the leg, and matching hairstyles.

"Angie's here to pick up her car. Todd was just going to get the keys for her."

"Hey, man, that's not cool. Tell him to get the fuck out of here, Todd."

"Tell me to get the fuck out of here, Todd." I stepped past Dutch.

"I said I'd kick your ass the next time I saw you, remember?"

"So, kick my ass."

"Yeah, kick his ass, Todd."

The whole thing had gone far enough. Angie had said her piece, Todd had demonstrated his lack of integrity, and the roommates were gearing up for the show. I bum-rushed Todd and pinned him against the wall with his feet barely touching the carpet.

"Now listen, dipshit, I seriously doubt you could kick my ass. I am absolutely certain that you couldn't kick Dutch's, and you might have trouble with Angie in a fair fight. If you like, I will be happy to mash your face right through the wall behind you and then have a similar discussion with these other two boys." I let that simmer for a few heartbeats. "I'm going to let you go now, and you and Dutch are going to find Angie's keys;

then in an hour or so we are going to come back with the paid title to the car, and you are going to sign it. All right?"

"I'm not signing anything."

"Well, that'd be a mistake, for you, and that sweet little ride out in front."

"You wouldn't do anything to my car." He was doing his best, but he was seconds from wetting himself.

"How long would you like to have to look over your shoulder to see if I'm behind you? I got lots of time, and I don't really like you very much."

"Okay, okay, let me go. I'll get the bitch her fuckin' car keys."

"What was that?"

"Nothin'."

In under a minute we had the keys, and the three boys were sullenly sitting on the wrap-around sofa in the living room, the football game in front of them forgotten.

"Anything else?" The fight had gone out of Todd.

"I believe you owe Dutch an apology."

"No fuckin' way."

I'd been simmering but now I was just mad. I stepped in close and got hold of a handful of polyester and hauled him to his feet. I gave him the slap across the face that his father should have ten years ago. It stung him to the core, and he slumped to his knees holding his face.

"Dutch? Come over here."

The look on the women's faces registered shock and righteous satisfaction. Dutch stepped in front of Todd.

"I think Todd has something to say to you, don't you, Todd?"

There was sniffle, then a little choked intake of breath.

"I...I...I'm sorry."

"That's all right, Todd, someday you'll get some hair on your little ball sack and then maybe you'll grow up." Dutch was not about to let him come up for air.

After I paid off the car at the bank with most of my cash stash, we took the Monte Carlo to Milwaukee and partied all night at a wild place called the Milwaukee Underground, then spent the night in a too-expensive hotel by the river. Angie smiled the whole night, and for once she didn't drink herself into oblivion.

The next day we shopped and bought swimming suits. Angie's was a Day-Glo orange bikini, Dutch's a more conservative beige. They presented a contrasting pair together. Angie's full figure was stunning at any given time, but in the bikini it took your breath away. Dutch's figure was long, leggy, and slim, with small boyish breasts and almost no waist. I bought my first pair of swim trunks. I felt ridiculous, and the girls laughed at my white legs and farmer's tan arms.

We went to the beach. Lake Michigan in Milwaukee is far too cold to swim, especially in early November, but we waded and splashed each other until we started to turn blue, then sat on new towels and stared out at the horizon, all talked out.

Later, as the sun started to set behind the buildings and the temperature began to drop, Angie walked along the water's edge dipping her toes and lost in her thoughts, wearing my long-sleeved shirt open to the breeze. People universally stopped what they were doing and stared.

From her place on the towel Dutch observed, "Look at her. She's completely oblivious to the effect she has on people. She's so beautiful."

"I know, and innocent."

Dutch looked out over the water and asked, "You love her, don't you?"

"I'm not sure what that means."

"You better figure it out."

"I know."

There was another long pause while she maintained her gaze and I watched Angie break some more hearts.

"So, you're gonna have to know sooner or later… I'm pregnant."

A Whole New Set of Problems

After the newsflash from Dutch, the atmosphere in the car was somber in comparison to the exhilaration of the ride up to Milwaukee. Angie sat in the back and babbled, trying to reignite our enthusiasm. Dutch gazed out of the passenger window, and I drove mechanically with my thoughts churning.

"What?" Angie finally asked.

"What what?" Dutch asked.

"What's with you two? We've been having a great time all day. I can't wait to get home. What's the matter?"

"Nothing, honey, just tired I guess."

I said nothing.

"Well, humph." She leaned back in the corner behind me and was asleep in minutes.

Dutch turned sideways in her seat, leaning against the door. Evening had turned into night and the inside of the car was in shadow. She leaned into the back and covered Angie with our coats, and then poked me with one of the toes of her long feet.

"There's more news, if you want to hear it?"

"Better or worse?"

"Depends."

"Depends on what?"

"Depends on how you're going to take it. I'm sorry,

Emmett, things have been pretty crazy lately, and I've known for a while, but I kept thinking there'd be a better time to talk about it. There just wasn't going to be a good time."

"I'm sorry, Dutch, it's a little hard to get my head around it right now."

"Well, then you better hear the rest of it."

"Shit."

"You remember when I did those photographs last month? The ones that I mailed out all over the place?"

"Yeah, kinda."

"Well, I got an offer."

"No kidding? That's great!"

"Not great, fabulous."

"Fabulous then. What's the catch?"

"No catch, they want me to screen test for some commercials. It's really exciting, in LA, they want me to come out in a couple of weeks and be there for a few days. They're paying for all of it."

"Wow!"

"If it goes well, I'll be the spokesperson for some baby shampoo. The one that says, 'No more tears.'"

"That's pretty big! Like, nationally, right?"

"Yes, but I'd have to move there."

"Oh."

"And I can't do it if I'm pregnant."

"Oh."

"I'll either have to do something about it, or I'll have to turn it down."

"That's what you've been working so hard for all this time. How can you turn it down?"

"I can't. My body is my ticket to the place I want to be. I can't be getting stretch marks, and babies, and the whole nine yards, Emmett. I'm going to have an abortion."

"Is that legal?"

"In Illinois it is, for now. I've already made the appointment."

"Dutch, I don't think I can let you do that. Don't I have any say in it?"

"You can't let me do that? Who do you think you are?"

"I'm the father of the baby. I should have some say in it."

"You don't have to live with the consequences, but I do."

"That's murder, Dutch, not self-defense, pure murder. You don't know what that can do to your head. You'll be a murderer."

"Shut up, Emmett. You should talk about murdering people."

"I can talk about it. This is a defenseless little human, not someone who's trying to kill you back."

"I've made up my mind already. I just wanted you to know."

"But, Dutch, shouldn't we just get married and have the kid?"

"You? Marry me? Hah!"

"I would, I really would."

"And what about Angie? Sorry, Angie, I got a better offer, see ya."

"I'd need to do the right thing."

"Sure, why not ruin three lives instead of just one or two."

"You're not looking at this the right way."

"I'm looking at it the right way; you're looking at it through those Irish Catholic eyes."

"Dutch."

"I'm leaving for a long run the day after tomorrow. I'll be gone almost ten days, Europe, then South Africa, then on to the South Pacific and back home. When I get back, we'll talk again, okay?"

"When is this appointment?"

"Three days after I get back."

"What's to talk about?" I sounded sullen, and I felt the same way.

"I want you there with me, at the appointment, for the procedure, and I want you to decide once and for all. Angie or me. I want your answer when I get home."

"I do too" came the voice from the backseat.

Ten days is a long time to spend in purgatory. In a completely different sense, it isn't long enough when judgment is waiting for you at the other end. I was a father, at least for now, and I wasn't ready. I was supposed to decide between Angie and Dutch, but it wasn't like deciding if I wanted strawberry or blueberry pie. It was deciding about life and where it went from this point forward. It was about manning up, doing the right thing, or continuing to let life happen to me. It was about being a Casey, or being something less.

In truth, it wasn't really up to me to decide. It was up to them. I recognized that either of them had far more worth than I did. They were both too good for me, and I had been a parasite in their lives. Angie, so full of youthful exuberance, would slowly darken and sour if she was to stay with me. I knew that I couldn't keep the balloon of her energy perpetually inflated, and deep inside of me, I knew that I was too shallow to try.

Dutch, with all of her calculated planning, had a future, and that future looked pretty bright. I couldn't identify the strange feelings that told me to let her go, let her become, and let her soar. It dragged at me like the boat anchor I was convinced I would become if we were together. I wanted what was best for her to my core. I wanted what was best for both of them, and I was pretty sure it wasn't me.

But I was selfish too. I wanted Angie because she was fun, delightfully innocent, with a touch of toughness that you didn't see right away. If I was totally honest, I wanted Angie because she was beautiful, sexy, and it made me feel special to be seen with her. But I couldn't find the truth of how I felt about her emotionally. I wanted Dutch because something inside of me yearned for the strength she radiated, and because I felt joy in her presence. In truth, I also wanted her because she was beautiful and made me feel special to be seen with her. They were each in their own way what every other man wanted as soon as they laid eyes on them, and they were both mine. But that time was about to end.

The Wages of Sin Is Death

It had been one of those better days that you occasionally have at work. The tasks had been relatively easy to perform, and the coffee had been good. Department managers were beginning to ask my opinion, and I enjoyed the attention. I had developed a solid grasp of what the company was trying to accomplish and I had dedicated myself to helping. It was starting to pay off for them, and for me. I had started to like the job.

It was only three more days before Dutch got back from her trip, and although I was dreading the talk that she wanted to have when she arrived, I was looking forward to her return. Angie had been more reserved in her absence, pensive and waiting for the verdict. We'd watched television on the couch together, and played the game of shared domestic duties that come when couples live together long enough. We'd settled into a routine of daily life.

On the way home from work, I stopped at the grocery store and picked up something to make for dinner and as an afterthought some flowers. I didn't think beyond the fact that it was just something nice to do, but I also knew it would warm the situation. After that I stopped at the liquor store and bought beer. It's always better to cook with an open beer handy.

The November weather had been atypical, warm and

sunny; the trees were bare and the leaves rustled and blew across the streets and piled deep along the curbs. Flurries of them chased passing cars down the streets, rattling their way to a new resting place. Along the streets, homeowners struggled to keep up with the influx when the wind changed and blew their neighbors' leaves into the yard. Piles of leaves smoldered here and there creating a haze of pungent smoke that hung in the bare trees. Thanksgiving was a week away and this year I'd been invited to deer camp with the Quinns and Caseys. It would be my first time.

When I arrived home, I filled my arms with grocery bags, beer, and flowers and walked briskly to the door, trying to remember which pocket I'd dropped my keys into. I shouldn't have worried; the door stood ajar when I got there. Angie was already home. Pushing it open with my foot, I entered and shut it behind me with a backward kick and headed for the kitchen, where I deposited the load. Picking up the packaged bouquet of flowers, I went to present them to her.

Dusk was already advancing, it would be fully dark in only a few more minutes, and the apartment was dark. I'd missed her when I walked past; she was sitting in Dutch's oversized wing chair, curled in a ball. When I did, I thought she was asleep at first until she sniffed. Turning on the lamp on the side table across the room revealed ruined makeup and puffy eyes. She was still dressed in her work clothes.

"Jesus! Angie, honey, what's the matter?"

She sobbed, took a breath. "There's been…an accident…a crash…"

"Oh God, who? Are they hurt?"

"She's dead… Oh god, Emmett… Dutchie's dead."

The Worst News Bulletin Ever

On November 20, 1974, Lufthansa Flight 540, a Boeing 747-100 carrying 157 people (140 passengers and 17 crew members), crashed and caught fire shortly past the runway on takeoff in Nairobi, Africa. The flight was on its last segment of its Frankfurt-Nairobi-Johannesburg route. All souls on board were lost.

There was one additional soul that was not listed on the manifest.

After Dutch

I was hungry. As hungry as I ever could remember being. But the truck was almost out of gas, and I only had seventeen dollars left. My last job had been a week and a half ago, shoveling foundry sand at the Warsaw Foundry in Warsaw, Indiana. The road beyond that ended in Fort Wayne. I couldn't go any further, and I didn't really care. Food was a problem, gas was a problem, and life…life was a problem.

I wasn't really tired of life, I just didn't care anymore. Tomorrow would come whether I liked it or not, and when it did, I'd find a way to see the evening. When the evening came, or maybe the next day, I'd move to the next dot on the map, but it didn't matter which dot it turned out to be.

At the funeral Dutch's family had been cold and stoic, wooden figures in a tragic play. Angie had wept through the funeral, the trip to the cemetery, and throughout the graveside services. I watched them all from a far-off place in a surreal state where life looks like a television show and you can't change the channel you're watching.

Afterward Angie and I introduced ourselves to pay our respects; I had never met them before. Anna DeBoer threw her arms around Angie, and they both cried together for a long moment. Heinz patted her on the shoulder. Anna ignored me and Heinz, taking my hand, leaned in and spoke into my ear, his words harsh to match his face.

"I hope you are satisfied; you were never good for my daughter."

After that we were just two people living in the same rooms. Silently going through the motions of life. Any intimacy would have felt like a betrayal to the memory of Dutch; any joy—unfair. I had never been on very good terms with the emotion of joy, and now it was an inconceivable anomaly. I dressed in the morning and went to work each day, but I had no stomach for it anymore.

At home the phone would ring—my father or mother or one of my adult siblings, most often Kate wanting to know if I was okay. After assuring them that I was, I resolved to stop answering the phone. Finally, I just stopped being home. I took long drives in the truck, recently retrieved from impound. I would tell myself to go someplace interesting, but when I arrived, I would realize I didn't care enough to get out of the truck and look around. Instead I would sit behind the steering wheel and watch other people coming and going, oblivious as yet to how much life could actually suck if you gave it a chance.

The company tried to be patient, they even changed some of my duties, then gradually began relieving me of them when I didn't respond. Then I missed a day, then I missed a couple. Finally, we had the talk and it was decided that it would be mutually beneficial if we parted company. That prompted the talk at home.

"This isn't working anymore, Emmett, is it?"

"I don't know what you mean."

"Yes, you do—you're not the same; you're not you these days."

"Well, I'm just tired. I'll get over it."

"It's been eight weeks; that's too long to be just tired. I want the old Emmett back. I'm in love with that Emmett."

"So…what you're really saying is that you're in love with the thought of me, but you aren't in love with me?"

"No! I'm in love with you, but I want the Emmett that's in there, not the one that's dragging his ass around these days."

"So?"

"I want us to get married. I can make you happy again."

"Oh my god, that's all I'd need right now, Angie! Honey, I do love you but I don't think that's a good idea right now."

"Yes, it is. We've been sleeping together for a long time, and I love you. I just want you to be the other guy you were before."

"So, you want me to pretend until I get back in the habit of being what you think I should be?"

"No! Well, yes…"

"Listen, sweetie, I can be what you want for a while, but I won't be what you like, not right now, and maybe—I don't know, I just don't know. I'm having trouble just giving a shit right now. I'm sorry. I don't want to lose you, you know?"

"I don't want this, I didn't want any of it, and now I'm just so sad. Why can't you be there for me?"

"I can't be there for myself right now. It's not just Dutch—well, maybe, I'm not sure. I just don't know how to be who I am anymore. I don't think I know who I am supposed to be."

"Does that mean…maybe…we should take a break for a while?"

That had been two months ago. I hadn't called or gone back, I just left. I knew I should call but I didn't know what I would say. I should have but I also knew that I wouldn't. I disliked myself even more because of it.

Now I was in Fort Wayne, Indiana. I'd slept in fleabag motels and more often than not propped into the corner of the truck seat. The winter months had been long and cold, but it was now warming into spring, with sunny days and cold nights.

I found the local public library and parked. Inside, it was a little too warm, like all libraries seem to be, and smelled like old books that people had handled too often, sneezed into frequently, and fallen asleep with. The librarian had given me a jaundiced eye when I asked her where the newspapers were, but she'd directed me nonetheless.

Turning to the Help Wanted pages, I scanned for a place that was hiring. The field was somewhat narrowed because it also had to be a job that I wasn't going to mind walking away from when I felt like it. With my back to the front desk, I quietly tore out the likely prospects from the local paper and pocketed them. I didn't have a pencil and paper.

In spite of the enforced quiet of the library, there was plenty of talk. Immediately to my right a hallway led down to a room that a small engraved sign identified as the public conference room. There had been a steady flow of people in twos and threes down the hall for a while and then a person had begun to speak. In the enforced silence of the library, I could hear every word of what he was selling.

"Did you ever wonder why it is that your life is never perfect?"

I knew where this was going right off. A medicine showman, selling the latest snake oil panacea. People were such sheep.

"Did you ever stop and think that it actually is perfect? Perfect in every way? Well, it is, but people don't see it that way. They think to themselves, *If I only had this car or that television set. If I only got that promotion, well then, I'd be happy. My life would be perfect*. Instead of realizing that it's already perfect."

He was speaking with enthusiasm, engaging his crowd—pissing me off.

"Well, folks, consider this—each and every one of us is the author of our own experience. Each one of us is responsible for the paths we walk, the turns we make, and the forks in the road that we decide to take or not take."

Not if life keeps finding ways to shit on you, I thought.

"If we take responsibility for those decisions, then where we are in this life is the natural outworking of those decisions. It can't be anything else because the decisions we made are what brought us to this particular point. Therefore, since it can't be anything other than that natural outworking, then it must be perfect. Perfection!"

This guy must have been living under a rock for the last century. I'd lost all ability to concentrate on vandalizing the newspaper. Instead, I seethed at how such a misguided fool could have the audacity to mislead these people seemingly without conscience, or consequences.

He continued in this vein of lecture for almost an hour. By the time he was finished, I had resolved that I was going to have a little chat with him when he finally wound down. Moving down the hall and to the doorway, I watched as, instead of leaving, people moved forward to exchange greetings and thanks to the man standing near the podium.

He was nothing special. Dressed in a white shirt and tie

with a buttoned blue blazer that matched the tie, he was average height and weight with big horn-rimmed glasses and a toothy smile. People hovered near him, and he engaged each one as they presented themselves, making eye contact and, apparently, listening to them sincerely. Many of the people in the room seemed familiar with him, giving me the impression that he was a local personality. My face was flushed and I wasn't any more impressed by the shortened proximity.

Eventually the group thinned and made their way out past me and back down the hallway. Entering the room, I was met with the smiling face of a woman about my age with a pleasant smile blocking my path.

"Hello! I'm Jamie, Jamie Claire. Did you come for the talk?"

"Nope, just listened from the Reading Room."

"Isn't he great!?! We're so lucky to have him; it's not too often he's in this area."

"Who is he?"

"He's David Dean. He's such a good speaker."

"I'd like to talk with him for a second."

"That's great. There are snacks in the back if you'd like something. David's going to be leaving right after, and he wants to get going as soon as he can though."

The hint hung there for another second, but the mention of snacks had gotten my attention. Free food should never be passed up. I moved to the back of the room where I didn't recognize a single thing as edible. There was a panful of congealed something that the little card identified as yogurt sponge. Another bowl of congealed spit-up had a card that read spinach and garlic dip. A plate of crackers sat next to it that read, sesame seed. There were three pitchers along with cups; one looked like water and didn't have a card, and the other two were labeled Alfalfa and Red Zinger respectively. I opted for the pitcher that looked like water. I took some of the yogurt sponge and tasted it; then I took the rest of it. It was good whatever it was.

While I was inhaling the food, I hadn't noticed that the rest of the group had emptied, leaving only Dean and Jaimie. Both of them were standing right behind me when I turned around.

"Hello, I'm David."

"Emmett Casey." I took the proffered hand and gave it a shake. The grip was firm and dry.

"Thanks for coming, Emmett," he looked over my shoulder and added, "and helping with the cleanup. Jaimie said you wanted to have a word with me?"

"I don't really know how to put this politely. But I have a problem with what you were talking about."

"Really? How so?" He smiled a big smile. I couldn't tell if I'd amused him, or if he was finally glad someone had called him on his bullshit.

"That 'perfect' thing. That's just baloney." I was trying to be polite. "Life's not like that."

"You don't think so?"

"Life is a never-ending step from one stone to the next across a great big pile of shit." So much for polite speech.

"But we decide on which stone to step to, don't we?"

"Life pushes from behind, and the steps aren't marked with little signs that say Easy or Stupid. Unless they're all stupid, then I'd understand, because all of mine have been."

He appeared to be at least listening; his face looked

thoughtful and he cupped his chin with one hand and folded the other across his body, rocking back and forth on his heels. While he listened, his eyes ran from the top of my head all the way down to my dirty boots and then back up. All the time the small smile never left his face.

"I don't think it's right to sell that line to people. People need to know that life pretty much sucks, and that if you let your guard down, it'll flatten you. Life's tough enough even when you're expecting it."

"Life can be pretty tough, but don't you think that most of the 'pretty tough' is because we fight so hard against it? Instead of letting it flow around us?"

"That sounds like some kind of hippie nonsense to me. You know, 'Love—love is the answer.' That's baloney too. Love is just another roadblock; love isn't an answer. I'm not sure that love actually is a thing, more like an excuse to sell Valentine's Day cards. The Age of Aquarius, really?"

"Love has an incredible power for sure, but that's not what I mean. Life is like a river; it is in constant motion and always moving forward. If we let go and float in the current, we can see all the wonderful things that life has in store for us. If we keep grabbing on tree limbs and rocks, the water pulls us under, takes our breath away, and we suffer."

"That's the view from the riverbank, not the view from the river."

"Those rocks and branches are just the things that we want to hang on to in our lives. The things we can't let go of because we want them; we don't want those things to ever change. But life changes constantly, things change, situations that we think are comfortable change, and when we fight against the change—it hurts, and we suffer the consequences of choices that we don't want to make. So, they are made for us. Even no decision is still a decision. Don't you think?"

"You're awfully old to have lived this long and still believe that. I've learned that it isn't that way."

He looked at Jaimie with an arched eyebrow.

"Jaimie and I are staying a ways down south. We are in a bit of a time crunch to be on our way, and I believe the library is getting ready to close. This is a really great conversation and you've raised some valid points, so I'd like to keep discussing them with you. Before we leave town, we were thinking about getting something to eat. Would you be interested in coming along? My treat?"

Jaimie took her cue. "That would be great! Why don't we do that."

Different Isn't Always a Bad Thing

I woke up to complete silence. I'd slept in a bed for the first time in two weeks, and this bed had been comfortable and the room hadn't been freezing for a change. Bright sunshine shone outside the window, and beyond the glass a shady tree swayed in the breeze. I could tell it was still early but not that early. I looked up at the white ceiling and tried to work out my exit strategy.

The night before, David Dean, Jaimie, and I had convened at the local Denny's for a late dinner. Next to the two of them, I looked like a vagabond just out from under a bridge somewhere. Jaimie had ordered a salad and a glass of water. David had a cheeseburger. I knew I'd never lay eyes on either one of them again and David had offered to buy, so I ordered almost everything from the right side of the menu. The food came to the table in waves, and they both exchanged amused glances as I worked my way through the final stack of pancakes and a plate of corned beef hash as big as my head.

For all his proffered deference, there was very little conversation until I couldn't eat any more of anything. Then he ordered coffee, tea for Jaimie, and opened the floor for discussion. He was polite enough not to comment on my appearance, or demeanor; instead he picked up where he left off at the library.

"It's changes and the consequences that change brings that are so difficult for most people. There's a saying, 'A man marries a woman because he thinks she will never change, but she does. A woman marries a man because she thinks she can change him, but she can't.' When that realization occurs to them, then the real work of a marriage actually begins. It's also most likely to be the reason that divorce is becoming such a popular recreational activity."

That actually made sense to me. I sipped my coffee and looked somewhere else.

"Changes like that, they don't happen with ease most times. It's uncomfortable, gets hot, and we squirm. Change is the fire that burns away the garbage, the things that need to go away, but fire for all the good it does can be bad if we stand too close to it."

"That's some pretty cerebral thinking. Most people, me for instance, don't have the gift of perspective that you have. I'm not even sure if it applies, but it sounds nice."

"We have a choice, we ride the current of change, or we fight it and get what we get."

"Sometimes we get what we get, no matter how hard we try to do the right thing. For every joy there is a corresponding despair. Better to not have either, I'd say."

"I didn't say it was always an easy thing. It's just that people who refuse to become the person that life dictates soon become irrelevant. Even to themselves."

The food had started to kick in and I had slumped down a little. No amount of coffee would have kept me awake much longer. David noticed it immediately.

"We're headed to some friends for the night. In the morning I'll have some business to attend to, but I can see you're tired. Why don't you come along with us? There's always room for one more. You can get some rest, and sleep on what we've talked about. In the morning maybe you'll have a few more questions? Either way, a good night's rest and breakfast in the morning by one of the best cooks I've ever met? What do you say?"

I was tired enough so I didn't even think about it. Much. I followed them in the truck, after I put half of my remaining seventeen dollars in the fuel tank, and they waited patiently. The drive had been almost an hour and consumed half of what I'd just gassed up on. In the end, we had entered a long, rural driveway and driven up to the typical white-sided farmhouse that stood in a grove of mature oaks. The house was dark, and as we stood in the driveway, David pointed to the side door.

"Inside, Jaimie will show you. See you in the morning."

Then he'd struck off in the opposite direction and into the darkness beyond without a backward glance, walking and whistling. Inside the house, Jaimie directed me into a first-floor room with two twin beds near the back of the house. The house smelled like Murphy Oil Soap and fresh bread, clean and healthy. There were no sounds, and only a small light down a hallway to the left.

"Take either bed and have a good night. In the morning, come on out when you're ready. Breakfast will be ready."

Now it was morning and I didn't know what was on the other side of the closed bedroom door, but I could smell breakfast. With the benefit of a good night's sleep, my mind was much more rationally capable and I decided that I needed to have my head examined at my earliest convenience. Different is almost never good, but I'd spent my life stepping through doorways before they could close. Some of the times the experience had been good, and some of them had been pretty bad, but always the experience had a lesson. I was ready for a different lesson than the one I'd been studying lately.

I'd slept on the outside of the bed covers, concerned about my recent lack of hygiene and not wanting to impose any more than I might already be doing. I threw my feet over the side of the squeaky bed and pulled on my boots. Getting up I tried to arrange my hair and finger-combed my two-week-old beard. I left my knife on the bed next to my kit and opened the door. To my left was the entryway where I'd come in last night, and to my right was a short hallway that turned left and right at the end. It was the source of the small light last night when we'd arrived. I headed down to the right.

It didn't matter which way I turned at the end of the hallway because they both opened into the same room. The room was brightly lit and large enough that it gave the impression that it had been two rooms at one time. Which explained why the hallway opened into two different directions. Where they weren't taken up by large spotless windows, the walls and ceiling were painted bright white, which made the entire room sunlight bright. Directly opposite me a large country-style kitchen with a pass-through window occupied the entire left side of the wall. The right side opened into a room-sized alcove where a few chairs and a sofa were arranged in front of a television in the corner.

The room featured three rows of trestle-type tables about

twelve to fifteen feet in length with folding chair seating on both sides. All the seats were full. Two women, one blond and one auburn haired, and wearing jeans and aprons, walked between the tables clearing or adding water or milk to glasses. Other women similarly attired bustled back and forth in the kitchen. One of the women holding a large stainless pitcher quickly approached.

"Hello, you're Emmett, right? I'm Kathy. We're so glad you're visiting. Let me find you a seat. I bet you're hungry."

How she knew my name was a bit of a puzzler, but where all these people had come from was an even bigger one. They couldn't all have fit in this house, even with a shoehorn. Several of them smiled and waved a greeting.

"Um...hi, Kathy. Are you sure it's all right?"

"Oh, of course, I'll get you a seat."Turning she tapped two young boys on the shoulder. "You two are finished; you're just fooling around now. Take it outside."

"Can we turn on the television? It's Saturday."

"Not until the other kids are done eating; otherwise, we'll never get them to finish. Go outside for now. David's here."

"David's here!?!"

With that they grabbed their plates and glasses and hustled them to the pass-through window, scraped them and placed them in the tub that was apparently there for that purpose, and headed out through the side door. Several of the other children who had heard the conversation did so as well.

"Here you go. Right here on the end. There's food on the table, and eggs being kept warm in the kitchen. I'll bring those along right away. Would you like coffee?"

"Please, um...Kathy. Thanks."

The food was basic. Granola and plain yogurt, raisins, scrambled eggs festooned with green and red peppers and filled with cheese and onions. Homemade bread toasted and slathered in butter, and pancakes with thin syrup. I had never tasted yogurt before, and I found the slightly sour taste very appealing when mixed with the granola and raisins. Everything was delicious, and there was more than enough to satisfy me. As I was finishing, David came in through the side door riding a wave of small boys and carrying a little girl whose face was impossibly dirty considering the time of day.

The other woman in the apron and scarf moved over and said, "Where on earth did you get so dirty?"

"She was throwing dirt at the boys." He laughed. "With both hands, I might add."

That got a general laugh in the room, and a few smirks and good-natured tsk-tsks from the ladies in aprons.

"Good gravy, c'mon, Effie. Let's get you in the kitchen and wash your face."

Handing the young one off to the woman, David spied me in the far corner and headed over. As he approached, he hooked a coffee cup off the table and sat down across from me. He was wearing a crisp oxford shirt and tan slacks; the shirt had suffered several muddy insults compliments of Effie. After attempting to brush off the worst of it, he offered a greeting.

"Good morning, how'd you sleep."

"Actually, pretty good. I was tired."

"I bet you were."

One of the women passed by and filled our cups.

"Have you thought about what we talked about last night?"

"Not yet, I'm still getting oriented. This is a little hard to take in."

"That's why I thought it would be better for you to see it. It would sound a little strange if I tried to tell you about it. A little cultish maybe."

"Isn't that what it is?"

"Not at all. It's something so far from that that it is hard to describe, and easy all at the same time. Depends on the opinion that you had when you came through the gate really."

"So a commune...like hippies?"

"Again it depends upon your opinion at the gate."

"No offense, David, but opinions are like assholes. Everybody's got their own."

He threw back his head and laughed a good hearty laugh.

"Well, that's one I'd never heard before. But you're right. We are a community, an intentional community here, not a commune like your preconceived notion, but a group of people who came here to live with purpose, to live on purpose."

"Everybody lives on purpose...once they get the hang of it."

"No, most people live under their circumstances. Isn't that what people say? Well, under the circumstances I had to do this, or I had to do that. They pretend to give up their free will so they aren't responsible for the outcomes that they ultimately get."

"So, what's the alternative? Joining a cult, or intentional community? Leaving society behind?"

"Absolutely not! These people are all well inserted in society. John there works for Delco Battery; Anne there in the kitchen teaches at Ball State. All of us in one way or another contribute but by a different code."

"In it but not of it."

"Exactly...very good."

"Boy! I can certainly understand that, but does it really work?"

"It's not a group thing, except for the reinforcement that it provides; it's an individual thing. People trying to live up to what their highest vision of themselves is. Living with honesty about themselves and attempting to express integrity into everything they do. It takes a very momentary consciousness to accomplish something like that. It takes living on purpose."

"So like self-improvement."

"You mean like those gurus who give classes? No, not like that. Just simply being conscious enough in any given moment to see what is needed, and then doing the needed thing. Whether it is about you personally, or the group, or the situation. It takes practice, and places like this provide a safe place, behind the hedge so to speak, so that they can practice."

"Places like these? There are more."

"We are an international group, comprised of many such centers as this one. There are these focal centers across the globe, all with like-minded ones who are living to their highest vision."

"So? That's weird and wonderful all at the same time."

"In the true definition, yes."

"Amazing really. Thank you, David, I learned something that I didn't know yesterday. And thanks for breakfast, and the bed last night. I'll be honest, I really needed it, but I'll be pulling out now and let you folks be."

"Really? Why not stay?"

"Stay? You can't be serious, David, you don't even know who I am. Once you find out you might not like what you see."

"I see a man who's searching and I see a man that is running away."

I took a drink of my coffee to hide my feelings, but my hand shook a little, so I didn't pull it off completely.

"I'm not looking for anything. I'm not even sure if I'm that interested, but I'm not running away from anything. If anything, David, people run away from me."

"Can I ask you a question?"

Not really.

"Sure, go ahead."

"How long does it take when you run from your enemy before you realize that you brought him with you?"

"You mean, how far is far enough when you're running from yourself? I've heard that one before."

"You should have listened."

Guilt or Shame? You Choose

"Get down off the ladder, Effie! Now!"

The ladder that I was standing on continued to shake, and I didn't have to look down to know who was trying to climb it. Effie Kane was almost busy enough for two four-year-olds. She was into everything—always. The shaking stopped and I risked a look down to see Effie already on her way to my truck, where two boys were trying to get the dog to jump into the rear bed and two five-year-old girls were arguing about which one could pretend steer while the other got to wrestle with the transmission lever. Effie barged in and wormed her way onto the truck floor and started pushing the foot pedals with her hands.

"Jameson and Caroline, quit messing with the transmission lever! If you get it out of gear, it might roll over someone. All of you out of the truck!"

The response from the truck cab was a cacophony of squeals of laughter and renewed effort. The boys in the back quit fooling with the dog and started trying to rock the truck. Either they were trying to scare the girls or get the truck rolling. Both efforts were equally unappealing, and with a sigh I began my descent from the second-story eave where I had been installing an attic vent.

As soon as my foot touched the ground, I was gang tackled

by the boys who'd abandoned their efforts in the truck.

"Quit it, guys, for god's sake get off me!"

They made no effort to curtail their obnoxious activity, and were joined by the three little girls, who simply piled on the pile and giggled their way all over the pile. I gave up all pretense of trying to adult the situation and began to wrestle back. When possible, I'd tickle one girl or the other until she was helpless and threatening to pee her pants. That made the boys try to tickle them too.

"Okay, okay…that's enough, boys. I've got to get my work done. If you keep pestering me, I'm going to be up there until it's dark."

The pile began to disassemble, and I climbed back up on my feet, shaking the grass out of hair and shirt. One girl each fastened herself to a leg, pinning me to the spot. The boys immediately started trying to push me over, all the time laughing hysterically.

"Boys!"

The voice carried from beyond the garden fence. All activity froze. There was something about Jaimie Claire's voice that demanded immediate obedience. She pushed the straw hat she was wearing back and leaned on her hoe.

"Leave Emmett alone for once, will you. Christopher and John, come over here and help me straw the berry rows. Effie, go get your britches changed, you've wet them again. Jameson and Caroline, you two go pick up your things that you left in the driveway."

And just like that they scattered like chickens in a rainstorm, all to their newly assigned chores. Except Effie, who began to climb back into the truck to escape.

"Oh no you don't. C'mon, little miss, I'll take you up to the house."

"Okay, Arie, up, up…on your shoulders."

"Not until you get your pants changed."

The Saturday had turned into Sunday. After breakfast a group meeting of sorts took place with the tables pushed back and the folding chairs set in rows. Once again, I was surprised at the number of people in attendance, until I noticed that there were several cars pulled up in the lane and realized that some had traveled just for the group meeting. David had presided with another one of his "under the circumstances" discussions. Afterward a general discussion of what it meant to different people personally. From my vantage point near the doorway, I was impressed. Not one cynical comment was made, every opinion seemed well thought out, and each one had depth. I was not particularly convinced of the genuineness of the sentiment, but the people all seemed pretty nice anyway.

The weekend had stretched a week. On Monday I had replaced the gate post and rehung the cattle gate. Tuesday I rehung a gutter on the south end of the farmhouse. Wednesday I hand weeded the longest row of green beans I'd ever seen in my life, all because it looked like it needed doing to me. Thursday and Friday, Old John and I had changed the water pump on the tractor. Old John couldn't lift anything bigger than the cigarette which perpetually hung out of the corner of his mouth. I finally had unpacked my knapsack and used the top drawer of the dresser in the backroom of the farmhouse.

The week had blossomed into a month, then longer. Now it was mid-summer. The Indiana sun was just as hot as the Illinois or Wisconsin sun, and my shirt was sticking to me thanks to my recent wrestling match. In the house, I handed Effie to Margaret, a lively seventy-year-old with a gift for whimsy.

"Oh, not again, Miss Muffett! I'm not sure why I'd thank you for this, Emmett." She whisked off down the hallway, but called back over her shoulder, "There's iced tea in a pitcher in the kitchen pass-through. Have some before you go back out in the sun."

I had developed a taste for herbal tea.

Since the first week of my time at the farm, David Dean had been away. I was told that he traveled extensively, his gifts as a speaker and motivator were in high demand, and he was often away lecturing at various schools and colleges. He was often a guest speaker at weekend symposia and only visited rarely. He was also a physician and had a practice somewhere. In fact, he actually lived in a completely different state. He was often a topic for discussion around the dinner table, but not the only one. Lively discussions surrounding the superiority of Indiana basketball, the Cincinnati Reds, the price of beef, beans, and whether some of the younger men would be asked to go out west where a large construction project was being organized at one of the other focal centers.

There had never been anyone trying to sell me on a different belief system. The women were extremely polite, kind, and not adverse to an affectionate touch, but also careful to avoid entanglements. I kept my distance from them. I'd ruined enough people's lives already, and I didn't want to start doing it all over again. I was still skeptical, and my bullshit detector was never turned off, but I couldn't find anything that didn't seem to ring true. I began to think that they might be on to something.

After a week I had asked if I could use the phone and called my father. My mother had answered and given me the third degree. Where was I? What was I doing? Where was I? Was I in trouble again? After that Da had come on and listened without comment. After I finished, he was silent for a half minute.

"You do what you think you need to. Get your shit together. As long as you think a cult is the answer though—you stay away from my family." And he hung up.

In August I was called into the house for a phone call. After my first use of the phone, I hadn't touched it again until now.

"Hello."

"Emmett! I'm so glad you're still there. I'd heard you were. I'm glad."

"Hello, David, how's it goin'?"

"Splendid! Of course."

"What can I do for you?"

"There's a big project that's being organized; they need good hands, and ones that know which end of the hammer is the business end. They need men like you, Emmett. How'd you like to go to Colorado?"

"I've never been to Colorado. Why would they want me?"

"Because you're Emmett. Are you doing something else right now?"

"I'm setting fence posts for the new pasture ground."

"No, not that—any reason you should stay in Indiana?"

"Not really."

"Any reason why you wouldn't want to see Colorado?"

"I guess not."

"Great! See you in a week or so."

And that was the end of that. I went to Colorado; for a job

that took two months. I enjoyed the scenery of the mountains and I enjoyed the hard physical work which gave me time to work off the energy and anxiety that had wound me into knots and freed my mind to think objectively. I actually started to have fun.

There was plenty of time for good-natured joking and teasing while we worked together. There was time for games and sports in the evenings and weekends. I gained back the weight I'd lost when food stopped having taste, and I stopped sitting on the edge of the group and began to actively listen to discussions of success and failure.

I met many people. Some were permanent residents on a working ranch, and some had come for the building project. I enjoyed working with men and women who seemed to have a handle on life that I envied. Some were upright, stalwart, and strong leaders because they couldn't be anything else. They reminded me of Seamus and Charlie, leading by example with integrity and that radiated their honesty. I met people who fancied themselves leaders because they thought they shouldn't be anything else, but were in fact only bad examples. I saw people fail and pick themselves up and carry on, determined to try again, to achieve whatever their personal highest vision might be. I watched myself fall, and I witnessed firsthand how hard it is to get up when you don't think you can. I watched myself from the sidelines as I pushed myself beyond introspection and self-pity, each little step a victory, and each backslide a lesson.

I felt the fire that David had talked about. The fire that burned away the trash that I carried around with me, my personal identity—the guilt and shame that had been my personal burden. With each revelation, I saw how I had owned the negative vision, lacking worth, only capable of the next sinful act, unable to accept credit for any good one. It burned and cleansed me from the inside, and it hurt. The concrete foundations of my belief systems went to war with my rational thought processes. It was a battle far more harrowing than a firefight in Vietnam. That had been a simple live-or-die scenario. This was a fight that I picked with myself, and either way it went, I was going to have to live the rest of my life by a new standard and leave Hole behind. With blazing clarity, a different view of who I might be began to emerge. I began to understand the lesson of my father and the consequence of not being able to evolve beyond that burden of despair.

I wasn't a leader, and I wasn't a drone. I didn't entertain the egocentric requirement of becoming a person at the forefront. I began to see it as a tool. David had said it provided a hedge, a place to operate where it was safe to practice being honest with others and myself. Life had handed me a great gift when I needed it most, and when I grasped that simple idea, I resolved to use it. With the benefit of distance and time, I glimpsed the Casey inside of me. I began to see the edges of what I might be capable of. I began to hope.

After the building was done, I heard there was a need for people to pick apples in British Columbia, so I picked apples for a season. A hotel in California needed a new adobe roof and skylights. I learned how to install the fired clay tiles without breaking them and without falling off the roof. When that job was done, an irrigation pipeline needed digging in Arkansas. Then spring found me in the Catskill Mountains of upstate New York, another crew, roofing an entire hotel. I had traveled from one side of the country to the other and from the top to the bottom. All of the projects had been affiliated in one way or another with the people from the farm in Indiana. I watched as the others practiced whatever version of integrity was for them, and I practiced my own, attempting to integrate my foundations of guilt and shame to a new sense of personal values. It was the real task while my hands were kept busy.

The hotel was one of the old early century wooden structures, set on a pristine lakeside, glowing bright white in the sun and stretching an impossible length by any current construction standards. Three stories of small, tight rooms, squeaky wooden floors, and cozy sitting rooms with plush, dated furniture throughout. The hotel was quaint, the location perfect, and the visitors, up from New York City, returned year after year. The third-floor rooms were tucked up into the roof, each with its own individual gable and window. The project was a big one, and the gabled units required a long, tedious, one-by-one shingle placement. The job promised to last well into the summer.

The nights were still chilly in the late spring, but the days had gotten hot all at once. The cool nights provided long, quiet walks in the woods along the ice-cold streams that ran downhill in crystal-clear cataracts. The days were hard physical work moving scaffolds and climbing endlessly up and down with bundled shingles over my shoulders. It tired my body and freed my mind for reflection. I was satisfied, for now.

At the end of the day, I'd come down off the scaffold and directly into a small crowd of children who swarmed me immediately. At the edge of the group, Jaimie Claire stood, white apron tied around her waist, her white blonde hair covered in the standard kitchen scarf of the hotel staff. She was holding a glass of iced tea in one hand and a now five-year-old Effie, her daughter, in the other. Effie's eyes were big and a smile animated her little face. Jaimie watched as the mob searched my tool belt for possible treats and chewing gum.

"Hello, Emmett."

"Jaimie! Is that for me?" I pushed through the crowd as they dispersed, passing out the remainder of my pack of gum. I had quit cigarettes months ago.

"Yes, it is. I see you haven't lost your touch."

"I don't know why they torment me so much. I don't even like them."

"Your lips say 'No, no, no' but your eyes say 'Yes, yes, yes.'" She laughed.

"That's not true, they just are too young to know any better."

"Hmm…" Then remembering, she handed me the glass of tea. "Hot up there."

"That it is, plenty hot. And we're only about half done. At least another two weeks at the rate we're going. Moving the scaffolding all the time slows the progress considerably."

I unbuckled my tool belt and set it on the concrete slab step that served the back door of the kitchen. Jaimie took a seat next to me. Effie climbed into my lap and started picking sawdust out of my beard. Like me, Jaimie moved where she was needed. She was managing the hotel kitchen and staff for the upcoming tourist season.

"How goes the scullery duty?"

"All right. Some of the staff is pretty experienced; some of them couldn't find their butts with a flashlight."

"Such a way with words you have."

"We'll see."

"Is David going to be around?" Jaimie seemed to have a handle on just about anything related to David Dean.

"No, but I'm sure we'll see him sometime soon. So? How's it going?"

"Good, I guess, working on my tan, you know, taking the breeze."

"You've filled out some since last summer. You need a little help with your wardrobe though."

"What? You don't like bib overalls?"

"I do, but those have got a few too many miles on them. You need to trade them in."

"I need to do a lot of things; new pants are pretty far down the list."

She leaned against me and I leaned back.

When In Doubt, Turn Right

I sat across from David Dean drinking coffee. Dinner had been in the hotel dining room. The guests had all finished and moved off to their evening leisure pursuits. The sound of clatter in the kitchen was loud in the now empty space as dishes were washed and banged into the big dishwasher. David had poured the coffee himself and brought it to where I was sitting. Now he leaned back in his chair and ignored his, watching me. I fidgeted under his gaze.

"You've stopped running."

"From myself? I guess, but I'm still waiting for the rest of me to catch up and spoil it."

"So? You haven't entirely let that identity go yet. That can only happen when you embrace a new one."

"Well, David, that's pretty easy to say when you're you."

"You can't hide here forever, you know."

"I'm not hiding here."

"What would you call it then? There have been plenty of opportunities for you to go. Even more for you to stop moving and stay somewhere, but you've kept moving every time any permanence reared its head."

"I like the challenge of a new place, or a new job. I like learning new things."

"So I've heard, but you don't get very far out of your

comfort zone. You keep your experiences pretty guarded, don't you? You don't try and challenge yourself."

"I don't know what you mean by that."

"You like to learn new things, you say, but what you're actually doing is developing new ways to do the same thing that you've always done. So, it's not really learning, is it?"

"Isn't that what learning is about?"

"Learning is more about seeing things in a different way than you previously thought. Puzzles that open up when you suddenly learn how to solve them."

"Like math?"

"Not really. Did you ever look at a picture that you'd seen a hundred times, and then you notice something in the picture that you hadn't noticed before, and then you can never see the picture the way you used to again. It will always be the way you see it now."

"It's ruined a lot of pictures for me over the years."

"That's what real learning is."

"So, what? What should I do, or where should I go to learn new things?"

"I have no idea, where or what. That's up to you. But I have something in mind."

"Okay, we'll be done with the roof by next week. I'm ready to move on."

"Jaimie might think otherwise." He gave me an arched eyebrow and a little smile.

"Jaimie is good people. She's much too good for me, I wouldn't—couldn't drop a millstone like me on her."

"Isn't that up to her?"

"I know me better than she does. I can't keep this act up

forever; sooner or later, the old Emmett is going to surface."

"You think all this has been an act?"

"No, but kinda yes. The old Emmett, the inner Emmett isn't all that far away. He still wants his say, every day he wants his say. That Emmett is not a good person."

"That Emmett?"

"Yeah, that guy, he was a bad guy; he is a bad guy. That guy can't go back and undo the past or apologize enough for it. That guy is still in here somewhere." I tapped my head. "I could be the patron saint of good deeds for the rest of my life, but that Emmett, the old Emmett, would still be there."

"So, written in the book, at the gates of heaven, Old Saint Peter will deny you entry because you made mistakes?"

"Exactly. Not just mistakes, mortal sin mistakes."

"You can't wear your sins like some people wear their clothes, Emmett. You can't deny affection because you did something hateful years before. You can't accept love if you continue to believe you don't deserve it."

"Well, I don't. There are lives behind me that were left in ruin," breaking eye contact I added, "and some that I've ended."

"So, you don't deserve something better because you think people should see who you really are?"

"They'd find out sooner or later."

"One of the things that adults often lose is the ability to see true character. They get so wound up in making a living, making the grade, or just getting by that they haven't got time to look too closely at the people right next to them. It's something that children innately possess."

"It's probably because people learn to guard themselves."

"Yes, they do, but children don't bother with that. They

just see joy, love, and goodness. They are attracted to it like bees to flowers. Children see magic because they look for it."

"Yes...so?"

"There is a connection that they sense. Everywhere you go, children can't seem to get enough of you. The climb all over you because they can't get close enough. And you return the kindness. Oh, you pretend to not like it, but you do—everyone but you sees that. You have a gift," he leaned across the table and poked me in the chest, "and it's right in there."

"A gift? Maybe a curse."

"Suit yourself, but either one is only a fact depending on how you express it. You hide your light under a bushel basket, like you're afraid someone will notice it. Like you're afraid they'll exploit what you think is just another weakness. You need to shine your light, not as a weakness but as a beacon of strength, and you need to find a way to give what you so desperately want."

"Oh sure, like there's an on/off switch for that."

"There is! Isn't that terrific? Just throw the switch, Emmett."

"How does one throw the switch?"

"I think it's time that you stopped hiding here behind the hedge. Time maybe to step out of this comfort zone and start learning new lessons."

"Like what, any suggestions? I could maybe try something new." Maybe.

"So many people could benefit from that gift that you carry. You could be a service to so many people if you can find a way to express how much you actually do care for them, I believe."

"So many people?"

"But you just need to find a way for them to come to you instead of trying to find the ones you can help one at a time."

"How does someone do that?"

"By learning how to be a service to them. Offering them something they need, while quietly slipping them something even better under the table."

"And what would I be slipping to them under the table?"

"Heartfelt caring, genuine acceptance. Unconditional love."

"Geezus, David, that's a little out there, even for you."

"Not really. I think you could become a physician, I think you'd be a bang-up doc, Emmett. Want to give it a try?"

"Me!?! A doctor? I can't even feature that in my head."

"I'm not kidding. You are very intelligent; the kaleidoscope of learning that you'd encounter would fill in corners in your mind that you can't even imagine. At the very worst, you would stretch your scope as far as the horizon. You could grow. And when, if, you came out the other side, think of the possibilities that you might be capable of."

"I don't want to be a physician. I don't want to patch bullet holes or help people die on the installment plan."

"Don't then. Don't be a physician, be a lawyer, a counselor, be of service. Become something, but become. I think you should learn to heal with your hands, because that is where your gift lies. It's in your hands—in your heart. If you can find it inside of yourself, then it will appear in your hands soon enough.

"Leave your comfort zone, maybe go to Davenport, Iowa, go to Palmer College like I did, take a look at it. If it's right for you, you'll know. If it's not then find the thing that feels right and leave your comfort zone behind. I think it's time you let yourself become who you really are. I think you'll find the heart of a healer."

I emptied the top drawer of the little dresser and handed it to Jaimie, who refolded it and rolled it tight so that it all fit snugly into my old canvas knapsack. There wasn't much to pack, but it filled it almost completely once I'd added my toothbrush and shaving cream. I was wearing my new bib overalls, and the old ratty ones were destined for the rag pile. When my bag was packed the only thing left was my hat, jacket, and .38 Ruger long-barreled revolver.

I picked it up and hefted it, feeling the burnished handgrips and how it fit my hand. Spinning the cylinders, I smelled the gun oil and smiled at the smoothness of the action. Then I laid it on the bed next to the worn-out denims. They were both staying here. I had no use for either anymore.

Jaime had stayed with me the night before. We both felt a little guilty about it, having never done something like that before, and we had talked long into the night. In the morning, she had slipped out of my room as the light was coming up in the east. Now we worked in silence, not wanting to overwork the situation. Afraid that we might try to change it.

My future was a mystery. Hers, out of necessity, needed stability for both herself and Effie. I had nothing to offer in that regard. I also knew what kind of person I had been at one time, and feared I might become again. She couldn't go and I couldn't stay.

In the hotel drive I tossed my knapsack onto the floor of

the passenger side and set the monstrous sack of sandwiches, bottles of tea and water, and Good Luck notes from the staff I had gotten to know on the opposite end of the bench seat. I gave Effie a long squeeze and Jaime a hug.

Climbing in I started out the driveway, and at the gate I looked in the mirror one last time. Jaime stood at the kitchen doorway, her apron and scarf in place, her hands folded in front of her. Her head bowed.

When in doubt? I turned right at the end of the lane.

Book 3
The Heretic

The light is slow to come on the winter mornings. The biting cold presses in from the outside, causing the old house to groan and crack as the cold seeks to compress it into a smaller colder space. Standing at the kitchen sink, I wait for the coffeepot to boil and feel the cold's frigid touch pressing against window glass, frosting its way onto the inside without asking permission, making beautiful snowflake landscapes in thick Jack Frost patterns. Even in my woolen socks and slippers, I feel the chill of the wooden floor under my feet, causing them and my calves to itch with chilblains, and I shift my weight, patiently waiting for the little percolator to sputter and drip my coffee, filling the small chilly kitchen with the aroma of fresh coffee.

The electricity is off again. The storm that blew in Friday and stayed through most of the weekend took care of that. It is not uncommon for us living so far out in the country, even in summer, to lose power once or twice a month. With winter, outages are more frequent and for my old bones, more inconvenient. Thankfully I still have gas in the LP tank out in back of the house, so the stove still works. Taking a cup down from the cupboard, I pour coffee and the dogs follow me as I shuffle to the front room, where the fireplace fire crackles cheerfully, filling the room with welcome warmth and the pleasant faint smell of wood smoke. The darkness of the early winter morning creates a sense of warmth and coziness in the comfortable little room. With the electricity off, the fireplace is the only source of heat in the house unless you count the dogs, both of whom throw themselves down on the hearth with a thump and a sigh. Pulling an afghan blanket off the back of the recliner, I wrap it around my shoulders and ease my aching knees down into the high-backed wing chair close to the fireplace, trying not to spill the coffee. Cradling the cup between my hands, I lean forward and stare into the fire.

I am an old man now. Aged by the mileage of experience and the erosion that years bring. The frenetic energy that fueled my life has finally burned itself out. My body, the vehicle that I have used all these years, has arrived at this point broken and patched, only now at the far end of my life appreciated for its former abilities and accomplishments. The end of my life is much closer than the beginning, and I marvel at the dependability this body provided and wish as all old men do that I had taken better care of it. The doctors smile and tell me that I am doing "just fine," but the look in their eyes tells a different story and I understand.

We are alone now, the dogs and I, both of us too old and worn for any more adventure and hopefully too smart as well. My children, grown and gone to lives of their own making, call on Father's Day. She, too, has been gone many years now, and the passing of time has softened my memory of the hard years that we spent together and have brightened those memories of the good ones. I stare into the fire and reflect, turning back through the chapters of memory. I recall the different lives that I have lived, and the lives that I have touched all in this one lifetime. The memories arrive unbidden; random and not in ordered sequence but instead each one connected to the next by the emotion it stirs, triggering the progression to the next one. They are not sequenced by time or date and yet they are not random but related at a deeper level. I try to recount these lessons and victories that came with a cost. I now recognize that every person's journey is storied with tragedy and love, sorrow, pain, and joy, and mine is no different in that regard. I think about the people who have passed through my life and the impression they have left on me, and consciously give thanks—for all of them.

I take a mouthful of too-hot coffee. Setting the cup down, I lean forward toward the fire and rest my elbows on my aching knees as another memory begins the progression of thought.

CPSIA information can be obtained
at www.ICGtesting.com
Printed in the USA
BVHW071751010519
547089BV00001B/14/P

9 781977 208569